Revenge

From the author of

The Key to the Street

Revenge

Anne Willingale

Matador
9 Priory Business Park,
Wistow Road, Kibworth Beauchamp,
Leicestershire. LE8 0RX
Tel: 0116 279 2299
Email: books@troubador.co.uk
Web: www.troubador.co.uk/matador
Twitter: @matadorbooks

ISBN 978 1788038 591

British Library Cataloguing in Publication Data.
A catalogue record for this book is available from the British Library.

Printed and Bound in the UK by 4Edge Limited
Typeset in 11pt Minion Pro by Troubador Publishing Ltd, Leicester, UK

Matador is an imprint of Troubador Publishing Ltd

I have to thank my family and friends who have given me their endless support and understanding while I was writing this book.

A mother, even one who lives her life in the peaceful wisdom of the Goddess, will take her revenge when her child is defiled.

1.

It was April, yet the sky was still heavy with ominous black clouds. Winter, in a bullish mood, was reluctant to give way to spring and threatened more snow. Heading through the silent lanes towards the village of Haddenford, a young woman, swaddled tightly in a shawl, picked her way carefully over the deep ice-covered ruts. Usually, Martha Tilby walked with her head up, a look of peace on her face, absorbed by the nature that surrounded her, but today she was muttering to herself, reciting important words.

Normally placid by nature, Martha was angry. Angry with William and angry with herself but, more than that, humiliated by what she was now forced to do. This she perceived as her failure to support her children in a life that she and William had believed that they could achieve.

As she approached the village green and the church that stood beside it, snow flurries danced in the air, settling on the shawl that now covered her head and shoulders. Although dressed in all the clothes that she possessed, the cold still bit painfully at Martha's bones.

The rough, grey wood of the lychgate creaked beneath her hand as she pushed it open. An unfamiliar sound to her ears. Standing beneath its roof, she remembered when she had accompanied William here in his box. Then, the gate had been open for the small funeral party to pass through. They faced the formidable presence of the elderly vicar, who had met them at the

1

gate with a prayer, as was the tradition, before leading the small group along the path to the church door. Although William had not practised it, he was a Christian at heart, and Martha felt that, whatever her views, he should have a Christian burial.

Her booted feet now moved reluctantly along the churchyard path towards the large oak door with its black patterned ironwork. A door that was not inviting to Martha. Its heavy blackness rejected her, yet all too soon she had stepped inside the building.

A large candle burnt brightly in the inner sanctum, flickering and forming shadows on the stone floor and wall. The air, which smelt of candle wax and incense, was as cold inside as it was outside. The bleak emptiness of this interior touched her with hard, unforgiving alien hands that bore no comfort, no love and no belonging.

Shivering beneath her damp clothes, Martha prayed that she wasn't going to be ill. She couldn't allow herself to be ill; what would happen to her children?

As she stood slightly apart from a small group of silent women that had also gathered, she wondered how people came to this austere place and found God. The worn granite slabs on which she now stood, gave no relief to her painfully cold feet, and as her body shook, it was all that she could do to keep control of her teeth which were gritted, but not only against the cold.

Three people sat behind a black oak table in front of the women, at one end Jacob Rudd with a large book of reference. When he spoke, his voice reflected the importance of his role as clerk on behalf of the church widows' and orphans' fund. Two other people sitting stiffly in the freezing air were the sharp-faced widow Fearling, and the new vicar, the Reverend Ernest Draycott. He, a young man, smiled warmly and raised an expectant eyebrow at the sad group of women that stood, heads covered, shivering in the chancel, beneath a suffering Jesus pinned to his cross.

'Next!' Rudd's voice grumbled through the beard that hung from his jowls in a wide black, tangled mass, that reached to his stomach and occasionally interfered with his writing.

Martha stepped forward, conscious of the mud on the bottom of her skirt and boots. The clerk nodded stiffly in her direction, and there was an audible intake of breath from the widow Fearling.

'Name?' Rudd didn't look up. Quill poised, he continued to stare down at the book in front of him.

'Martha Tilby, sir.' She tried to keep her voice even and not let her shivering be heard.

Rudd wrote deliberately, his quill scratching slowly on the parchment before him. 'What is your need?' he addressed her sharply, not seeing the pain and embarrassment that fell about her shoulders like a curse, biting into her courage. She felt no kindness and there seemed no understanding of what it had taken to come here and ask for help. On her difficult journey through the icy lanes, Martha had been rehearsing her words, but had now forgotten the first line, and for a moment was speechless.

Rudd raised his voice. 'Well? Speak up!' His breath formed a small white cloud on the air in front of his face as the elderly woman and the new vicar stared at her with emotionless eyes, waiting.

When Martha spoke, her voice seemed small in the chasm of this unfamiliar place. 'I am a widow with five children, sir. My husband died in the early part of the year. I have managed through most of the winter on our vegetables, but now I have nothing. I need money for food, fuel and rent.' She pulled her shawl tighter about her shoulders as her muscles danced uncontrollably beneath her damp garments.

The group behind the table put their heads together and mumbled. The word *church* reached Martha in the woman's sharp elderly voice.

3

The young vicar nodded in understanding, before turning back to Martha, with a look of disbelief upon his face. 'You don't attend church, Mrs Tilby!'

'No, sir.' Martha's chin rose, her voice held steady. She was not going to explain her reason to these people who she knew without doubt were hostile.

The elderly widow whispered in the vicar's ear and he nodded in acceptance of her words. His face looked pained as he prepared to speak to Martha. 'You understand,' he said, 'that this church fund is for residents of the village, Mrs Tilby?'

Martha felt degraded, yet held her nerve. 'I live on the edge of the village, sir, I am a resident and so are my hungry children.'

'And!' interrupted Mrs Fearling accusingly. 'You are an outsider. Not born here and you don't attend the church.'

Martha felt the eyes of the women behind her boring into her back, and heard the mumblings of unrest. Her back straightened. Her voice when it came was strong. 'My children, madam, are as cold and hungry as any other children in this village without a father.'

'Mrs Tilby.' The vicar's voice was firm as he cut in. 'You may have decided to burn in the flames of Hell by not coming to church. As a mother, you should want your children to go to Heaven and rest in the arms of the Lord.' He rested his arms on the table in front of him, waiting for a reply.

Martha's mouth tightened, as anger rose in her chest. She wanted to respond, but kept her counsel. Dangerous times had not long past and fear lay deep in the hearts of many like her. She had no wish to shake hands with the ducking stool, nor warm her feet on a pyre, something she felt that these reverent people were not beyond resurrecting. She knew them to be a law unto themselves, hiding behind their book for an excuse to reprimand any that didn't conform to their way of thinking, and collaborating with their idea of divinity. She didn't trust them,

4

any more than they trusted her, and it irked her greatly to have been forced by the hunger of her children to come into this building and ask for assistance.

'We will provide you with help if you and your children attend church.' The Reverend Draycott spoke directly at her, raising one eyebrow as though he were asking a question, but this, Martha knew, was an ultimatum.

'A docket will be handed to you on Sunday after the service. Mister Rudd will issue the docket, which you can spend with him on fuel, fat and flour. You will have to find the money for your rent elsewhere.'

'But, sir,' Martha was quick to protest. 'If I cannot get help with my rent, I will lose my home.'

'Madam,' intervened Rudd harshly, 'you must find work. It is not our job to support you entirely. Next.'

She was dismissed without another thought.

As she walked home Martha felt the pangs of failure deep in her soul. She and William had been so sure of his skills as a carpenter that they'd believed he would always be in work, and so had called their last child Charity. William had laughed as he had named her, smiling and stroking the baby's soft head. 'You will be the only Charity we will ever need.' A small tear ran down her face as she remembered how sick William had become. More tears followed as the grief of not being able to heal him surfaced in her heart. She had failed William. She had failed their vision of the future and she had failed herself having to ask for help from the church. And worst of all, if she didn't soon get work, she would fail her children.

~

On Sunday, amidst the stares of the congregation on their way to the morning service, Martha moved slowly with her five children along the path that twisted through the graveyard. Her children looked nervous and dragged their feet. She felt James clinging to her skirt and saw that he was close to tears.

The Reverend Draycott stood outside the church welcoming his new congregation with small nods and smiles as they passed through into the dark belly of the church.

As Martha approached the man, who was dressed in his Sunday robes of office, she pinched Charity's leg. The baby howled loudly. When they reached the preacher, Martha smiled a greeting while at the same time pinching the child again. The baby's howls carried far beyond the door and into the church, where those who had just entered turned and frowned. The preacher looked concerned. 'What is wrong with your child, madam?' he enquired as the family stood before him.

Martha hushed her child and rocked her, but the baby was in full flow and working up to a crescendo. 'She is ill, sir, and not fit to come to the church.'

She could see that her words had vexed him, and she knew why. This was his first sermon to his new flock. His words of wisdom would not be heard above Charity's yowling.

He frowned, looking from the child to the inside of the church, where his congregation packed tightly together awaited him. 'Perhaps it would be better if you took your child home.' He nodded, accepting the situation and it was clear to Martha that he wanted her and her disruptive baby gone.

'Thank you, sir, but I need the docket to buy my children food.' She again pinched the baby through its clothes. Charity responded, screaming loudly, purple in the face and kicking her legs. It was obvious to the vicar that the child was not going to stop.

'Please, madam,' he raised his voice above the noise, 'take your child home. Your children can receive the docket on your behalf after the service.'

'Thank you, sir.' Martha nodded. 'You're very kind.' She rocked Charity, and kissed her wet face to show the baby that she still loved her. Needs must, she justified to herself.

Martha ignored the frown that Emma, her eldest daughter, flung in her direction, as Robert, who was younger but nearly as tall, took hold of his sister Nona's hand. James, the smallest, hugged his mother's skirts, before they were ushered into the church porch, from where they stepped warily together over the threshold. 'Just copy everyone else.' Martha whispered an assurance. 'But don't come home without the docket.'

~

Three weeks later, Martha lay silently in her bed, listening to the peaceful breathing of her children. It was early. The light had not yet penetrated the cracks in the wooden shutters that covered the window. But the birds had already begun their dawn chorus in praise of another day. This morning, the joy of that sound did not touch Martha's heart. A great dread ran unchecked through her body. The sun was rising on a day where she would lose one of her children, and she was already feeling the pangs of loss. Everything around her seemed bleak. That desperate feeling was enhanced by the smoke-blackened ceiling over her bed in the recess beside the fireplace, and the faded and patched grey curtain hanging from the ceiling that pulled across to keep out the draught. Upon her bed lay a drab cover which had once been woven with beautiful shades of red. Now faded and thin, it barely kept her warm. On the pillow, her oval face, the colour of milk, was framed in a sea of long black hair. This morning her large brown eyes carried an expression of deep pain, as she went over the event that was to come. Life was going to get harder. But they would survive, she told herself. Through this opportunity she would be better placed to provide for her remaining children.

Martha eased herself from the warm hollow that her body had made in the straw mattress. She was careful not to wake the baby who now slept soundly in the folds of the bedcover. Silently she padded across the bare floorboards and dropped some fresh coal and sticks onto the fire.

A spillage of water spat for a few seconds, breaking the silence as she pulled the blackened kettle back onto the iron rack that straddled the coals.

Then, closing the latch door behind her, she stepped outside. The air was cold and fresh upon her face and spiders' webs sparkled with the diamonds of early dew. In her special part of the garden, hidden from the view of her neighbours by tall shrubs, Martha turned her face skyward, raising her arms to the frail morning sun as it rose above the trees. Here, she tried to find peace, as she immersed herself in the energy of the new day, breathing in its fresh fragrance. 'I welcome the energy of the life-giving sun,' she spoke quietly. 'I understand that you, like all living creatures, are part of a greater force and that it is because of your warmth that life survives on this earth. I ask the greater being to help me to honour all that I do this day and to be with those I love.'

Stooping, she let water run over her hands from a water-filled dish from which the birds drank, and in conclusion whispered, 'So mote it be.' She stood quietly for a time thinking nothing, absorbing the peace and the energy, until the cold penetrated her clothes and sent her back indoors.

In the kitchen she found that Emma and Nona were up but not yet dressed for the day. Emma was giving her younger sister her daily glass of milk. It was the only help they had against the rickets that plagued the thin child. 'Are the others still asleep?' The question was aimed at Emma, who nodded.

'The tincture seems to have helped Charity, Mother.' Emma looked towards the bed where the baby lay silently in the recess. 'When will the tooth be through?'

'A few days, I think.' Martha checked the fire. 'It's hard on Robert and James. I may have to change the sleeping arrangements.'

Nona screwed up her face. 'What does that mean, Mother?'

'It means that Charity will be in with you. She'll sleep better in a larger bed.'

'But I was going to have Emma's bed to myself, Mother,' Nona whined.

'Oh, were you, young lady, and who told you that story?'

'I thought...'

'Well, you thought wrong; we'll discuss this later. We have things to do right now that are more important.'

Nona sulkily laid the table for breakfast, while Emma dragged the pot onto the rack above the hot coals. Martha knew that her daughter would not eat with them again for a very long time, and she had mixed feelings about where Emma was going.

As the large bone that flavoured the stew from last night's meal was boiled to flavour the morning broth with half an onion, Martha cut a piece of bread and laid it next to each bowl. Since their fortunes had changed with the death of her husband, food was the only area where she could cut back to pay the bills. What she received from the widows' and orphans' charity barely kept them in coal and fat. She'd gleaned the forest of fallen wood, for their fire during the winter, and now the land behind the cottage was almost bare. They had eaten the last of their produce that had been planted to get them through the winter, vegetables that should have accompanied their meat. But they had long since eaten their pig and four of their six chickens. With William's death, there had been no money to replace the pig, or his lovingly planted vegetables that had become the main part of their diet.

'No! Not that much salt, Nona, just half that amount,' Emma's voice scolded as her sister seasoned the broth, standing on a stall to reach.

Nona shook some of the salt back into the stoneware pot and looked at Emma for confirmation. She nodded approval.

9

Martha tidied her bed in the recess and pulled a bag from beneath the solid wooden structure. Looking across the kitchen she said, 'Emma, I want you to pack your things in this. It will remind you of home and give you strength while you are away.'

Taking the canvas bag, which had been her father's, Emma held it gently to her chest. Her lip trembled; she could say nothing, as tears rolled around the rim of her eyes and the smell of her father engulfed her. Throwing her arms around her mother's waist, she hid her face, and screwed her eyes up tight against the tears she had promised that, at twelve, she was too grown up to show. The moment was brief before she ran to the ladder, climbing into the open roof space, where she fell upon her bed cradling the bag and sobbing silently into the rough material.

'I don't want Emma to go. Please don't make her go.' Nona's mouth puckered. She had been counting the days, and now that dreaded day had dawned.

'We've already talked about this, Nona, and you know it's not what any of us want. We are all going to be brave, aren't we?' Martha pulled her pale daughter towards her. As she wrapped her arms around the small girl, she was made aware of the sharp outline of the child's shoulder blades through the smock. 'We don't want Emma's last morning to be sad, do we?' she spoke kindly. 'You go up and wake the boys. We will all have breakfast together and say goodbye properly.'

With a heavy heart Martha watched Nona slowly climb the ladder into the roof to wake her brothers. Everything was relevant, she thought. Life would be much tougher for Nona from today. She would have to take up Emma's chores and take care of Charity and James, while she and Robert worked on Farmer Tate's land. How she thanked the higher energy that ruled her life, for her neighbour, Dolly Mott. Dolly had put a word in for her at the Tate farm, after she'd heard Mrs Tate saying that they needed more labour. 'It's hard work, Martha,'

Dolly had said, as her eyes searched Martha's face. 'Long hours hoeing in the fields between the rows. Picking fruit, stacking corn or anything that needs doing on the land. Do you think you're strong enough?' Martha wasn't sure; she'd been in a privileged position with William always in work. She hadn't had to work like her neighbours, but had said that she was strong enough.

From now on she would be relying heavily on Nona.

2.

It was still early as two female figures, the smaller dressed for travel and weighed down with a large bag, made their way across the fields towards the lane that eventually joined the road to London.

Emma clutched the bag that had been her father's, as she settled herself close to her mother on a flat stone at the side of the leafy lane. Here, accompanied by birdsong, they waited for the carrier, Mim Buckle, and his cart.

Long before the cart came into view, the sound of slow-moving cartwheels creaking over rutted earth and stones reached them. Martha put her arm around her daughter, knowing that they had very little time left together.

'Emma, I want you to do whatever Mrs Ames the housekeeper asks of you. Without question. Understand?' She looked into her daughter's pale brown eyes and marvelled at the green flecks that seemed illuminated in the early light. 'Just do as you're told, don't bring attention to yourself and all will be well.'

'Yes, Mother. I'm going to miss you all.' She wanted to say, I wish I didn't have to go, but she knew there was no choice. The money paid to her would if managed well, get the family through next winter.

Sliding her arms around her daughter, Martha pulled her close, kissing her golden head and smelling her fragrance.

Suddenly Martha shivered. On the road in the direction that the child would be travelling was a single magpie, a bad omen. Martha couldn't let it pass. 'Good morning, Mister Magpie,' she called, 'I hope your wife and loved ones are well?' The magpie didn't fly away, nor did any of his loved ones join him. Martha felt disturbed, but she knew that there was nothing that she could do to alter destiny.

At that moment Mim Buckle and Lady came slowly around the bend in the lane. The cart lurched and creaked over exposed tree roots and Lady shook her nose against her leather harness and snorted.

Mim muttered as the cart lurched. Known in the village as a rough, tough man, he dressed as other carters did in a brown leather coat, matching breeches and wide-brimmed hat. Except that in Mim's case it was rumoured that his hat was made from the skin of a highwayman's horse, the rogue having unsuccessfully asked him to stand and deliver with an unloaded pistol. It was also alleged that Mim, carried the highwayman's trigger finger in his pocket for luck. Mim Buckle was a legend on the roads and Martha knew her daughter would be safe travelling with him.

'I put a piece of bread and some cheese in your bag in case you get hungry on the journey.' Martha smiled lovingly at her daughter. 'And don't worry about us. Robert and I will be able to get some of the rent together.'

The cart pulled up beside them as she spoke, already loaded with goods for the day's deliveries. Martha spoke to Mim while Emma climbed up onto the front seat.

'You did me a great service, sir, in letting me know about this position for my daughter. I am most grateful to you and your sister.'

'I'm glad to have been able to help you, Mrs Tilby. My sister will be happy to know that she has been of some help to someone else. Good day to you, ma'am.' He turned away, flicking the reins. Lady strained against her harness and the old cart creaked as it moved off.

Martha watched them until they were out of sight, hardly daring to blink and lose the picture of her daughter's tiny frame and long golden hair as she sat high at the front of the cart. How strange it should be Claydon House where Emma was going to work. Martha felt uneasy but then thought, it had been so long, who would recognise her name? No, Emma would be safe and Martha had done all that she could to keep her daughter protected.

~

In the late afternoon, a blackbird sang in a tree above the hedgerow edging the fields. Emma felt far from home but the slow clip-clop of the horse's hooves made a comforting sound. Lady had struggled to the top of a hill, pulling the rickety old cart and its passengers in a ragged rhythm. The sun showed its face for the first time and now the horse stood sweating. Snorting hard, she shook her huge head. One hoof scraped the ground impatiently as Mim pointed to the valley below. 'There's Claydon House, down in the trees.' He waved his arm to the right. Emma strained to see. Below them, in a wide valley, a forest covering several acres of land was surrounded by a high wall. A roof and chimneys could just be seen amongst the greenery, and beyond that a farm and fields.

'Claydon!' Mim grunted through his teeth, as he bit on his pipe, moving it to the centre of his mouth and back again.

'It's big!' Emma's voice sounded small, uncertain. She couldn't remember living anywhere but her parents' cottage. Mim expelled some air and looked as though he was going to speak again but didn't. He flicked the reins and the cart jolted forward.

It was another two hours before the horse and cart, having made two deliveries, came to a halt outside the open gates of the Claydon Estate.

'This is it.' Mim pulled the horse to a stop and indicated Emma dismount the cart. 'I'll fetch your bag.' He descended stiffly, shuffling to the rear of the cart he picked the bag up and left it beside her on the ground.

Emma looked through the pillared gateway at the avenue of trees and shrubs and realised that the house couldn't be seen from this position. Behind the gate on the left a small lodge seemed to be hiding under the shadow of overhanging trees. It looked desolate, with a curtain of cobwebs hanging at the windows and the thatch in need of repair. She also noted that tall weeds and ground ivy, surrounding the porch, spread along the bottom of the faded door. The abandoned loneliness of the building unnerved her and she turned to Mim. 'Are we not going any further, sir? I can't see the house.'

'No', he grunted. Having dropped the bag at her feet he'd turned away, walking to the front of the cart.

Emma peered uneasily at the dark avenue of trees that drifted away into the distance and wondered if it was just the strangeness of this unfamiliar place that made her feel so unwelcome?

Seeing the look on Emma's face, Mim called across the back of his horse. 'I'm sorry. I tried it 'afore but Lady refuses to go up that path.'

Emma looked at the long-suffering horse in disbelief. But Mim was already climbing into the seat and flicking the reins to be off. And so she was left, in lonely solitude, a small figure standing in the dusty road.

The weed covered path felt lumpy beneath her feet as she stepped just inside the gates where a silent atmosphere enclosed her. She puzzled about it and then realised that there was no birdsong. Standing still, she listened.

There were so many trees and yet no birds, how strange! Walking slowly, her eyes scanned the darkness between the trees as she wondered how far ahead the house stood.

Suddenly, an unseen spider's web touched her face and hair. She panicked. Petrified of spiders, she dropped her bag, waving her arms about her head trying to free herself. The thin strands were invisible to her, but she could feel them so strongly that she thought the spider must be huge. Crying out, she ran in circles, eventually falling dizzily at the edge of the path. Although she knew that she was no longer in the web, she sat on the ground pulling at her clothes to rid herself of it. It was some time before she realised that she hadn't seen one strand of a web. She looked at her hands, her clothes: there was nothing to see. Trembling, she got to her feet. Stepping towards her bag, that now lay in the dirt, she studied the air above the path and saw nothing. Sighing in relief, she shuddered. She hated spiders more than anything else she could think of. Brushing herself down, she bent to retrieve her bag and walked straight into the web again. This time it wrapped itself around her head and moved down her neck. Screaming, she tore at her hair with one hand and tried to protect her neck with the other. Tears streamed down her face. In her giddy frenzy she fell over the bag, hitting her head on a large stone hidden in the weeds.

When she eventually opened her eyes they still held the fear. She was lying face down on the path and could taste its gritty dirt in her mouth. Turning her head slowly to the side, she could see that her bag was within reach and moving her arm slowly in its direction she grasped the strap. Pulling it towards her, she felt comforted by its familiar fabric and lay with it cradled in a hug as though it were her father. Eventually, she knew that she had to move and on hands and knees she made for the edge of the path. Standing up slowly, she looked down at her clothes in dismay. They were covered in dirt and her only skirt was torn at the hem. Her head ached as she stepped between the trees to get off the path and decided to walk through the forest to the house.

At first she found the walking easy and was able to keep sight of the path. The ground was made soft underfoot by layers of rotting leaves. It was easy to push through the emerging ferns that stood to attention like little green soldiers. But gradually the ferns gave way to tight bushes and thorns that barred her way. Disorientated by her constant detours, she became completely lost. The pain in her head was getting worse as she wiped a trickle of blood from the cut above her eye. The sweet aroma of the occasional fir was lost on her as the bag became heavier and heavier. As the light faded under the thick canopy she began to shiver in the cold air. Never had she felt so desperate and alone. In fact, she had never in her short life been alone. With the silence hammering at her ears she fell, exhausted at the base of a tree. Her face became smeared with dirt as she wiped the tears away with her hand, and she would have cried harder if her head had not hurt so much. Gradually her eyes lost focus and although she fought it she was sinking into unconsciousness. Her last thought was of wanting her mother.

3.

Claydon House

The flagstoned kitchen at Claydon House was large, although cosy and warm. Wiping her hands on her apron, Nell Ames, the cook and housekeeper looked out of the window into the yard. The night was closing in; she hated this time of evening.

Moving her ample frame towards the warmth of the fire, she edged the singing kettle away from the heat. She had hoped that the new girl would arrive today; the mistress wasn't going to be pleased. Nell shivered, as the cold chiselled face of Amelia Brack, the master's sister, flooded into her mind. Poking the fire, she inspected the coals and was glad of the warmth. I'll soon be banking it down for the night, she thought with a sigh.

At the sound of scraping boots outside she took a plate and a mug down from the dresser. 'You want supper, Matt?' she asked her son as he entered the kitchen.

'Please.' A dark-haired lad in a worn leather jerkin sat heavily on a chair beside the door removing his boots onto the mat.

His supper was placed on the table and he moved wearily towards it, but didn't eat it straight away. He looked at his mother, asking, 'Where's the girl?'

Nell threw up her hands. 'Where's the girl? Wouldn't I like to know where the girl is? She didn't arrive.'

The eyes narrowed in the young man's face and his tone when he spoke was meaningful. 'Mim dropped her off at the gate, about five.'

Nell's heart froze in her chest. 'She's out there somewhere at this time of night, alone?' her voice rose on the word, alone.

Matt turned towards the door picking up a boot. 'I'll have to go and find her.'

'No! You can't enter the woods, Matt. You can't go against the mistress. We daren't disobey her.'

'We can't leave the girl out there all night, Mother.'

'I don't want to leave her out there! Do you think I'll get a wink of sleep knowing that child is lost somewhere in the forest?'

Fear of what she had heard about something evil lurking amongst the trees, and the mistress's strict instructions that they should not enter after dark, pounded in her head. Nell was afraid for the girl. Afraid for her son if he went, and, afraid of Miss Brack if she found out.

'I'll find her.' Matt started to lace his boot.

'Don't be silly, Matt. If the mistress finds out you entered the forest, something terrible will happen to you, just like it did to Jake Poleshore.'

'Don't worry, Mother. I'm quick and I'm strong. I'll find her.'

Nell put her hand on his shoulder. This boy who looked so much like his father was all she had in the world. 'Matt, look through the window. There's no moon tonight and dark as pitch. You'll never find her amongst those trees.'

He sighed, dropping the boot to the floor. His mother was right. He wouldn't find her in the dark, and he wouldn't dare light a lamp to find her, or call out her name. 'I'll go out at first light.' His face was grave, his lips drawn tight as he wearily approached the table.

Nell wondered at the strength of her son's character. He was just fifteen and had done a man's job since the age of twelve. She remembered it as though it were yesterday, his father lying crumpled in the stable yard having been thrown from the master's favourite horse. After his burial, the mistress had called them to her drawing room and informed them that they must be gone by noon the next day. Standing like rigid grey marble, with eyes as heartless and dead as mussel shells, she'd said, 'I need a couple to run this house, Mrs Ames, a man for the stable and a woman for the kitchen. You'll have to get your charity elsewhere.'

Nell had returned to the kitchen distraught; she had a son, no money and nowhere to go. This fear she knew would never leave her.

~

Matt lay on his bed in the darkness of his small room above the stable block listening to the silence of the night. He could not sleep for thinking about the girl. Bile rose in his throat as he acknowledged how much he hated this house and its mistress. If only he and his mother could get away. He had tried over and over to make a plan, but there was always a flaw in it. His mother was no longer young; how could he look after her with no place to stay? Miss Brack gave them very little money. He'd been frugal, saving a little, but it wasn't anywhere near enough to journey far, or to house them. There was no question of him leaving alone, leaving Nell homeless.

Unconsciously he took a deep breath as he remembered Miss Brack's look of scorn, when three years ago after his father's funeral he had gone to ask for his father's job. She had towered above him like a black vulture and when she spoke there had been no pity in her voice.

'You have two days to prove that you can do his job.' Her voice rose and she spat. '*Two days*.' She had leaned forward, her eyes narrow slits, her nose almost touching his young face. 'And then you're out, understand?' His mouth had become dry. He'd not been able to reply, so he had nodded. '*Go*,' she'd shouted at him, but his feet had become glued to the floor. He'd wanted to move them, he'd wanted to run from the room, but his legs wouldn't move.

'*Get out!*' she'd screamed, reaching towards a table on which were an ink bottle, a heavy ornament and a knife. Suddenly he'd been galvanised, flying for the door, not waiting to see which she was going to pick up.

The next morning his mother had cried as he had gone to the stables to see to the horses.

Having helped his father every day since the age of six he knew the routine. It was a hard job for a man, but a seemingly impossible task for a boy. The horses trusted him as he scratched their ears, whispering to them, telling them what had happened. After grooming, they'd been turned out into the field. Then he'd set about cleaning out the stable and cleaning the tack. It had been a hard day. In the evening they came to his whistle and were stabled on clean straw. At the end of the second day he was told that he could have the job until she could find someone else. That day had never come, yet it hung over him like a sword.

Matt's body jumped. Opening his eyes he looked around the bare room. He must have fallen asleep. Still dressed he swung his legs over the side of the bed. It was dawn and the light was just creeping across the top of the chimneys.

Outside in the yard he splashed his face with water from the horse trough. The water was cold. Taking a horse-blanket he made his way past the vegetable plot towards the forest. He went at a run, as though the girl's life depended on his speed. But, in reality, he knew that if something was going to happen to her it would have happened hours ago.

Matt had seen Jake Poleshore after he'd stumbled from the forest where he had been poaching. Alf Freeman the gardener had found him wandering near the edge of the estate, his face white and expressionless, his eyes staring as though he had seen a horror. The man heard nothing that was said to him, and had uttered no word from that day on. It was enough to scare all those employed at the house to do as they were bid and none dared enter the forest for fear of both the mistress, and whatever had sent Jake Poleshore mad.

Matt hoped that the girl might be saved by the fact that she didn't know about the danger she was in, and that Miss Brack didn't know that she had arrived. He frowned. It was the first time that he had thought in any great depth on the subject. Was his mind telling him that the master's sister was the cause of what went on after dark? He had not seen anything except the poacher before or since, and he was almost sure that most of this fear originated in village gossip. Almost sure.

During the night Emma's senses had returned. Opening her eyes, she could see nothing. Lying very still she listened for a while to the sound of branches creaking around her. Slowly she stretched out her right arm; it connected with a tree just behind her head. Searching the ground with her left hand she felt the rough bark of tree roots. As she eased herself onto her knees her head swam and fear banged in her chest. The rustling of the forest floor beneath her made her hold her breath; anyone lurking in the darkness could have heard her movement. But apart from the vague creaking, there was nothing else to hear. Slowly, leaning forward, her hands searched the ground around her, feeling tentatively for her bag. It was only a short distance away and pulling it to her she opened it. Her hands moved blindly over the contents, recognising the textures of her shawl and coat. Removing them, she closed the bag and pulled it close to her. Folding the shawl for a pillow, she lay down again, pulling the coat across her body as a blanket. Her head ached. Her trembling fingers found a large bump over one eye. She cried quietly, but that action made the bump throb. As she waited for morning the tears ran silently down the side of her face and into her ears. Holding her hand up just in front of her nose in the darkness, she could just make out the shape of her fingers and was relieved to know that she wasn't blind. 'I'll wait until first light,' she thought, 'and then try to find the house.' Her stomach growled. She had not eaten for a long time.

She slept lightly, her exhausted mind drifting to the cottage where her family were asleep. In her dream she stood looking at her mother in her familiar bed. Transporting herself to the roof space, she saw that the baby was lying peacefully now beside Nona. The boys, Robert and James, were topped and tailed in their bed, their faces pale with sleep like little angels. Returning to the kitchen, she tried to warm herself by the fire. But the fire in her dream gave off no heat. Her eyelids fluttered as she awoke for a moment, the weight of her coat giving her some comfort. Feeling its warmth, she drifted again into sleep.

Almost immediately a sound like rats burrowing amongst autumn leaves made her open her eyes wide. Some way from her feet she could see a white mist. As it moved, dark spaces appeared like eyes. Frozen with fear, she watched it swirling above the ground. Suddenly, it swooped towards her. Her scream was silent, a facial expression of horror. Pulling the coat over her head she felt a pressure moving along the fabric from her feet towards her shoulders and the hair on her body stood upright on clammy flesh. Gripping the coat tightly, every muscle tense, she curled herself into a ball beneath it. Instinctively she knew it was after her mind, her identity. Biting her lip she held her breath, this wasn't going to happen.

'I'm Emma Tilby. Emma Tilby, Emma Tilby,' she repeated over and over in her head. 'The Great Energy protects me. The Great Energy is my protector. The Goddess protects me.' The words forming in her head came faster and faster, blocking out the feeling of the pressure on the coat. I will not give in. I am Emma Tilby. I am protected.

4.

In the morning, when Emma stirred, the forest had a different feel about it. A shaft of fragile sunlight now penetrated the canopy and she could see between the trees. Gathering her things together slowly in the stillness, she decided to walk towards the light in the hope of finding the house. As she tiptoed between the trees in the eerie silence she felt exposed. Was she the only living being in this forest? Yesterday, she had seen the whole estate from the top of a hill and remembered that a high wall surrounded the trees and that the house was in the centre. If she could find a part of that wall, put her back to it and then walk in a straight line she should come upon the house.

She thought that she was hallucinating when a familiar smell of pipe tobacco reached her nostrils. For a moment, instead of elation, she felt cautious. Where was the smell coming from? It was only a short time later while walking warily between the trees that she saw the smoke, its position given away, as it rose upwards like an ethereal snake dancing in a ray of sunlight. Her hopes rose. She was saved. There was someone else in the forest. But something stopped her rushing towards it. Like a fox, she was using all her senses: ears, eyes, smell and something else imperceptible that made the hair on her head crawl.

Between the leaves she saw a man dressed in fine clothes, a man of means, casually smoking his pipe. The help that she needed and hunger drove her to ask him for assistance. Stepping clumsily out from the trees she startled the man, who she now saw stood beside a rocky stream.

'Excuse me, sir, can you help me? I seem to be lost.' The muscles beside her mouth started to twitch. But she would not cry; she wouldn't. The man stared, and then looked around as though he were looking to see whom she was addressing.

'Are you addressing me, mistress?' He seemed surprised.

'I have to find the house, sir. Can you set me in the right direction?'

'The house?' He repeated her words as though he were in a dream. Then a flicker of understanding appeared in his eyes momentarily. 'What is your business at Claydon House?'

'I shall be working in the house, sir, but I don't seem able to reach it.'

'How long have you been lost?' His voice did not convey any care; it was just a question.

'I've been all night in the forest, sir.' She wanted to cry, but lifted her chin in defiance.

'Lost in the forest, and you were in there, all night?' He frowned.

Her voice wavered. 'Yes, sir.' Tears welled in her eyes as the man showed no sign of sympathy for her. Desperate for a drink, she asked, 'Would you mind, sir, if I drank from the stream?'

'Help yourself, mistress, but mind you don't fall in; it's very deep below where the water swirls around the rocks.'

Emma lay on her stomach, cupping her hands to hold a little water. The smell of rotting and damp vegetation rose into her nostrils and the nuttiness of the soil brought memories of home and a feeling of peace. After splashing her face, she stood and brushed her skirt and retied her hair.

The man, now standing with his back to a tree, raised his chin like an animal sniffing danger. 'Someone is looking for you,' he said simply. 'I'll take you near to where he is, and then you will be found. Come.' He turned suddenly, and marched along the bank before ducking into the trees. Emma ran after him, not wanting to be on her own again. Her strides were short with an intermittent skip as they pushed through the foliage and she tried to keep up.

'Do you live here, sir?' Her question went unanswered.

It felt as though they had covered a great distance, when he suddenly came to a stop. Grabbing her arm tightly, his cold fingers bit into her flesh.

'Don't tell anyone about me,' he warned. When she didn't speak, he bent down to her, his eyes holding a threat. 'Don't tell anyone that you have seen me, understand? You found your own way out.'

She tried to pull away, but his grip was like a vice as he shook her arm. 'Do you understand?' he spat.

'Yes, I understand,' she stammered, afraid of his sudden threatening behaviour. His manner immediately changed and he let go of her arm.

'I'm sorry. Miss Brack denies me access to the house.' He frowned as though he were deciding what to say. 'She would be angry if she knew that I was here.' He raised his eyebrows. 'She has something that is mine and I want it back.' His voice had become a whisper and Emma felt his sadness. 'You can help me to get it back.' He looked hopeful.

Emma felt horrified at the thought. 'I can't,' she almost choked. 'I couldn't steal what isn't mine!'

'I don't want you to steal it, only to let me know where it is.' His manner became impatient. Thrusting something cold into her hand, he said, 'take this small piece of silver; hide it in your pocket. When you are near what is mine it will get hot. Take a piece of cloth or ribbon and tie it to the outside of the nearest window. You need never know exactly what it is that I want. One favour deserves another.' He smiled unconvincingly.

He was right: she had an obligation; he had rescued her. Now, she should help him. She dropped the silver into her pocket.

'If you walk straight ahead,' he pointed, 'someone is looking for you; you'll be found.'

Emma looked in the direction that he pointed and then turned back to thank him, but he'd gone, melted away into the early-morning greyness of the forest.

There was a little flicker of hope in her heart to think that someone from the house was out looking for her. Dizzy from hunger, she no longer cared about fear, just so long as someone found her and gave her something to eat.

The branches covering the overgrown path ahead moved and the mumbled curses, together with the sound of cracking twigs, were sweet music to Emma's ears.

'Hello,' she called. 'I'm over here.'

Matt broke through the undergrowth looking scratched and dishevelled, his face showed concern as he stared at the slim girl before him. 'Are you all right?'

Emma found herself staring into the deepest brown eyes of a boy only a little older than herself. 'I am, thank you, sir, just hungry.' A spike of pain jagged near her eye and she put her hand to her head feeling dizzy.

'Let me look at that,' he said, passing his thumb over the lump. Emma flinched. 'Nasty bump!' he exclaimed, gripping her shoulder with hard fingers. His voice had a matching hard tone as he spoke again. 'What did you think you were doing going for a walk in the woods?'

Emma could feel his hot breath moving the hair on the top of her head. She felt like crying: after all that she'd been through she now found herself surrounded by angry people. But before she could reply he dismissively walked away, saying over his shoulder, 'Let's get you back to the house. Can you walk?'

'Yes, I can walk.' She felt annoyed. Her chin rose and her face flushed with anger at her seemingly sudden abandonment.

As they stepped carefully, pushing their bodies through the tangle of foliage, his manner changed. 'I'm sorry to hurry you but there's good reason.'

'I'm Emma Tilby,' she ventured. 'I'm going to be working here.'

'Yes, I know. We've been waiting for you.' He sounded angry again. 'You'll be working with my mother.'

'Miss Brack?'

'No! Not Miss Brack.' He spoke sharply. 'Mrs Ames, the housekeeper.'

Emma felt confused by his anger and wondered why he kept being so nasty to her. She knew that she was in trouble for being out in the forest all night, but it wasn't as though she'd enjoyed it. She decided to stay quiet until she understood who was who and what she would be doing.

As they climbed over the fence into the horses' field Matt stopped. 'I don't want to frighten you, Emma. I know you've been through a lot since yesterday, but I have to hide you in this blanket to get you into the house.'

'What?' She was stunned. 'Why should I hide; they're expecting me?'

'Miss Brack doesn't allow anyone to go into the forest, and I pray that you may never experience her displeasure. She may not know yet that you are here. I thought that I could smuggle you into the kitchen in this blanket, so you don't get into trouble.'

Emma looked at the smelly blanket and pulled a face. 'Won't she see me walking?'

'Not if I put you over my shoulder.' He shook the blanket out and as he spoke the air was filled with dust and the smell of horses.

Reluctantly Emma nodded agreement. It was obvious that she was already in trouble. She stood obediently as he wrapped the coarse material around her. When he pulled the blanket over her head she sneezed suddenly as the dust mites entered her nose. His voice came to her through the thick wool, muffled but sharp. 'Stop making a noise.' And without any preamble he lifted her roughly into the air. With a small squeal of fear she felt herself going over his shoulder.

~

As Matt pushed through the door into the kitchen, Nell, who had made the kitchen ready for a casualty, went into shock at seeing the bundle on Matt's shoulder.

'Dear God no! Don't say she's dead.' Nell flapped her arms like a chicken, sitting suddenly on the chair and getting up again immediately, crying, 'Oh no! She's dead, poor little thing, poor little thing.'

'Mother stop,' Matt shouted. 'She's not dead.' But Nell continued to howl. 'Will you listen to me, Mother? She's not dead.'

Laying the bundle on the floor, he unrolled it. Emma's groan brought Nell to her senses and she found herself looking into a pale oval face, surrounded by long golden curls and a bump the size of a blackbird's egg over the girl's right eye. Quickly recovering the situation, Nell took charge.

'Matt, go and get a cloth from the scullery, dip it in cold water and bring it here.' Rubbing Emma's hand, she said softly, 'You're all right now, dear; come and sit beside the fire and get warm.'

Emma's hands were put into a bowl of warm water and washed. Her face was also washed as Matt held the cold compress to her head.

'We've got to make a plan, Matt,' Nell whispered. 'The mistress can't see her in this state.'

Putting the compress down, Matt started to leave. 'I should see to the horses, Mother.'

'Yes, you should, but not before you've both eaten.'

Taking two plates from the warm brick oven at the side of the fire, Nell dished up fried meat, potatoes, egg and mushrooms from a flat pan. A weak beer was served in large mugs before Nell cut thick chunks from the bread that sat on the table. Emma cleared her plate almost as quickly as Matt while Nell sat silently thinking in her armchair beside the range, her fingers tapping absent-mindedly on her mouth.

'Matt, as soon as you're finished I want you to go upstairs to Brier Rose and get the uniform hanging in the cupboard for me.'

Matt wiped the last of his bread around his plate before he left the room.

'I'm sorry to have caused so much trouble, Mrs Ames. I got lost.'

'How did you come to be lost in the forest, Emma? Why didn't you stay on the path?' It was a question that had kept Nell awake most of the night.

Emma explained all that had happened. It seemed so lame now avoiding a spider's web. Nell shook her head and Emma couldn't tell what she was thinking. Matt arrived with the clothes, which he handed to his mother before leaving the kitchen for the stable.

Nell held a brown dress up against Emma and sucked air in between her teeth. 'It's a bit big, but you'll grow into it. I'll pull it up at the waist and hold it there with your apron ties until we can shorten it tonight. This white apron' – Nell thrust white material towards Emma – 'is for going to see Miss Brack, or anytime that you go into the house other than to clean. Otherwise you will always wear this grey one.'

Emma nodded; she was becoming frightened now. She really didn't want to meet Miss Brack. Her life would be happy if she could just stay in the warm kitchen with Mrs Ames and earn her money to send home.

'I'd better tell you what your duties will be, Emma. You will get up at four-thirty, wash and dress, come to the kitchen and rake the coals, wearing your grey apron.'

Emma nodded again. She did that at home, although not so early. 'You will take the ashes outside and dispose of them. I will show you where. You will fill the coal baskets for the day and fill the kettle and that churn with water.' Nell pointed to the corner of the room, where a large milk churn stood. I will show you later where the well is. Miss Brack rises at seven-thirty and so does Mrs Shillabeer. You will take a pitcher of hot water before that time to Miss Brack's room and leave Mrs Shillabeer's on a table on the second landing. Don't worry. I will show you this morning. You must *never* be late and the water must *always* be hot. Their breakfast is left in the dining room in covered terrines. While they eat their breakfast you will visit their rooms and remove the dirty water, putting it back in the pitcher and remove the chamber pot from under the bed. I will show you where you dispose of the contents. Then take them to the scullery and wash them before putting them back where you found them.'

Emma turned up her nose. Nell raised an eyebrow.

'Did you think that they would do that for themselves?' Emma shook her head. She had never before thought about what rich people in big houses did.

'Who is Mrs Shillabeer?' she asked, to get a better idea of her importance.

A good question, Nell thought. There was something very strange about Gertrude Shillabeer. She decided only to tell Emma what Miss Brack had told her. 'Mrs Shillabeer was at school with Miss Brack in France and is staying here as a friend and companion.' Emma nodded, accepting all the information.

Later, carrying two pitchers of hot water, Emma was shown the servants' route to all the rooms in the house. She was led from the kitchen into an arched passage that ran through the basement. It was cold and badly lit. Green paint peeled from the walls, where large damp patches mouldered. And the uneven flag stone floor, worn away by the hurrying feet of servants over many years, could now trip the unwary. The wooden stairs from the passage to the upper part of the house creaked under her feet and the banister moved and groaned like an elderly servant. Emma was amazed that all parts of the house could be reached without her being seen.

31

'The whole point, Emma,' Nell explained, 'is that the house runs smoothly and that the servants are seen as little as possible.'

'How many servants work here, Mrs Ames?'

'Four. There used to be around thirty when old Mister Brack was alive. We had a butler and two footmen then. There were upstairs maids, downstairs maids, two scullery maids, three working in the stables, four gardeners and the farm workers. Things changed suddenly when the master died. He was a lovely man.' For a moment, she seemed lost in her thoughts. Then, turning around at the top of the servants' stairs, Nell pushed backwards through a scuffed green door. Emma followed and stood gaping at her surroundings. On the other side of the green door the passage was lined in dark wood. There were matching doors the length of a long landing. Large pictures of people in fine clothes looked down on her and heavy drapes hung at large latticed windows. She followed, mesmerised, behind Mrs Ames, who stopped outside a door.

'This is Miss Brack's dressing room,' she whispered, and Emma's stomach lurched. 'Just follow me in and watch what I do.'

The room that they entered was small and dark. Nell placed the pitcher of hot water on the marble washstand and hung a towel on the rail at the side. She then quietly opened a door into a larger room, where in the gloom a large bed could just be seen, its drapes half pulled across. Emma was close on Nell's heels as the heavy drapes that covered the lattice windows were pulled back, letting light into the room and exposing the gardens below. Emma didn't look towards the bed. She didn't want to see Miss Brack if she was there, especially not without her clothes.

Hurrying back along the landing, Nell led in another direction, until they came to a small flight of stairs, at the top of which was another passage leading to the West Wing.

'Put the pitcher on this table, Emma. Mrs Shillabeer likes to look after herself.' Now come; we have a lot still to do.

Back in the kitchen Emma was put to work helping with the breakfast and setting the trays that would be taken upstairs to the breakfast room. Nell made a dish of scrambled eggs, one of fried meat and another with mushrooms; all were covered in silver terrines. Bread was cut thinly and put in a basket lined with a white cloth, whereupon the cloth edges were turned back, covering the bread to keep it fresh. Emma was instructed to put butter in a little white dish and some red preserve in another. The tray was heavy and Emma struggled under its weight. Nell realised she would have to find a way to help Emma; she just wasn't as strong or as old as Polly. Nell blew out her cheeks in frustration; she'd like to know why Polly had run away without any explanation. It had really made life difficult; she'd tried to carry on by doing Polly's work so that Miss Brack wouldn't turn them out: a threat that she felt still hung over her head.

Nell liked Emma; she was small but she had a strong character, and she'll need it, she thought. Later Emma was instructed on cleaning the house from top to bottom, a job that would progress throughout the day. She was shown many rooms, but it was the library that had the biggest influence on her. As the door was opened a huge portrait dominated her view. It was of the man in the forest and he was looking straight at her in a manner that dared her to speak. Nell had bustled in ahead and hadn't noticed Emma's shock.

'Who is the man in the portrait, Mrs Ames?' she asked, unable to look away from the eyes that stared at her in, she thought, recognition.

'That is Oliver Brack Emma, brother of the mistress and the master of the Claydon Estate. A good likeness, I think. He was a bit younger then and old Mister Brack was very pleased with the painting. Mister Oliver became the owner of Claydon when his father died and he and his sister live here quite alone. They don't seem to have any living relatives and that's a real shame.'

As Nell pointed out several items that she must be very careful with when cleaning, Emma felt Oliver's eyes on her back and wondered what he was doing in the forest and why he couldn't come home. Nell noticed the look on her face. 'I know what you're thinking. It's quite unnerving the way his eyes follow you around the room. Come on, Emma, we're done in here, let's go and pour some hot water on the tea leaves I saved from the mistress's teapot.'

~

Miss Brack and Mrs Shillabeer took their evening meal together in the dining room. Whilst in the kitchen, Emma was setting the table for four when Matt entered sitting heavily on the chair to remove his boots. 'I'm really hungry, Mother. What's for supper?'

'Meat pie, potatoes and cabbage. How much do you want?'

'Pile it up. I've had real trouble with the horses. I had to move them from the field near the woods. Something down there is spooking them.'

'Could it be a fox?'

'No, I don't think so. I had a quick look around but I couldn't see any signs.'

'Another mystery then.' Nell was putting the plates on the table as the yard door opened again and an elderly gentleman entered the kitchen, removing his cap and his boots.

'Emma, this is Mister Alf Freeman, our gardener. I'll be sending you over to him for the vegetables most days.'

Emma smiled and nodded in greeting. 'Good evening, sir.'

Alf chuckled, 'Sir, that's a good 'un. You're going t'get on well 'ere, Emma. Call me Alf. We'll get on fine.'

'Have you seen any foxes hanging around, Alf? Something's spooking the horses down in the lower field.'

'No, I've not seen anything unusual, Matt.' Alf's face took on a troubled look, but his eyes didn't leave his plate. 'Chickens are good. I'll keep watchful. Talking of horses, I need some manure.'

Matt nodded. 'I'll bring some over when we're finished here.'

As they sat around the table, Emma found it hard to believe the amount of food that was piled on their plates. What Matt was tucking into would have fed her whole family for a day or more.

'Come on, Emma, eat your food. You have to keep your strength up; there's still a lot to do before bed,' Nell said kindly.

Emma ate, wishing that she could share the feast with her family and imagining the amazed hungry look on the faces of her brothers, who she knew had never seen such a huge pie.

Alf ate his food head down over the plate in complete concentration. The knife, dwarfed in his huge brown hand, took Emma's attention. She watched as he cut his pie and the potatoes with it, before scooping the food up into his creased mouth on its blade. She blushed and looked away as she realised that she was staring at his gums and his long thin tongue that stretched out towards the knife, guiding it home with each mouthful. Cutlery scraped on plates until Alf broke the spell. 'Anyone know when the master's cum'n back?'

'No one bothered to tell me he was leaving.' Nell sounded hurt. 'You'd think they'd say he didn't want his dinner. Gone to town, just like that. All I can say is that he must have a property in town to stay in as he didn't take his clothes with him.'

'How'd you know that, Mother?' Matt stared at Nell, eyebrows raised.

'Since Polly ran away I've had to clean his room and all his clothes are still in his cupboard. And, that's another mystery, why did that girl run away without saying first what was wrong?'

'Ah, but she'd been peaky, Nell, white as a sheet she was last day she came for vegetables.' Alf looked around the table at the serious faces.

'She'd been peaky or lazy for some time,' Nell said, frowning. 'She was doing less and less and it was beginning to show upstairs. The mistress must've said something to her. If only I hadn't gone to bed early.'

'You can't blame yourself, Nell. You were like a mother to 'er.' Alf pushed his plate into the centre of the table.

'But if I'd been awake I might've stopped her leaving.' Nell was feeling guilty and the pain of it was heard in her voice.

Matt pushed his empty plate away. 'Not if Amelia Brack chased her out of the house you wouldn't.'

'No, she wasn't chased, Matt; she had time to pack all her things. The cupboard was completely empty apart from her uniform. She must have planned it.' Nell looked around the table. 'Baked apple?' Three heads nodded and a thoughtful silence ensued as they ate.

~

Two hours later Emma emerged from the scullery, wiping her hands on her apron. They were already turning red.

'Well, that's your first day over with, Emma. You must be weary. Come and sit with me by the fire and I'll make you a nice hot drink. That's it, dear, settle yourself in that chair.'

Nell heated milk for the two of them and got two mugs down off the dresser shelf. 'Now tell me all about yourself, Emma. Do you have brothers and sisters?'

'I have two sisters and two brothers.' She took the milk that Nell offered to her. 'Nona's eleven; she's not very strong. Robert is ten and he's going to work in the fields with Mother. James is eight and Charity is five months old and just teething.' Nell wondered why they were such a small family, but then it wasn't unusual for a woman to miscarry between births. She stared at Emma for a moment, trying to gauge the strength of the girl's emotions. After all, she'd been through a great deal these last twenty-four hours. The fire crackled loudly between them as they hugged their warm drinks in the candlelight and the furniture made long shadows on the flagstone floor as they sat companionably in the warm glow of the fire.

'And your father?' Nell was interested.

'My father was a carpenter, a very good carpenter. He died of pneumonia three weeks after Charity was born.' Her eyes filled with tears and Nell was wise enough not to stop her. Better out than in, she always thought.

'I'm sorry, Mrs Ames, I miss him.' Emma dabbed her eyes on her grey apron. 'Everything changed after he died because we had no money being earned. We lived for a while on my parents' savings and the vegetables in the garden. But the money has gone. Mother received some charity money from the village elders, but it wasn't enough. She has managed to get labouring work in the fields with my brother, but I don't know how they will manage.' She dabbed her eyes again.

'Well, your mother's found work, Emma. Things have a way of working out. I'm sure they'll be fine with the help that you will give them.' Nell put her mug down. 'How old are you, Emma?'

'I'll be thirteen next week, Mrs Ames.' Nell nodded. She wasn't too young to be out to work; after all, boys of ten were working down the mines and she'd heard that children as young as six worked in the mills up north. But it was young to have fallen into such a hard job. By rights she should only be the scullery maid, but as things were in this house she was now the maid of all work. Nell felt sorry for the child for a fleeting moment, but it passed quickly, there were a lot worse off than her.

It was eleven o'clock before Emma left the kitchen, where Nell was sitting comfortably next to the fire with the sound of the kettle singing gently as she altered Emma's brown uniform.

Emma reached her room by climbing a bare wooden staircase from the servants' passage to the top of the house. Three doors led off the landing and on one someone had painted a stem of roses. The words *Brier Rose* were painted in blue beneath the picture. The room was basic, with a bed, chair, cupboard, and a table holding a jug and bowl for washing. A few days ago she would have thought this a luxury, but tonight it was the loneliest place in the world. She hung her few garments in the cupboard. Then, clutching her father's bag, she climbed into the bed. Her body ached. She hadn't known she would have to do so much. She thought about Polly, who Nell had said was fifteen. Did she run away because she had so much to do? And then there was Miss Brack. She didn't want to meet the mistress and wondered if she could scurry about the passages for the rest of her time here, never meeting her at all. She was just linking with the energy, asking for the strength to be able to do the work and that her family be kept safe, when sleep won the battle for her mind.

5.

Haddenford

Martha answered the knock at the door and then wished with all her heart that she hadn't. A knot of fear gripped her stomach as she looked into the face of the rent collector, whose bulk now filled the space, blocking out the light. 'Well, Mrs Tilby, do you have the rent this week?' Spittle dripped from his lip and bubbled white in the corner of his mouth. As always, he stood on her doorstep as though he owned it. Martha pulled herself up straight and faced the sweating man in his heavy blue-flecked jacket. 'I will have it, Mister Beemer, on Friday.' She nodded and smiled trying to convince him.

Beemer's flabby pink mouth parted, showing his uneven yellow and brown teeth. 'Not good enough, Mrs Tilby. Today is Friday and you couldn't pay last Friday. Why should I believe that next Friday you will suddenly have three weeks' rent to give me?'

'I have a job, Mr Beemer. I start on Monday. I will have the money, I can assure you.'

'It must be a well-paid job, mistress, for you to be able to pay three weeks' rent at one time.'

His small eyes looked her over from head to foot. She understood what he was implying and wanted to slap his flabby face, but instead clenched her fists and held her peace. When she shut the door she was shaking with anger and fear. The job was not well paid and it would be very hard work for a woman still breastfeeding.

Sitting by the fire, she put her head in her hands; what else could she do to bring in money? There had to be something.

Robert came in from the garden, where he'd been digging and playing with the coloured stones he liked to collect.

'Look what I found, Mother!' He was proudly holding up a muddy coin. 'I dug it up.'

Martha stared at it and had the seed of an idea. When you're desperate you clutch at tiny straws, she thought; any small amount of money would help. Taking a bowl from the shelf, she called James from the garden, where he was feeding their last two hens, and Nona from the roof space. They stood before her waiting with interest. Martha stood like a schoolteacher at the front of class.

'Robert has just found some treasure buried in the garden and just now we need a lot of treasure to pay the rent. How would you like to play a game looking on the ground for money? Anything you find we will put in this bowl and give to Mister Beemer on Friday.'

Nona screwed up her face 'Mister Beemer?'

Yes, Nona, Mister Beemer to help with the rent.'

'Barmy Beemer, barmy Beemer,' the boys sang as they jigged around the room, pulling at each other's clothes. 'Barmy Beemer,' they giggled.

Martha clapped her hands. 'Outside, all of you, let's see who can find some treasure.' The boys raced noisily from the room, each wanting to be first.

'Can we look anywhere, even along the lane?' Nona asked.

'Of course, as long as it's on the ground and doesn't belong to anyone.'

There hadn't been this much excitement for a long time and Martha realised that they were going to get even less attention from her once she started work. Washing Robert's coin, she put it in the bottom of the bowl, where it looked very small and lonely. It's a start, Martha thought, as she tied her apron around her slim waist.

She'd just put the bread to rise when Charity needed a feed. Sitting beside the fire with the baby cradled in her lap, she opened her bodice. Soon the child was contentedly sucking, her small fingers stroking her mother's breast. A ringlet of silky black hair worked loose from Martha's bun, and as it slipped down onto her breast Charity held onto it. This is the best feeling in the world, she thought, as Charity sucked contentedly. Oh, how she didn't want to give this up. Stroking her daughter's soft head absent-mindedly, she watched the baby close her eyes. So much of William could be seen in her. She was a little miracle, born too early and so small she'd had difficulty feeding and breathing. Now that she was doing so well Martha was loath to take her from the breast. She'd fed each of the others until they were over two years old. But on Monday she would express milk for Nona to give to Charity, and if that didn't work she would have to start the baby on broth. She sighed. And then there would be another mouth to feed.

A knock on the back door brought Martha out of her thoughts. Dolly's face appeared in the opening, her red hair burning like fire with the daylight behind it.

'Not disturbing you, am I?' She was already crossing the floor, where she settled herself into the armchair that used to be William's.

'Come in, Dolly, and tell me what's new.' Martha smiled at her neighbour, knowing that she would come in anyway and always had the local gossip.

'I just came to see how you were going to handle Monday.'

'I'll give Charity her morning feed. Nona will stay here and look after the baby and James. She'll feed them both and watch them until I get back. I'll breastfeed Charity when I get home. I can't say more than that until I know what work and hours I'll be doing.'

'I feel I should be helping you more, Martha, after you looked after my children when me and Tom were ill.'

'You finding me this job, Dolly, has saved my home and my children. You can't imagine how much you have helped me; please don't say any more.'

'Are things that bad?' Dolly looked worried.

'I'm behind with the rent two weeks, three on Friday.'

'That's bad.' Dolly looked worried. 'Mister Bullock isn't a forgiving man and his henchman Barney Beemer enjoys clearing houses.' Dolly thought for a moment and her face became brighter. 'Do you have anything you can sell?'

'Sell?' Martha looked around the room. She needed everything and nothing was in good condition. Her pots and pans were black with soot. Feathers were coming out of cushions and the curtain next to her bed was faded. All the bedding was needed.

'It's May Day tomorrow,' Dolly continued, 'and the village is holding a feast. The celebrations are being held in the church grounds.'

'Feast?'

'Yes, feast! So called by the sharp tongued widow Fearling, who arranges the flowers at the church and knows everyone's business.'

'Dolly, that's not nice.' Martha transferred Charity to her other breast.

'Sorry, Martha. You and me could, lay a cloth down and sell some things,' she said hopefully.

'But I don't go to church; they won't let me do that, will they?'

'Course they will. The feast is for the villagers. I heard that the more that come the more success it will be.' She had turned on the pleading look that Martha found hard to resist.

Martha sighed. 'William made one or two things in wood when he was an apprentice that someone might buy.'

'That's settled then.' Dolly got up to leave. 'Oh, I forgot to say, it's tomorrow morning; will you be ready?'

'Thanks, Dolly. I'll see what I can find to sell.'

When the children were in bed and Charity settled, Martha took a bundle from a cupboard. Opening it carefully, she revealed the nut-brown wood. A small wren exquisitely carved by William for an exam was wrapped in an inner oily cloth. It was Martha's favourite bird and William had been given good marks for it. In another cloth was an apple with the tighter wood grain skilfully placed on one side, giving it a darker hue, as though it had a rosy bloom. She stroked the pieces, smelling the linseed oil, and for a moment William seemed very near. He would want me to sell them and pay the rent, but how much could I ask? There were other pieces, but most were not finished. Not fully carved, or not polished. She put the apple and the bird on the table. It was as she was pushing the bundle back into the cupboard that she saw a small box. Frowning, she pulled it out. It was from her childhood but she couldn't remember what was in it. Opening the lid, she gasped, having forgotten so many years ago sitting at the table learning to make lace. 'One day,' her mother had said, 'if you're very good, you could make collars for the dresses of fine ladies.' But Martha was too slow; it took a very long time to make a piece of lace in-between doing the chores and looking after her sisters. But there were several pieces that were finished. She unrolled four lengths of lace and remembered practising the different patterns. They were just practice pieces but there was enough in each length to decorate a baby's gown, or child's bodice. Would these do? They joined the other things on the table.

She banked down the fire and went to her bed. Tomorrow she would look for other things to sell.

As she linked with the energy in which she believed, she gave thanks for Dolly's friendship, and asked for the protection of her daughter Emma, and help with raising the money for the rent. As she drifted into a fragile sleep, one part of her brain was searching the house for saleable items and the other half was listening for Charity's teething cry.

43

Next day the children were all excited about the village feast. They had never been to anything like it before. Breakfast was eaten and the children were washed and put into their best clothes. Martha had added a quince cheese and some bundles of herbs to her saleable items. It still wasn't much, but then she didn't have much.

Dolly arrived on the doorstep, arms stretched wide, carrying a box of assorted objects. 'Ready?' she asked.

'Yes. I'm really nervous about this, Dolly.'

'Why? It will be a day of fun. The children will love it, Martha.'

'It's those widows at the church. They really don't like me, Dolly.'

Dolly looked at her strangely. 'What do you mean?'

'I'm not sure, Dolly.' Martha felt uncomfortable; she'd said too much. 'Forget what I said, it's just a feeling. I'm being silly.' And pushing the nagging feeling to the back of her mind she shut the door and followed the chattering children up the front path. She could feel their happy expectation and wished that she could feel the same. But, whatever she felt, she needed the money for the rent and she would have to face whatever was put before her.

They took the lane that wove between the high hedgerows towards the village. Bees hummed amongst the wild flowers and herbs that grew on the sides of the steep banks. A profusion of primroses lined their walk with a joyful yellow light. Blackbirds sang from the tops of the trees as the families walked, and a shy wren flitted low down amongst the foliage, looking for food. Martha thought of William and clutched her bundle closer with some regret.

Dolly's children, Dan, her eldest, a little older than Robert and Alice at fifteen a young lady, ran ahead with Robert and James, while Nona, moving slower, carried Charity. 'It's going to be a great day out,' Dolly laughed.

The church, at the centre of the village and the lychgate that led off the village green, were decorated with wild flowers and white ribbons.

'It's just like a wedding day,' Nona told Charity, her eyes glowing excitedly.

Men and women were milling around in the grounds, putting their wares onto tables. Dolly had at the last minute decided to use her mother's light table and transported it on her hand barrow. 'What fun,' she'd called as they passed the black-faced Mollies dancing on the village green to the accompaniment of a man playing a pipe and banging a tabor with a stick, the drum tied to his leg.

When they entered the church grounds they were amazed at the transformation. People were touring the stalls set along the path, viewing the goods on display and children were playing games, their laughter filling the normally silent air. It was all so colourful and joyful that Martha was glad to be a part of the crowd as Dolly set out their pitch. It didn't take long for Martha to set her few items out on the table. But then she sighed: she had a dilemma. 'How much should I ask for my items?'

Dolly came and stood next to her and looked at the items placed one end of the table. 'I'm not sure! Go and have a quick look at the other stalls and get an idea from them. And be quick, you don't want to miss a sale.'

As Martha moved from one stall to another she was amazed at the variety of items on sale. It was obvious to her that some of these women had been preparing especially for this day. There were good used clothes, herb bags and embroidery, embroidered handkerchiefs and petticoats. A table displaying root vegetables was being run by three ladies who were surrounded by eager buyers. Mister Savoury, a maker of farming tools, was selling second-hand tools and another man was sharpening knives. There were many women around the edges of the feast with goods for sale on the ground. Martha recognised the wife of the vicar standing behind a table and although they had never spoken Martha felt safe, looking to see the price of her preserve. The young woman, with yellow curls pushed neatly under a bonnet, was wearing a pale blue dress. She was just giving a pot of strawberry cheese to an elderly parishioner when Martha approached. She can scarcely be twenty, Martha thought, and so unlike the last one, who dressed only in black and was as old as sixty if she had been a day.

'Hello, would you like to buy some strawberry cheese? I boil it down with honey and a little vinegar, it's very sweet.' The wide smile exposed teeth like pearls and for a moment Martha was lost for words.

'Err, no, thank you.' Martha flushed. 'Would you mind if I just asked you how much you're selling your preserve for? I have a pot for sale and I haven't sold anything before.'

'Of course I don't mind. Mistress?'

'Tilby. Martha Tilby.'

'Martha, how nice to meet you. I'm Emily Draycott, wife of the new vicar. But I expect that you already know that.'

Martha smiled and knew that here was a young woman who cared about people.

'I'm selling my preserve for one halfpenny a pot.' She smiled again.

Martha thanked her and hurried back to Dolly. On her return she priced her own quince cheese at a halfpenny and her lace was priced reasonably by the strip. The carvings done by William were another matter; to her they were priceless. Dolly saw her standing holding the wren, in deep thought.

'Don't know what to charge?'

'No, I really don't, Dolly.'

'What about threepence?'

'Threepence! Are you mad? That's a lot of money. Who would pay that much for an ornament?'

Dolly's face was serious as she pointed at the crowd. 'Look around, Martha; we may all be wearing our Sunday best, but it is plain to see that some of these people are not as poor as us.'

Martha looked closer for the first time at the gathering. There were people from the big house. Major Laddisbrock and his wife, dressed in their fine clothes, were arriving in their black carriage pulled by two magnificent chestnut horses. Their servants, walking behind the carriage, looked more affluent than Dolly and Martha. Gentleman farmers and their wives were also supporting the event and even the new school governor and the teacher were there.

'All right,' she said reluctantly, knowing how much that amount of money would help with the rent. 'I'll put threepence on it.'

They did a good trade; Martha sold her lace and was complimented on the patterns and fineness of the work. A young man bought the apple for his love and that made Martha happy. Interested buyers were crowded around their table when a plump, hairy hand pushed through the crowd and removed the wren for inspection. Horrified, Martha saw her precious wren being pawed by Barney Beemer. She felt as though she, were being mauled as he turned it over and over in close proximity to his swollen, sweaty face.

'How much?' He held it aloft.

'It's sold, sorry.' It was out before Martha could stop herself. All the muscles in her body tensed, she wanted to snatch it from his fat fingers.

'If it's sold, why's it still on the table?' He stared over the heads of the crowd, his eyes becoming slits beneath his frown.

'The buyer's coming back for it,' she lied. 'Please put it back on the table.' He put it down heavily and walked on.

'You could have sold that.' Dolly was aghast. 'That would have got you out of a lot of trouble, Martha.'

An anger that Martha didn't know she possessed rampaged in her body and showed in a sudden flush on her face. 'I'd rather be homeless than have him owning anything that belonged to William,' she hissed through her teeth.

'You daft woman. If you don't pay the rent he will turn you out and take goods to cover the amount. He'll end up owning *all* that belonged to William.'

Martha knew that she had been stupid. It was a sudden reaction that had surprised even her. But she wouldn't go back on it. She couldn't stand that man and the way he looked at her each time he stood on her doorstep.

Dolly's voice interrupted her thoughts 'Look out, heads down, here comes the dark widow. That woman could cut air with her tongue.'

Martha was about to chide Dolly when she also saw bearing down on them a thin, severe-faced woman in grey, followed closely and purposefully by two nicely dressed churchwomen. The widow Fearling was looking straight at Martha. Clutching her purse tightly in a gloved hand, she now stopped in front of the table.

'And what do you think that you are doing on church land?' Her voice was high and rasping as she glared at Martha.

Dolly and Martha were both taken aback and stared at the women in shocked silence. It was Dolly who recovered first. 'Would you like to explain that remark, Mrs Fearling?' Dolly's voice was angry and defending, her face becoming as red as her hair.

'This woman,' she pointed at Martha, 'is causing a blasphemy on church land. How did she get a table at this feast?'

Martha still had her mouth open; what was this woman saying and what did she mean? But deep down beyond the shock Martha knew just what the widow was inferring. She looked at the faces of those standing at the table and those passing by. Thankfully, all she saw was curiosity on their faces but that, she knew, is where it would start. Ignorant people gossiping about differences and then making up what they didn't know.

'I brought this table,' Dolly was saying, 'and, this is a village feast, not a church feast. As far as I know, any villager can sell his or her wares here today.'

It was at this point that Emily Draycott intervened. 'Mistress Fearling, could you explain your remark to me, please?' She waited expectantly.

'This woman' – a long scrawny finger was waved shakily in Martha's direction – 'has been seen walking the fields when the moon is full.'

'And?' Emily was as puzzled as Dolly.

'And she doesn't attend church.' The widow's voice had risen and people were now crowding around her watching and listening.

The vicar pushed through the crowd, his clothes wet from having clumps of wet straw thrown at him by the children while he was locked in the stocks by his arms.

'Thank you, ladies.' He used an authoritative voice. 'I will deal with this.' His face was serious as he stared at his three elderly parishioners. 'Thank you, ladies,' he said again, and bowed to them, leaving them in no doubt that they were being dismissed.

The women walked away, their noses in the air. Clucking like justified hens, they swept along the gravel path between the stalls.

Embarrassed, Martha took the wren and her money from the table. She'd leave the herbs with Dolly. She no longer wanted to sell anything. She would find her children and go home. The show being over, the crowd moved on. The vicar, however, stepped towards Martha.

'Please accept my apology, madam. Ernest Draycott, new vicar of this parish.' He bowed to Martha.

'I know who you are, sir; we have already spoken.' Martha was not surprised that he did not remember her. Some of the villagers, the gossips, gathered closer to hear more. Mortified at all the attention, Martha was pink with embarrassment at having become the focus of attention. Then gathering herself, she looked straight into his eyes and spoke in a clear voice for all to hear. 'I wonder just what it is that the people who attend your church learn about love and kindness, sir, for I have felt none of it here today.' Her face flushed again with anger because of the unjustness of what had just taken place.

'Yes,' he acknowledged quietly. 'Yes. I think I know just what Sunday's sermon is going to be about. Please accept my humble apology for any embarrassment caused.' He was about to go on to admonish Martha for not attending church when a look from his wife made him think again.

Later that evening, when her children were all in bed, Martha sat in meditation on the day's events. In her hand she held a crystal given to her by her mother. She'd learnt all that she knew about herbs and natural medicine from her. Salanda had taught respect for all living things and for others' thoughts. 'We have just found different ways of expressing our love for the energy,' she would say. 'Don't let it disturb you, Martha, when others do not understand you. They have to walk their own path.' How wise her mother had been. Martha became still and, as always when she linked into the energy, it gave her the will to release the tension and to be silent. She forgave the churchwomen, although she remained sad that they could not accept the differences in people. In her forgiveness she retired to her bed and slept a disturbed sleep. In her dream she was barring the windows against a mob with torches. They hammered angrily on the door, calling her name. A ball of fear grew in her stomach.

6.

Claydon House

Emma woke with a start. The room was getting light. Nell had left the brown dress on the landing. Putting it on quickly, she hurried down to the kitchen and was relieved to find it was still early. Filling the kettle with the last of the water, she hung it on the hook above the fire. After raking the grey coals and emptying the cinders into a bucket, she struggled with it out into the yard.

'Hello, skinny ribs, you're about early. Let me give you a hand.' It was Matt, who was just entering the courtyard from the direction of the stables.

Emma frowned. 'Skinny ribs?'

'Well, you have to admit you've not got much meat on you.'

Emma's nostrils flared and her head came up higher. 'You're very rude to someone that you've only just met.'

'Well, you are part of our family now, Emma, with Mother, Alf and me, so I'm treating you like a sister. Tell you what,' he said, taking the bucket. 'I'll empty this and fill it with coal. You fill the pitchers with water and we'll soon have breakfast ready.'

Standing in the silent courtyard watching him walk away with the smouldering bucket, she smiled. She liked Matt, and she liked him very much. It felt good not to be the eldest.

By the time Nell came down everything was prepared in the kitchen.

'You ready to take the hot water upstairs?' Nell asked as she looked around her domain, feeling pleased with Emma's efforts.

The girl had made a decent start; she was going to be a good worker and a great help.

Emma lifted the two jugs one in each hand. The weight was heavy for her small wrists and she wondered if she would be able to get all the way upstairs with them, but said bravely, 'Yes, I'm ready, Mrs Ames.'

Nell opened the door and watched Emma walk carefully along the passage trying not to spill the hot water. 'Take them up the stairs one at a time, Emma,' she called after her.

At the top of the stairs Emma walked backwards through the green door pushing it with her back as she'd seen Mrs Ames do. Walking quietly along the landing, she was soon outside Miss Brack's dressing room door. Her arms began to shake as she stood holding the pitcher and the towel. The dreaded moment had arrived, as she knew it inevitably would. Taking a deep breath, she knocked very quietly on the door and listened. No sound came to her ear pressed against the door. Opening it slowly she stepped inside and found the washstand easily. Putting the hot pitcher down beside the wash bowl, she hung the towel on the bar. With heart thumping she opened the door that led into the darkness of the bedroom. The noise of her heart banging in her chest was so loud in her ears that she was sure it would wake her mistress. Tiptoeing past the bottom of the bed with her eyes fixed on the drapes, she didn't see the dressing table chair holding her mistress's clothes. As her knee hit the chair she knew it was going over. In a split second she had grabbed for it and lost her balance. As she lay across the chair, her face buried in her mistress's undergarments, she watched the bed with one eye. The body in the bed rose like a silent monster, snakes writhing about its head in the gloom. It was Medusa, the Greek goddess that she'd learnt about from her mother.

'Who's there?' The voice was full of annoyance and constricted by sleep.

Silence cloaked the room as Emma lay immobilised with fear. The figure of Medusa peered around for what seemed like an eternity and then lay back muttering. Emma continued to lie amongst the clothes until the breathing from the direction of the bed indicated that Miss Brack had returned to sleep. With eyes that had now become accustomed to the darkness, Emma rose silently, corrected the chair and opened the drapes. Back on the landing, the water for Mrs Shillabeer was no longer hot. Emma hurried back to the kitchen for a replacement. Red-faced she rushed from the kitchen and back to the second landing just in time to hear a door opening somewhere in the distance.

Nell was putting laden breakfast plates in front of Matt and Alf as Emma ran again into the kitchen.

'I can't stay here any longer, Mrs Ames. I've seen her. It was awful. She's got snakes coming out of her head.' Emma's lip trembled; after all she had been through since she had arrived here, this was the worst. They all stared at her. 'Miss Brack! Miss Brack.' Emma shouted as though they were all daft.

Nell started to laugh. 'Was she in her bedroom?' she asked with difficulty.

Emma nodded. 'I fell over her chair in the dark. She sat up and she has snakes instead of hair.' Tears fell from the frightened eyes that looked around the kitchen at the grinning faces.

Alf and Matt were soon howling with laughter and Nell was holding her sides. Tears rolled down their faces as they dabbed at their eyes. 'Stop me laughing,' Matt groaned. 'I'm in pain.' Alf started to catch his breath and Matt banged him on his back so hard his teeth flew out. That made them laugh even more and Emma joined them, although she didn't know why.

'Come here, girl.' Nell was having more luck than the men at controlling herself. Putting her arm around Emma's shoulders, she said, 'The mistress used to have a maid' – Nell indicated upwards with her chin – 'but no longer. You see, Emma...' and now she laughed so hard she could hardly speak. 'I... put madam's hair... in rags at night, so she has curls in the morning. They must have moved about a bit in the night.' As the laughter broke out again, Emma joined in, seeing the funny side of the situation.

Later, while Miss Brack and Mrs Shillabeer were having their breakfast, Emma removed the pitchers from their positions in the dressing room and the landing. It was as she carried the covered porcelain pot from the West Wing landing that she made a discovery. Walking towards the disposal area, the wind took the linen cover from the pot, exposing its contents. Before throwing it into the earth closet, Emma stared at it in confusion. Was Mrs Shillabeer not alone? Emma knew very well the difference between adult waste and child waste. But why had nothing been said about a baby? She decided that Mrs Ames thought she didn't need to know and, frowning, got on with her task.

~

Emma had been at Claydon for seven days and the work had been so hard and constant that she had had no time to think about home, except on this day. She awoke knowing that from today things would be different. It was the day of her birth. A day that her mother celebrated, and this year she was no longer a child. She was thirteen. Creeping from her bed, she took a small packet from the shelf. At first she stared at the little gift, wondering what it could be. Then with great happiness and expectation she undid the tie and stared in disbelief at the locket sitting within the finest lace square. Taking it from the soft lace, her thumb caressed the small opal embedded in the lid. Flashes of iridescent colour coming from the stone seemed to acknowledge her, and she was filled with wonderful memories, as she was transported to her grandmother's home. Salanda was making cake for the Beltane celebrations and had given Emma the locket to hold. She remembered Salanda's beautiful face coming close to hers, and the shots of light leaping in her eyes as she said, 'No one can wear this, Emma, apart from the person who owns it and the person who one day will receive it. One day, it will help you to concentrate your mind as you connect to the Goddess. When it belongs to you, you will be able to ask for insight into the past, the present and the future.' As Emma now inspected the precious gift, she was aware of the light that burnt within the pale opal and she wondered at the symbols engraved in the silver surrounding it. Then she remembered something else and with trembling fingers turned the locket over. Sudden tears blurred her vision as she stared at the small plait of hair encased in the back. A plait now in a tighter circle than when she had seen it last. The hair in the centre had belonged to her great-great-grandmother, who had been hounded and drowned by ignorant neighbours in her village. Her hair had been a deep rich auburn and plaited onto it was the almost-black hair of Emma's great-grandmother Liannda. But it was the new piece of hair added to the plait that had brought the tears. Salanda's hair, taken from her as she passed from this world to the next, had been added to the locket by Martha with great love and dexterity. Kissing the locket, Emma held it to her heart, swaying gently around the room in a rhythm only she could feel. Her tears flowed freely, knowing that Salanda could reach out from the other side and be with her, that she was no longer alone in this dark place. The question was, she thought, why had her mother negated her own inheritance of the locket? Placing the locket and the soft lace back on the shelf, she hid them amongst her clothes, knowing that at thirteen a maid having a silver and opal locket would possibly bring questions. Questions that she would not want to answer as she could never divulge the secret of why she had it. She had been grown up for only half an hour and was already facing the complications of being an adult.

7.

Haddenford

It was just getting light as Dolly, Dan, Alice, Martha and Robert entered Farmer Tate's farmyard, joining around thirty other labourers, men, women and children. The group stood awkwardly in the cool morning air awaiting their instructions for the day. Chickens scurried everywhere, pecking in the dirt. A gaggle of geese with necks stretched, walked slowly in a tight group, complaining amongst themselves and nervously watching the workers from the protection of an open barn.

When Andrew Tate appeared, his clothes were as ragged and dirty as his workers. His dark beard was as long as his shoulder-length hair. His weathered skin, pulled tight over high cheekbones, gave him a skeletal look which Martha found unsettling.

They were soon divided into working groups and headed towards a barn to collect their tools for the day's work.

'We need those two Dutch hoes, Martha.' Dolly indicated the long-handled implements hanging on the wall.

Martha took one from the wall and then looked at her son. 'What about Robert? This hoe is larger than he is.'

'He will have to use this hand hoe and pull the tough weeds up by hand. Don't miss any, mind.' Dolly looked sternly at Robert. 'Your row will be walked and inspected, because you're new. They won't pay you if the job's not done properly.'

With this warning in their ears they boarded the cart that took them out to the fields. Martha put her arm around Robert as they rumbled along in the back with the other workers. For the first time in a long while, she smiled in relief and thought how lucky they were to have work.

Martha faced her first row of cereal with Dolly on her left and Robert on her right. Alice and Dan, on the other side of a contour, were hidden from sight. None of them could see the other end of the field that stretched away towards some trees. Dolly had instructed Robert, 'Hands and knees, pull up every weed and leave it lying on the surface to die in the sun.' He smiled, excited and happy with the importance of his job. Martha watched Dolly's technique and copied it, pushing the long handle of the hoe away from her, pushing the blade into the soil and under the roots of the unwanted weeds. Then she dragged it back through the soil, leaving the roots lying on the surface to burn in the sun. The weeds growing between the stalks had to be pulled by hand.

By midday they were all hot, dusty and blistered. Martha's breasts were hard with milk. Each push on the hoe brought her pain, until the milk began to flow. At first it soaked into her bodice but soon, reaching saturation point, it soaked into the waistband of her skirt. When the sound came for them to stop for their lunch, the milk was running over her belly and down her legs. The milk-soaked bodice had stiffened as the sun baked it dry and the hard material chaffed her nipples. As they sat at the edge of the field for their rest, Martha was aware of the sour smell. 'This is awful, Dolly; I don't know what to do.' She screwed up her nose.

'There's nothing you can do today, Martha; you'll have to work something out for tomorrow.' Dolly made herself comfortable in a small amount of soft grass growing almost under the hedge, leaving a good amount of space between herself and Martha.

Mrs Tate and her children, two boys and a small girl, made their way around the field, carrying the cider so necessary on such a hot day. The workers gladly held out their mugs for the liquid as they ate their bread. Margaret Tate held the container towards Martha and filled her cup. She said nothing, but her eyes held the understanding and compassion of one mother for another.

When the short break ended, Martha returned gladly to the isolation of her row, where she could work unseen in her soiled and uncomfortable clothes. The work was back-breaking and the day seemed to go on forever. When the drum was beaten for the end of the day, calling the workers from the fields, Martha felt as though she would never stand straight again. Her heart almost broke with compassion as Robert emerged from the field unrecognisably grey from the dust. His hands and legs were covered in large red and white lumps caused by stinging nettles. The dust on his face was streaked where he had bravely cried his silent tears. Alice was in much the same state and threw her arms around her mother. Dolly rubbed her daughter's back and tried to comfort her. Dan, who was older than Robert and Alice, stood to the side, showing no feelings as he leant on his hoe. His hooded eyelids hid any expression of pain that might have been in his eyes. The journey back to the farmyard was born in silence as the jerking of the cart painfully pierced every aching muscle and bone of its occupants. Slowly the tools were cleaned and put back in the barn.

The sun was low in the sky as they walked painfully into their cottages. The bread Nona had made that day was in pride of place in the centre of the table and a broth was bubbling in the pot over the coals. The kettle was not over the fire, as Martha had hoped.

'Tomorrow, Nona,' Martha said as kindly as she could to the girl standing proudly beside the table, 'set some water on to the heat so that we can wash the dirt from our eyes before we eat.' Martha was aware of the tiredness in her voice and tried to smile at her daughter, who looked worried.

'Yes, Mother. I'm sorry, I didn't know you would need water.'

'Nor did I, darling, nor did I. Let's put water in every pan that we can find and we will wash now before we eat.' After Robert had bathed and Martha had washed her arms, legs and face, they sat at the table with their bowls filled.

James complained. 'This bread's hard, Mother. I don't like Nona's bread. I want Mother's bread.' And he started to cry.

'Dip it in your broth, James, and soften it,' Martha suggested. But he ignored her and sat unmoving, his mouth pulled in a downward curve. 'Please don't complain, James,' she said more strongly. 'Can't you see we're all tired and Nona has done her best; she'll get better at it.'

At first he didn't budge but sat arms crossed ignoring his food. But when he realised that no one was taking any notice of him he took a piece of bread and dipped it into the broth.

Robert was too tired to eat and had to be encouraged. Martha put him to bed and when all the children were asleep she sat beside the fire, still dressed in her soiled clothes, and fed Charity, grimacing as the small mouth sucked eagerly on her sore nipples.

By the time Martha had washed her body, it was getting late. She pushed her soiled bodice into the dirty water they'd washed in, and then hung it by the fire to dry. How, she wondered, was she going to keep this up? She hadn't realised how hard it was going to be or how long the hours. Although desperate for sleep, she made up the first stage of the bread dough, putting it near the banked-down fire to rise for the morning. Exhausted, she fell upon her bed in the alcove. After pulling the curtain across the gap her arm fell limply to her side and she slept without moving until morning.

8.

Claydon House

It was mid-morning and Gertrude Shillabeer sat quietly brooding with her teacup in her lap. A shaft of sunlight poured in through the closed windows and although it brought warmth and colour to the library floor it made no impression on the atmosphere building within the room. The two women sat on comfortable chairs before the small fire that flickered in the huge carved oak fireplace.

'We have to agree on a plan soon, Amelia; it's becoming very difficult to be away from my family.' Gertrude spoke while still looking into her teacup.

'Your sister said that she would be pleased to have your children Gertie.' Amelia sipped her tea elegantly, the smoothness of her movement belying her irritation.

Gertrude put her cup and saucer on the small table in front of her. 'Yes, Amelia, she did agree to take my children under her wing for a short time. But I miss them, especially my baby, who I haven't held for four weeks and fear she will soon forget her mother.'

'How do babies know their mother, Gertie, when they are brought up by their nanny or nurse?'

'Every day that I am with Tobias, feeding him, I am reminded of my own child. As I see him growing, I know that my own dear child is growing without me.'

Amelia's voice had an edge to it as she rose from her chair and paced the room. She didn't understand this attachment that her friend seemed to have for her children. It was degrading. What were servants for if not to look after the miserable children that seemed to endlessly appear. 'You agreed to do this.' Her voice held an accusation. 'You are as involved as I. After that night, in which you played as big a part as me, you agreed on this action. You can't change your mind now.' She faced Gertrude accusingly. 'I can't wet-nurse him and I can't get someone else in without explaining about Tobias. The staff and everyone else in the county will know he isn't mine and I am not in favour of saying who his parents were. The scandal would put the last nail in the coffin of this family.'

'It will get harder and harder to conceal him, Amelia. He can't stay hidden in the West Wing for ever.'

'If he doesn't know any different, I don't see why he can't stay up there.' Amelia's cup landed heavily in its saucer.

Gertrude was amazed at Amelia's lack of knowledge. Having had six children herself and watching the nurses who brought them up, she was well aware that a child could not be kept in the house all day without air or sunshine, or indeed without something to stimulate its mind. And Gertrude was also well aware of Amelia's temper; she had witnessed it at school in France too often and witnessed the terrible results. The authorities were unable to find the cause of the odd madness and suicides that happened at the school and, eventually coming up against a wall of silence, put it down to pressure of youthfulness in young ladies. A wall of fear had kept them all silent and obeying Amelia, who exercised her strange power over others with impunity. Gertrude was the only friend Amelia had and, although she didn't want to admit it, it was a friendship rooted in fear.

After the events of that terrible evening to which Amelia referred, Gertrude now regretted having continued the friendship. She wanted to go home to her family. Wanted to escape the trap she now found herself in. But she had to tread carefully and, after watching Amelia's face for the right moment, tried again to help the woman understand the position more fully.

'What about schooling? How would you keep a tutor from the staff? And a child needs to play.'

Amelia knew that Gertrude was right. But the anger that raged within her made it impossible for her to make a plan. The speed of her pacing increased as she damned the servant girl and damned her brother even more. How could he let this happen, on top of everything else that he had done to this family? Was there to be no peace in this house?

'Could we not involve the staff? Impress on them the secrecy that is needed. With their help, I could set a date to return to my family. At least a date would appease my sister.'

Amelia's voice had a dangerous edge to it when she replied. 'And just what do you imagine that I am going to tell Mrs Ames? That her maid was about to have a child, my brother's child, and wanted her standing in this family noted? That she thought, that under the circumstances she should no longer be my servant? Do you not think that they would want to know what happened to her?'

'Yes. Well, of course they would.' Gertrude could see Amelia's anger rising and having seen it before at its worst she was becoming afraid. 'Couldn't we agree on something to tell them?'

'No' Amelia's voice was sharp. 'Mrs Ames will want to know why we didn't call for help.'

'I have been going over and over this, Amelia. We should have got help as soon as that girl started her labour and she might have been saved.'

Amelia's face was shot with anger. 'We have been over this so many times, Gertrude.' A threatening light now danced in her eyes and a thin note of tolerance was hardly masked as her mouth set in a hard thin line.

'I know Amelia, but I feel like a criminal. If we had called the doctor, even though it was too late, things would be so much better.'

Amelia ignored her words, not able to see the point of this constant and dangerous retrospection. 'What has to be done, Gertrude, is that you must not allow this to play on your mind.'

'But if someone finds her body, have you thought of that?'

'That will not happen. No one goes to the forest now, not even poachers.'

The niggling fear that had been building within Gertrude's unused brain suddenly realised itself, like a bright dawn breaking after a moonless night. Her voice hardly left her throat as she whispered, 'Having the child implicates us. If the maid's body is found, the authorities will want to know how we came by the baby.'

Amelia nodded her head slowly, her mouth still drawn into a thin line. 'Yes, Gertie, I realise that and we will think of something before that time comes.'

'And what about the other matter?' Gertrude whispered, as though the walls had ears. Her face paled as the vision of Amelia wielding a spade acted out like a nightmare before her eyes, as it often did in the middle of the night. She still heard the thud, the silence, saw Oliver on the forest floor lying dead at their feet. Her voice was so thin it hardly left her mouth as she said, 'Your brother must already be missed by his friends. How could we have let this happen? I have never before done a wrong deed.' She was becoming hysterical, but still managed to whisper.

'Pull yourself together, Gertie; no one would suspect two well-bred, genteel women of such a thing. No, we will be able to put the blame somewhere else, like that poacher who saw us.'

'What if he talks, Amelia?'

'Have no fear about that, Gertie. I have dealt with that possibility; he is too afraid to ever speak again.'

Gertrude stood up, trying to pull herself together and moved towards the door. 'I must return to Tobias. His morning sleep will soon be at an end. I don't want his cries to be heard. We will speak again tonight. We have to do something.'

There was a long silent pause. With a sigh Amelia turned to her friend of so many years. 'Yes, I know, Gertie; we will talk again after I have seen Mister Redfern. I have forgotten to tell Mrs Ames that he will be here for lunch.'

~

A bell rang in the servants' passage and Emma went to see which one it was. 'It's the library, Mrs Ames,' she called.

'Put on your white apron and go and see what the mistress wants.'

Emma paled, her eyes becoming huge. 'Me?'

'Yes, you. Who else is going to do it? She won't bite you, Emma. Open the door, do a small bob, like I showed you, and say, "Yes ma'am?" Then come and tell me what she wants.'

Changing her apron, Emma hurried up the stairs; she had heard that it didn't do to keep Miss Brack waiting.

As the door was opened and Emma gave her little bob, she was amazed at the transformation of her mistress. A tall, elegant lady stood before her in a beautiful bottle-green outfit. The dark curls piled high on her head tumbled down the back of her neck.

'Yes, ma'am?' Emma managed in a small voice.

'Would you tell Mrs Ames that Mister Redfern is expected for lunch. We will have cold meat and bread and in case he prefers it fruit and cheese. Tell Mrs Ames that I would like a selection of her pickles available and some wine.'

'Yes, ma'am.'

'And show Mister Redfern into the morning room on his arrival.'

Yes, ma'am.' Emma bobbed and withdrew, shutting the door. Her first encounter had not been as bad as she'd imagined. When she reached the kitchen Nell was busy preparing pastry for the evening meal.

'Well, what did she want?' She didn't stop rolling out the pastry or look up.

'A Mister Redfern is coming to lunch, Mrs Ames. Could they have cold meat and bread?'

'Did they want anything else?' Nell was banging and turning the pastry on the table with a force that made the loose skin above her elbows wobble.

'Fruit, cheese and a selection of your pickles, and wine.'

'Take that basket.' Nell indicated a thick woven basket that sat near the door and carried on talking. 'Find Alf and ask for some vegetables. Be as quick as you can so that I can get on with this pie.'

Taking the basket, Emma ran as though her shoes were on fire towards the vegetable patch.

Around lunchtime Emma opened the heavy front door to a very fine gentleman. So fine an authoritative figure was Mister Redfern, dressed completely in black, that she could not speak.

'Miss Brack is expecting me.' His voice was warm and mellow as he stepped boldly through the door. Removing his hat, he gave it to Emma, who placed it on a silver tray that lay on the hall table. His topcoat removed, he handed that to Emma along with his cane. She bobbed politely and laid them on a chair before leading the way to the morning room.

'Mister Redfern, ma'am,' she managed to announce. He entered without a thank you to the sound of Miss Brack's gushing.

'Mister Redfern.' Holding out her hand, Amelia glided towards him. 'Will you stay to lunch?'

Emma closed the door behind him. She had received her first important person and must now get back downstairs to help Mrs Ames with the food.

~

The solicitor took a seat opposite Amelia as indicated and noticed that she looked pale. 'Are you unwell, Mistress Brack?'

'I am a little apprehensive about the nature of your visit, Mister Redfern.'

He nodded sagely. 'I am most remorseful, madam, that I could not give you more information. I come about a delicate matter, and as your family solicitor I wanted to speak to Oliver most urgently. I have tried in vain, but have not been able to locate him at his club or in town.'

Amelia's heart bumped in her chest as she fought to keep control of her feelings and quickly concealed any change in her face with a slight nod of her head.

'I have called at a bad time and I can see that you are unwell.' He made to stand.

Amelia held her hand up to him. 'Please, be seated, sir. I am quite well. I have not seen my brother for some months and I was but worried that you may have brought me bad news.'

'My dear madam, I am so sorry. It had not occurred to me that you would think that I was the bearer of tragic news.'

Amelia took her lace handkerchief and pressed it to her cheek. 'It is a relief, sir, that you are not.'

'I am afraid, madam, that my news is not good.' He sighed, feeling some pity for the spinster. 'I feel somewhat at a disadvantage in the absence of your brother as this does affect you both. But time is short and we have to get the legal papers signed.'

'Legal papers?' Amelia was mystified.

He nodded solemnly. Being unused to dealing with women, he continued quickly with his speech. 'Oliver, your brother, is the owner of the property and land known as the Claydon Estate.' At Amelia's sudden intake of breath he paused, noting that her eyes held a momentary flash of fear that was gone as quickly as it had arrived and he appreciated that she was trying to understand what he was saying. 'Miss Brack,' he continued quietly, 'I am afraid that your brother has gambled and lost the farm known as Foley Farm, bordering this estate, and... the surrounding fields to various other gentlemen who now wish to redeem their wagers. They want to take ownership legally and I require your brother to sign the various papers. I have been waiting for him to contact me, as a gentleman would, to let me know the extent of his debt and to whom he owes it. But this he has not done.' He hesitated. 'I cannot – at this stage – tell you if the house or the forest are still safe from the debt.'

Amelia felt drained. Could things get any worse?

'Do you have any idea where your brother might be, Miss Brack?' he continued.

'I am sorry, sir; I cannot imagine where Oliver might be. I, like you, imagined he would be at his club or with friends.'

'Could you give me a list of his friends, madam?'

'I wish that I could, sir, but Oliver and I move in different circles. There were a couple of gentlemen who spent several weekends here with my brother who, I am afraid to say were, for gentlemen, rather vulgar.'

'I can see that this is very difficult for you, madam, but can you remember their names?'

'I wasn't introduced to them, sir, but one was called Barty by the others, and another was referred to as Pompy.'

The solicitor nodded his head. 'These two gentlemen are on the list of creditors against your brother. They also do not know where he is.'

'Then what is to be done, sir? As you know, I own none of this property but am allowed to live here with my brother until I marry. All that I inherited from my father was two hundred pounds a year, which, Mister Redfern, without the goodness of my brother would not go very far.'

'Yes, I understand your position. But your brother's debts must be paid. Do you have any living male relative of whom I am unaware, and who might be called upon in this matter?'

'I am afraid that I cannot help you, sir, for I believe that Oliver is the last of our male line. In fact, we have no other relatives at all. But should my brother return, then I will inform him that you called. Now, let us take lunch together before you return to London.'

9.

Haddenford

Since that uncomfortable first day, Martha had taken Charity with her to the fields. The child was fed at the breast in the shade of the hedgerow and then laid on a blanket to sleep. The baby slept well in the open air and when she did wake her voice carried to Martha, who gathered her up using the blanket to carry her under her breast. It was a system that worked, although Martha was even more exhausted with the extra weight when bending.

When the gang of workers arrived at Tate's farm on Friday morning, Martha found herself in a different group. She was taken with a dozen others to the orchard, where they were instructed to clear grass and weeds away from the base of the fruit trees. Martha moved Charity on her blanket from tree to tree keeping her by her side. The baby kicked and cooed, mesmerised by the movement of the leaves above her head. There were several other women there with babies and during the break Biddy, a woman with a black eye and shiny blue cheek, said, 'I heard that the farmer's wife had a hand in moving us mothers with babies to the orchard.'

'Well, Gawd bless her,' called Beth, a buxom woman with a red-headed two-year-old and a baby. 'She's a good woman is mistress Tate; she's got three children and lost as many. She doesn't have an easy life any more 'un the rest of us.'

'Does anyone have an easy life?' questioned Biddy. 'I'm not sure I'd recognise an easy life if it crept up and bit me in the bum.'

'Yes, you would.' Beth continued, laughter in her voice. 'It's the sort of life where you do nothing all day and someone else cooks and cleans your house, while you visit friends and eat all the food you can see until you're as fat as a pig.'

The women's laughter floated amongst the trees in a companionship born out of the need to survive the harshness of their lives.

The day passed quickly and the women worked well in the shade. For the first time Martha felt strong; she was, she thought, getting stronger by the day. Robert proved to be a good worker and she knew she could rely on Dolly to keep an eye out for him. Looking up at the sun, she could see that it would be another hour before the cart came to collect them. She felt excited about receiving her first wage. Although she knew she hadn't enough to pay Master Beemer the full rent, she hoped that she would have enough to stay in their home until she could get the rest of it.

~

James came running in from the lane banging the front door against the wall. 'Don't make the house in a mess, James, I've just finished the chores.' Nona had worked hard and wanted her mother to notice what she had done.

'What can I do then?' he whined.

'Go and play in the fields, look under the hedges for eggs.'

Taking the small basket that always rested beside the back door he turned and ran back outside. She smiled. He was easily distracted and might find an egg if they were lucky.

Nona had just taken the bread from the oven and sat it on the table when a knock came at the door. On opening it, she found herself looking at the blue-flecked jacket and stained waistcoat of the rent collector Barney Beemer. His body filled the doorway, blocking out the light.

'Is your mother home? I've come for the rent.'

'She isn't home yet, Mister Beemer. Can you come back later?'

His manner changed; anger flooded across his face. 'Do you think that I can waste my time by coming back to people's houses to collect their rent? I told your mother if she didn't have the rent today I would turn you all out into the lane.' Mauve veins stood out on his flushed face and sweat glistened under his eyes. His large hands held the door posts as though he were about to tear the house down.

Nona was afraid of him. He wasn't like her daddy, who had been quiet and polite, never threatening. The tears welled up in her eyes; she wished that James were here.

'Don't turn the tears on. I tell you what. You let me in and be nice to me and I won't throw you all out. It can be your way of helping your mother and our little secret.'

Nona hesitated, not knowing what he meant; did he want some of the bread? She flinched as he shouted into her face, suddenly irritated, 'Do you want to save your family or shall I come in and throw all your furniture out into the lane?'

She began to cry and out of fear she let him in.

~

Martha joined Robert in the farmyard, where everyone queued for their wages. Tate sat behind a table with a book in front of him ticking off names. As he counted the money from a box, the queue gradually got shorter until Martha and Robert stood before him.

'Name?' He didn't look up.

'Martha Tilby, sir.' His finger moved down a line of names written on the page, then moved across several columns. After calculating he counted the money carefully from the box and handed it to Martha.

'Thank you, sir.'

'Mister Tate will do.' His voice was flat and dismissive. 'Next.'

'Mister Tate,' she replied slowly stepping aside, but stood beside Robert as he approached the table.

'Name?'

'Robert Tilby.'

'Six days at fourteen hours a day on child's pay.' Robert was handed his money.

'Thank you, Mister Tate.' Robert spoke strongly.

The farmer looked up and raised an eyebrow. 'You're a quick learner, Robert. I like that. Next.'

The first week was over. There wasn't enough money for three weeks' rent but they had made a great effort. Barney Beemer would surely see that they would soon be able to pay all of it.

'Does it feel good to receive your pay, Martha?' Dolly smiled a weary smile, as they walked home.

'Yes, it feels good, Dolly. I just hope it will make a difference.'

'How much did you say you owed?'

'Three weeks.'

Dolly was silent and felt sad. She knew Barney Beemer, and she was sure that, whatever Martha managed to rake together, it wouldn't be enough to stop him evicting them.

~

James rushed through the back door as Martha, Robert and Charity came in the front. In all the mayhem of removing clothes and washing the dust from their faces before the evening meal no one noticed how silent Nona was. With eyes lowered, she moved slowly around the room picking up clothes and dishing up the evening meal.

Later, while the children cleared away the plates and James and Nona went to the well for water and to clean the dishes, Martha went to her box and removed her money. Laying it on the table she counted it out. It was still a long way from the three weeks' rent that she needed. But look on the bright side, she said to herself. That's nearly two weeks' rent, with the money from the fair. If we can earn the same amount next week we will be almost clear. Her limbs were stiff as she moved to look in the cupboard; they were nearly out of fat and she'd used the docket for this week. She removed two pennies from her wage. They would need at least a couple of bones. She could get a large bone with some meat on it if she was lucky, for threepence. It was going to be a struggle. How could she feed her family on so little? The money earned wasn't nearly enough. Jumping at the sound of heavy thumping on the front door she opened it quickly. Beemer stood on the step, a leering smile on his face. 'Well, Mrs Tilby.' He raised his eyes expectantly. 'Do you have the rent?'

'I have a lot of it, Mister Beemer, but not quite all.'

'How much?' His voice was sharp; his face twitched.

'I have nearly two weeks' rent, sir.'

'Two weeks isn't three weeks as promised, is it? You still owe the landlord and he is not a forgiving man.' He smirked contemptuously.

Martha watched a bead of sweat roll from his hairline down the side of his face. 'By next week you will owe as much again. Are you not out of your depth, Mrs Tilby?'

'I'm doing my best as the only provider, sir. I have also to feed my children.'

'None of that moves me, madam. I'm only interested in collecting the rent for my employer and your landlord. I will be back next week and I will expect to receive it all.' He took the money from her hand and turned away. She was surprised that there hadn't been more of a fight. For a moment she watched his wide frame swagger down the path and with relief she shut the door. Another week's reprieve but how long could they go on like this? It would be another three weeks before she would have any money from Emma and that would only be if Emma managed to catch Mim as he passed the grounds of Claydon House.

Before going to her bed, Martha checked her children. Robert and James were still sharing top to tail in the narrow bed. She would have to do something about the sleeping arrangements. Robert worked so hard he needed a good night's sleep without being kicked by his restless brother. She checked the girls, who looked lost in the double bed. Nona so thin and Charity so small; yes, she would change them. It was as she pulled the cover up over the girls that she noticed a large bruise on Nona's arm. She must have knocked it, she thought to herself. Strange she didn't mention it. She must be growing up, with all the extra responsibility; she smiled proudly and stroked her daughter's head.

10.

Claydon House

At the end of her first month Emma received her wage as arranged. Mrs Ames had been called upstairs and returned to the kitchen with the money for herself, Emma and Matt. 'Here's your wage, Emma, less your bed and board,' Nell said, handing Emma a small brown envelope.

Emma had never had money, and could hardly believe it was hers. A small tear ran over her cheek as she stared at it.

'What's wrong, Emma? Not enough for you?' Matt quizzed.

'It's the first money I ever had, Matt,' and she smiled at him with moist eyes.

Nell put her arm around Emma's waist. 'You've earned it, Emma. You've worked hard. Done all that I asked with a will and never complained once. You are a good girl to work with.'

Emma could only nod at the praise, for now the tears were streaming down her face.

'I'll put the kettle on.' Nell bustled about the kitchen, retrieving from a small box some dried-out tea leaves that she kept for herself from the mistress's teapot, while Emma pulled herself together.

'Matt, would you take my money to the gate on Sunday and give it to Mim as he passes?' Emma asked. 'He has agreed to take messages to my mother.'

'You haven't been off the estate since you got here, Emma; wouldn't you like to give it to Mim yourself?' Matt replied.

'I can't walk down the drive,' she shuddered. 'I just can't.'

'Why would you want to do that? That's for the rich and mighty; there's another path for us slaves around the back of the house.'

'Oh, Matt, I would love to go for a walk. I really need some fresh air.' She hadn't realised until that moment how much she had been starved of air and the outside world.

'Of course you do, dear.' Nell put the weak tea in front of her with a little cake. Emma looked questioningly at the housekeeper whom she was growing to love.

'So!' Nell smiled. 'We are having a teatime cake in the morning; who is going to know? We are celebrating Emma's first month's wage.' The kitchen was filled with warmth and laughter as Emma tucked her money into her apron pocket and reached for the small cake.

~

On Sunday, Emma awoke with a warm glow in her heart. The sun was shining as she pushed the lattice window open. The air smelt sweet even at this early hour and was filled with the gentle drone from the bees that were already at work on the rose that climbed the wall.

Dressing quickly, she got on with her chores. Today she would have the afternoon to herself and she was going for a walk. It was this thought that made her realise how starved her soul was for the nature that she had grown up with.

The morning passed quickly as she raked the coals, brought water to the kitchen, took water to the mistress and Mrs Shillabeer and laid out the breakfast. It was while picking up the chamber pot from the West Wing landing that she again witnessed the contents. There was indeed a child in the wing, but why had no one seen it?

'Mrs Ames, did you know that there is a baby in the West Wing?' she asked as she passed through the kitchen.

'A baby you say? How would you know that, Emma?'

'There's evidence in the chamber pot in the mornings.'

'You know that you're not supposed to look in there, Emma.'

'I don't look; the cover sometimes comes off in the wind when I'm walking.'

'Um, well.' Nell screwed her face into a look of concentration. 'Perhaps it's Mrs Shillabeer's baby. I know she has one, although it's strange' – Nell continued to frown – 'we haven't heard a baby crying and no one has taken it for air.'

'Should we ask the mistress about it, Mrs Ames?'

'Good Lord, we can't do that.' Nell's eyes widened in horror. 'You will learn that the mistress will tell you what you need to know. Don't ever question her. We don't exist and that's how she likes it – and so do I.' When Emma looked puzzled, Nell sighed. 'To them' – she tipped her head towards the ceiling – 'the chamber pots empty themselves. The house cleans itself. The food gets itself ready and miraculously arrives on the table and clears itself away. That's why we scurry around like little mice in the servants' passage, unseen. We are looked upon as not wholesome, unclean, without a brain. Do you see now?'

'Yes, Mrs Ames, I do see.' It suddenly came home to Emma what the word servant meant. Unclean, anonymous slave.

'What they don't know,' Nell smiled, 'is that we usually know a lot more about what is going on upstairs, and that is what is puzzling. Keep your ears and eyes open, Emma, but don't say anything to anyone, only to me. I should know what's going on in this house at all times.'

~

Mid-morning Emma sat with Nell, Matt and Alf behind Miss Brack in the family pews. The vicar, a large man with a ruddy face and red nose, stood in a flowing black robe beating his fist on the lectern as his voice carried furiously around the church, informing them all that those who do not come to God with pure hearts and thoughts will burn in the fires of Hell and damnation. That their bones would be picked over for the Devil's dinner.

Mrs Shillabeer did not attend. A pain in her head that always arrived on a Sunday stopped her from doing so. Emma was suspicious and believed that she stayed to look after the mystery baby, but said nothing.

After a cold lunch and still wearing her Sunday best dress, her curls piled up under her bonnet and her money wrapped safely in her pocket, Emma met Matt in the stable yard. He had washed his face and was still wearing his Sunday suit. He quite took her breath away; he was, she thought, very handsome and noticed that his tanned skin glowed against the white of the collar at his neck.

He'd seen her standing in the yard waiting for him. There was something about her. He couldn't put his finger on it; she had an unusual peace, a gentleness that was not of this world. He chastised himself for being so sloppy, but she was going to be a beauty when she grew up. As he passed through the stable door into the yard, an excited smile lit her face; even at thirteen she was beautiful and his heart beat faster. They walked towards the back of the house, cutting through a neglected garden with its dry fountain and overgrown paths. Between two weed-choked beds near the corner of the house was the start of a track that led through trees that were nothing like the forest. The path was brought to an abrupt end by a gate, through which they passed and were soon walking on a track flanked by fields. Matt pointed out different species of butterfly, moth and beetle to her. He was surprised at how quickly she learnt them by name, colour and shape. Reaching the road that Emma had not seen since Mim deposited her outside the gates, they walked following the estate wall, looking over their shoulders often for Mim.

Matt started the conversation, as walking in silence unnerved him. 'Tell me about yourself, Emma. I don't know anything about you.'

'There isn't anything to tell.' She shrugged.

'There must be. Tell me about your family, where you come from.'

'We moved from London to the edge of a village, Haddenford, because my father, who was a carpenter, got work on the Laddisbrock Estate.'

Her mind flitted back to the cottage and she tried to describe it. 'We live in a small cottage with a little garden. Father felt that this was a great step up. Before that, we had been in London living in one room off an alley near the wharf and the Thames while he completed his apprenticeship. We were poor and Mother was always worried about us. My parents thought that their fortunes had changed when my father was recommended for this position through his tutor. Life had been hard for Mother living in London: she loves nature,' Emma qualified.

'Was that the first time you'd been to the countryside?'

'Oh no, my grandmother Salanda lived in a little village near here and I sometimes stayed with her.'

'Salanda? That's a strange name.'

'Is it, why?'

'Because I've never heard that name before and it feels strange.' He shrugged.

Her eyes looked straight into his, challenging. 'I'd never heard the name Mathew before, but I liked it straight away.'

The deep, clear pools of colour that were her eyes made his head spin, capturing his young soul, and in his confusion his cheeks flushed slightly pink and he looked away.

Mim and Lady arrived, breaking the moment, and Emma handed the package to the carter when he came abreast of them. 'Please tell my mother that I am well and well looked after. Have you news of my family?'

'Your mother and brother are working for Farmer Tate and they're all well. 'Tis all I can tell you.'

'Thank you, sir. Please pass on my good wishes to my mother.' He nodded and flicked the reins to be off. Lady moved forward and part of Emma wished that she could be travelling with them. But another part of her was glad to stay with Matt.

As they stepped off the road onto the dirt track on the return home, Emma felt the fun and excitement of life rising in her body. 'Beat you to the field gate,' she challenged Matt and ran off down the track, removing her bonnet and holding it in her hand as she ran. Her bouncing curls became unpinned and she felt wild with the freedom and Matt's company.

'What? Come back, Emma. This is no way for a lady to behave on a Sunday.' He laughed as he ran after her. She was quick, but not as quick as him. She tried to stop him overtaking her on the path by holding out her arm, but he jumped a log at the side of the track and, accompanied by her shrieks of laughter, was first at the gate. They leant on it, gasping for breath, faces aglow with the exertion and fun.

'Oh, Emma, I'm so glad you came to work here. I don't think I ever had so much fun.'

'Then that is a very sad state of affairs, Mister Ames, and we must put that right whenever we get the opportunity.' Emma smiled as she replaced her bonnet and she also couldn't remember a time when she had ever been so happy.

Supper was a cold affair and the high spirits of Matt and Emma infected Nell, who hummed a tune as she placed the plates on the table.

At the evening service, the candles had been lit, giving the church building a different mystical ambience. Emma sat with Matt, Nell and Alf behind the mistress and felt that, although life had changed, it was for the good. She didn't understand the church service, but put her hands together when everyone prayed, and gave thanks to the Goddess for her new position and the chance to help her family.

11.

Haddenford

It was the end of the month and Martha was relieved to receive Emma's money brought by Mim. She would at last be straight with the landlord and able to buy food as well as pay the rent. There would be nothing much for clothes and soap, but they could struggle on a little longer. She was, she had to admit, finding it hard to keep them all fed. Her hair, which had once gleamed with health, was now dull and dusty from working in the fields; her white skin was tanned where it had been exposed to the weather. A tanned skin had become a class symbol and she knew that she had joined the lowest in society. But she had no time for worrying about unfairness; her whole being was concentrated on feeding her family. If only Nona were stronger, she could also have worked in the fields with Robert. Next year James would be able to join them. She worried about Nona, who was very pale and walking badly. Her joints, she thought, must be more painful than usual and decided to talk to the child that evening when she got home from the farm.

As they were leaving for the fields, a serious-faced Nona asked, 'Can I come with you tomorrow, Mother? I won't get in the way.'

'I'm sorry, Nona, it just isn't possible. You can't work if you haven't been taken on, and if everyone brought their children it would be like a fairground and who would look after James?' Martha was disturbed by the look on Nona's face. Something wasn't right with her. She must find the time to talk with the child. But not now; there wasn't time, and she hurried out.

The day promised to be beautiful, with a clear early-morning sky. The workers, gathered in the usual area between the barns, were shuffling their feet, talking quietly. But after half an hour when no-one had come to give them their work the crowd became restless. There were quiet mutterings, a man next to Martha asked, 'Where's Mister Tate? Should someone go and find out?' No one wanted to go, but they knew that they couldn't stand in the yard all day. The men pulled straws and a hapless Gerald Badcombe was sent to the house, cap in hand. He soon returned looking sheepish, with the news that the farmer's wife had died in the night. People gasped. Everyone was shocked and confused. What would happen to them now? Were they going to work today or tomorrow? Faces changed from shock to sadness and then to fear in the space of three breaths. Then, suddenly, Andrew Tate was amongst them, standing tall. His chiselled face was pale under its usual tan, his eyes empty and red-rimmed. He chose a gang master for each group and sent them off to different areas of the farm. Martha was once again placed in the orchard with the women, who looked troubled and gossiped together.

'What do you think she died of?' Biddy asked the question that was in everyone's thoughts.

Beth called over her shoulder as she tied her two-year-old to the nearest tree. 'I don't know, but we'll be the poorer for it, you mark my words.'

The women had their pinafores tied up at the corners and wore outsized hats as they harvested the early plums. Huge wicker baskets stood at the end of the orchard and each woman had a large basket standing by her tree. The scene was colourful and the day would have been cheerful but for the news they'd just received. 'What do you think he'll do without a wife?' Biddy called from half-way up a tree.

'Biddy, you're always so practical; what do you think he'll do?' said Beth.

Biddy blushed. 'I don't know, but surely he can't run the farm, the house and the children on his own, poor man.'

Yes, Martha thought, poor man indeed. Life was a constant struggle.

The day was harder than expected, probably because the buoyant atmosphere that usually kept them going was missing. None had the heart for the usual banter; all were lost in their own thoughts. Even the children seemed subdued and as a result the women harvested more baskets than yesterday. All through the day the flat carts were loaded and removed by men with patient horses, until the last cart returned for the tired workers.

'Do you think we'll be taken on tomorrow, Martha?'

'I hope so, Biddy; there's still a lot to harvest. But I could understand if he put us off.'

'Let's hope not; we need every penny.' Beth looked worried. 'I've seven more children at home and a husband with the crooked bone disease.' Martha realised it was probably worse having a sick husband than no husband at all. In the end it all boiled down to how many mouths there were to feed.

'Well,' Martha ventured, trying to be cheerful, for she had liked Margaret Tate. 'If we're taken on tomorrow we'll have a full week's pay coming.'

'She's right.' Biddy sounded relieved. 'We have to be paid for the days we've worked.'

~

That evening as Martha sat quietly by the grate, she contemplated how lucky she was to only have five children and one of those in service and one in the fields. Although it wasn't the life she'd envisaged; no, that was very different. She and William had dreamt one day of renting a large house. They were going to be comfortably off and their children educated. William would always be in employment because he was a talented carpenter. They would be well dressed and have friends to the house. She smiled sadly: such a rosy picture. Renting this cottage had been their first step towards that dream. Now it was far too expensive a rent for a woman in her present position. Over these weeks she had gradually realised that she was paying the price to keep their dream alive. On Sunday afternoon she would look for something cheaper.

'Oh no,' she sighed, 'I forgot to talk to Nona.' Getting wearily to her feet she dragged herself up the ladder into the roof space to check the children. The air was hot below the eaves and the boys, now in the double bed, had kicked off the covers and lay nude and hot on the bare mattress. She didn't wake them. The girls were now in the single bed. Charity slept against the wall, to stop her falling out of the bed. Nona lay in a crooked position; her cotton slip had ridden up and the covers were pushed off, exposing her swollen joints. 'Poor child, I must think of some other salves to help her with the pain.' As Martha bent to straighten the child and pull her slip down, she noticed black and yellow marks on the inside of the child's thighs. 'What's this?' She looked closer. 'Bruising? How could she bruise herself there? Perhaps if she'd fallen off a stool, but no, not like that, not there on both legs.' Martha shook Nona gently awake.

'Nona, is there something that you want to tell me?' she whispered. The child looked sleepy and confused as she opened her eyes 'You have bruises on the inside of your legs: how did they get there?'

Nona blinked at her mother, whose face was set firm as she waited for a reply. Nona started to cry but wouldn't answer. A niggling suspicion that another person was involved rose in Martha's throat. She went straight to the point. 'Has a boy been coming to the house, Nona?'

Turning her face away from her mother, the thin child lay on the bed and cried silently. Martha was worried. 'Will you answer me, please? Have you been seeing a boy?' A feeling of dismay pressed on Martha as she awaited an answer.

'No, Mother.' The sound was small, but Martha heard it in the stillness of the hot roof.

'Then how did you get those marks, Nona?'

'Please let me come with you to work tomorrow, Mother.' Nona's small body jerked with the violence of her sobs.

'Tomorrow?' Martha was surprised and suspicious, but tried to stay calm.

'Yes, please, Mother.' The child's eyes were swimming with tears and a look of pleading that could not be ignored.

'Do you mind being here on a Monday, Nona?'

'No.' Another sob racked the small body.

'Any other day?'

'No.' The word was almost whispered.

'Just Friday?' A horror was forming in Martha's mind as she saw the vision of Barney Beemer standing on the front step, leering at her.

'Yes, please, Mother, I won't be any bother.'

'Is it Mister Beemer?' There was a knot in her stomach as she heard herself voicing her suspicion, in a voice that didn't sound like her own. Now she watched the reaction of her small daughter, aghast at the idea that she'd just proposed. Nona confirmed her suspicion by looking terrified. 'Why?' Martha tried to understand. 'Did he attack you?'

Nona could hardly speak; her sobs choked her. With her heart breaking, and anger rising through her body, Martha sat on the bed and took her daughter in her arms. 'Ssh now.' She stroked the damp hair. 'Tell me in your own time. You're not in trouble.' The child shivered, and yet she was hot and her skin was damp. 'Ssh, ssh now, it's all right. I love you. Tell me when you are ready.'

'He said, if I was nice to him he wouldn't turn us out.' Nona gulped for air. 'He said it was my way of helping you.' Now she cried the deepest unstoppable sobs. 'It hurt, Mother, it hurt.'

Martha held her daughter close as the child's frail frame jerked with each sob. Shock and anger ran through her in a way she had never experienced before, as a primeval, animal emotion rose in her soul. A need to kill the person who had injured her child invaded every cell in her body. She had known grief and hardship, but never anger like this. For Nona's sake she had to control herself, had to control the shaking in her own limbs. Now she understood why he hadn't thrown them out when they were so far behind with the rent. Laying Nona down in the bed she pulled the cover up over her. 'It's over, little one. Get some sleep. You won't be here tomorrow when he calls.'

She stayed awhile, stroking the child's head, until her sobs subsided and she was asleep. Then, quietly, Martha slipped downstairs and out of the front door.

~

At the vicarage the lights were just being extinguished when a furious knocking was heard at the heavy door. In the darkness the vicar tried to find the means to relight his candle but gave up as the knocking became more urgent. Slowly he made his way along the dark passage in his billowing white nightshirt and on opening the front door was surprised to find Martha Tilby, the woman from the fair, on the step in what he described later to his wife as a troubled state.

'Vicar, I have no one else to turn to, I need your help. I know I don't go to your church. But please… help me.'

'Come in, come in, Mrs Tilby. Please forgive my attire. I was just retiring to my bed.'

'It is I who should be apologising to you, sir. I wouldn't have come if it were not so urgent.'

'Tell me what has happened. Here sit yourself down, let me get you a sip of brandy; you are shaking.'

Martha sat on the offered chair, with a small glass of brandy that did seem to help when sipped.

Putting his candle on the table, he sat on a chair opposite Martha and watched her until, in the long, uncomfortable silence, he raised a questioning eyebrow. Martha tried to control the anger that was still overwhelming her. 'Since my husband died,' she spoke slowly, looking into the brandy glass avoiding his eyes. 'I have been trying to keep a roof over our heads.' She nodded, trying to hold back the threatening tears. 'Mistakenly, I now believe, I left my sick daughter to look after the house and her brother while my son Robert and I worked in the fields.' For a moment she couldn't go on. The vicar looked puzzled – many of the women worked in the fields – but he did not interrupt.

'While I was away my daughter was attacked.'

The vicar gasped. 'My goodness, is she injured?'

'She is injured in a way that I can't speak about.' Tears of anger welled up and she swallowed loudly before going on. 'I need somewhere safe for her to be tomorrow while I'm away from the house. Please, could she come here, and her brother James? I can't think of a safer place.'

'Of course we will take them in, Mrs Tilby. Do you know who attacked her?'

'Yes, I do, and I will deal with it myself.' There was such strength in her statement that he felt it reject him and any offer of advice he might give.

'Of course, of course,' he said quickly. 'These children and their squabbles, sometimes only the parents can help. We will be pleased to have them keep us company, Mrs Tilby.'

'Thank you, sir, thank you.' The relief was so great that Martha felt like throwing her arms around him, but didn't. It was bad enough speaking to him as he sat in his nightshirt.

At the front door he asked, 'Will we see you in church, Mrs Tilby?'

Martha turned and stared straight into his large blue eyes: a stare he felt searched his very soul and uplifted him while taking his breath away.

'One day, sir, we will discuss religion,' she said quietly, and, turning away, disappeared into the night, leaving him on his dark doorstep wondering what she needed to discuss.

12.

Claydon House

Emma liked to walk in the overgrown garden at the back of the house and down the lane to the road. It was her escape on her Sunday afternoon off. Sometimes Matt joined her, but today she was alone and on a mission. She'd felt it was time that she had her own altar, where she could link with the Goddess. She would have loved to build it in a corner of the wild garden, but decided that perhaps it would be wiser to build it in her room. There were things to collect and it made her walk even more enjoyable. Today was going to be special; she was looking for a stone to represent the Goddess. She hoped that to any observer she would appear to be walking idly around the garden, but all the time her eyes were on the ground. At the base of an old cherry tree she found her stone. It was long, oval and pinched in the middle like a waist. It was fat and rounded at one end like a female belly and slightly rounded in the shape of a head at the other. To her it looked feminine. Yes, this would be her Goddess stone. It fitted comfortably in her hand. After picking a few wild flowers she returned to her room. Washing the stone, she placed it gently on a low shelf. The wild flowers were put in a cup of water and also placed upon the shelf. She was more pleased and excited than she had been about anything in a long while. Taking the locket from its lace covering on the shelf above, she laid it in front of the flowers and sat cross-legged on the floor in front of her first altar. She became still, breathing gently as her mother had taught her. Linking into the energy, she prayed. 'I call on the Goddess, who dwells in all things. I reach out to you in love and ask you to smile upon my altar. I ask for your blessing, your strength and wisdom. So mote it be.'

At that same moment sunlight streamed through the window touching the flowers as she sat in meditation. Taking the locket, she held it gently in her hands and thought of her grandmother. A voice came as a whisper in her head, one that she recognised, and her being was filled with so much love she wanted to cry.

'Grandmother,' Emma whispered, 'I miss you; thank you for the locket, which I will treasure always.'

'Your mother has given the locket to you, because you were going to be alone, and so that you could link with your ancestors for advice. We cannot interfere in your life, Emma; your decisions can only be your own.' In the silence of the room Emma nodded her understanding.

'One day, Grandmother, I will return it to my mother and wait to inherit it in my turn,' she whispered.

'You are already a wise child, Emma and very much loved.'

Choked with emotion, Emma realised that she was no longer alone and kissing the locket placed it back on the altar. Lifting the flowers from the cup, she poured a little water into her hand. Reverently sprinkling the water over the altar, she whispered, 'I dedicate this altar to the Goddess. So mote it be.'

Now feeling complete and uplifted she hid the locket in the lace and placed it under the linen on her other shelf, before returning to the kitchen to help Mrs Ames with the tea.

'My, my, Emma you look very pleased with yourself. You're almost glowing,' Nell complimented as Emma entered the kitchen.

'I have had a wonderful walk, Mrs Ames. It's so good to get out of the house. Here, let me take the tea things upstairs for you.' Emma picked the tray up from the table.

'You are such a good girl, Emma. I don't know how we ever managed before you came.'

On the landing Emma knocked on the door of the library where the mistress took her tea, but the room was empty. Laying the tray on the table, she left. Wandering along the landing towards the servants' door, she looked at the portraits. The people, she noticed, all looked alike, with their sharp noses and hard eyes, except one man. He stood erect in his black clothes, a dog at his feet. The white lace at his cuff was crisp and matched the lace at his chin. Unlike the others his face was soft and his eyes gentle. She stood, head on one side, staring at him; there was something familiar about his face. She looked at the brass information plate: 'Hanwell Brack Esquire. 1743.'

Hearing footsteps on the stairs leading to the West Wing, Emma slipped silently through the servants' door. Not letting it close completely, she looked through the crack and saw Mrs Shillabeer heading for the library and moments later the upright figure of the mistress followed her. When the library door had closed, Emma stood again before the picture, with one ear listening for the library door to open. Walking along the landing she noticed at the bottom of the stairs to the West Wing another, smaller portrait of Hanwell Brack, this time sitting on a seat in a garden surrounded by trees. Painted into the distance was a church spire. Her eyes shot wide open as she recognised the spire. That's in Salanda's village, I'm almost sure of it.

The distant sound of a baby crying reached her from above the stairs and looking towards the library she thought better than of informing Mrs Shillabeer. Creeping on tiptoe, she slowly climbed the steep stairs. The cry became louder as she reached the landing and was not difficult to follow. Pushing a door open, she found herself in a comfortable sitting room with heavy pink drapes. Crossing the room to a closed door, she opened it and found a small nursery with a sobbing baby in a cot.

91

'Hello.' The baby stopped crying for a moment, looking surprised, and then continued louder. Bending over the cot she said quickly, 'If I pick you up, will you stop crying?' Reaching down, she lifted the child and as she did so it released the wind that was trapped in its chest. 'There, isn't that better? Your mother won't be long; she's just taking tea with the mistress. Would you like to have a little look out of the window?' Walking to the casement, she held it up to the window but it was too young to look through the glass and its head dropped to Emma's shoulder. She smiled at it as she laid it back in its cot. 'I wonder if you are a girl or a boy. Now be good. I have to go.'

As she was leaving the room she became aware of a burning sensation at her hip. Putting her hand into her pocket she felt the forgotten silver and remembered the man in the forest. Looking about the room, she wondered what could belong to him in a room like this. The silver had become so hot that she couldn't touch it and she wondered again what he would want from a room with only the bare necessities for looking after a baby. What could she tie to the window as promised?

On the dressing table she came across a piece of dark blue ribbon and hurried to tie it to the window handle on the outside of the baby's room. Although it was very old, the leaded window opened easily. Having completed her task, she closed the window, trapping a large fly inside. I am no longer beholden to the man in the forest, she thought, as with a feeling of relief she waved at the droning fly with her hand. Now she could forget him. She tried to reopen the window to let the creature out but no matter how hard she tried she couldn't move the handle and noticed now that it was rusted over. As the fly threw itself against the glass, Emma looked across the gardens to the forest and saw a momentary flash of light. The sound of the fly brought her attention back to the room, where she saw that it was lying on its back, legs flailing in the air. Its wings frantically vibrated, but, unable to lift itself, the fly was carried up and down the windowsill in demented circles. Several times she tried to flick it over, but it was soon dead.

As the baby was now comfortable and asleep, she hurried back down the stairs, closing the servants' door behind her with relief. Should she tell Mrs Ames of her discovery? But in the next second she answered her own question. She already knew what the housekeeper would say. If the mistress had wanted us to know she would have told us. So Emma decided to wait and see what happened. She would throw the silver away next time she was in the garden. Putting her hand into her pocket, she was surprised to find it empty and the silver gone.

13.

Haddenford

At midday the workers were called from the fields and orchards. They weren't happy to be working half a day, but said nothing as they received their pay. Mister Tate sat in his Sunday suit to pay the line of men, women and children. None said a word as they shuffled in silence towards the table. Margaret Tate's funeral was to be later that day and the man had enough on his plate. He handed Martha her pay and then Robert his, without looking up. Martha felt truly sorry for him. 'I'm sorry, sir, about your wife. I truly liked her. She was a good woman.' His finger stopped sliding down the column of figures; his body stiffened and his silence was felt. He didn't chastise her for calling him sir, but nodded that he'd heard and continued with his task.

As they walked home Martha was making a plan. It suited her very well to have a half-day off. 'Robert, I have something that I have to do. I want you to take Charity with you to the vicar's house and stay there with Nona and James until I come for you.'

'Oh, Mother, do I have to? What will I do there? I don't know the vicar.'

'Robert, he is a lovely man and you will like his wife; they won't mind.'

'But…' Robert started to complain, a bloom of indignation on his cheek.

'What *is* this, Robert? I thought you were becoming a man. Now do as I ask. Please.' She had never used such a determined voice to any of her children before and was sorry that she had to do it now.

Robert looked shocked at the anger in his mother's voice and set off down the lane, carrying his sister and kicking at the stones on the path as he went.

Martha's anger was immense as she concentrated on her plan for Beemer. Walking directly through the cottage, she went to her special part of the garden and sat on a wooden stool next to a long, flat slab of rock. Taking up a swan's feather, kept for the purpose, she swept the stone until it was clean. Pouring water into a small bowl, she set it on the stone. From a box she took a small amount of charcoal and fashioned it into a pile before lighting it. She blew the flame until its smoke rose into the air and waited until the charcoal was hot and grey. From a small bag hanging at her waist, she took dried herbs and pine resin, placing it carefully onto the burning charcoal. Inhaling the soft grey fragrant smoke of the incense, she breathed deeply. Then laying her hands on her special stones, she addressed the energy.

'Oh, Goddess who lives in all things, who moves the oceans and the fluid within the bodies of women. I ask for wisdom to overcome my anger so that I may know exactly what I am doing. I ask for strength to see me through the consequences of my actions. I understand that I cannot stay here any longer and that things have become difficult because I did not move with the energy. Give me the courage to move towards the next opening door in my life and to have the faith that we will be provided for. I know that your way is love and peace and I honour that. But I cannot let this man get away with what he has done to my child. I honour the gift that you have given to me and ask for understanding of what I am about to do.'

Tipping the water into her hand she sprinkled it over the altar, then placed a spot of the water on her forehead.

'So mote it be,' she whispered.

Inside the cottage she placed her heaviest pan on the table. Taking her sharpest knife from a box on the dresser, she went to her bed in the recess and pulled the curtain across.

It was mid-afternoon when a knock came at the door. The silence in the cottage was tangible. When there was no answer, the knock came again, harder. The door was pushed violently open and she heard Beemer step into the room. He walked to the back door and looked out and then he shut it again, returning to the foot of the ladder. 'Where are you?' he called. 'You'd better not be hiding. I'm not in the mood to play games.'

'*What a pity,*' said a cool voice behind him, 'for I have a game that I want to play with you.'

Martha watched Beemer freeze and saw all the muscles in his back tense. She could almost see the hairs on his back rising under his clothes as he felt her presence. Turning slowly from the ladder, his eyes settled on the knife in Martha's hand.

He smirked. 'What do you think you're doing with that?'

'I understand that you have been touching my daughter,' she said, ignoring his observation.

'She was happy to do it,' he sneered. 'She wanted to help her mother.'

Martha gripped the knife's handle as anger throbbed in her chest, threatening to choke her, yet somehow she managed to calm herself enough to speak. 'Do you know how old the child is?' she asked, in a voice that wavered with the emotion of her anger.

Beemer's face twisted in an insolent smile. 'Does that mean something?' His eyes followed the movement of the knife as Martha made small round circles with its tip in the air.

Taking several steps backwards, she gave him space. He followed, as she knew that he would, looking for his chance to overpower her. She could see it written in his small eyes. She could also see the excitement of possibility lighting his face.

'I'm going to give you a taste of what I've given your daughter,' he said. 'Although I like them younger. Then, I'm going to thrash you soundly for daring to confront me. You forget, madam, that I have the power of the landlord behind me and he would throw you all out onto the lane.'

Martha moved backwards again to the end of the table. Beemer followed, still watching the circles that the blade made in the air. Suddenly he lunged, but Martha's hand was already on the heavy pan. It connected with the side of his head with such force that it took him off his feet.

He lay silently on the floor in front of the fire; a trickle of blood ran from a cut at his hair line towards his hairy ear. Martha worked quickly. Pulling down his breeches she took the knife and cut slits along the inside of his thighs to his groins as though preparing the fat on the pork before it's pushed onto the spit. Trembling, and fighting the need to hack it off completely, she took his penis between her forefinger and thumb. Her hand gripped the knife as she shook with anger. The knife hovered. The blade was sharp. Everything in her being screamed for the ultimate retribution. But in the end she covered it in small deep cuts and nicks before rubbing salt into the bleeding mass. Rolling up his sleeves, she quickly did the same to his inner arms.

Outside, the day had turned darker and thunder echoed behind the clouds. Pulling his clothes straight, Martha dragged the heavy body with difficulty to the door. There was no one in the lane and, if anyone was going to see her, it would be Dolly and she would understand. Martha managed to pull him a good way up the lane away from the cottage before the rain came. Exhausted, she dropped him in a heap. She could go no further.

Running back to the cottage she spent time washing his blood from her floor before pulling on her shawl and going to collect her children.

When she returned, he was gone. Now, she realised that Beemer would not rest until he got his own back. She had acted out of anger, without wisdom. She had not listened to the Goddess wisdom; she had only stated her intentions and asked for the right to take her revenge. A human right, that she felt that she had, but a spiritual right she knew that she had not. Taking the children inside, she secured the door.

Her children had been fed at the vicarage, for which she was very grateful. They were put to bed early with the promise of a day out on the morrow. Martha could not settle. Full of nervous energy, she was cleaning her grate when there was a tap on the back door. She grabbed the knife, fearing the worst, but it was only Dolly and she was in a state of excitement.

'Have you heard the news about Barney Beemer? He's been attacked. The men who found him say it's really odd for the attacker didn't take the rent money he was carrying. It must have been a grudge. He was covered in blood, they say. It must have been more than one person; he'd taken a real beating, and they say that he was hollering like a stuck pig.'

'I'm sure he deserved it.' Martha found it hard to look at Dolly.

'You're right, Martha, but I wouldn't want to be in the shoes of the person who did it when he recovers. Their life won't be worth living. Let's hope he doesn't know who it was.'

Martha lowered her eyes and wondered how far-reaching the consequences might be. Perhaps she should confess to Dolly in case something happened. 'Dolly, I have to tell you something, in case anything happens to me or my children.'

'What do you mean?' The excitement in Dolly's eyes faded, replaced by a frown of concern.

'I mean that I attacked Beemer.' She saw the confusion on Dolly's face and then the disbelief.

'You? Why? And how could you have done it?' Dolly stared at Martha.

'Pour some cider, Dolly; you've been a real friend to me and I'm going to be sorry to lose you.'

Going to the shelf, Dolly took down the stone jar in which the apple juice was kept. 'You're frightening me now, Martha,' she said, returning to the table, where Martha lay two cups.

It was a shocked and angry Dolly that listened to the story that Martha told, her voice at times trembling. When Martha had finished, Dolly said earnestly, 'We should tell the men what he's done.'

Martha shook her head. 'I know him, Dolly; he will tell them she was happy to go along with it.'

'They wouldn't believe him, Martha.'

'Wouldn't they, Dolly? Can you be sure of that? My child has been through enough. She's only eleven. How could she live with everyone knowing what he'd done to her? Their sympathy and watching her walk down the street. The gossip behind closed doors. What young man would be allowed to marry her once his parents know this? People are cruel, Dolly.' Martha fought to keep the tears from her eyes.

'Oh Gawd, Martha. I don't know about this. Are you sure you're right to run away? You'll be on your own. Never knowing when he'll turn up. Tell someone, let us protect you.' She gripped Martha's hand.

'I've told you, Dolly, please, only tell my story if you have to.'

When Dolly had gone, Martha thought about her words. Dolly was right: they were in danger; she would have to leave. While the children slept, she looked at the things that meant anything to her and the useful things they would need. Tomorrow they would go out for the afternoon and she would try to think where else they could live.

14.

Claydon House

Emma was beginning to feel at home in this strange house, where most of her time was spent out of sight avoiding the mistress or happily in the kitchen. Matt had become a good companion on a Sunday afternoon walk, something that she had never done at home. It felt to her young heart that this was what Dolly referred to as walking out. Of course, nothing had been said, but her heart gave a jump whenever she saw him. Some Sundays Matt was in a dark mood and on those days Emma walked alone. She didn't mind. Although she loved Matt's company she was also glad to spend some time walking quietly amongst the trees and the fields, breathing in the air, happy to be out of the house.

It was a fine hot summer day when half-way through her walk she saw Matt sitting moodily on a field gate. As she approached him she decided to try to keep the atmosphere happy by being cheerful.

'Isn't it a wonderful day, Matt? I wish we could stay here forever living together like a family.' He looked at her with eyes as deep as black pools, but said nothing. 'What's wrong?' she asked, and then wished that she hadn't spoken. Her mother had often told her to keep the silence, to let others be with their thoughts.

'Nothing that you would understand,' he replied; 'you're just a child.'

Emma was shocked. Is that how he saw her? She felt embarrassed by the thoughts that she'd had of them walking out, but how could he think her a child? She was thirteen.

'I don't see myself as a child, Matt, I'm thirteen,' she said defensively and remembered that when she was twelve that she had felt like a child, playing with her brothers and sister. But now at thirteen she was a working woman. How was he so blind?

'And does that make you an adult?' he retorted sharply.

'No, I think it makes me a young woman,' she returned sharply back. 'Do you think, then, that at fifteen you are a man?' Her eyes flashed with indignation.

His expression was grim as he shouted back at her, 'I've been doing a man's job since I was twelve. Yes, I see myself as a man.'

'What has made you so angry, Matt? Sometimes I can't talk to you, you're so horrible,' she retaliated.

'That's because, while you think we are a family and are happy here, I want to get away and make my fortune.' He got down from the gate and kicked at a clod of turf.

'Where would you go?' Her heart plummeted.

'I can't go anywhere,' he shouted. 'How can I leave my mother? Our jobs are tied.'

'What's that mean, tied?' she frowned.

'The job is for a man and a woman, one to look after the stables, the other to run the house. In taking on my father's job to stop us from being replaced, I've thrown away my chance of a future.'

'But you're very good at your job. What else could you do?'

'I'll never know, will I?' There was a bitterness in his voice again and she was sorry to hear it.

'I don't understand you, Matt; there are so many people without work, without homes, and you have both. You don't have to worry about where the next meal is coming from, or if you will freeze to death in the night, or if the rent man is going to throw you out.'

'And how much longer do you think that's going to last?' he spat at her.

Emma was puzzled, shocked. What could he mean?

'For goodness' sake, look around you, Emma. The place is falling down. No money has been spent on it since the old master died and his useless children took over.'

Emma was horrified. He shouldn't be talking about the master and mistress like that, but said calmly, 'Didn't it always look like this?' She looked towards the house and could see nothing amiss.

'It's nothing like it was, Emma. Once upon a time people called at the house in their carriages. My father looked after the late master's horses and stabled the visitors' horses. There were maids and scullery maids doing all the jobs that you do. There were footmen and a butler who had rooms along the servants' passage. There were lots of gardeners and the gardens were beautiful. The house was alive with visitors and laughter. People went shooting and fishing at weekends. Mother made huge picnic hampers. When there was a ball, we were loaned staff from other houses and the kitchen was full of fun.'

Emma couldn't take it all in. It was a world she couldn't imagine. She couldn't see the mistress being a part of a world like that, and said so.

'Surely the mistress wouldn't have joined in all the jollity?'

'She was away at school for many years. And was a woman when she returned home. Her friends came to the dances but one by one they married. She was left here running the house after the death of her father.'

'Didn't anyone want to marry her?' Emma felt sorry for the woman.

'They came and looked. But she was so sour they changed their minds and after the master died things changed. Mister Oliver came home from abroad because he'd inherited it all. They are brother and sister but the two of them are so different, they don't get on. Fire and water they are, fire and water.'

What is he like, the master?'

Matt shrugged. 'Hard to tell. He wasn't here much. When he was, he was sullen. When he brought gentlemen with him, they acted like fools. They shot their guns into the river at the fish. They raced their horses across the fields, destroying the crops. Mother hated him being home. He ordered food he was too drunk to eat and did a lot of damage to the furniture. They had no respect for the maids. Gradually the staff for one reason or another left.' He looked at the ground. 'Except, Mother, Dad and Polly. Oh, and Alf, of course.' Matt kicked a stone. 'He doesn't get a wage; he works for his bed and food.'

'That's terrible!' She was truly shocked.

'Not really: at his age he'd have been going to the workhouse. He's happy to live here in exchange for his work.'

They were walking slowly back to the house while talking and were just rounding the corner of the building when they smelt smoke.

'That's strange,' Matt said, increasing his pace. 'Alf wouldn't have a bonfire on a Sunday.'

At the next corner, he almost ran into Alf, jerking along with a bucket of water.

'Matt, the West Wing's on fire,' Alf called, seeing them suddenly appear.

'Where's Mother?' There was panic in Matt's voice.

'In the kitchen, I think.' Alf could barely speak as he hurried with the heavy bucket, trying not to spill the water.

'Give me that.' Matt snatched it from Alf's bony fingers, spilling water on his feet. You go and get more water. Emma, you go with him.'

Emma ran towards the kitchen door and then remembered the baby. She screamed after Matt. 'There's a baby, Matt; find the baby.'

But he was gone around the building and through the front door, racing up the stairs two at time, spilling water on the wood and carpets. As he reached the top, Miss Brack appeared on the landing.

'What do you think you are doing in this part of the house?' Her eyes held a fury that Matt knew only too well, but he found the courage to shout at her.

'Get down the stairs; the house is on fire.'

'How dare you speak to me like that?' she demanded, but Matt had turned the corner at the end of the landing and was heading for the stairs to the West Wing. Smoke was already making its way into the lower corridor as he raced up the stairs two at a time. Somewhere along the passage in front of him he could hear a woman shouting for help. Finding the room, he opened the door and as he did so flames shot out, catching his hair. Pouring a little water from the bucket over his head, he peered through the smoke and located the screaming woman. The air was hot. Small sparks amongst the flames were spreading the fire into the corridor behind him. He could just see Mrs Shillabeer making her way to the door across the room. He shouted to her, 'This way, this way, you're going the wrong way.'

The fire was becoming fierce; his shirtsleeve was on fire and he plunged his elbow into the bucket. 'Over here, madam.' She turned her face to him, full of determination. 'There is a baby. We have to save him.' Her dress was beginning to smoulder.

Unable to hear her voice above the noise of the crackling flames he shouted to her, 'Come this way or we'll both die.'

Throwing the bucket of water over himself, he charged through the flames and grabbed the woman, who was screaming and beating at her dress with her hands. The flames, devouring the material, were soon licking around her waist. Matt ripped the garment from her and pulled her with him back to the door. The smoke and heat were intense.

Emma stood in the doorway with her bucket of water, her arm over her face, screaming, having seen Mrs Shillabeer on fire. As Matt reached the door, he poured some of the water from Emma's bucket over the blackened woman and the rest over himself and Emma. Draping the woman over his back and blinded by the smoke, he crawled, choking, with Emma, on hands and knees along the corridor floor. The flames had leapt ahead of them, licking the post at the top of the stairs and the carpet along which they crawled. Emma's hand was following the wall when she came upon a door. Hardly able to breathe, she reached up for the door handle. As the door swung open, Matt pushed Emma in and dragged the unconscious woman with him. The flames leapt above their heads, racing along the ceiling as Matt slammed the door shut. The hungry flames had already caught the curtains. Working together, they ripped them down, while behind them flames licked around the bottom of the door. They were both choking, desperate for air, as Matt grabbed a vase containing slimy green water that stood on the top of a tallboy. Tipping the water along the bottom of the door made the flames hiss and increased the fumes in the room as they coughed uncontrollably. Sitting on the floor, gasping for breath, Emma's eyes streamed painfully. Mrs Shillabeer lay silently, unmoving, blackened on the floor where she had been dropped.

'Emma,' Matt coughed, 'we have to find a way out of here. Help me move that tallboy in front of the door.'

Getting on one side of it, she tried to push. 'It's too heavy,' she wheezed, unable to draw a full breath.

'Get on your knees, stay near the floor. Put your shoulder against it.' His eyes were streaming, leaving white channels in a blackened face. Removing the bottom two drawers, he pulled while she pushed and it started to move. Wedging it against the door, he grabbed Emma's arm and dragged her towards the window. 'Keep breathing, Emma, we'll be all right.'

Eventually the ancient window creaked open at his insistent pushing. Through smarting eyes he could see that there was no way down from this point. If they jumped they would certainly be killed. If they stayed, they would die a worse death, everyone was on the other side of the house; there was no one to help them. Then he noticed a small ledge just below the window. It was only the width of a brick and ran decoratively around the house. With a bed sheet taken from the drawer of the tallboy, he pulled it under Emma's arms, tying her to him. Stepping up onto a linen box that was under the window, he felt Emma's weight. Her lovely blackened face lay limply on his chest. He realised then that the ledge wasn't wide enough for two people, and the only finger holds were small holes in the old brickwork. They would surely fall. Untying the knot, he let her slide unconscious to the floor as the heat in the room intensified. He worked quickly, knowing the nature of the flames and their need for oxygen. Tying all the material he could find in the linen box together, he made a rope, then, tying it around Emma's chest, lowered her slowly out of the window. When his hands came to the end of the last piece of sheet, he let her drop, not knowing how far that was. Behind him the door and the tallboy were on fire; he only had a matter of minutes. He felt below the smoke for the woman. She didn't move. He had no time to save her; she was in God's hands now, as was he. With eyes almost closed from the acrid fumes, he stepped out onto the narrow brick ledge. Seconds later a fireball burst through the open window.

Alf and Nell were staggering back and forth from the well with full buckets and throwing the water up the narrow stairs that led to the West Wing. But their progress was slow. They kept calling Matt and Emma's names, but nothing could be heard above the crackling of the flames above them. 'It's no good, Nell,' Alf said sadly. 'We have to shut the door to save the rest of the house.'

Nell screamed the name of her son as Alf slammed the door.

~

Having seen the smoke, the local squire and some of his men arrived on sweating horses, followed by workers from the area estates on foot. Alf directed the men, who had come armed with buckets, towards the well. But it was too late to save the West Wing. The roof collapsed just as the heavens opened, and heavy rain aided the men in dousing the flames.

Wringing her hands in grief, Nell cried out to the passing men, 'My son is inside, and our maid. Save them, please save them.'

They looked at the building and shook their heads. No one could have survived the inferno and they knew that it was their sad duty now to look for bodies. The squire walked sadly towards Amelia, who stood silently in front of the house. 'Is there anyone else to your knowledge in the house, madam?'

'I had a friend staying, a Mrs Shillabeer,' she replied without hurrying.

'Anyone else?' he asked as she seemed vague. 'It's important, madam,' he pressed.

She didn't hesitate. 'No,' she said, 'only Mrs Shillabeer.'

'So we are looking for three people,' he said, looking directly into her eyes for confirmation.

'It seems so.' Her face, set like a mask, showed no emotion.

The squire noted the coolness of this woman, of whom he had heard but until now had not met. She was, as gossip said, nothing like her brother. People had died in her house and she was showing no emotion. He watched her turn towards the house. But what he missed was the momentary smile that flitted across her face. Providence, she felt, had smiled upon her; there was no one now to know her secret. After the fierce fire there would be no trace of Tobias. The West Wing would be closed and forgotten for ever.

A shout from the other side of the house galvanised the men into action. 'Squire, I found a body on the ground, a young girl.'

Nell screamed in anguish, 'Emma!' and her tears flowed as she covered her face with her apron.

'Get the tarpaulin sir, there's another,' a man shouted.

Nell fainted at Alf's feet as the men rushed towards the voice.

'She's barely alive, sir,' the labourer said as the squire arrived.

'Where's the other one?' the squire asked, looking around.

'He's there, sir.' The man pointed upwards. 'He's on the ledge; he'll have to jump. We'll catch him in this.' They gathered around the tarpaulin, holding it out just as Matt lost his grip on the brickwork and fell unconscious towards the ground.

15.

Haddenford

It was a pleasant Sunday afternoon when Martha and her little family left the cottage for a walk through the fields. James ran here and there, looking for rabbits. But Nona dragged behind, while Martha and Robert took it in turns to carry Charity. At midday they sat by the river and Martha watched her children paddle and soak each other with water. She didn't complain; how could she when they had so little fun? While Charity was having her afternoon nap, Martha lay back in the grass, watching the sky above her. It was so blue, so deep it seemed to go on forever. She wondered carelessly how deep it was; could anyone ever know? Lying half asleep on the grass, she felt the energy of the earth as though it were breathing and she acknowledged the Goddess. I am at a crossroads, she thought her communication to the energy. I don't know where to turn. I dearly want to keep us all together. A tear rolled down the side of her face. 'Oh, Goddess of perfect love,' she whispered, 'who dwells in all things, see my desperate need. Lead me in the right direction. Give me the wisdom to know where I should be.'

Mid-afternoon they passed the Tate farm and a daring idea formed in Martha's head. 'Robert, take the children home. I'll be there soon. There's something I need to do.' As she watched the little group walk together down the lane, she knew it was a crazy idea and her heart pounded as she visualised the forbidding figure of Farmer Tate. But, she thought, she had nothing to lose by talking to him.

~

Martha stood, a lonely figure in his yard. A place she had no permission to be. She'd stood in this yard many mornings with the other workers, but now she felt exposed standing alone. The yard appeared wider than she'd noticed before and surrounded by the barns on two sides and the house on the other she was intimidated by its silent emptiness.

The geese, taking an interest, waddled towards her in a neck-snaking group, their shiny eyes watching her warily. Two boldly broke free and, hissing, pecked at her heels. She wasn't fond of geese and tried to shoo them away, while continuing nervously towards the farmhouse door. There was nothing attractive about this plain two-storey house, a brick square with large windows that seemed to watch her approach with empty eyes.

Lifting her skirt, she picked her way through the mud and manure to the doorstep. A strong smell of animals hung in the air and a dog barked at her from the end of its tether, at the edge of the farthest barn.

There was no answer as she nervously knocked on the door with her fist, her heart thumping. As she waited on the step it was the sound of children's high-pitched quarrelsome voices that reached her ears from the other side of the door. It seemed as though they were fighting. When one started to cry, Martha pushed the door open slowly to reveal a kitchen in turmoil. A small girl with long, brown, unruly hair was standing on the table screaming and throwing food at her brothers, who rolled on the floor beneath her, fighting. Stepping cautiously into the room, Martha stopped abruptly at the sight of Andrew Tate sitting in a chair staring into space. He seemed neither to hear nor see what his children were doing. Her heart skipped a beat as she wondered if he was even alive. A louder yell from one of the boys brought her attention back to them. A boy with brown hair and a cut on his lip was about to hit his brother on the head with his father's shoe. Martha rushed around the table and took the shoe from the small hand. Taking each boy by the back of their clothes, she pulled them to their feet.

'Now stop this fighting,' she said firmly. The boys looked at her in amazement and struggled again to punch each other. 'No, no, this isn't right; this isn't how brothers behave. Now tell me what happened.'

'It was his fault. He started it.' The smaller boy accused the other and tried again to kick his larger brother.

'No, I didn't; he fell over and wanted his mother,' the larger boy shouted, red in the face. Martha was shocked at their behaviour. 'I told him, we haven't got a mother, she's gone away, she doesn't love us anymore.'

'It's not true,' the small boy cried. 'It's not true. She is coming back.'

And he turned his face into Martha's skirt and sobbed. Sinking to their level and with a boy in each arm Martha sat on the floor amidst all the food and pulled them to her. Farmer Tate still sat in his chair, staring into nothingness. Nervously she smiled down at the grubby faces.

'Tell me your names and how old you are.' It was the larger boy who responded first.

'Jack. I'm nearly nine. He's George.'

'I'm nearly eight,' came a voice from her skirt as a piece of bread, thrown from the table where the girl had been holding it in her hand, hit Martha on the head. Martha looked up into a worried face that became defiant.

Ignoring her, Martha turned back to the boys. Looking from one to the other, she said, 'Let's go outside and I'll tell you a story.'

She had seen on her arrival a low-walled, thinly grassed area, where the washing was hung, and she led them there. 'I'm Martha Tilby,' she said, getting them to sit on the grass beside her.

'I saw you, in the field.' The smaller of the boys spoke with such a serious expression on his face that he looked like a wizened old man.

'Yes, George, you did,' Martha said softly, to take the tension out of the air. 'I work for your father.'

'Our mother's gone away,' a small voice called from the wall.

'That's Sarah. Father says she's gone wild,' Jack informed Martha.

'Would you like to come and sit with us, Sarah?' Martha asked, looking up at the girl, who shook her head vigorously.

Martha looked away. At least the girl was listening. She turned to Jack. 'Did you know that your mother wasn't well, Jack?'

'She couldn't breathe,' George interrupted.

'She was talking to me, not you.' And Martha was just quick enough to catch the little fist that travelled towards George.

'That is enough fighting.' Martha's voice was firm. 'I want you to apologise to each other.'

'I'm six.' Sarah stood in front of her with shoulders lifted and chest pushed out. 'I'm a big girl.'

'I can see that you are, Sarah.' Then, with her voice a little sharper, 'Please sit down.' The girl sat and Martha turned to the boys.

'I'm waiting for you to say sorry to your brother.' She looked from one to the other. 'I'm waiting.'

'Sorry, Jack.' George looked sheepish and pulled at the grass, avoiding looking at his brother, while Sarah looked on bemused.

'Sorry, George.' Jack looked down at his feet and squirmed.

'Thank you,' Martha said before anyone else could say anything. 'Now let's start again. Tell me about your mother.'

'She went away because she doesn't love us anymore and she's not coming back.' It was Sarah that spoke, sitting dirty-faced and dry-eyed, looking straight into Martha's face.

'Who told you that Sarah?'

'George was crying and father told him to stop because Mother wasn't coming back and he would have to grow up.' The girl continued to look straight into Martha's face.

Inwardly, Martha was furious at the insensitive way the children had been treated. 'You know that your mother loved you very much!' She looked from one to the other with raised eyebrows. The children were silent. 'Do you remember that she cooked you nice things to eat?' Three serious faces nodded in agreement as they remembered.

'I had bacon for breakfast and nice bread,' George remembered.

Sarah tried to better that, her voice rising. 'Mother made me a cake for being good.'

'She kept you all clean,' Martha continued. They nodded. 'She kept the house clean.' Again they nodded.

Jack pulled away angrily. 'So why did she leave us? Why isn't she coming back?'

Martha didn't know what to say. Surely they knew that their mother was dead? She looked at Jack. 'You're the eldest, Jack. You tell me what happened, if you can.' Sarah opened her mouth to speak but Martha was quick to bring some order to these children. 'I'm sorry, Sarah. I've asked Jack to tell me. Jack?' She raised her eyebrows. He hesitated, trying to recall the last time he'd seen his mother.

'Mother wasn't well,' he started. 'She sat at the table with her head over a bowl of hot water and a cloth over her head.'

'Go on,' Martha encouraged when he stopped.

'Father said, put yourselves to bed. We wanted to kiss Mother goodnight but we couldn't because she was under the cloth. She squeezed our hands. When we got up in the morning, Mother wasn't there. We wanted our breakfast and, when George started to cry, Father shouted at him and said we'd have to look after ourselves 'cos she wasn't coming back.'

'Do you know where she went?' Martha asked.

They shook their heads. This was incredible. Their father should have told them. Would he be angry if she told them? But she'd gone this far, she surmised, and wondered how to start. She remembered how she had told her own children of their father's death and how difficult the decision had been to tell the truth. It was natural for a parent to want to protect their children from terrible grief, but in the end it was a part of this fragile life. It couldn't be avoided, but she felt uncomfortable taking on the responsibility. Would she be in trouble? He was her employer, after all, and she needed the money; she didn't want to lose her job. Three upturned small faces were looking at her with expectation.

She started slowly, looking at each face in turn. 'That night,' she started, 'after you had all gone to bed, your mother became very ill and your father couldn't help her. He couldn't make her better and she went to sleep and didn't wake up again.' The little faces continued to stare up at her. 'Do you understand what I'm saying?' Their faces were blank. Then a sort of dawning crossed Jack's face.

'Like Jep our dog?'

'What happened to Jep?'

'He went to sleep and father said he'd died. He lay in the yard and wouldn't get up.'

'Yes, just like Jep, your mother died. She didn't wake up. She didn't want to leave you. She loved you all very much. She wasn't well.'

'Did they put her in a hole in the ground like Jep?'

'Yes, George, there was a funeral and lots of people were very sorry that your mother had died. She was well respected.'

'Did you like my mother?' The eyes of an innocent child, who spoke straight from the heart, having no understanding of any embarrassment that might be caused by such directness, stared into Martha's face.

'Yes, Sarah, I liked your mother very much. She was very kind to me and many other women. Now, shall we go inside and clear up some of the mess before I make you something to eat?'

The children nodded. Although they were shedding no tears, she could see that they were now coming to terms with what had happened.

In the kitchen, Farmer Tate's chair was empty. Relieved that for the moment she did not have to explain why she was in his house, Martha suggested that the children get a bucket and put all the broken things and food into it.

'Not the food,' Sarah told her. 'We have to put that in a bucket outside for the pigs.'

'I see,' said Martha acknowledging the information. 'If you pick everything up, then I will wash the floor.'

The children worked well and were soon sitting at the table in a tidy kitchen, hands and faces washed, eating bread and dripping.

'You stay here and eat your food,' Martha directed, 'and when you're finished, clear it away. Jack, you will wash up. George, you will dry the plates and, Sarah, you will wipe the table. Can I leave you with that while I go and find your father?'

'Yes, Mrs Tilby,' they chorused.

Martha searched the large, untidy house with a heart that was beating too fast. She felt particularly vulnerable upstairs, where she knew that she should not be, and felt the possibility of his angry presence behind every door that she opened, but found the house silent and empty. Out of an upstairs window she looked across the fields to where she had so often worked but saw no human movement.

Going out into the yard she noticed a barn door ajar and made her way in that direction. The geese, necks stretched, grumbled to each other, suspiciously watching her from their tight group, threatening.

It was dark and warm inside the barn and smelt of wood and straw. As her eyes adjusted to the darkness, she saw him sitting on a bale of hay, a rope between his knees, its length hanging on the floor. He stared in her direction as she entered, but didn't move.

'Mister Tate?' Her voice wavered. She'd always been a little afraid of the tall, severe figure. He'd given the orders and given them their pay, but apart from that had little to do with the workers. He seemed aloof; his mind always somewhere else. He was shown a great deal of respect by the older workers and that in itself made the newer workers show deference when he was around.

'What do you want?' His voice was barely audible.

This obviously wasn't a good moment to ask about a roof for her and her brood. So she said, 'I gave the children their supper.' He was silent and she wondered why he was sitting on the bale holding a rope.

'What are you doing?' she asked quietly. He lowered his head and didn't answer. Her heart froze. Surely he wasn't about to hang himself? Moving towards him she covered the floor quickly, and knelt beside him, placing a hand on his arm.

'Your children need you.' She looked at his face, but could hardly see it in the half-light and his beard made it hard to judge what he was thinking.

'I don't need them.' His voice was distant, gruff.

'You loved your wife?' she encouraged, hopeful that he would engage. He said nothing as tears rolled into his beard.

Martha continued, trying to keep her voice from shaking. 'She loved you and the children.' He hung his head but now she'd started she had to go on. 'She wouldn't want you to leave them on their own.'

He didn't lift his head but spoke into his chest. 'I can't deal with them. I run the farm. She cared for the house and the children.'

Afraid for him, Martha whispered, 'What's to become of them, sir?'

There was agony in his voice as he replied, 'I don't know. I don't know.'

With a sudden movement that frightened her, he threw out his arms, almost toppling her.

'Sir,' she said quickly, 'I am about to become homeless. Would it be of use to you if I came and lived here? I could run your home and care for your children. I wouldn't want a wage, just a roof and food.'

He stared at her as though seeing her for the first time, his eyes screwed up into an expression of deep pain. 'I don't know. I don't know what to do. I have no heart in anything now.'

'Let me look after the children, sir, while you deal with the farm.' Martha's heart was racing. This was her last chance.

'I don't know you.' His voice had lost all its energy and his head drooped.

'I don't know you, sir, but I am willing to help you in your hour of need, even if it is only for a short time.'

He nodded slowly, and she took it for agreement. She could see that he was too worn down to argue as he put down the rope and walked, shoulders bent, from the barn.

~

A weight had lifted from her shoulders as she hurried along the lanes to the cottage, and as she went she blessed the Goddess for her help.

Nona was at the door to meet her. 'I was getting worried, Mother.' Nona looked drawn and tired. 'Why have you been so long?'

'I was talking with Mister Tate. He has agreed to let us live at the farm for a while. We move in tomorrow.'

'Hooray,' James yelled, jumping around the room and making a nuisance of himself.

'Tonight,' Martha said, ignoring her son, 'we will gather all the things we will need. This is our last night in this cottage.' She put her arm around Nona. 'All is going to be well, little one,' she said, kissing Nona's head.

117

When the children were all in bed, she surveyed the few possessions that they were taking with them. Gathered together on the table were her needlework box, the wren and their clothes. Not much to show for a whole lifetime. There was no point in taking the furniture as the farmer had a houseful of that. She wrapped her cutlery and some plates and bowls in a cloth and took them next door to Dolly.

'Use them or keep them for me in case this doesn't work out,' she said, placing her few possessions on Dolly's table.

Dolly had tears in her eyes as she gathered them up and placed them inside a cupboard. 'I'll keep them for you, Martha; you may need them later.'

But Martha was more concerned about something else; a feeling of doom was invading her soul. She felt as though she had set something in motion that she had no control over. 'Don't tell anyone where we are, Dolly. I don't want Beemer to find out too soon.' She tried to keep the fear out of her voice but the look that Dolly tried to hide told Martha that she understood.

'What about the children?' Dolly asked. 'How will you keep them safe from Beemer?'

'I'll be teaching them myself; there'll be no need for them to leave the farm.'

'I'm worried about this, Martha. Perhaps you should tell Mr Tate why you're there.'

'I can't do that, Dolly! He has such a lot of worry and pain at the moment. I can't burden him with my worries. Why would he be interested anyway?'

'Because he has a daughter!'

'At this moment he can't take any more, Dolly. I will look after Sarah and you must watch Alice.' The women embraced, holding each other tightly.

16.

Claydon House

In her sleepy state, Emma became aware of Mrs Ames leaning over her bed. Her usually kind face looked concerned as she shook a small bottle and removed its stopper.

'Come, Emma, take a spoonful of this medicine; it will soon have you feeling right.'

Emma winced as she tried to move. 'My back hurts.'

Nell put a motherly arm around the girl's shoulders for support. 'Lean on me. Good girl, now open your mouth and swallow this.'

Emma pulled a face as the mixture entered her mouth. 'It's truly bitter, Mrs Ames. I… I don't like it.'

'Yes, I know it's a bit bitter, Emma, but the worse it tastes the more good it does you, that's what me old mother used to say.'

Emma swallowed the mixture with her eyes screwed up and was eased back onto the pillow, where she went into a spasm of painful coughing.

'Keep coughing, Emma; we have to get all the smoke out of you.'

'How is Matt?' Emma asked between coughs.

'He has blisters, the size of duck eggs on his back and shoulders,' she exaggerated. 'The medicine is making him sleep and while he is sleeping he's repairing.'

As Nell pulled the covers up over her, Emma realised that she was wearing a clean shift. Someone had been in her room. 'Where are my clothes, Mrs Ames?'

Nell looked uncomfortable. 'I'm sorry, Emma. I wasn't able to save the clothes that you were wearing. I had to throw them away.' Nell knew that this moment would come and she had been dreading it. Not knowing how to explain to Emma what she had done. But then she'd had no option. If the mistress found out that she had known that the girl had the locket and hadn't said anything, then she would be out in the lanes with nothing but a hedge to sleep under. Nell watched the look of panic cross the girl's face and was sorry to see it.

Emma stared up at her. 'You've given me clean clothes?'

Nell had been trying to work out an excuse for the little maid having such expensive jewellery hidden amongst her spare garments. Perhaps, she'd said to herself, the girl hadn't known it was there. But now, sadly, she knew that she was wrong about that.

'I washed your undergarments, Emma. I did the best I could with them.'

Emma stared at Nell, biting the side of her mouth. She was on the edge of tears. Nell must have found Salanda's locket.

'You found my grandmother's locket, didn't you, Mrs Ames?'

'Your grandmother's?' Nell's eyebrows shot up in surprise. Emma nodded. 'Then why didn't your mother sell it instead of sending you to work?'

'It can't be sold Mrs Ames; it belongs to my family.' Emma searched Nell's face for some understanding. But Nell was wondering why Emma's mother would do such a stupid thing as to send a child out into this harsh world with such an expensive object about her person. No, the girl must be telling a lie and Nell felt sorry. She'd thought a lot of Emma; she'd had no reason not to trust her. She'd liked her.

'Where is my locket, Mrs Ames?' Emma was direct, her eyes holding steady on Nell's, causing Nell to bluster in confusion and some regret. Emma was not ready for the answer when it came.

'I had to show it to the mistress.'

Emma sat bolt upright in the bed, her heart beating like a drum in her chest and ears. Spasms of pain travelled up her spine and spread out across her neck and back. 'No!' she cried in agony. 'Why?'

The look of anguish on Emma's face was almost more than Nell could bear to see. She'd been telling herself ever since she had done it that she'd had no choice in the matter. 'Because it might have been hers,' Nell replied.

'But it wasn't hers. It's mine, Mrs Ames. It belongs to my family. How will I get it back?'

Nell was sorry to see Emma so distressed but there was nothing she could do about it now. The mistress had it and Nell knew very well that it could not have been Emma's.

Emma pulled the covers off slowly. Pain seared through her back as she slid her legs over the side of the bed. Her skin burnt and her head swam.

'My back!' she groaned and was almost sick with the unbearable pain but kept moving slowly.

'Hold still, Emma. That spine was jarred when you fell. And now look. The burns on your back and arms are weeping again. You must stay still. The apothecary said you shouldn't move for a few more weeks.'

'I have to get it back,' she whispered through the pain. 'Could you help me get dressed, Mrs Ames?'

Nell watched the girl get dressed in the oversized brown uniform and walk with painful steps from her bedroom to the back stairs and then make her way down them to the landing below and, with great effort, walk along the landing towards the mistress's sitting room. It left Nell wondering, would someone who had stolen jewellery be foolish enough to ask for it back? She just didn't know what to think anymore.

~

Knocking on the sitting room door, Emma waited; her leg muscles trembled as she struggled to keep her body upright. The voice that came from behind the door was sharp. '*Enter.*' The sudden increase in Emma's heartbeat took her breath away. Opening the door, she walked slowly forward, and with all her strength she fought the searing pain that overwhelmed her.

Dressed completely in black, Miss Brack stood behind a small table holding a book in one hand. Looking up and seeing it was Emma, she glared down her sharp nose. The long fingers of her other hand rested on the table in front of her. She looked, Emma thought, like a large black crow eyeing up the meat at the side of the lane. Emma knew all about single black crows and magpies.

'Well?' she demanded, her voice as rasping as a crow's.

Emma tried to speak but nothing came from her dry mouth.

'Speak up, girl.' The voice was short and sharp, the eyes held a gleam of knowledge. Emma took a breath and her determination returned, overpowering her fear of the moment.

'May I have my locket back please, ma'am?'

With a look of disgust, Amelia ignored the plea. 'Where do you come from?' she asked simply.

Surprised and confused, Emma flinched. 'Haddenford, ma'am.'

'I don't want to know where you live.' The voice was suddenly filled with anger. 'What is the name of your family?'

'Tilby, ma'am.'

The look that fell upon Emma was cold enough to cut her skin. And she shrank before the gaze of this woman who held all the staff in such fear. 'First names,' she bellowed with a power in her eyes that was not lost on Emma.

Emma shook as she tried to answer. 'Martha and William, ma'am.'

'How did you get here?' The fingers of the woman's left hand drummed on the table.

'In a cart, ma'am.' Emma answered quickly, still confused.

'That's not what I asked. Are you being difficult on purpose, girl?' Amelia's eyes flashed with anger and Emma could only look terrified as the woman moved around the side of the table as though she were going to grab her. 'Because if you are,' she continued, 'you will be very sorry for it.'

Emma was puzzled; what else could she say? She had arrived on Mim's cart.

'How did you get here?' the mistress shouted again, her eyes manic.

Emma couldn't answer; she couldn't breathe. There was nothing else to say and she was in pain.

Amelia slammed her book down on the table. Emma flinched but stood her ground. Amelia smiled inwardly, acknowledging the girl's fear. 'Who told you about the position here?'

'My mother, ma'am.'

'And how did she come to hear of it?'

'I… I don't know.'

'You don't know?' The eyebrows were raised, the voice now a quiet hiss.

Emma felt the power of the woman in front of her and could only shake her head, at a loss to know what the woman wanted from her.

'Where did you get that locket found by Mrs Ames?'

'It belonged to my grandmother, ma'am. It belongs with my family.'

Emma couldn't read the woman's face, but something had changed in the way that she held herself.

The voice was quieter as Amelia asked, 'And who is your grandmother?'

'She was called Salanda, ma'am.' At that moment a pain shot through Emma's back as the skin on her burns tightened and her muscles went into spasm. It was all that she could do not to cry out. Instead she gritted her teeth and her breath came in short gasps.

Amelia's fingers still drummed on the table while she thought about what to do. 'I don't believe that the locket is yours, and I don't believe this story of a grandmother. I will keep it until I can talk to the authorities.'

'No! Please, ma'am, it is mine. No one but me can have it. It's been passed down through the family.' Distressed, Emma took a step forward and felt the new skin forming on her burns split.

Amelia raised her voice. 'You are in no position to argue with me. You had stolen property in your possession. You see, the locket is mine.'

Emma's last ounce of forced energy slipped away like water from a jug. Her legs buckled under her and she fell forward into blackness, lying crumpled on the floor like a rag doll.

Amelia looked at the girl. There was nothing about her that she recognised. Why should there be? She had never met her aunt Salanda. There had been some sort of scandal before she was born. She had heard her father speak once to her Uncle Hanwell, before he left for the war, asking if he was going to visit their mother and sister. It had been a shock. Until that moment Amelia hadn't realised this other part of the family existed. When she'd asked her father about it, he'd said that she must have been mistaken. She remembered the look on his face as she'd told him that she would ask her mother about her father's relatives. And she recalled the look of fear that flashed into his eyes, quickly followed by rage, the only anger he had ever shown. 'I will not be cross-examined by you, young lady, nor will I creep around in my own house wondering if you may be listening to my conversations and repeating them to your mother,' he had shouted, red-faced, eyes bulging. 'It is clear to me,' he had continued, 'that it is time you left your governess and went to school.' It was soon after that day that she'd left for France, where she stayed until the death of her mother. She had returned briefly, but had been unable to settle and had returned to France, but not before she'd made enquiries about her grandmother and her aunt.

The sharp sound of a bell rang manically in the servants' passage. Nell groaned. 'What now?' she mumbled, bustling up the stairs. 'I hope she isn't dismissing Emma. I have enough to do. I need that girl.' Nell knocked and entered at the command, but stopped in the doorway in shock. Emma lay pale and unconscious on the floor at the feet of the mistress, who had a satisfied look on her face.

'Take her away and be rid of her, Mrs Ames. The locket is mine. I will be taking the necessary action in due course. We can't have a thief in the house, can we?'

Nell didn't usually question her mistress, but in this instance she had to ask, 'You want me to turn her out, ma'am?'

'Straight away, Mrs Ames. I don't want her about the house.'

Nell opened her mouth to protest, but the flame of anger that burnt in her mistress's dark eyes changed her mind. Taking Emma by the arms, Nell dragged her unceremoniously through the door and across the landing, leaving her at the top of the servants' stairs while she went for Alf. Between them they carried Emma to the kitchen table, where she was laid with her head on a cushion.

'What am I going to do, Alf? The mistress told me to throw her out. How do I do that when she can hardly stand with those burns? And the new skin is split and weeping.'

Alf shook his head, unable to believe the hardness of the mistress's heart. 'If I 'ad anywhere else to go, Nell, I'd leave meself, because in the end she'll be rid of us all.'

'And what good would that do her? No, she needs us to feed her and keep the house going and that's the problem. I can't do the work as well as the cooking. I'm getting too old, Alf. I need Emma.'

'So,' he shrugged, 'what do we do Nell, keep her hidden?' His face reflected the hopelessness of the question, to which there seemed no real possible answer.

'That's an idea, Alf, but would we get away with it?' Nell pulled the cider jug from the shelf and poured two mugs of the gold liquid. 'We could make her up a bed in the empty butler's room while she recovers; it'd be handy for me to have her close. The mistress never comes down here. Emma could still help me in the kitchen and do some of the work upstairs in the night, when the mistress is asleep.' Nell looked at the thin, elderly man sitting on the other side of the table. 'Why the frown, Alf?'

'Because she'll be like a prisoner, Nell. Working for no wages, which is why she came here in the first place, to help her mother.'

'But if she goes back to her mother,' Nell sounded frustrated, 'the poor woman will have another mouth to feed.'

Alf shook his head again, as they sat with their silent thoughts beside the body of the girl on the table and drank their cider. It was Nell who made the decision. 'Help me make her up a bed in the butler's room. She can stay there until she's recovered. Then, we'll rethink, and God help us if the mistress finds out.'

'Shouldn't you be doing something to wake her, Nell?' Alf looked into Emma's pale face and noticed that her breathing was shallow.

'It's just the laudanum in the medicine; it makes her sleep.' Nell stood slowly. 'I better go to the stables and have a look at Matt.'

~

The weather had turned hot and Nell found Matt in agony with his burns, in the heat of his small room over the stable. Taking the torn cloths that she was using to cover his wounds, she rinsed them out in cold water, and then laid them gently on his arms and legs.

'I don't know why I didn't think of it before, Matt. I'm bringing you to the house and making you up a bed in one of the rooms off the servants' passage.' Soaking the cloths again she laid them gently on the burns. 'I'll be able to nurse you better there.'

Later, Nell cleaned out the room that had been the footman's domain. It had a bed, an armchair and a fireplace and by the time she was finished it was adequate for nursing her son. Alf and Nell moved him as soon as they could. It was a slow process. He could walk, but the medication made his progress slow. After getting him onto the bed and re-dressing his wounds, Nell made him a herbal tisane. Life would certainly be a lot easier for her now she had everyone close to hand.

'Mother, who's looking after the horses?' Matt's voice was thin, drifting.

'Alf is, son; don't worry yourself.'

'How can he manage the horses? He's a frail old man.'

'He's left them in the field. He takes water to them.' She lovingly touched his hair. 'They'll do until you're better.'

~

A week later, Nell was surprised to find the mistress already in the dining room, when she entered with the breakfast dishes.

'I am going to the coast for a few days to attend the funeral of Mrs Shillabeer. I will give you a list of garments that I want you to prepare for my journey.'

'Yes, ma'am; when will you be leaving?'

'The day after tomorrow.' She spread her napkin on her lap. 'I trust that is enough time.'

The threat in the voice told Nell that there was no doubt that it would be enough time.

'Yes, ma'am, the garments will be ready.'

'Good,' she said, removing the lid from a terrine. 'Tell Ames to prepare the carriage for my journey.'

Anger rose in Nell's breast; as a mother she could not hold her tongue. 'I'm sorry, ma'am, my son is still suffering from his burns and the smoke that sits in his chest.'

'Is that so, Mrs Ames?' She spooned egg onto her plate. 'Are you telling me that he cannot do his job?'

'He will be able to do his job when he recovers, ma'am.'

Amelia's face contorted into a furious mask and when she spoke her tone was threatening. 'My carriage *will* be ready, Mrs Ames, and we will discuss the position of your son on my return.'

Nell's anger turned to fear and her courage failed her. Unable to speak, she nodded, backing out of the room.

When Alf arrived for lunch he found nothing ready and Nell crying into her apron. 'What's happened? Is Matt…?' He didn't get any further as Nell's howls filled the kitchen.

'Stop, woman, stop and tell me what's wrong.' To comfort her, he put his hand on her shoulder, and felt the action of her sobbing through her coarse clothes.

'The mistress is going to get rid of Matt.' Tears ran from her swollen eyes, running unchecked over her cheeks and dripping off her chin.

'No!' He exclaimed, and sat suddenly on the nearest chair, the blood draining from his face. 'Why?'

'She wants the carriage ready for Wednesday. I told her Matt was suffering from his burns. If he can't do his job then she's going to discuss his position when she returns.'

Alf's mouth dropped open showing his pink gums and his eyes were troubled. 'If Matt goes it's the end. What can she be thinking?'

'She's going away for a bit to the Shillabeers.' Nell dabbed her eyes on her apron. 'She's going to the funeral of that poor woman, though why she is going I don't know.' The sobbing started again. 'She's shown no sadness at all for her friend or the baby that Emma says was burnt in the fire.'

Alf went to her again and put his arm around her shoulders in a form of solidarity. He agreed, the woman was heartless. He wanted to say evil, but he didn't want words like that in his head. Words like that brought trouble to those who thought it.

'But what about the carriage?' Nell's howl broke into his thoughts. 'Matt isn't well enough to drive it. She'll turn us out if it's not ready.'

I'll get the carriage ready, but the horses, that's a different pot of fish. I can't drive them.'

'What's that about the horses?' The drowsy voice came from the doorway.

'Matt!' Nell was horrified. 'What are you doing out of your bed?'

Pale and weak from the medication, he gripped the door frame for support, looking from one to the other 'Tell me what's wrong.'

'The mistress wants the carriage for Wednesday but we can't manage the horses and there's no one else to drive them.' Nell started to cry again. 'I told her you weren't well enough, Matt,' she mumbled through her tears, 'and that made her angry.'

'It's all right, Mother, I can do it. I've only lost the tops of my ears, and the rest of me is only scorched. If I don't take any more of that medicine I will get my wits back.'

'But, Matt, how will you be able to bear the uniform on top of the burns? Now that the blisters have broken, it's a mess.'

'I'll keep the air to them; they'll harden off, don't worry.'

But Nell was worried, and she couldn't bring herself to tell him of the mistress's threat on his return.

Emma had instructed Nell in the making of the calendula ointment with the added ingredient of honey for burns, which was being liberally smeared on the mending flesh of both patients with miraculous results. While Matt was keeping the weeping flesh on his shoulders and back open to the elements, in the hope of forming a crust, Emma helped Nell with the laundry. The mistress's garments hung limply from every beam in the servant quarter and flapped on the line in the yard. By Wednesday, Matt was still moving slowly and trying not to crack the newly forming crusts.

It was early, and the morning mist that often sat in the valley was slowly lifting as Matt and Alf hitched the horses between the shafts. The horses were in high spirits and hard to control, having not worked for some time. Leaving them with Alf, who was giving each a nosebag, Matt went to put on his uniform.

In the kitchen, Nell and Emma smeared the new crusts forming on his burns with ointment, and laid clean cloth on top as padding. He was then helped into his uniform; the blue jacket was heavy and he flinched. The pain, however, was much worse when it came to forcing his sore feet into the boots.

When they were finished, Emma put her arm around the weeping Nell and her little heart swelled with love for Matt, who was, she thought, being brave. He looked handsome in the uniform with its gold braid and embroidered family crest and, before he left, Nell hugged him cautiously.

'Be careful with the burns, Matt; they could turn nasty. I've put clean cloth in your pack with the ointment. You will keep them clean, won't you?'

'Don't worry, Mother, I'll look after myself.' He turned towards the door as the high-pitched sound of a bell rang angrily in the passage. 'Sounds like she's ready to go,' he said sadly.

Nell wiped her eyes on her apron and nodded stiffly.

She and Emma couldn't go to the front of the house, so stood in the little yard outside the kitchen door and waved to him as he stepped around the corner of the building.

17.

Haddenford

In the village of Haddenford, Barney Beemer had recovered enough to take up his duties collecting the rent. He could feel the silent emptiness of the Tilby cottage as he walked up the path, but knocked on the door anyway. His mouth became tight with anger when, as he feared, no one answered his knock. He'd been looking forward to coming face to face with Mistress Tilby. Oh yes, he was going to deal with her. And enjoy it. She would pay for every cut she had put on his body.

Pushing the door open, he discovered the rooms empty. Roaring like a bull and blind with anger he stamped red-faced to Dolly Mott's front door. Spittle ran from his mouth as he knocked heavily on the wood and kicked the bottom of the door. Dolly opened it white-faced. Barney grabbed her by the neck of her dress, pulling her off her feet and up to his sweaty face.

'Where is she?' he bellowed.

Dolly's eyes were bulging with fear and the tightness of his fist in her neck made it impossible for her to answer. Then Dan was at his mother's side, kicking Beemer in the shins and shouting, 'Leave my mother alone.'

Beemer's fist came down on top of the boy's head, rendering him senseless in the open doorway. His attention turned again to Dolly, whom he slammed against the wall. 'You'll tell me, or you'll be sorry.'

Just as suddenly, his own head shot forward and hit the wooden doorframe. As his legs buckled, he dropped Dolly, who was dragged in one movement to safety by a strong arm.

As he lay on the ground, Beemer's head was reeling. But he wasn't there for long before someone holding the back of his jacket dragged him to his feet. Then, spun around, he came face to face with Tom Mott. Beemer's eyes bulged; in his fury he'd forgotten about Dolly's husband.

'Lay hands on my wife, would you, Beemer? Well, now I'm here, you can take it out on me.'

'I don't have any quarrel with you, Mott.' Beemer blinked.

'But you have a quarrel with my wife, Beemer, so the quarrel *is* with me.' Tom's face was close to Barney's and his eyes were as sharp as a wolf's coming in for the kill. 'Dolly, Dan, get inside.'

Not wanting to watch what might happen next, Dolly helped her son to his feet and took him inside and shut the door, behind which she stood shaking.

'Now,' Tom said through gritted teeth, 'you have the opportunity to tell me what this is about.'

Beemer's mind was working overtime, trying to think of something that Tom would believe. His eyes became shifty, his face contorted with the strain of thinking, but his mouth uttered no sound.

'It seems, then, that you just felt like attacking my wife and son,' Tom suggested, holding his fist up in front of Barney. 'Maybe I feel like doing the same to you, Beemer.'

Barney swallowed loudly and screwed up his face, but could not defend himself. The punch landed squarely in his stomach, folding him in half. As his buttocks hit the door he was propelled forwards into the oncoming fist aimed at his jaw, but which now connected with his nose. The resounding crack as his nose broke was heard the other side of the door. Beemer howled, dropping to his knees. His hands covered his face; blood poured through his fingers. Tom looked up at the sound of someone running up the path.

'What's going on, Tom?' It was Gerald Badcombe.

'I caught him manhandling my wife and hitting my son.'

'Why?'

'He won't say. So I gave him a taste of his own medicine. Help me with him, Badcombe. I'm taking him to the landlord. I want an explanation.'

The two men dragged Beemer down the lane to a small house with a faded door wherein their landlord lived, and he did not have a forgiving nature.

Tom's knock was answered by a maid, who, alarmed by the blood covering the landlord's man, ran screaming directly to her master without being asked.

The generously proportioned Mister Bullock filled the doorway seconds later, wearing a brown wig, long dark jacket and black breeches. He was still holding his quill and his yellow waistcoat was covered in small splashes of ink. 'What is this? Explain yourselves,' he demanded.

'No, sir.' Tom Mott took charge. 'It is I who have come for an explanation and, unless you wish the whole village to know our business, I suggest you let us in.'

The portly gentleman stood for a moment as though deciding, weighing up the situation. 'Peachy,' he bellowed at the maid hovering at the end of the passage, 'bring some cloths for Mister Beemer's face. I won't have blood on my floor.'

Several minutes later Beemer stood in front of the landlord's desk, his face hidden behind some reddening rags.

'Well, Mott, Badcombe, perhaps you would like to tell me what has happened.'

Gerald Badcombe looked at Tom; he would also like to know what had happened. In the silence that followed Barney groaned, and held his head back, trying to stem the flow of blood that had almost filled the cloth. 'Well!' Bullock's voice boomed again, his face flushed with annoyance.

Beemer began to buckle at the knees and Tom pulled him sharply upright. 'I arrived home, sir, to find your man holding my wife by the front of her dress against the wall of my house. I was just in time to see him bring his fist down on the head of my boy, who was trying to release his mother, and the blow knocked him out. I am the one wanting an explanation, Mister Bullock, and as your man refuses to tell me what this is about, I have brought him to you for an explanation.'

The landlord looked at Badcombe. 'Where does Mister Badcombe come into this affair?'

Badcombe looked uncomfortable. People tried to live without the landlord being aware of their existence and his legs began to tremble.

'He was passing, sir, and helped me transport Beemer to your door.'

'Then you may go.' The dismissal was sharp and Badcombe quickly left the office. Hoping never to see the inside of it again he almost ran home.

'So, Mott, let me see.' As he spoke Bullock took a large ledger from a shelf. Placing it heavily on the desk he opened its leather cover and began to turn the pages, slowly running his fingers down the columns of figures.

'You were only behind with your rent when you first arrived here. Since then you have always paid on time. So the quarrel between Mister Beemer and your family must be personal. I am not interested in your personal lives, Mister Mott.' He slammed the book shut.

'This man is employed by you, sir, and as far as I know Mister Beemer has no reason to attack my wife and child. He had, I assumed, come for the rent. We *had* the rent.'

The landlord looked across the room at his man. 'You will explain yourself, sir, to Mister Mott this instant. I would also like to hear why you were satisfying a grievance in my time on people who had the rent.'

The pain in Beemer's head was almost more than he could tolerate. He was aware that his eyes were puffing up and he could hardly see the two men before him who were waiting for his version of events. Unable to tell them the truth he said nothing.

'You leave me no option but to let you go, Beemer. I am known as a hard man, but I hope a fair man. I won't have the wives of those who regularly pay their rent manhandled.'

Going to the safe, he removed a small paper envelope. 'Take your wage, Beemer. I don't want to see you again.'

'That is all very well and noble, sir, but I still do not know why my wife was attacked by your man.' Tom felt irritated, as his need to know why Beemer attacked Dolly was being dismissed.

'Perhaps, Mister Mott, you should go home and ask your wife. Good day to you, sir.' As he spoke, Bullock slammed the reference book back on the shelf and stared at Tom belligerently. The meeting was at an end.

~

Dolly had never before felt worried about Tom arriving home. She felt sick to her stomach and jumped when the latch lifted sharply. 'Where are the children?' His face was strained, his voice sharp.

'To their beds.' Her mouth was dry as she watched him nervously.

'Let's get this over with.' Tom stood stiffly before her. 'I want to know why you were attacked.' His words had never been so sharp when spoken to her, and now that Martha's troubles had come between her and Tom she would have to tell him and break her promise to Martha.

'I think he was angry because Martha has gone.' Tears welled up in her eyes and she bit her lip. 'He thought I would know where she was. When I said I didn't know he grabbed me by my dress.' Now the tears began to flow.

'You know where she is, don't you, Dolly?'

Dolly looked up; her thick red hair framing a face in which huge wet eyes stared out in defiance. Tom knew that there was nothing on God's Earth that would make Dolly tell a secret. He opened his arms. 'Come here,' he said, pulling her towards him. As she sank into his chest he believed that he was the luckiest man alive.

18.

The farmhouse kitchen was warm from her cooking and Martha hadn't been so fulfilled in a long time. James was sitting at the table with his slate. 'How long have we lived here, Mother?' he asked as he tried to do a sum that Martha had set.

'Eight weeks, James, why?' she asked, wiping her hands on her apron.

'I don't want to live anywhere else. I want to stay here forever, Mother.'

'Well, that would be wonderful, James, but Mister Tate may not want us here forever. Nona, would you get those pies out of the oven for me, please?'

Martha watched her daughter go to the oven with a thick cloth to remove the pies and marvelled at the way she was recovering. The first few weeks had been difficult for Nona, who'd been silent and withdrawn, a small shadow at Martha's side, not wanting to be left alone, afraid of Farmer Tate. But now, as the weeks had passed in the safety of the farmhouse, she was becoming more like her old self. Martha didn't expect that Nona would ever forget the menace that had been Barney Beemer, but she hoped that the girl would be able to live with it and without it ruining her life.

The outside door opened sharply as Sarah entered with a basket of eggs, followed by Jack and George, who had been feeding the pigs.

'Put the eggs in that corner, Sarah, you can deal with them later. Who wants some bread and dripping?'

A great cry of 'me, me, me' went up and each was given a piece to take outside.

'The kitchen's the best room in the house,' Robert exclaimed as he arrived and kicked his boots off into the corner behind the door, where they joined a pile of assorted shoes. He moved to the table for his food, where Martha put a plate of bread and cheese before him.

'Is Mister Tate coming, Robert?'

'I don't think so, Mother; he's gone with the foreman to look at fencing on the edge of the farmland.'

Martha was very aware of the disappointment rising in her heart. She'd caught herself lately thinking up dishes that would make Andrew happy and had cooked a pie and several small pies that could be taken to the fields for lunch. She had cooked them joyfully in the brick oven, filling them with meat, herbs and vegetables, wanting him to enjoy her cooking. Pulling herself together, she watched Robert eat his lunch, his face glowing with health.

'Is it all right with you, Mother, that I'm not being paid for the work I do?'

'Of course, Robert, that was the arrangement. I look after the house and children and you work on the farm for our keep. It's a good arrangement and we have no worries here.'

'But what if we have to leave? We wouldn't have any money.'

'Then we would be in the same position that we were in before we came here. And I am sure that someone would help us.' She stroked his hair. 'You are a good boy to worry about us, but there's no need.'

Could I have a little more?' Robert pushed his plate forward.

'All right, as you're working so hard and growing so fast, but we must be careful not to eat all Mister Tate's profits.'

Martha was careful with the rations. They were eating regular meals of eggs, meat and vegetables and it was her silent way of helping with the farm debts.

~

Since Martha and her children had moved into the farmhouse Andrew had moved into the farmworkers' cottage with his foreman, John Brisket, where he slept, but continued to eat his meals in the farmhouse dining room alone. Martha was, as usual, disturbed by his silence. He extended a curt nod in her direction as she entered the heavily panelled room, which she found dark and depressing. His quietness and unkempt condition didn't fit into the new cheerful atmosphere of the house. Pleasant as always, she said nothing about his appearance as she placed the food before him. She knew herself the pain of grieving.

After the meal, his children were allowed to show him the writing that they had done with Martha during the day. He nodded and grunted, but Martha could see that he was taking nothing in. George and Sarah didn't seem to notice his lack of interest and adoringly chatted on regardless. But Jack, who had tried so hard with his work, had tears in his eyes as he slunk away out of the room.

Martha found him in the yard, his head buried in the coat of the farm dog. Slipping her arm around him she said, 'Do you want to tell me what's wrong, Jack?'

'He doesn't like me.' The boy's face was wet with tears.

'Of course he likes you, Jack; it's just that he has a lot on his mind at the moment.'

'What?' The question was delivered with a directness that unnerved her.

'Well, he misses your mother very much and it must be very hard coming into the house when she isn't there. He doesn't feel a part of it any more.'

'Why?'

'Why what, Jack?'

'Why isn't he part of it?'

'It's nothing that you or anyone else have done. He's having a great struggle with himself.' The boy said nothing, his face showing that he still didn't understand. 'Your father,' she tried again, 'has a lot of worries with the farm, Jack. It's not easy to make it pay its way. He needs money to buy seed, and if the weather isn't good he loses his crop. When he makes no money he still has to pay the workers and find the money for more seed. Life for your father is a constant battle for survival. He's just very tired, Jack. He loves you all very much but he can't stop thinking about his worries.' She turned his little face up to hers. 'Come on inside and see a bit of your father before you go to bed.'

~

At Martha's suggestion, Andrew had begun visiting the kitchen in the evenings after eating his meal and now sat, eyes closed, in a chair by the hearth with Sarah at his feet playing. Nona was clearing the table and George was making a nuisance of himself trying to trip her up. James, who was still afraid of Andrew, sat in the far corner of the kitchen washing the eggs in a bucket. Martha smiled, seeing Robert sitting in the armchair opposite Andrew, emulating his sitting position, his eyes also closed. It was good that Robert had a man to look up to, and a good man at that.

The peacefulness of the kitchen was broken by a sharp knock on the door. All heads turned. It opened slowly, almost apologetically, revealing the rosy round face of the foreman, John Brisket.

'What is it, John?' Andrew was already on his feet.

'It's the new sow, sir. I think you should come and take a look.'

Andrew pulled on his boots and left the kitchen, his family instantly forgotten. The children stared silently at the door after he had left and Martha felt the emptiness of what might have been a cosy evening. 'Bed I think, children,' she said gently. 'Go quietly; don't wake Charity. I'll be up to see you soon.'

Later that evening, as Martha sat in Andrew's chair by the hearth, hot tears welled up in her eyes as she was devoured by angry thoughts. It was time for him to start showing some interest in his children. Yes, he had his worries, but he couldn't ignore his children's need of him forever. She resolved to try harder to be both mother and father to them, talking about Andrew, so that he was part of their lives whether he wanted that or not. As she thought of Andrew a great emotion swept over her. Her heart was opening to him. What was, this, she asked herself? Was it gratitude for being given a home? Was it an understanding of his pain? Was it her motherly love, seeing him as a child that needed the love of his family but he, always being on the outside? With a heavy heart she took up her mending.

The summer evening was humid and the kitchen was still warm from the baking when Martha decided to wash her body symbolically before retiring to her bed, thinking it might improve her mood. At around midnight, in the glow of the kitchen fire and the light of numerous candles, Martha stood in the tin bath. Pouring warm water over her head, she felt herself relax as it trickled over her breasts and down her back. Water and candlelight always improved her mood. She could relax, reach the Goddess and be at one with the energy. Lifting her hands into the air, she spoke quietly.

'Gracious Lady, whose wisdom guides me on my path and protects us, I ask that harmony fill my troubled heart.' Lifting a jug of warm water, she again poured it over her head.

'I remove all negative thoughts. I acknowledge that life moves on. I ask that I be cleansed and blessed in your name.' Stepping out of the bath, she approached the largest candle. Raising her arms, she addressed the Goddess as the water ran in rivulets over her naked body and dripped upon the floor.

'May the mother who dwells in all things hear my thoughts. Share with me your wisdom. Guide me for the good of this family. Help me to understand my feelings and to own them. Andrew is a good man. Please help him to come to terms with the changes in his life. I ask for the strength to help the children in their pain and growth.'

She stood silently for a moment, linking with the energy, breathing slowly and feeling the blessing of pure love that she was able to reach. 'I thank you for your love and wisdom. I ask a blessing on all those that abide on this farm. So mote it be.'

Snuffing out the candles, she stood for a moment in the darkness breathing in the blessing and the fragrance of the candle smoke.

~

The new sow was hot. Andrew was not a praying man even though he attended church on a Sunday. But right now he prayed to God that this sow had not brought infection onto his farm. As a new animal she'd been kept in isolation on straw, something Andrew had learnt from his father. He and John spent the evening keeping her cool with cold-water washes. By midnight she seemed over the worst and was again a normal colour and her breathing had eased.

'I think the crisis has passed, sir. But I'll stay with her tonight just in case.'

Andrew inclined his head. 'Thank you, John. If you need me...'

'I know where you are, sir.' The two men nodded an understanding. Andrew looked around for his cap and realised that he had left it in the kitchen. Grunting at John, he stepped out of the barn and made for the house that was now in darkness. As he passed the window he realised that Martha might still be up as candles were still lit. Before he could turn to the door, Martha's naked form stood before his eyes, her wet body glistening in the candlelight. He had never seen a woman completely naked before and stood spellbound, unable to breathe. Her black hair, normally worn up in a knot, was now hanging loose and damp, reaching below her waist. As she stepped gracefully out of the bath, the flickering candlelight threw shadows on her large breasts, making them seem to appear and disappear. As he watched her, framed in the window, she raised her arms above her head. The cloak of black hair hid her long back but left her buttocks and long legs exposed. He had never seen anything so beautiful. How long he stood there he had no recollection but when she snuffed out the candle, he stepped back into the darkness of the yard, embarrassed by what he had seen.

~

Next day as the weather was so good Martha decided to take the children to the dew pond after their chores had been completed. They travelled along the causeway, which ran in a straight line between the fields. Martha gave thanks for the bounty that grew all around them. A bounty that she had asked for on May Day, at her Beltane celebration, when she had broken bread infused with herbs while asking for a good harvest. Now she smiled at the sheaves leaning against each other in the sun, drying. She felt a secret joy at the sight of a field clothed in its earthy bristling stubble, which had already been gleaned by the poor. The children looked through a hedge at some pigs grubbing and snuffling in the stubble of another field. Turning the earth with their snouts, they loosened it ready for the plough. The group meandered to the edge of a large copse and to a natural pond where the dragonflies dipped and dived in their green and blue iridescent coats, where bees visited the pond lilies and spiders walked on water, where two young ducks nearly as big as their parents waddled and frogs watched from the weeds with only

143

the rounds of their eyes breaking the surface. Nona and Sarah sat close together in the long grass making daisy chains to wear in their hair. And it was, to Martha, as though a bountiful peace had touched the world.

'Can we put some flowers in your hair?' Sarah asked Martha.

'Yes, make me a circle of daisies; that will be lovely, Sarah.'

'You will have to put your hair down like ours to look like a princess,' Sarah said. Her face was serous as she concentrated on making a hole in the stem of a daisy, to add it to the chain she had started.

'All right, but it will have to go back up before we go home.'

Martha skimmed the pond water into a bucket, after which they all stared at the captured wildlife in awe. 'Each creature has an energy of life that you can see if you look hard enough,' Martha said. The children jostled to look into the bucket. 'Do you know how we know they have energy running through them?' she asked, feeling like a teacher, although she knew that she was an unconventional tutor.

''Cos they're alive,' George piped up, poking at a stickleback and making it swim to the bottom of the bucket.

'Yes, well done, George,' Martha laughed. But what about the earth and air that support all this life? Does it have energy? They all stared at the ground and George shrugged his shoulders.

'I want you all to lie on the ground and feel the energy of the earth,' Martha instructed, tipping the creatures back into the pond. They all eagerly lay in the grass. 'Shut your eyes, listen and feel,' Martha said, kneeling beside them.

'It's moving,' Sarah laughed. 'The ground's moving.'

'How is it moving, Sarah?' Martha felt joy at the child's response.

'In a circle!' Her voice sounded dreamy, as though she was going to sleep.

'You're moving with the energy of the earth, Sarah; you are being part of this wonderful nature.'

'I feel like I'm flying if I open my eyes and look at the sky,' Jack said quietly, spreading his arms out on the ground beside him like a bird in flight.

Martha smiled. 'You're feeling the energy of the earth and sky, Jack.'

The children were quiet for a while until George got bored and, sitting up, asked, 'Can we play in the water now?'

'Of course you can, but only stay on the edge and don't get too wet.' The day was warm and she didn't want any accidents.

With whoops of joy the children ran to the pond and were soon splashing each other. The end of summer, thought Martha as she dipped Charity's toes in the water, was as wonderful as the beginning of it, when the weather was just right.

~

The widow Fearling had been to visit her sister and was taking a short cut home along the causeway. She loved this time of year. Walking between the harvested fields, she gave thanks to God for the abundance of food. Soon it would be harvest festival and she would be making her special bread in a huge plaited sheaf. The last vicar always gave it pride of place in the harvest display and she imagined that this vicar would do the same when he knew how magnificent her centrepiece was. Her sharp face twitched in a tight smile. She visualised the end of the harvest ceremony, when the bread was always cut up and given to the poor. She was very proud of her bread. The goodness of God and the harvested fields, the excitement of being able to show the new vicar how important she was to this ceremony filled her with joy. Opening her mouth, she sang in her high-pitched elderly voice. A hare dashed off across the bare field, disturbed by the noise. As she stopped to watch its swift zigzagging progress she thought that she heard the sound of children's voices. Looking around she frowned, sure that the fields were deserted. The voices came again on the air, screaming, high-pitched sounds that rose and fell. Knowing the pond was in the direction of the sound, she thought it her duty to investigate. After all, their parents might not know that the children were there. Older children should be at home or working, not getting into temptation, and younger children should be with their mothers.

Breaking out of the copse of trees, she stood stock still, unable to believe her eyes. Before her was the figure of Martha Tilby, black hair flowing freely down her back, ankle deep in the pond with her children and those of Farmer Tate. 'Well, madam,' she muttered, 'so this is where you're hiding.' Unseen, tight-lipped and resolute, she turned back towards the causeway.

~

The day was dry yet slightly cooler as the bells rang out over the village and across the fields, calling the faithful to church on Sunday morning. En route along the lane to St Mary's Church, the rich in their carriages, followed closely on foot by their servants, mixed with the poor in their Sunday best. Sunday was an event for the community to get together. For some, it was the only day to meet friends and relatives. Washed and scrubbed, they arrived at church in the clothes they kept for this day, weddings and funerals. Men, caps in hand, and women ushering their broods like mother hens entered the church. The young girls and boys who looked across the path at each other shyly were not encouraged to speak. Whole families took their places in the pews and the church was full to bursting. Major Laddisbrock, wearing a richly embroidered coat, his hand resting on a silver-topped cane, cut a fine picture of prosperity, accompanied by his elegantly dressed wife and son, equally richly attired. Andrew Tate had made little effort with his appearance, but his children were clean and smart in the new clothes made for them by Martha.

Ernest Draycott delivered a sermon that was of a kinder nature than his predecessor, who liked to bring his fist down hard on the pulpit and watch the guilty jump. Ernest was a good man who wanted the community to love and help each other. 'After all,' he said, 'where would we be without the love of our brothers and sisters, or the kindness of our neighbours in these hard times? We should aspire to the teachings of Christ in our everyday lives. He abides in us all. So how can we be anything else but helpful and loving to our neighbour?' He looked across at his wife, a picture in pale blue, who smiled back at him, nodding encouragingly.

Towards the end of the service the widow Fearling and Beemer passed the collection box amongst the congregation. The money that was brought before Ernest at the altar was blessed, truly blessed, as he knew how little most of this congregation had to give.

His parishioners filed out after the service, to an uplifting tune played by the musicians sitting in the gallery. He was thanked for a wonderful service as each person shook his hand at the door. But in his heart Ernest knew that if he'd asked any one of them what the service had been about they probably wouldn't remember.

As always, little groups of people gathered in front of the church to gossip and to catch up on news. Mrs Fearling was deep in conversation with some of the ladies of the church. 'And there she was,' she said, 'like a... a...' She couldn't say the word. 'Wearing a headdress of daisies and her dress open at the neck, exposing her flesh.' Ignoring the gasps of her horrified friends, she continued her story. 'And with her hair loose, like a woman of the night, she stood in the pond shouting and screaming with her children and those of Farmer Tate.' To this there were more gasps from the well-dressed women.

'What should we do about it?' asked Celia Tuppence, a twig-like spinster of seventy. 'In my day she would have been publicly whipped and cast out, acting so in front of children. It's a disgrace. We should tell the vicar.'

Mrs Fearling looked over at the vicar, standing with his lovely wife talking to the parishioners. She really didn't trust that Ernest would have it in him to do anything about it, unlike the Reverend Stanley Osborne, his predecessor, who would probably have taken the whip himself and dealt with this woman personally. He would have wanted to know why she didn't attend church. He would have had suspicions when told that the Tilby woman walked in the moonlight, that she stood holding her arms up to the moon. That she played in the middle of the day with her hair loose, bedecked with flowers. No, she would have to think about this; she was sure they had a witch in their midst and she couldn't ignore it. Oh no, not while Martha Tilby was influencing Andrew Tate's children.

A rather large widow, Lillian Blatch, suggested that they approach Andrew and tell him what had been seen and their fears for his children. But, as Andrew Tate passed by with his children, none of the ladies was brave enough to speak to him, his manner and his appearance being so unapproachable.

'We will bide our time.' The widow Fearling's left cheek twitched as she felt a flutter of fear caused by Farmer Tate's distasteful manner. 'She will reveal herself in time and we will be ready, ladies.' She said this more to reassure herself than anything else.

Beemer had seen the group of women in a huddle and knew them well enough to know that they were gossiping about someone. He had played eavesdropper many a time on this little group, finding out valuable information that had helped him in his job as rent collector. It was habit and boredom more than anything else that made him sidle over and pretend to be inspecting the grave of Thomas Shaw, elder of this parish. What he heard made his mouth turn dry. *He had her.* He was elated. Knowing now where they were, he quickly realised his advantage. She was in a happy state of ignorance. He had time to plan his revenge.

As they left the church, Dolly was aware of Alice blushing and looking coyly at her feet. She recognised the signs and quickly looked around for the focus of her daughter's attention. Standing close to the path was Stanley Smith, son of the village blacksmith. Stanley was a tall, good-looking boy with little brain or vision. Not his fault, she told herself, as he had never been to school. Yes, he was definitely staring unashamedly at Alice. Dolly stepped in front of her daughter to show that she had noticed his attention, and he quickly moved away. It was as Stanley moved that Barney Beemer was revealed, bending over a grave. It was obvious to Dolly that he was eavesdropping on the widow and her cronies. 'I wonder who they're gossiping about now. Poor devil,' she muttered with feeling.

'What did you say, Dolly?' Tom came up beside her.

'Oh nothing,' she said, rubbing his arm affectionately. 'Let's go home and have some food.'

~

Martha had been making new clothes for the children out of material found in a cupboard. There had been enough over for her to make a shirt for Andrew. She had stitched it lovingly as she sat each night by the fire. It had been her intent to give it to him one night after supper when the children were in their beds, but he hadn't been to the house since leaving to look at the sick sow. It had been more than a week since she had last seen him. Enough time for her to believe that he could be offended in some way.

'Robert,' she called to her son as he walked to the barn, 'I want you to wear your new shirt and take this shirt to Mister Tate. Tell him I have made all of you new clothes.' She held a bundle out to Robert.

'Do I have to say that, Mother?'

'Yes, Robert, it's very important that he knows that you *all* have new clothes.'

'Why can't you give it to him?' Robert looked annoyed and clearly didn't want to take the parcel.

'Because he is so busy, Robert, that he isn't coming to the house.'

'I don't want to give it to him, Mother. He's been very strange lately. Even Mister Brisket is worried about him.'

Martha's stomach tightened in alarm, remembering only too well the sight of Andrew sitting downcast in the barn, staring into space, with a thick rope dangling from his hands.

~

Since the night of the sick sow, Andrew's mind, waking and sleeping, had been plagued by the vision of Martha naked in the candle light. He saw her walking naked through the fields when he looked out across the vista of his land. He saw her rising from the water trough in the yard, her body glistening with water in the sunshine. He saw her lying naked amongst the drying corn sheaves, her beautiful body being caressed by the sun. Feelings were stirring in his body. Shutting his eyes tight, he drew in a sharp breath and felt as though he was going mad.

'Is something wrong, sir? You don't seem yourself.' Andrew jumped and his cheeks just visible above his beard took on a glow. He didn't make eye contact as he rebuffed John's enquiry. 'I'm fine; get on with your work, John.'

But as John walked to the other end of the field to check the fences he was worried. There was a lot to do before winter. Andrew had always been the one pushing the pace and yet lately John had noticed him standing still, distracted, staring into space. Something was wrong with the man. He would have to watch him closely. If the boss went down then they were finished. They were walking a tight line.

Robert found Andrew stripped to the waist in a far field swinging a hammer at a fence post. For an old man, Robert thought, he's very strong. 'Excuse me, sir.'

Andrew took his last swing and turned to the boy. 'What can I do for you, Robert?'

'My mother sent you this.' He pushed the package forward. 'She made us all new clothes from some material found in a cupboard and there was enough for a shirt for you.'

Andrew stared at the loosely wrapped parcel and then at Robert. In the silence, Robert felt uncomfortable. 'She'd have given it to you herself but you've been very busy,' Robert offered.

Andrew took the parcel slowly from the boy's hand. 'Yes, Robert, we are very busy this time of year. Thank your mother for me.' And, taking the parcel, he walked away, the long-handled hammer resting on his shoulder as though it weighed nothing.

As Robert watched the retreating figure of this man that he was slightly afraid of, he suddenly craved the company and humour of his father.

Sitting beside the repaired fence, Robert pulled absently at the long grass, having a vague memory of sitting on his father's knee before bed. His mother was stitching clothes, perhaps for him, perhaps for his father. It all seemed so long ago. Tears filled his eyes as he realised that he could no longer remember what his father looked like. He wanted to go home, but where was home? It wasn't here living with strangers. Home was in the past with his father and mother in a place that no longer existed, a place that was a fragment of memory, and that was fading. Desperate for the love of his father, he lay down beside the fence and cried.

19.

Claydon House

Although they were all worried about Matt, a wonderful freedom was now being felt in the house. Suddenly the building could breathe. Windows were thrown open and stale bedding hung from the airy openings. Drapes were beaten where they hung at the open windows. Floors were cleaned and singing filled the house. There was no more hiding in the passageways and Emma and Nell brazenly walked up the forbidden front staircase. At the first opportunity Emma went into the mistress's rooms and searched for Salanda's locket. She looked in every box, every pot, every drawer and on every shelf, but it wasn't to be found. With a heavy heart she knew that she would never get another opportunity as good as this. It was clear that it was not in the house and she felt its loss deeply.

Later, in the kitchen, Emma asked Nell, 'When do you think the mistress will be back?'

The question was ignored. 'There's something I have to tell you, Emma, before she comes back. You had better sit down.' Nell hesitated. 'The mistress doesn't know that you are still here.'

'What do you mean, Mrs Ames: *still* here?'

'It was the day you went to see her about the locket, Emma, she was very angry and told me I had to turn you out. But you were so ill I couldn't do it. So Alf and I hid you in the room off the passage, where we could look after you.'

Emma was stunned. 'So these past weeks I've been hidden?'

'Yes, I'm sorry. We didn't know what to do. You couldn't walk and you would have died of exposure outside alone without help.'

'What am I going to do, Mrs Ames?' The enormity of her situation dawned very quickly on Emma.

'My idea was that you could help me in the kitchen as usual. The mistress wouldn't know. And you could clean at night when she was asleep.'

'But I wouldn't be able to go out! I wouldn't have any wage.'

'Yes, that is true.' Nell had a painful look on her face as she admitted it.

Emma felt desperate. 'I have to have money, Mrs Ames, to send to my mother. Have I no money for these past weeks?'

'I'm sorry, Emma. You must decide, now that you are better, what you want to do.'

Emma stared at Nell in shock. 'So the choice is to stay here and secretly help you, and be fed.' She summed the situation up. 'Or walk to the next town and without a reference try to get work.' Emma felt deflated as she realised that her option was no option at all, and if the mistress found out! She dare not think what that woman would do.

Nell removed the meat from the jack and transferred it to a dry dish, and then proceeded to make gravy from the fat in the dripping pan with stock.

'It won't be easy to get a job at this time of year, Emma.' She added flour to the fat and stirred vigorously to remove the lumps. 'The number of people looking for work increases as there's less and less to do on the land.'

Emma bit her lip. She wasn't ready to leave. 'Thank you for hiding me, Mrs Ames. I'll stay a little longer. I can't go without my grandmother's locket.'

'So it really is your grandmother's locket?' Nell was still feeling very bad about that situation.

'Yes, it has her hair and her mother's hair plaited into the back. It has to stay in my family.'

'Why did your mother give it to you? It feels strange to me.'

'I'm not sure. Perhaps because one day it would be mine. She might have thought life so uncertain that I may not receive it if I didn't have it now.' Nell nodded. She agreed with Emma's mother about life being uncertain. She and Matt might also soon be looking for work. But there was no need to worry the girl with that.

The door opened as Alf arrived with a basket of vegetables and Nell chastised him. 'What are you doing picking so much? After all, there's only the three of us.'

During the meal, which was the happiest they had eaten together, Emma felt restless. Driven by the thought of not being able to go out once their mistress returned, she decided to get out of the house.

'I'm going to take a walk in the forest,' she suddenly announced.

Both Alf and Nell gaped at her. 'Why?' Nell asked, wide-eyed.

I want to walk amongst the trees, Mrs Ames, and smell the river, while I have the opportunity to go outside.'

'I can understand that.' Alf nodded. 'I've been an outside man all my working life.'

'All right, Emma.' Nell frowned. 'But be out of there before it starts to get dark; it's not safe.'

'I haven't forgotten my first encounter with the forest.' Emma shivered. 'But I should be all right in daylight.' Her heart soared at the thought of walking amongst the trees, smelling the pine and the wild blackberries.

~

After clearing away the lunch, Emma left Alf and Nell sleeping in the armchairs beside the fire. The day was full of late summer warmth and walking from the yard to the stables she basked in the sour smell of the horse waste. As she passed the nursery beds outside Alf's little hut she felt the energy of the growing plants and was tempted to sit in Alf's old chair, with its well-worn cushions, and enjoy the sleepy silence. But she moved on, stretching out her arms in ecstasy, as she walked between the rows of vegetables and herbs that grew in the rich soil of the walled garden.

As she made her way across the field towards the forest, she saw the horses sheltering under a tree on the far side of the field. They flicked each other's faces with their tails and lazily watched her. Wild herbs, crushed beneath her feet as she walked, threw up their scent and she valued every ounce of the aroma as though she would never breathe air as fresh or as fragrant again.

As she climbed the low fence and stepped between the trees, a serene silent atmosphere immediately enclosed her. The peaceful atmosphere of the forest was like a comfortable blanket, wrapping her in its safety. Walking to the nearest tree, she stroked the bark gently and looked up into its leafy canopy. The sun flickered between the branches, and beneath her feet the ground was soft and spongy, a token of years of fallen leaves and rotting vegetation. Autumn was coming; she could feel the change and the evidence of that was upon the forest floor already. Her heart was light as she touched the ferns and inspected the fungus that grew on fallen logs. Why couldn't life be like this every day? She didn't want to go too deeply into the forest in case, like last time, she couldn't find her way back. So, when she heard the sound of running water, she had no option but to move towards it.

She came upon it in an area so thick with trees that their top branches formed an arch across the river, forming a tunnel through which the water flowed across a stony bed. It frothed and gurgled around black rocks mid-stream and caressed the edges of moss-covered rocks at the bank. The light, where the warmth of the sun's rays penetrated the leaf canopy overhead, gave off a curious luminous green glow. It was, to her childish mind, as though the place had been touched by magic. Moving away, she could still hear the water when the thickening foliage barred her way, until once again she broke out of the trees and found herself on a gently sloping riverbank with a small shingle beach further upstream. Removing her shoes and lifting her skirt a little, she walked carefully into the shallow water. Mesmerised, she watched as it ran crystal clear, sparkling, and shot with rainbows over the gravel and over her feet.

The hairs on the back of her neck started to move. It was an uncomfortable, creeping movement that she had felt before when something beyond her control was taking place. Seeing the shape of a man watching her from the bank, reflected in the water, she turned sharply and was almost unbalanced.

'Good afternoon, Mister Brack, sir.' She felt embarrassed, and at a disadvantage being caught with her feet bare. He didn't answer but walked towards the forest, beckoning for her to follow. She didn't want to go. She didn't want to be asked to do any more favours for him. She would have to explain that she was also now in hiding. His beckoning became more insistent as she hurried to push her wet feet into her shoes. He walked quickly, keeping a good way ahead of her amongst the trees, always just in sight, leading her on. When she eventually broke out of the undergrowth into a large clearing, Oliver was standing on the other side of it, holding a bundle.

Emma gasped as he held it up and the bundle moved. Small pink arms waved in the air, reaching for his face. *A baby?* Emma's eyes were wide with shock as she recognised it as Mrs Shillabeer's baby. But that baby had died. Oliver said nothing, but held up a piece of silver and smiled. His words flooded into her head. '*I want what is mine.*' A horrible realisation swept over her. If she had known it was the baby he'd wanted she would never have tied the ribbon to the window handle.

'You killed the baby and you continue to hide here? Why?' she shouted across the space. Then realised that the baby was pink and alive as its little arms continued to reach for his face. It couldn't be the one that died in the fire. How could it now be pink and alive? It must be a different baby. But why was he here with a baby at all? This was a trick. But why show it to her? He watched in silence as she battled with her thoughts. Then, kissing the child tenderly, he walked towards a patch of soft bare earth at the edge of the clearing and laid the baby on it. To Emma's horror the earth began to move and the baby sank gradually out of sight.

'No!' Emma screamed running forward. When she reached the spot she fell to her knees on the patch of earth, desperate to save the child. But the baby couldn't be found. With her bare hands she dug deeper and deeper into the soil until she felt something and her hand involuntarily pulled back. Yet the picture of the baby sinking into the ground drove her on. Scratching more soil away, she grasped the object and pulled it from the grave. As the earth fell away she saw with horror that she'd uncovered a decomposing hand as large as her own. Her wide-eyed scream caught in her throat as the hand fell from her fingers back onto the soil. Gasping for breath, Emma stumbled from the scene with heavy legs that held her back; shocks of fear ran down her spine and gripped at her stomach. As she entered the trees the sound of screeching wheeled around her head and her heart pounded with terror. It wasn't until her breath became laboured that she realised that the unearthly shrieks were her own. Careering blindly through the forest, she panicked as scrambling bramble leaders caught in her clothes, holding her back. Their sharp barbs tore her fingers as she tried to release her clothes from their tight grip. In her desperation to get away, ignorant of her torn and bleeding flesh, she felt only the presence of the ghost that she thought followed her as she tried to outrun it.

~

In the warm kitchen, Nell and Alf still slumbered in the armchairs beside the fire. The mantel clock ticked a constant rhythm, accompanied by a gentle unstructured chorus of heavy breathing and occasional snorts.

The sleepers were brought back from their dreams with a jolt when the kitchen door suddenly flew open, banging against the wall. Nell, who was facing the door, stared horrified at the sight standing in the doorway. Alf's eyes also shot open at the sound of the door crashing against the wall and, seeing the expression on Nell's face, he turned slowly in the chair, wondering what he was going to see.

Emma stood just inside the kitchen door, physically shaking. Her face was white with shock, her arms, legs and face were bleeding and her tangled hair stood out at all angles. It was Nell who recovered first.

'My God, what has happened?' She got out of her chair, her hands flapping in exaggerated movements of panic. Emma's mouth was moving but no sound escaped and there was a look of horror in her eyes that frightened Nell.

'She's got the same look as Jake Poleshore, Nell. I'll get her to the fire while you fetch the brandy.' Staring into the girl's vacant face, Alf tried to speak calmly. 'Emma, come and sit here by the fire.' As he pulled at her arms she followed as though in a dream and sat heavily in the chair just as her legs gave way.

Nell, who had hurried for a blanket, wrapped it around Emma's shoulders and poured the brandy. 'What can have happened to her, Alf?' Her eyes appealed to him for an answer.

'I don't know, but we have to get it out of her.' He took charge as Nell was at a loss. 'Tell me what happened, girl. It will be better for you if you can tell someone.'

His question brought the unwanted vision of the lifeless hand in hers, grey, partly stripped of flesh and covered in soil. Emma's eyes increased in size as she relived the fear accompanied by the sound of her own screaming. Her body shook out of control until Nell put her arms around her and held her tight. Emma was aware of Nell stroking her hair and heard her words: 'You're safe now Emma. You're safe now. Relax, nothing can hurt you here.' The trembling in her limbs slowly subsided as she laid her head against Nell's ample bosom and sobbed, feeling safe.

'Drink the brandy, just a nip.' Alf put the cup to the pale lips. The sweetness of the drink and the warmth and safety of the kitchen brought Emma from her shock. Her voice was barely a whisper in the quiet room when she eventually found enough energy to speak. 'There's a dead body in the forest.'

Nell and Alf both recoiled, looking at each other for confirmation that they'd heard correctly. 'Whose body?' Alf was first to speak.

'I don't know.' Tears rolled over her cheeks. They stung her scratched face and dripped off the edge of her jaw. With hands fluttering like leaves in a breeze, she tried unsuccessfully to wipe her tears away as her crying turned into howling and fluid ran from her nose. She couldn't stop, even though the sobs brought pain to her chest and her jaw. There was no stopping the flow as she visualised the baby being swallowed up by the earth and then the dreadful dead hand in hers.

'Let her cry, Nell; it'll be the shock coming out.' Alf nodded sagely, although in truth he was out of his depth with the situation.

Nell held Emma close until the sobs stopped and she cried no more.

'Are you feeling better now?' Alf asked, holding the brandy to Emma's lips once more, and was relieved when she took a sip. At least she could communicate.

A pale face covered in scratches, eyes swollen from crying, looked up at them and Nell and Alf both smiled reassuringly at her.

'There you are, dear, all better.' Nell's voice was motherly. 'I'm going to wash those scratches and you must tell us what happened.' Pouring water from the kettle into a bowl on the table, she pushed a soft cloth into the warmth that steamed gently.

Emma looked at Alf, a reassuring figure in her life, who had become the grandfather that she had never known. She swallowed and spoke slowly. 'I followed the master into the forest and he took me to a clearing.'

'What would the master be doing in the forest?' Nell interrupted as she squeezed water from the cloth and pressed it to Emma's face.

'He's hiding there.' Emma winced as a thorn stuck in a scratch pierced deeper.

'Why would he be hiding in the forest? It makes no sense.' Nell removed the thorn with her fingernails and dabbed at the scratch again.

'I don't know,' Emma groaned. 'He told me he couldn't come to the house.'

'That doesn't make any sense either. This is his house.' Nell was exasperated.

'Stop questioning her, woman, and let her tell us what happened.' Alf sounded irritated and glared at Nell.

'Sorry,' she said, annoyed at being told, 'but it does seem strange that...'

'Nell!'

'Sorry, sorry, Alf.' She held up her hands. 'Go on, Emma.'

'I was paddling in the river when I saw him. He wanted me to follow him into the forest. I didn't want to, but couldn't help myself. Eventually I came to a clearing and he was standing the other side of it holding Mrs Shillabeer's baby.'

'*What!* Not that baby again, Emma!' Nell could not contain herself at this piece of information.

'Nell!' Alf warned. 'Let her finish.'

160

Nell's mouth settled into a tight line to stop another interruption. But the look of disbelief stayed on her face.

'The master walked to a clearing, where there was bare earth,' Emma continued, 'and laid the baby down.' Tears flowed as she spoke, making it hard for Alf and Nell to hear what she was saying. 'The baby... sank... into the earth... and I... I ran to get it out... before... before it suffocated but I couldn't find it,' she howled. 'I kept digging until I felt something and when I brushed away the earth...' the sobbing started again and her words were almost inaudible. 'It was a hand.'

The crying was again uncontrollable and Nell's face was a picture of horror. Yet none of it made any sense. It sounded more like a dream. Yes, that was it. The girl had fallen asleep and had a nightmare because she was in the forest again. That had to be it.

'If you can talk about it, Emma, how big was the hand?' Alf was asking.

'The same size as mine,' she shivered and sobbed.

'Not a baby's hand?'

'No!'

'What did the master do when you found the hand?' Alf asked.

'I don't know. I didn't see him anymore. I just ran away.'

As the kettle sang on the hook above the fire in the cosy, secure kitchen, it belied the fear that the three people within its walls felt. 'Give her more brandy, Nell, and let's go over this again.' Alf patted Emma's hand to reassure her. 'And you put me right, Emma, if I get it wrong.' He started slowly, not wanting to miss anything out. 'You were paddling in the river when the master asked you to follow him.'

'No,' Emma interrupted, 'he didn't speak, just beckoned.'

'I see. And you followed him until you reached a clearing.' Emma nodded. 'The master was holding a baby.' She nodded again. 'When you saw him first, by the river, did he have the baby then?'

'No, he just beckoned me to follow him.'

Alf frowned, his mind trying to understand, but there were gaps in her story. Even so, he continued. 'Was it a real baby? Was it alive?'

'Yes, Alf. I saw its little arms moving. I recognised it as Mrs Shillabeer's.'

'But if that baby ever existed, it's dead!' Nell's voice was frustrated.

Alf ignored her and carried on. 'Then for some odd reason,' Alf continued, 'the master laid it on a piece of bare earth and it disappeared into the ground.'

'Yes, yes, and I tried to save it!' She felt the tears rising again.

'And when you dug into the earth looking for the baby, you dug up a hand?' She nodded. 'All right, Emma. This is what we will do; tomorrow we will go into the forest and find this grave. We have to know for certain if someone is buried out there. Nell, can you make a broth for our supper and warm her bed? We'll all start out early tomorrow.'

'What do you mean by all?' Nell asked. 'Do you mean *all* of us?'

'You don't have to come if you'd rather not, Nell.' He turned back to Emma. 'We'll follow your route and try to find the spot.'

Emma nodded an agreement, but in her heart, she was frightened about seeing a whole dead body. He must have read her mind as he tried to reassure her. 'We won't be digging it up Emma. If we do find something, I'll fetch the squire. He'll know what to do.'

~

All three spent a restless night chased by frightening dreams. The next day got off to a dark start, as a chilling mist blocked out the morning sun. A silent breakfast was eaten and warm clothes pulled on. As Nell closed the door behind them, the mist had started to lift, leaving everywhere dripping and dank. When they passed the out buildings, Alf went to collect a spade. Emma and Nell shivered in the chill dampness awaiting his return. As they all crossed the field, the forest ahead of them appeared dark and forbidding. The trees at its edge, and the small wooden fence that they climbed were dripping and sullen, slippery and green with algae. Yet only a short distance into the dark interior the forest foliage was dry. Emma walked in front, trying to remember her route and feeling desolate. They at last reached the sloping riverbank where the day before she had experienced so much pleasure from the water on her bare feet. Today, wrapped against the dampness, she could not imagine taking off her shoes.

'This is where I saw him.' Her voice was small and thin. 'He led me in that direction.' She pointed into the trees. They followed her directions in silence, with Nell stumbling from time to time and getting hooked up on brambles. Although she muttered a lot to herself, she didn't complain out loud and kept a sharp eye on the gaps between the trees. When they reached the clearing, Alf stepped into it, followed by Emma and then Nell looking dishevelled. 'Is this it?' Nell whispered a bit too loudly.

'Yes,' Emma whispered back.

They stood hesitantly, almost reverently on the edge of the clearing, looking about them, half expecting Oliver Brack to appear. The silence of the empty forest was deafening, and as the weak sun fought through the mist and touched their chilled skin it brought little comfort.

Alf looked at Emma and spoke one word. 'Where?'

She pointed to the far side of the clearing and Alf set off alone with his spade. Nell pulled her shawl tighter around her neck. Neither woman spoke as Alf stopped suddenly in front of the far trees. They watched as he knelt, brushing at the earth with his hand. Nell shivered as he stood up and lifted the spade. It made a hollow thud as it hit the ground. The sound echoed around the space, threading in and out of the trees. They saw him drop to his knees and again brush at the earth. Then, standing up, he removed his cap in a stance of honouring the dead. Nell groaned, her innards turned to ice. 'He's found someone, my God, he's found someone,' she whimpered.

They didn't go forward to look, but waited for Alf's return. He was deathly white as he took a flask from his pocket and drank the liquid hidden within.

'You look like you could do with some of this.' He handed the flask to Nell.

'Who is it?' She took the flask with a hand that fluttered and put it shakily to her lips. Pulling a face, she coughed and wiped her mouth on her sleeve, looking at him.

'I think it's Polly, but I can't be sure.'

Wide-eyed, Nell started to shake, physically rocking and yet set rigid in her stance. Both Emma and Alf grabbed her before she could collapse to her knees but she was in a shock that had solidly set her joints.

'What are we going to do?' Emma looked to Alf.

'Give her a bit of time and another slug from my flask,' he said, putting it to her lips again. This time she drank deeply and there was no reaction to the brandy that flowed into her numbed body.

~

Later, both women sat huddled in silence beside the fire each with her own thoughts and still dressed in their outdoor clothes. Alf had gone to the inn to procure a messenger to go for the squire, who also acted as the Justice of the Peace.

Nell's thoughts were with Polly and her sudden disappearance. And all this time she was dead, she mused glumly, shaking her head. What awful thing could have happened to the girl? She remembered how at first the girl was very willing to work and how after a year, when she should have been at her best, she took a long time to do chores, disappearing for long spaces of time, sometimes returning not having done the work at all. Nell had her suspicions now, that maybe she was getting out of the house and meeting a boy. She remembered then how the girl was becoming cocky in her manner, as though the work was beneath her station.

Emma thought about the girl in whose room and bed she slept, and whose uniform she had been wearing. The tears ran again over her face and she wished that Matt was here; she wanted to talk to someone her own age. He was the only one that she could have a conversation with. A warm feeling swept into her heart as her young thoughts visualised Matt, but no longer as a brother. She loved him. He had saved her from the fire. They had suffered together the pain of the burns. They had a bond. She needed him, right now.

The Pickerel Inn was busy as Alf pushed through the noisy smoke-filled room, weaving his way between the tables of men with their pots of ale. Some drank alone, seemingly morosely immersed in their thoughts. Others sat in groups and laughed and spoke loudly. Few eyes watched his progress across the room until he addressed the large pigtailed man behind the bar. A hush fell on the tables nearest the bar as Alf asked for a messenger to go to the Hall for the squire. The barman, known as 'Black Dog', shouted to a ragged barefoot girl who was sweeping the floor.

'You, wretch, get yer no-good brother. This man needs a messenger.'

The child paled under the smears of dirt that covered her skin and dropping her broom ran obediently from the room. Moments later a young boy of about ten came from the back of the bar, wiping his mouth with the back of his hand. He looked put out. Dressed warmly in a dirty jacket that was too large for him, he carried the marks of a hurriedly downed pot of ale. He walked slowly. Black Dog grabbed the boy roughly by the shoulder and pushed him towards Alf.

'Jobe's yer messenger. He's a fast boy.' Black Dog's deep voice crackled with years of misuse. Large red hands stroked the boy's head, harshly. Fingers, fat as rolled meat, pinched the flesh on the boy's neck, and Dog's voice held a promise of retribution as he whispered into the boy's ear. 'Y'listens to what the man 'as to say, an' y'listens good.'

As neither Alf nor the boy could write, the message was given to Jobe verbally. 'Ask the squire to come to Claydon House,' Alf whispered. 'We found a body in the forest.'

The boy stood for a moment staring at Alf, trying to absorb the words. Black Dog's huge red hand connected with the side of Jobe's head and the force pushed the boy sideways into a table, almost upsetting a man's ale. The man, a field worker, stood up sharply, glaring at Black Dog and, removing the boy from his table with one sweep of his arm, shouted,

'Mind whatcha do with y'pup, Dog.'

Dog ignored him and shouted at the boy. 'Get going, y'lazy brat, or I'll give y'a good seeing to when y'return.'

Galvanised into action the boy took off, weaving between the tables and out of the building. Dog held out his hand for payment and Alf handed over the money, asking for a large brandy. The last few hours had caught up with him and he needed a drink more now than he'd ever needed a drink in his life.

20.

Haddenford

The mornings and evenings were becoming cooler. Patches of yellowing leaves were lying upon the ground, forerunners of the autumnal tapestry to come. Martha felt excited; she loved this time of the year. The making of jams was almost finished and the children were helping in the gathering together of the last of the apples and nuts for storing. Vegetables were being pickled and set on shelves. Apples and pears were taken to the loft, where they were set on straw for easy access during the winter, and where they would be carefully watched in case any became bad. All this autumnal effort made Martha feel bountiful, wholesome. Like any wild animal she was setting her store for the winter.

At suppertime the children were already at the table as Martha removed the meat from the metal spit that she had been turning in front of the fire.

Hearing the children gasp as the door opened, she looked up and almost dropped the dripping pan that she was then putting to cool on a small table. Just like the children she gawped for a brief moment at the sight in the doorway.

Andrew was standing uncomfortably, just inside the door, wearing his new shirt and holding his hat. He was almost unrecognisable. His hair, which had been washed and combed, hung free. But more than that his beard had been removed, revealing a strong jaw and high cheekbones in a face that was both handsome and rugged. Martha's heart flipped like a young girl's and as she felt her cheeks flush it took a great effort to pull herself together. She hoped that Andrew would think that the sudden blush upon her cheek was because she was so close to the heat. 'Come in, sir. Would you like to eat with us? It's almost ready.'

Andrew walked self-consciously towards the table, accompanied by the stares of the children, and sat next to Nona.

'You look different, Father.' Sarah was the first to speak. 'You don't look like my father.' And she frowned as she looked at him from under her eyebrows. Andrew winced and avoided their eyes. The boys all stared, not knowing what to say.

'I think you look lovely.' It was Nona who voiced her mother's thoughts. 'And you smell nice too.'

At that the ice was broken and everyone was laughing, because no one else would have dared to say that to Andrew Tate.

There was something softer about Andrew and it wasn't just his new appearance. After the meal he addressed his children. 'Would you like to show me your written work?' They ran happily to get their slates.

'Look at mine, Father.' Sarah held up a chalk drawing. 'It's a stickleback, and it lives in the pond.'

'Does it now?' And he looked at it for a long time. 'It's very good, Sarah. I can see you're learning a lot about nature.'

George was pushing his slate under Andrew's nose, but Andrew turned to Jack, who was lurking half-heartedly behind his brother and sister.

'Come, Jack, let me see what you've been doing.' The boy stepped forward, taking in the face of this man who no longer looked like his father.

'I have been writing, sir,' he said quietly, placing the slate in Andrew's hand.

'Come here next to me so we can look at it together.' He put his arm awkwardly around the boy and together they read the work.

Martha couldn't believe the breakthrough and wondered how it had happened. Happy for the children and Andrew, she could have kissed them all. But instead she busied herself clearing the dishes from the table, accompanied by sly glances at Andrew.

When the children had gone to their beds, Andrew didn't seem in any hurry to leave, although he didn't speak.

'Would you like cider, sir?' Martha held out his mug.

'Thank you.' He took the offered mug.

The silence continued as he watched her move about the room. The stillness in the kitchen seemed exaggerated as they later sat peacefully with their mugs of cider. Sitting opposite him, Martha watched him through lowered lashes as he looked around the kitchen as though seeing it for the first time. Her heart throbbed as she saw him notice the jams and the pickles on the shelves.

He saw how clean and feminine the room had become. He also noticed the soft black hair that fell a little out of place near Martha's ear. The beauty of her oval face and the dark brown eyes that seemed huge against the creaminess of her skin, a skin that he longed to touch.

She spoke, breaking the moment. 'Thank you for allowing the children to show you their work, sir.'

'I didn't know that you could read and write so well, Martha.' His face was serious and his eyes, which stared at her mercilessly, were warm and suddenly she felt safe to speak.

'I learnt from my father, who believed all children equal and that girls were as able as boys to learn.'

He nodded, taking in what she had just said, for girls were not thought of as being as intelligent as boys. 'I can see that your father was correct in that; a wise man.'

'Sadly, he died before I could learn enough.' Talking of her father made her sad; she had loved him so much. 'Your children, sir, are very bright and next year I feel that they would benefit from the new village school, where they will learn a lot more.'

He nodded and the warmth in his eyes was replaced by sadness. 'It seems, the way things are going, that I may need Jack as well as Robert to help with the farm next spring.'

'Is something wrong, sir?' A niggle of worry started up in Martha's breast.

He sucked in a deep breath and frowned before speaking slowly. 'Like most farms a lot of money needs to be invested in it. Money I can never find. This is almost a hand to mouth existence. I can't afford to keep John Brisket, but I can't run the farm without him.' Andrew shifted in his chair, unable suddenly to understand why he was telling her so much.

In the silence that followed, he watched the beautiful hands of the woman in front of him, the long fingers that entwined around the mug. He noted the look of understanding in her eyes and knew that like many others she had known hardship. Feeling suddenly overwhelmed by the need to gather her up into his arms and push his face into her soft hair, kissing her neck, his breath quickened and realising the danger that he was in, he stood suddenly. 'I have to go,' and putting his mug down sharply on the table he strode quickly from the room and into the yard.

Stunned, Martha stared at the closed door, trying to understand why he'd left so abruptly.

Sleep didn't come easily to her that night as her mind went over and over the events of the evening and their conversation. Surely, she hadn't said anything wrong?

John Brisket had seen Andrew leave the house in a hurry. He'd earlier seen him without his beard and watched him walk towards the kitchen door wearing his new soft shirt, cleaned up like a man going courting. Seeing Andrew's nervousness, John now knew exactly what had been ailing his employer. But he said nothing. If it meant Andrew could now get back to work he would be glad, for there was still much to do before the weather turned.

~

Next day, while the children were doing their chores around the farm, there was a gentle knock at the door. Martha called, 'Come in!' and was puzzled. Who would knock? Then was delighted as the familiar red hair and Dolly's face came around the door. 'Dolly!' It's so good to see you. 'Come in, come in.' Martha indicated a chair for Dolly to sit.

'Oh, Martha, this room is so comfortable.' Dolly looked at the array of jams and pickles, sitting colourfully on the shelves around the room.

Martha was overwhelmed with joy to have Dolly sitting in her kitchen. 'I can't tell you how good it is to see you, Dolly. I haven't had an adult to talk to, really talk to, since I left the cottage.'

'That is why I came, Martha; people at the church seem to know where you are. Which means Beemer now knows where you are.'

'Well, it was only a matter of time, Dolly. I knew they would find out in the end. But I feel we are protected here. The children and I haven't been off the farm since we got here and we want for nothing.'

'Should you not tell Mister Tate why you are here, Martha?'

'What do you mean?'

'Barney Beemer!' Dolly's face was serious. 'You know what I mean.'

'I don't want to rake that up again, Dolly, for Nona's sake.'

'I can understand that, but what if Beemer comes calling?'

'Why would he do that? He has nothing to gain by people knowing what he is, or what he has done.'

'I have to tell you.' Her face was earnest. 'He came looking for you and attacked me and Dan.'

Martha put her hand to her mouth. 'Are you all right, Dolly, and Dan?'

171

'Tom dealt with him, took him to the landlord. Beemer lost his job because of it. Oh, Martha' – she held a trembling hand towards her friend – 'I think he'll be after revenge.'

Martha took the trembling hand and looked into Dolly's troubled eyes.

'We are safe here, don't worry, Dolly. I promise to be vigilant.'

Dolly sighed and shook her head. She had at least warned Martha; she could do no more and changed the subject. 'Tell me about life here on this rather bleak farm.' Dolly glanced through the window towards the barn walls as she spoke.

'It doesn't feel bleak anymore, Dolly. I must be getting used to it.' Martha smiled. 'It was really a wonderful place to be during the warmth of summer and the children are thriving.'

'And what about the frightening Mister Tate?'

'He is changing, softening towards the children. But he has his problems with the farm. He barely makes a living after all the bills are paid.'

'So he is no better off than the rest of us then?'

'No, Dolly, in fact for him it is worse because he is in a constant cycle of paying for what he can't afford, growing what he may lose or may not be able to sell in the face of all the imports from abroad.'

'If he goes down, Martha, many families will go hungry.'

'I truly believe he feels that responsibility, Dolly. Now, enough of this, tell me about your family; how are Alice and Dan?'

An hour passed very pleasantly until the children came in bringing milk to be made into butter and eggs to be washed.

~

That night, barefoot, Martha went outside and lit a candle to the Goddess. She knelt awhile in a space behind the house that she had created. The air smelt of night, clean and warm, as it often did after the day had passed into the silence. As the moon glided silently from behind a walnut tree, bathing the house and barns in white light, Martha laid a flower upon a small wall where she kept a bowl of water for the birds. Her breathing, deep and relaxed, became shallow and hardly noticeable as she linked with the Goddess energy.

'Sweet Goddess, who resides in all things,' she started in her usual way, 'I thank you for this wonderful home that was offered to me in a time of great need. I thank you for the food we have been able to eat and for keeping us all together. Help me to keep the children safe and to stay aware of the energy. I will listen for your guidance and your wisdom and I thank you for the knowledge that you have imparted to me.'

Raising her arms towards the moon, she let the light fall upon her face, breathing in its essence and feeling the depth of her meditation. 'Help me to accept what is ahead on my life path and to remember that everything that happens is for my greater good and learning. So mote it be.' Breathing in the energy, Martha listened to the sounds around her. Farm animals moving in their pens. Bats clicking, wings rustling above her, small darting shadows in the night air. Something small rustled in the leaves nearby and a sheep somewhere far away let out a plaintive bleat that carried hauntingly on the night air.

~

Breakfast next morning had just started when James rushed through the kitchen door, shouting, 'Mother, Mother, Bess won't get up, she won't lick me.' His cry dissolved into sobbing as he stood unmoving in the centre of the room as though he already knew the terrible truth. All the children left their breakfast, bursting out into the yard, and surrounded the lifeless body. Bess lay where she'd been tied up the night before, but, instead of looking eagerly for her breakfast, she lay limp and silent, her eyes glinting, unfocused. Martha knew that she had gone.

'I'm sorry, children, she was an old lady.' Martha stroked the black-and-white coat. 'She just went to sleep. Robert, will you go to the barn and get me a sack to cover her up? We will bury her later.'

It was a sad morning as Robert pushed Bess on a handcart to the edge of the drying area where he and Jack had already dug a hole near the wall. The children, walking solemnly in pairs, followed behind the cart, holding their flowers at chest height. As Bess was lowered into the grave, tear-stained faces turned to Martha expectantly. In that silence, as they all looked at her, she was greatly aware of the three children who, with their father, attended church on a Sunday, as well as of her own three who did not. How could she combine both faiths without appearing to make any differences? Looking up at the sky she put her hands together, as she knew that they did in church, and started a prayer.

'Oh, Great One,' she started, 'who looks after all animals, we ask you to take Bess, our wonderful companion, whom we will miss so much, into your loving arms. Please cuddle her and take her for walks amongst the clouds. We ask this with all our love.' She looked around at the bent heads.

'Would anyone else like to say something?' George put his hand up.

'Go on, George.'

'Oh, Great One,' he said loudly, following Martha's lead. 'Bess likes to chase rabbits, so I hope you won't mind. Amen.'

Martha smiled lovingly at his serious face.

'Sarah?' Sarah stood solid, her feet a little apart, hands clasped in the praying position, one eye closed but the other squinting up at the sky.

'Oh, Great One,' she said loudly and solemnly. 'Please take Bess to visit our mother, so that they both have someone to play with. Amen.'

174

All the children followed with 'amen' and placed their flowers on top of the earth after Robert had filled in the hole. It was a sad group of children who entered the kitchen for a drink and slice of bread. An hour later, Martha marvelled at the resilience of children as they worked happily together. Life had already moved on for them.

She had just started to think about what to get for the evening meal when Andrew burst into the kitchen.

'I need everyone's help,' he shouted. 'The pigs have got out.' For a moment no one moved. 'Come on. Don't just stand there or we'll never find them.'

Shaken from their stupor, the children rushed to the door for their boots and for a moment were caught up in a tangle of arms and legs.

They were excited as they were despatched to look for the pigs. Robert and James found one in the barn, snuffling in the straw. They tried to herd it towards the barn door but it wouldn't move. Robert smacked its rump; it squealed but continued to eat the muck ignoring him.

'Let's just shut the door, James, and trap it in here; we can come back with Mister Tate later and get it,' and, doing that, they went to look for another pig. Sarah, Martha and Nona found two pigs digging part way up the dung heap, grunting happily, scooping up muck with their noses and throwing it over their heads, where it lay steaming on their backs.

'They smell awful.' Nona screwed up her face.

'Never mind that,' Martha said. 'We have to get them back to their sty. Sarah, you go and stand next to Nona and clap your hands, that should frighten them and make them move.' The girls clapped loudly, but the pigs were too happy in the dung pile to be bothered about clapping.

'We'll have to climb up on the pile and push them off.' Martha sighed at their lack of success. 'Nona you climb up that side while I come up behind them,' she suggested.

'I don't want to, I'll smell of dung.' Nona whined.

'Oh you are flipperty, Nona.' Sarah took hold of Nona's arm. 'You can't live on a farm without getting dirty.' And with that she climbed the heap like a true farmer's daughter, pulling the reluctant Nona with her, slipping and sliding in the manure. After a lot of pushing the pigs ran off the mound, sending the muck flying beneath their trotters in all directions. Martha and the girls drove the pigs before them, flapping their skirts and slapping the pigs' rumps. Eventually they got the squealing pigs back into their sty and shut the pen door. Andrew found three pigs out in the lane heading for the village and with the help of John Brisket turned them around. Jack and George came upon a pig lying in the hen house happily covered in straw, feathers and broken eggs. Seven of the eight pigs were found, but no amount of searching uncovered the eighth. At his evening meal, which again Andrew took silently in his dining room, he wondered how the pigs could get out of a secure pen.

'Are you worried about the missing pig, sir?' Martha asked as she cleared his table with the help of Nona. His brow furrowed as though he were deciding what to say, but he didn't answer. Martha felt she shouldn't speak of it again and left the room quietly. There was trouble brewing; she could feel it.

Later that evening Andrew strode suddenly into the kitchen, banging the door against the wall. His eyes took in each and every one of them as they turned to look at him. 'Did any of you go near the pigsty?' His mouth was tight as he tried to keep his anger under control. They all stared at him in silence. He asked again slowly and in a lowered voice that sounded threatening, 'Were any of you playing near the pigs?'

Martha was alarmed for the children, who hadn't understood the inference behind Andrew's question.

'I wouldn't go near the smelly pigs.' Nona was the first to speak.

'She's scared of all the ani—' Sarah started to chide, but didn't finish.

'*That's enough,*' Andrew shouted. They all flinched and the anger in his voice frightened them. 'I want to know. Did any of you touch the gate to the sty?'

Wanting to protect the children, Martha said, 'It's one pig, sir, and we may find it tomorrow.'

'It's not just a pig, Martha, it's my boar. Without him, there will be no more piglets. This could finish us.' He ran is hands through his hair. 'Tell me, I want to know. Did any of you go near the pigs?'

Frightened, the children shook their heads; none admitted being near the sty.

Andrew stared at them all as though trying to read their minds. Then he turned and left quickly, saying that he had to check all the animals were safe before going to bed. The hairs on the back of Martha's neck stood on end. Something was wrong; she could feel it in the energy.

~

At nine months old Charity was crawling and into everything. Sarah had made it her job to play with the baby and keep her amused. Martha took advantage as there was so much to do with seven children to look after.

Before breakfast Nona went to the milking shed with a jug for the day's milk, but returned looking worried.

'What's wrong, Nona?' Martha asked at the girl's sudden reappearance.

'The women have already gone, Mother.'

'I don't understand. What are you saying?'

'Emi and Aida have gone and the cows are still standing in the shed?'

'Have they been milked?'

'Yes, Mother.'

Then I don't understand. Come, put the milk on the table and let's break our fast.'

Before the breakfast was finished Andrew walked into the kitchen unexpectedly. The look on his face disturbed Martha. 'Would you like something to eat, sir?' She hoped his reason for joining them was hunger.

'No, but thank you, I have something to say. I have had to let Emi and Aida go.' He looked around at the blank faces. 'Although they only came for a short time in the morning and evening, I can no longer afford to pay them.' As he looked about the room; everyone sat in silence, waiting for him to continue. 'It means that two of you will have to take on the milking.' He watched them as they looked from one to the other. Robert will bring them in from the field and return them either to the field, or the barn in winter. You will have to decide who is going to do the milking.' And he turned and left the kitchen, closing the door quietly behind him.

Nona started to cry. 'I can't do it, Mother. The cows frighten me, they're so big. They will step on me and squash me and they smell.'

George was quick to address Nona and Sarah. 'It's girls' work. You'll have to do it.' Pandemonium broke out as they all found good reasons why someone else, other than themselves, should do the milking.

'Let's not argue about it, children.' Martha had to raise her voice to be heard. 'I have to give this some thought.' She looked around the table at the worried faces. 'You will have my decision tonight.'

~

During the day Martha took the time to visit the milking shed as she hadn't seen it before. She had previously had no need, as the

178

milk had arrived daily in a jug. Pushing the door to the milking shed open, she stepped into a large space with iron rings set in a line on the back wall. As the sun streamed in through a window in the roof, warming the wooden walls and straw, the smell, a mixture of animals and sour milk, reached her nose. The floor was covered in straw and cow muck; milk churns stood against the wall near a far door. Milking stools and buckets stood in a corner next to a trough of water. She was trying to work out what the children would have to do when a movement behind her made her jump.

'Oh! You startled me, sir,' she said on seeing Andrew.

He stood just inside the door staring at her and she was aware of the shaft of sunlight that fell upon her face. At first he didn't speak. His lips had parted but no words came from them. His eyes, she noticed, held a soft light as they roved over her hair and alighted on her face. She could hardy breathe.

'I'm sorry, Martha. I hope I didn't frighten you.' His voice was soft. 'I didn't know that you were here.' A pink blush crept across his cheeks as she watched him, not knowing why he looked so embarrassed, or why that look was melting her heart and making her feel like a young girl. He took two steps towards her, his eyes not leaving hers. Her heart pounded in her chest. She wanted him to come closer. Her breathing quickened as she felt a need long forgotten. Then, mortified that she was letting something so precious be seen, she took a step backwards, trying to take charge of the situation.

'I came to see what the work entails,' she said, dragging her eyes away from him. 'So that I can choose the right child for the job.' She turned her back to him, surveying the shed, intensely aware of his presence, his closeness. His voice held a slight tremor and was softer than she had heard it before, as he said, 'The animals are driven in through this wide door from the yard. After the milking they leave by the other door into a holding pen. The milk in the buckets is tipped into the churn.

Then the buckets are washed and the shed swept through ready for the evening milking. The house is allowed one large jug of milk a day. Some of the milk is sold to Major Laddisbrock, who only keeps a beef herd, and to Mister Rudd for the village store. The rest goes to the community dairy.' He stood so close beside her that she could feel the warmth of his body, his arm almost touching hers. Wanting his arm to touch hers, she waited breathlessly for that moment. But it didn't come. He nodded his good-day and walked away leaving her alone and confused. For goodness' sake, she chastised herself; this is just what the gossips would want. No, she wouldn't give them the satisfaction. Fighting the need to follow him, to stand and watch him working, she hurried back to the house.

As darkness fell the boar hadn't been found and Andrew didn't appear for his evening meal. Martha prepared herself to tell the children of her decision about the milking rota, knowing that they'd been waiting expectantly and that Nona had hardly eaten anything all day. She fed them before she stood at the top of the table and looked at their troubled faces. She was sorry, but there was no way around it, this had to be done. 'We will all get up an hour earlier tomorrow,' she started. The announcement was met with groans from the children. 'Robert,' she continued, ignoring them, 'will see the cows in and out of the shed. That job will take all his time. Nona and James will do the morning milking and wash the buckets. Jack and George will sweep the floor ready for the evening. Jack and George will milk the cows in the evening and Nona and James will sweep the floor.'

'What about me?' Martha looked gently towards the smallest child.

'You, Sarah, are going to help me in the house and with Charity.'

'That's not fair, Mother, Sarah's a farmer's daughter and she should milk the cows.' Nona had tears in her eyes. 'I won't do it, I won't.'

'Yes, Nona, you will take your turn with everyone else. You are the eldest and we all have to work to help Mister Tate now.'

'They'll bite me or squash me. I don't want to do it. I won't do it.'

'That is enough, Nona. Mister Tate will show you what to do and nothing will happen to you.'

Nona ran from the room, crying loudly. The sound of her feet stamping heavily on the stairs made her presence and determination felt by everyone in the kitchen.

'I don't mind doing it, Martha,' Sarah said. 'Really I don't.'

'I know, Sarah, but you're so good with Charity it helps me get on in the house. If Nona really can't do it, then you can take her place. Now take Charity up to her bed while I get on with some mending.' Martha watched the small girl as she picked the baby up, placing her on her hip like any young mother. Martha knew that she had the courage of her father and would milk a cow happily if she had to. But Nona would at least learn how to do it.

Next morning they were all up early. The children got ready for the chores of the day and Nona cried as she sat at the side of her first cow, her hands on the soft warm teats. No matter how she tried, the milk wouldn't flow. Andrew stood beside her and showed her over and over until she started to pull the milk from the udders. His praise helped her relax and even enjoy it as the squirts hit the side of the bucket. She looked terrified as each new beast was herded in and tied to the ring on the back wall. They dripped slime from their mouths and noses, sweated through their mud-soaked coats and peed on the floor, soaking her feet. The smell made her retch. She was dismayed at having to lean her forehead against the dirty wet bellies to reach the udders. But it was James who got the bad-tempered cow that kicked him off his stool, landing him in the dung-spattered straw.

When the work was finished, Nona and James arrived in the kitchen stinking and plastered in muck for a change of clothes.

Martha was horrified as they trooped into the kitchen. 'Out,' she shooed them. 'Out into the yard and get your things off.' The pair did as they were told. Standing barefoot in the yard, they both peeled off their soiled outer clothes and left them in a pile near the drain.

'Wash your hands and faces in the bucket before you come in,' Martha directed. The water in the bucket that stood next to the kitchen door was cold and each child bent and washed the thick dirt from face and hands. When allowed inside, having passed inspection, Nona, James, George and Jack sat silently at the table while Martha gave them a drink.

'How did you get into such a state?' Martha said, looking from one to the other. 'Emi and Aida never looked like that.'

George started to giggle. 'James got kicked off his stool and fell in the muck.'

James glared at him. 'It wasn't funny, George.'

'The cows peed on my feet,' Nona complained, tears appearing in her eyes. 'And the pee was hot.'

The children fell about laughing and Martha sighed. 'It'll be better tomorrow. You had a lot to learn today.' And she hoped with all her heart that it would, get better.

Later, while the children went to collect the eggs and give the pigs their food. Martha removed the dirty clothes from the yard with the end of the washing stick and dunked them into the hot water in a large washing pot on the fire's gridiron to boil, then she got on with her own daily chores.

21.

A shadow crept slowly along the edge of one of Andrew's fields. In the darkness, a large, hairy hand used the hedge as guidance. Thick clouds covered the moon as the shadow picked its way over unseen obstacles, cursing quietly, the night a welcome cloak.

In the early hours, while it was still dark, it was the flickering light through the window that woke Martha. For a moment she stared sleepily at the bedroom wall, trying to make out the movement. When she heard the distant sound of crackling from outside she knew exactly what it was.

Running along the landing to all the bedrooms, she woke the children from their sleep, getting them out of the house and into the yard. By this time a yellow light played shadows against the walls of the house and lighted the yard and buildings. Burning straw floated in the air as Martha, with Charity grizzling on her hip, herded the children to safety in the furthest stone barn.

'What's on fire?' James and Jack asked at the same time.

'I don't know. Stay here while I go and look.' And she pushed Charity into Nona's arms.

'I'm coming with you, Mother,' Robert said, but was already running ahead towards the flickering light.

'Jack, James, you're in charge. Don't move until an adult tells you too. Do you understand?' They nodded as a roar came from the direction of the fire. 'Your lives may depend on any decisions you make,' she shouted over her shoulder as she ran from the barn towards the roar and glow of the fire. She already knew what was on fire from the direction of the burning airborne straw. It had to be the animals' winter-feed store but she wasn't prepared for the blast of heat that hit her body as she left the protection of the yard and barns.

'Martha!' It was Andrew, silhouetted against the glow. 'Where are the children?'

'They're safe,' she shouted above the roar.

'Go and get them. I need them to make a chain from the well to the fire with buckets. Get going.'

Martha ran back to the children, pulling her shawl over her head. James, Jack and Nona were standing at the door. Sarah was sitting next to George in the straw, holding the sleeping baby.

'Come, all of you, we have to help fight the fire.'

What about Charity?' Sarah asked looking frightened.

'Leave her in the straw and shut the door; she won't come to any harm.'

The children ran and gathered buckets from the house and milking shed. Forming a line, they passed the buckets of water from one to the other, while George ran back and forth with the empty ones to the well. Martha noticed smoke coming from George's hair and after emptying water over his head made all the children wet their hair. The water wasn't enough; the fire was burning too fiercely. John Brisket was suddenly beside Martha, coughing.

'Martha, we're going to move to the other end of the store. We're going to throw the water on the silage that hasn't yet caught. We might be able to save some of it.'

The line was reformed towards the other end of the feed-store as Robert and Andrew joined them. The pace was furious. The smoke was choking. With eyes stinging, they endlessly passed the buckets. Suddenly, half the store collapsed with a roar, sending burning straw and sparks into the air and across the land. Everyone ran before it, the children screaming. Andrew roughly doused the children's hair and clothes with water as they became singed in the heat, but soon fighting the fire had to be abandoned. There was nothing more that they could save. For their own protection they huddled in a group on the edge of the barns, helplessly looking through the smoke at the devastation as night turned to day. With the new day came a slight breeze and the adults prayed that it wouldn't become a wind.

'It's safe to go to the house now.' Andrew's voice was tired. 'Would you get us all something to eat, Martha?'

'Yes, of course, sir, I'll call you when it's ready.'

Half an hour later, the family, including John Brisket, were sitting around the kitchen table. For once Martha hadn't insisted on cleanliness and, with faces and hands black from the fire and clothes carrying the acrid smell that now seemed everywhere, they ate in silence.

Charity and Sarah were sent back to bed, but the older children were sent to do the milking while Andrew, Martha and John went back to the fire to damp it down. Andrew took stock of what was left of the feed while John kicked the straw about with his boot, stamping on smouldering embers as he took in the situation. 'We've lost over half the winter feed and bedding sir. What is left will have to be spread out and dried before being re-stored.'

Andrew stood forlornly looking at the charred mass. 'Will we have enough dry autumn days? He spoke almost to himself. I pray to God that there will be.'

John broke the following silence, for no one could answer with truth.

'How do you think it started, sir?'

Andrew drew in a deep breath as his own thoughts had just been voiced. He shook his head. 'I just don't know, John. I just don't know.'

'I suppose it could have been combustion,' John said quietly.

'It could have been. But why should that happen when we've stacked the straw in the same way for years without incident?

We're always careful that it's completely dry before storing it.' Andrew shook his head; everything seemed to be going wrong lately.

'Let's get on, John.' Andrew needed to do something. 'We'll have a good look around and see if we can find a reason.'

Later in the morning, Martha hurried to get Andrew's children from their beds, as she always did on a Sunday. Sarah was on her tummy, her thumb in her mouth. Martha smiled and felt sorry that Margaret Tate was missing her children growing up. 'Sarah.' Martha spoke quietly. 'Time to get up.'

'I'm tired.' The child whined, turning and pulling the blanket over her head.

'I know. But I have to get you ready for church.' Sarah groaned. 'Breakfast is ready, Sarah, and your clothes are on the end of your bed.' Martha spoke quietly. It was the same routine every Sunday but after the long night fighting the fire they were all tired. She'd hoped that Andrew would let them sleep on, but he hadn't given her any instruction to do so.

Jack and George were equally tired and Martha wished she could keep them at home. Each had been given their Sunday clothes and soon three sleepy children sat pale-faced over their breakfast plates.

Andrew arrived, standing in the doorway in his Sunday suit, his hair slicked back. He too looked pale, his eyes red-rimmed. There was a silent, detached atmosphere around him this morning that made him seem unapproachable. Martha saw it in his eyes, felt it in her being and decided against beseeching Andrew's better nature in allowing the children not to attend the morning service.

Martha felt weary as she watched them walk out of the yard, the stiff figure of Andrew leading, the children dragging behind and John Brisket bringing up the rear, his Bible under his arm. Good people, she thought, really good people. Going indoors, she lit a candle for Andrew, asking the Goddess to give him guidance and help to overcome his troubles. That this good man would find peace was the core of the energy that Martha exuded in her meditation and prayer that morning.

~

The night had seemed particularly quiet, almost eerie, as Barney Beemer had walked from the village and turned into the lane that led towards the Tate farmland. He'd spotted the location when stealing the boar and had made a small hole in the boundary hedge some nights after. He had moved slowly in the darkness, patting the hedge, searching for the hole, and cursed when a twig scratched his face. A bird had screeched, alarmed by the movement, and fluttered out into the night sky. His heart had pounded as he'd moved forward, cursing under his breath. Suddenly his hand had disappeared into a ragged hole in the hedge through which he then pushed the rest of his body, with difficulty. Crouching in the field on the other side, he had felt a difference in the atmosphere. It had left him feeling exposed and his intention dangerous. For a fleeting moment he had been intimidated by the space around him, but only for a moment as his passion for revenge overwhelmed him.

For guidance, he'd followed with difficulty the ancient quick-thorn hedge that edged the field. When he'd stumbled on the straw stalks, he had cursed Andrew Tate for being slow to turn it back into the soil, as Major Laddisbrock, whose land ran alongside the Tate's, had already done. Beemer had tripped many times on the uneven ground, tearing his jacket on the brambles that mingled with the quick-thorn and also tearing his hand. A slight smile had crossed his lips as his objective had loomed out of the night before him. Standing very still at the edge of the wooden storage barn, he had listened for any human sound. Adrenalin had pounded in his ears as, on hands and knees, his fingers had scratched at the ground, bringing together a pile of dry straw, which he had piled at the back of the barn.

His heart had thumped inside his jacket as he had struck his flint and got a spark. It caught in the small pile that he had held in his hand and he'd blown on it until it flared, then added it carefully to the pile on the ground and watched it crackle into life. Small flames had grown into large flames, spreading quickly up the side of the barn licking at its contents.

Beemer hurried back to the hole in the hedge and in the light of the fire could now easily see his way. Feeling exposed, he had crouched low along the hedge line and was relieved to reach the road just as the alarm was raised. On hearing voices he had looked back, the barn was well alight, glowing in the darkness. He'd been jubilant while thinking that this would finish Andrew Tate off and flush Madam Tilby from her hidey-hole.

Returning from his nights expedition he had crept in through the downstairs window of his room at the vicarage. The Reverend Draycott and his wife had been good enough to give him a room when he had been forced to give up his tied cottage on losing his job. He had felt satisfied as he lay on his bed, smiling at his success. The sleep that had evaded him for so long would come easily now and he would wait for events to unfold.

~

Barney was in church the next morning and was surprised to see Andrew Tate and John Brisket there as usual with all the children neatly dressed. As they took their seats at the back of the church, Barney had a feeling that the damage he had done had not been as successful as hoped. Seeing the widow Fearling take her seat next to Mrs Tuppence, he sidled over for a quick word before the service. In a low conspiratorial voice, he said, 'Good morning, Mrs Fearling, I wondered if you'd heard about the fire at the Tate farm?'

Her eyes widened. She had not heard and it irked to be last to know. So her voice was a little stiff as she answered. 'Really, Mister Beemer? How dreadful; was anyone hurt?'

'I think not, as the Tates are here as usual. They are, it seems, having a run of bad luck.' He frowned and tried to look sensitive about the situation.

'Bad luck? Are they, Mister Beemer? What else could have happened?' Her eyes were sharp as they searched his face and he noted her tight mouth pucker with disdain. It pleased him to see that she was upset at not being the first to know and he found it hard to hide his satisfaction.

'I heard, madam, that all their pigs got out and they've never found their boar,' he whispered, his face glistening with perspiration as he tried to smile sweetly at her. 'You are so well informed, my dear lady, that I thought you might be able to tell me more about the amount of damage caused by the fire.'

'No, I'm sorry.' She was indignant. 'I didn't know about the fire or the pigs. But, if I hear anything at all, I will let you know.'

As she sat back in her pew, the look on her face showed that she was determined to find out more. She knew exactly why Andrew Tate was having such bad luck. It could only be the influence of that Tilby woman.

The congregation became hushed as the minstrels started up a sombre tune and the Reverend Draycott walked slowly to his position at the altar and Beemer took his place at the side of the church. He knew he could rely on Mrs Fearling to find out what was going on. Yes, she would know if the damage was sufficient to finish Andrew Tate and if Madam Tilby left. She could also be relied upon to know where she would go. All he had to do was wait.

Ernest Draycott stood in the pulpit, observing his flock as they sang the last verse of the last hymn, accompanied by the merry fiddling of the musicians. The widow Fearling, surrounded by her fellow widows, sat rigidly in her usual seat on the front pew. Behind them, the rest of the village congregated in their Sunday best. Working people, who had very little, and yet he knew that they would give generously as Mister Beemer passed the collection box amongst them. In his heart he wished that he himself were Jesus Christ, for, if he were, he would be giving to these good people instead of taking from them. But what could he do about it? he thought. The church had to be maintained. His wage had to be found. He had to eat, while he saved their souls. The gentry, the Laddisbrocks and the squire and his family sat in their pews on his left and right and behind them their servants. Yes, indeed, these people also gave generously, but nowhere near what they could afford to give. He listened to the voices of his congregation with a mellow heart as they sang, high and low, young and old, rich and poor, raised to the rafters with much feeling as the last hymn of the morning came to an end.

Ernest held his hands up in a blessing. 'Whosoever cometh to the Lord,' he felt empowered, fatherly, his voice reaching across the church, hovered above their heads. 'Whosoever follows Jesus, loving their brothers and sisters as themselves, *will* sit at the Lord's right hand in Heaven.'

After the service, people stood in the churchyard as usual, talking in hushed tones in reverence for the dead who lay so near their feet. Andrew thanked the vicar and ushered his children down the path. He was not one to stand and gossip. As he passed the widow Fearling she caught his attention by flicking her hand as though warding off a fly.

'Mister Tate, sir, I just wanted to say how sorry I was to hear about your trouble.'

'My trouble, madam?' He stopped suddenly, a frown passing over his face. He was unaccustomed to people discussing his business. She looked confused.

'Your missing pig, sir, and the fire.'

'How, madam, did you hear of this?' Andrew glared at the woman, although he knew it was hard to keep any secrets from the villagers, who got to know everything in time.

'Why, Mister Beemer told me before church,' she gabbled, unnerved by his hostile stare, and, feeling overwhelmed, she retaliated with, 'You brought this on yourself, sir, taking in that woman and her brood. She's brought you bad luck; everyone knows what she is.'

'And what exactly is that, madam?' His eyes flashed, revealing the anger that he felt. Standing stiff as a board before her, he glared into the face of the nervously twitching woman in front of him.

'I can't bring myself to say the words, sir, not standing here on hallowed ground.' Then, stepping back from his ferocious stare, she made to look as though she were about to faint, at which point Mrs Blatch and Mrs Tuppence hurried to her assistance.

'What have you said to her, sir, that has thrown her into a faint?' demanded Mrs Blatch, having no trouble at all in supporting the thin frame of Mrs Fearling.

'I have no business with this lady, nor she with me,' Andrew said sharply. 'Good day to you, madam.' And he walked away, leaving them flapping and fussing over the widow.

'Oh, Dorothy, what did you say to him?' asked the frail Mrs Tuppence.

'I tried, as God is my witness, to warn him' – she pulled the back of her hand dramatically across her forehead – 'but he would not listen.' She sniffed.

'Come, dear, let us get you home.' Mrs Blatch took charge, leading the widow from the church grounds by her arm, with Mrs Tuppence walking behind, chattering like a frail bird.

~

That night as he lay in his bed Andrew pondered over the words of the widow. Bad luck taking in that woman. What did she mean by saying, *can't speak about her on hallowed ground*. The words went around and round in his head, making no sense at all. Martha's image came to him, as it often did, naked, damp from her bath, lit by candlelight. He groaned. Since he had seen that vision he had not been able to get her from his mind. He was, he realised, bewitched by her beauty; he was under her spell. It only took a second for the words he had just thought to be linked with the meaning behind the words of the widow.

'No!' he spoke out loud. 'I will not be party to gossip.' But then he thought, I have been plagued by bad luck ever since she arrived. But where would I be without her looking after my children, removing the burden from me? No, it is just vicious gossip because Martha doesn't attend the church. In the darkness he frowned. Why does she not go to church, or any of her children? People are naturally suspicious. This could be the basis for the gossip. Well, if it was, she had brought it on herself. But he would not have it involve him.

Three weeks later the bad luck seemed to be continuing as Sarah and Charity were burning with a fever. The other children got on with the milking, collecting eggs, feeding the pigs and their lessons in silence. All Martha's time was taken up nursing the sick girls.

It was James who answered a knock at the door, opening it to a stocky, well dressed man with a double chin. At Andrew's request his friend Dr Anderson, who had been at school with him, was making a house call, something he usually did only for the gentry and at a cost. He stood in the yard, his black medicine valise held tightly to his chest as the geese protected the step, pecking at his legs.

'Go in, Doctor,' James shouted as he shooed the creatures away and, shutting the door, took him upstairs to the bedroom.

Martha was relieved to see him as she crossed the landing with a bowl of water. 'I'm very worried about the children, Doctor. I seem unable to keep them cool.'

'Are they eating?' Mrs Tilby.

'No.' She shook her head. 'Sarah will take a little water but Charity is refusing everything.'

'You have to get them to have something.' He looked into Sarah's mouth. 'Her throat is almost closed. This is a very sick little girl.' Examining the baby, he said softly, 'Charity's condition is very serious Mrs Tilby, don't leave them on their own. I want them to have constant nursing. They must be made to drink and be kept covered even though they are hot.'

'Yes, Doctor. I will see to it.'

'And, Mrs Tilby,' he said as he packed his bag, 'pray like you have never prayed before.' He left, closing the door quietly behind him, and, as Martha stood alone in the bedroom looking at the two small children, fear clutched at her heart.

Calling Nona to stay with the them, she went downstairs and prepared all the medicinal herbs that she could think of. She made a tisane with thyme to make the children sweat and sweetened it with honey. Then she cut up some onion, covered it in honey and left it in a bowl to ferment.

Jack, James, George and Nona ran the house and milking shed, while Robert helped Andrew on the farm, leaving Martha sitting day and night with the girls. In the early hours of the third night, while Martha sat sleepily between the beds holding their hands, Charity began to fit. Martha screamed for Robert, while holding the baby tightly to her. 'Robert, get Doctor Anderson as quickly as you can. Run.'

But by the time he returned with the doctor it was too late. Charity lay limply in the arms of her mother, who sat on the floor cradling her baby, rocking back and forth as though to soothe the child. The doctor sent Robert from the room, with instruction to make a tisane for his mother, while he approached Martha gently.

'Martha, your baby has gone. I should examine her.' His voice was gentle as he bent to remove Charity from her mother's arms. But Martha hugged the baby closer, burying her head in the child's neck, sobbing.

'Come, let me help you sit in the chair. You can hold her a little longer, just until your son comes with the tisane, which you should drink for the shock. Do you understand what is happening, Mrs Tilby?' Martha nodded. Yes, she understood that this night would be the last she would ever hold her child to her heart. Ever stroke her little head or kiss her cheek. She didn't want to give her up or face that last moment. How could life have come to this? The emotional pain was the worst she had ever experienced. She thought her heart would break. But when the tisane came she did give Charity to the doctor, who removed her gently from Martha's arms and held her as though he cared.

After the doctor had examined Charity, Martha washed and dressed her daughter, singing quietly as she anointed the small body with scented oil, and then laid her back in her bed, where she looked as though she were asleep surrounded by herbs from the garden. While the doctor attended to Sarah, the children came to look at Charity for the last time. Standing at the foot of the bed, with silent tears wetting their pale faces, they seemed unable to believe that Charity was not just asleep.

It was the doctor who broke the silence. 'Would someone go for Mister Tate, please?'

Martha jumped from her seat. 'Robert, please go for Mister Tate. Is she worse, doctor?'

'I'm afraid so.' Martha approached the bed. Sarah was white, her lips and eyelids blue.

In what seemed the space of a breath, Andrew's frame filled the room. Leaning over his daughter's bed he stared at her pale face and wiped the wet hair from her cheek. Martha ushered the children from the room to give Andrew time with Sarah.

Returning with a bowl of water and a cloth after the doctor had gone, she instructed Andrew to wipe the child's face and hands. As he took the bowl, Martha could see that he was grateful to have something to do. When later she returned to the room, he sat quietly on the bed making comforting noises as he stroked Sarah's forehead. The sight of this rugged, reserved man having such depth of feeling for his child moved Martha to tears as she sat beside her own silent daughter.

Quietly his voice disturbed the silence of the room. 'She's gone.' That was all he said and Martha's heart froze.

'Are you sure? Shall I call the doctor?'

'There's nothing he can do; she's gone.'

Martha touched Sarah's arm. It was cool but still soft. She felt under the cover for a heartbeat. His voice came in a whisper. 'I've seen enough dead animals to know that she's gone, Martha.'

'I'm so sorry, sir.' Martha's eyes were wet with tears. 'I loved Sarah like one of my own.'

'I know.' His voice was choked. Without looking at her he stood abruptly and left the room, leaving Martha to cry alone.

Sarah was washed and laid out in her bed, her mother's small wooden cross placed on her chest. Jack put his head round the door. 'Can I see Sarah?'

'Yes, you can come in, Jack.' Martha made room for him next to the bed. He stood silently, holding his sister's hand, pale-faced and, with tears sliding over his ruddy cheeks, he asked, 'Do you think she is with Mother and Bess now, Martha?'

Martha put her arm around his shoulders. 'Yes, Jack, if there is a Heaven, and the vicar says that there is, then I believe that your mother and Bess are with her. She won't be on her own.'

'I'm going to miss her,' he whispered, and his voice broke with grief. Martha lifted him gently onto her lap where she cradled him, letting him sob until he had cried himself out.

22.

It was a cold, windy morning, although crisp and clear. The sky was the palest blue as autumn leaves floated in the air and covered the ground in a dancing carpet of amber. The wind pulled at the clothes of the small group that followed on foot behind the flat cart that carried the two small coffins. There was nothing to hear but the sound of the wheels on the hard-baked track and the slow regular clop of the horses' hooves.

In the village women stood at their doors, heads covered. And men, with caps removed in a sign of respect, stood silently at the side of the road or at their gates. The sad cortège passed slowly to the church. A single bell tolled continuously as they approached, ringing out across thatch and chimney, lanes and fields.

The inside of the church reflected Martha's feelings, grey and bleak. She shivered in these cold, unfamiliar surroundings and her heart ached at the sight of the two small caskets in front of the altar. She felt disturbed by the enclosure of the thick walls and stone columns reaching high into the wooden ceiling. It seemed a dead place, a place without colour, even more so today.

The words of the Reverend Draycott echoed around the walls, giving thanks for the lives of Charity and Sarah, gently soothing the families as he offered the souls of their children to God.

Later, the surviving children stood silently at the side of the graves, their hands filled with a ragged array of autumn flowers as the two little coffins were lowered into the earth. Sarah laid to rest with her mother and Charity with her father.

Martha was glad to be outside, in the air. She didn't hear the words of the vicar; she heard the song of the birds, the wind through the tall trees, and the whisper of those gone before who surrounded them with love. In her head she mooted her own prayer, in her own words, for her daughter.

Sitting silently in the cart that had carried the coffins the family returned to the farm. There was no wake, only John Brisket with hot broth and bread. He had made sure that the range belched heat and yet none could get warm.

After the chores were done, the children were in their beds and Andrew had returned to his cottage, Martha lit a candle for Sarah and Charity. Earlier she had made two small rounds from willow, into which she had woven small pieces of the girls' hair, autumn leaves and herbs. She laid the decorated willow circles that represented the continuation of life, even in death, in front of the candle. As she sat staring into the flame she had a feeling of impending doom. Something else was about to happen. She could feel it and, yet, what could be worse than today?

~

Andrew lay in his bed, going over the events of the past weeks, and in his heart, he now knew what he must do. He left it until the following evening to speak to Martha.

They were sitting together beside the fire, as they had got into the habit of doing after supper, but tonight Andrew looked uncomfortable and had not made eye contact all evening.

Eventually he said, 'Martha I have something very difficult to say to you.' He swallowed loudly as though something was lodged in his throat and still he did not look at her.

She sat quietly, not taking her eyes from his face. 'I have decided to send my children to my sister's.' He stared into the fire as though he were reading the words there. 'I don't know why I didn't do this before. She will bring them up with her own children, while I try with John to get the farm back on its feet again.'

There was silence as Martha waited absorbing what had been said. The fire crackled more loudly and she had to prompt him to continue. 'Go on, sir.'

He dropped his head until his chin lay on his chest and the words came muffled yet clearly heard. 'I have to ask you and your children to leave. I can no longer support you.'

The feeling of doom that she had felt approaching swept through her. Fear fizzed through her arms and legs, leaving her light-headed, robbing her of her senses. So here it was! The next stage of her life that had been waiting so closely in the shadows.

Her voice trembled as she spoke. 'When would you like us to leave, sir?'

'As soon as is possible. Perhaps you would be good enough to prepare Jack and George for their journey and pack their clothes. They are booked on the afternoon carriage tomorrow.'

'So soon, sir? Surely you can give them time to get used to the loss of their sister?'

'No!' His reply was sharp and by his tone she knew that his mind was made up. 'This is the best way for them. They will start a new life immediately.' He stood stiffly pushing his chair back with force. 'I'm sorry.' Still he did not look at her but walked to the door and was gone.

Martha continued to sit, her hands folded in her lap, trying to fight the shock and think where she could go with her children. She looked around the kitchen, with its warmth and tidy shelves. The vase of late flowers and greenery, sitting in the middle of the scrubbed kitchen table, the jars of preserve on the shelves that Sarah and Nona had helped her make for the coming winter. She knew that this home had never been hers and yet could she ever be as happy anywhere else as she had been here? Tears of fear and sadness wet her cheeks. Yes, she understood that this latest tragedy was too much for Andrew, who was also trying to hang onto the land that had for generations been in his family. But what of her tragedy? Was she not to be allowed time to mourn the loss of her daughter?

Next day it was a tearful goodbye as Jack and George threw their arms around Martha's neck before they were put on the afternoon coach. Martha tried to reassure them that their aunt would look after them and that one day they would all meet again.

On her return to the farm the house felt lifeless and Martha set about getting her own things together for their journey. Andrew didn't come for any more meals, preferring to eat with John in the cottage. Martha, Nona, Robert and James felt lonely in the large kitchen and ate in silence. When Martha told them that Andrew had asked them to leave, her children were also shocked.

'But where will we go, and is Robert coming with us?' James asked.

'I don't know yet where we will go, James, but Robert is staying on to help Farmer Tate.'

'What? For no money?' James was indignant.

'It will be best for Robert. He will be fed and learn to be a farmer. I'm sure that when Mister Tate is on his feet again he will pay Robert. If not, Robert will have gained enough skills to one day work for someone else and be paid. Mister Tate has also said we can stay until we find somewhere else.'

'Please let it be somewhere not so smelly, Mother,' Nona spoke earnestly.

They laughed, as only Nona could think of smells at a time like this.

That night Martha sat in the armchair and thought carefully about where she should head with her children. She couldn't just walk the lanes with no goal.

Closing her eyes, she asked the Goddess for help as she drifted into sleep in the chair. In her dream she was standing with William in a narrow London Street and they were happy. He had finished his apprenticeship and had been offered a job south of the Thames on a large estate. They were excited to be escaping the closeness of the congested London streets. It meant that they could afford to rent a home of their own. She saw herself standing outside a butcher's shop with two small children and a baby, saying goodbye to a large woman who was crying. In her dream William took her hand and led her away smiling, so full of hope for the future.

As she opened her eyes she knew that the dream had been a sign. But she couldn't imagine going back to the narrow streets of London. What if she couldn't get work? What if they couldn't afford a room? Martha knew only too well the sort of work she would have to do to support her children if she couldn't get employment, and she was afraid. She'd lived amongst the girls whose only support was the streets. She knew the dangers of being beaten up and robbed, or owned by a man who ran his girls' lives. She worried for Nona; she couldn't expose her to that. Taking some earth from a pot, she sprinkled it into a circle on the table then lit a candle, placing it in the centre of the circle. Marking the north, the east, the south and the west with autumn leaves, she sat silently in the candlelight, linking with the energy, until she felt peace open her heart.

'I call upon the Goddess, who understands the workings of the heart of a woman. Please help me to make the right decision, as I am at another crossroads in my life.' She breathed deeply, holding a crystal in her hand, and listened to the silence of the room. 'Mother of all life, above and below, whose gentle face I seek in the moonlight. Whose wisdom I hear on the wind through the trees. It is your gentle love that fills my being as I search within and feel your light that burns so constant. Guide me safely through this life. Fill me with your wisdom as I make decisions along my path. My ears will hear you. My eyes will see you. I will speak only your gentle words. My heart understands that all is experience. Give me the wisdom to judge no man and to forgive those that judge me. So mote it be.'

She sat a while longer in the silence before blowing out the candle, clearing the table and going to her bed. She would face tomorrow with strength.

Martha gathered their meagre possessions together next morning. One bag contained clothes and another several varieties of herbs separated into bundles. She had dried them during the summer, hanging them from the ceiling beam in the warmth of the kitchen. They were culinary, medicinal and spiritual herbs that she had tended lovingly and she couldn't go without them. The small carved wren that William had made was tucked carefully amongst the clothes. Now she knew that she could sell it to cover their needs.

Andrew wasn't around to say goodbye but Robert hugged them all, unable to imagine life without his family, and Martha could see that he was struggling with his emotions. 'You must be strong, Robert,' she said gently, 'and, if you are not, you must go to Dolly and Tom; they will look after you.' She kissed and hugged him, not knowing when she would see him again. 'This is best for all of us, Robert. I am doing this for you because I don't know what is ahead of us in London. I will think of you often.' She stroked his hair. 'Work hard for Mister Tate.' With a last embrace of her son, Martha turned and walked away from a life that had been both happy and sad.

As the small group made their way down the lane, Martha felt more alone than she had ever felt before. Everything ahead would now depend on her decisions. The lives of her children had never depended on her more than they did now and she was afraid, knowing that life was not always in the hands of its owner but most often in the hands of fate.

A cold, grey autumnal mist hung over the fields and wrapped itself around the thatched roofs as the family waited on the edge of the village green beside the church wall. Andrew had given her money, for she had none of her own, and with it she had paid for a place on a cart.

The carter was a young man and he made many stops on his way to London, delivering purchases to farms, inns and shops in little villages. Even exposed as they were, sitting with the goods in the back of the cart, Martha was glad to have a ride. It would have been too far for her children to walk and they would have been exposed to many dangers on the roads.

As the cart eventually rumbled across London Bridge the children stood up, holding onto the side of the cart, amazed at the width of the river below them and the many boats upon it. It was as though the river were another roadway, alive with people. The densely populated streets frightened the children, as did the sound of the many church bells and dogs barking and harsh voices calling. Like ants, hundreds of people were crossing back and forth across the bridge on horse and on foot, all going about their business. Nona and James were silent, taking it all in. When they alighted from the cart, Martha gave them strict instructions to stay close to her. 'Don't get left behind or I may never be able to find you again,' she warned as they tried to walk through the throng of people.

23.

When Barney heard of the death of the children he had been secretly pleased. He'd had to do nothing and the bad luck he had started seemed to be continuing without his help. He joined in with the many following conversations with sympathetic words. None could have guessed what was in his heart. Ironically, it was he who entered the names of the two children in the parish records, a job given to him by the vicar because he could write. He had hovered out of sight at the back of the church during the short funeral service, concealed in the shadows, then sat unseen, with his back to a gravestone, some distance from the mourners during the interment. Being near Martha's pain gave him satisfaction. Surely something would happen now if it were going to happen at all.

Events ran faster than Barney could have imagined. It was the following Sunday that Andrew Tate arrived at church with John Brisket and Robert, but without his other children. Barney watched the vicar hurry to meet them at the door.

'Andrew, so good to see you, but where are Jack and George?'

'They will be living with my sister, sir.' Andrew's manner was stiff, Barney noticed. It was clear he didn't want to talk about his business but on the other hand could not be rude to the vicar.

'I see.' The vicar raised his eyebrows and looked at Robert. 'It's very good to see you again in our church, Robert. I hope that you will become a regular worshipper.' His smile was warm.

'Thank you, sir.' Robert's face was pale as he looked around at the grey, cold interior, remembering the last sad time that he stood there.

Barney had hurried to the entrance, loitering in the background beside the font listening to the conversation and was irritated. Why hadn't the vicar asked about the Tilby woman and why was Robert Tilby now in church? Surely if Martha were still here he would be at home under her influence?

The Sunday service seemed endless. Barney sat with his eyes closed trying to hatch a plan, but the voice of the vicar was a constant interruption. A sudden dig in his ribs from Horace Lampwid, who at ninety had very bony elbows, made Barney open his eyes with a start. 'You goner do the collection?' Lampwid asked pointedly. The parishioners were already searching their clothes for their money and the vicar was staring straight at Barney.

Bowing to the vicar, he hurried self-consciously to the back of the church, where Mrs Fearling already stood with one of the collection plates. As the next hymn was sung they stepped forward to pass the plates up and down the rows.

'She's gone then,' she whispered as they stood back to back in the aisle.

'Who?'

The widow stared at him in disbelief, before sucking in her lips and turning away.

'You don't mean?' he tried to whisper.

'Yes.'

'When?'

'A few days ago,' she whispered back, taking the plate and passing it to the next row.

'And you didn't tell me?' His voice rose as his face reddened with anger.

'Do you think that I am going to be running around the village after you?' Taking the plate again, she gave it to a gentleman in the next row without a smile. He took the collection plate offered to him and after placing a coin gave it to a swarthy man who sat with his wife and six children all squashed together in the next pew.

'Do you know where she is?' Beemer hissed as the plate was taken from his hands.

'Oh yes.' She stared into the pew in front of her, watching that the money went into and was not taken out of the plate. With the collection taken, they both stood before the vicar with the congregation's offering. Then, bowing, walked forward, handing the plates to the reverend for his blessing.

'Where?' Barney whispered out of the corner of his mouth. But she had turned away and taken her seat with the widows. He cursed his misfortune as he also took his seat.

'You want to try to stay awake,' Horace Lampwid chided as he sat down. Barney ignored the comment and stared at the back of the widow Fearling's bonnet. He had to find a way to see her without all the others knowing.

Her friends of course surrounded her as she left the church, chattering like little birds. He hated these frilly old women with their strong opinions, but they did know everything that was going on in the village. They reminded him of his mother, who had kept him a virtual prisoner, always wanting to know what he was thinking, where he had been and what he was doing, and, worse still, letting him know in no uncertain terms what he should be thinking or doing. When she died he had become his own man and started to enjoy life, saying what he liked and doing whatever pleased him. He had made a vow at the side of her grave that no woman would ever again tell him what to do unless it suited him.

In the late afternoon, Barney was positioned outside the elderly woman's cottage ready to escort her to the evening service.

'Mrs Fearling, how nice,' he smiled as though he had just come upon her. 'Perhaps I could walk with you to the evening service?' He bowed before her and saw with satisfaction, the look of pleasure that crossed her face.

'Why, Mister Beemer, what a surprise and how kind, I should like very much to be accompanied as my sight is not as good as it once was at night.'

They walked a short distance before Barney asked, 'and where is it that Mrs Tilby has gone with her children, poor woman?'

'Poor woman, is it, sir?' Her lips tightened. 'She brought it all upon herself.' She stopped walking and glared at him.

'Yes, indeed she did. I must agree with you. But where could she have gone?' he said quickly.

'To London, Mister Beemer; she has gone back from whence she came.'

'London?' His eyebrows rose. 'London!'

'I believe she went with one of the carters a day or two ago.' And with that she gripped his arm a little tighter as they made their way up the path to the church door.

Barney was elated. *London*. He had never been but was in no doubt that he would find her. He took his usual seat just as the vicar's voice rang out across the church. 'Forgiveness is the key to a life of following the Lord.'

24.

London

Nona and James lost all sense of direction as they walked closely beside their mother through tight and winding back streets. Martha bade them walk under the first floor of buildings that jutted out over the narrow street and not out in the open. They understood why when a sudden shower of waste thrown from a window above hit the ground beside them, narrowly missing a man pushing a pig in a hand-barrow. Nona was holding her nose and complaining about the smell of the streets. 'It's worse than the farm, Mother,' she whined. But Martha wasn't listening; she had stopped in front of a butcher's shop where fly-ridden carcasses hung from poles across the front window. The ground in front of the shop was littered with offal, bone fragments and ants. Nona held her nose at the terrible smell of fat and dried blood that pervaded the air and was jostled by someone trying to enter the shop. As he pushed past he almost toppled Nona, leaving her speechless.

Martha knocked on a small door beside the window that was almost hidden by the carcass of half a cow hanging at its side.

The sight of the woman who opened the door frightened both James and Nona. The woman's bulk filled the doorway and her grey dress was stained with dried blood. Her lumpy face was as hairy as any man's and one eye had a blue bruise beneath it. 'Yeh, what d'u want?' The woman looked at the little group through tight lips and half closed the door when she didn't recognise them.

Martha stood her ground, ignoring the woman's aggression. 'Hello, Jane, I thought I might call,' she said, unperturbed by Jane's manner or the blood.

The woman frowned. 'And you are?'

'Martha Tilby. I'd hoped that you'd remember me, Jane.'

The grey eyes opened wide and the full mouth hung open. 'Well, I'll be blest on a Sunday. Martha Tilby, what are you doing back 'ere?'

'Can we come in, Jane? We've come a very long way.'

'My Gawd, what am I thinking? Come in, come in. It 'asn't changed much, except there are more of us.' She laughed as she shut the door behind them.

The children kept close to their mother's skirt, unable to take their eyes from the hairy face of the woman who seemed to know their mother. 'Sit down, sit down,' she encouraged the children as she moved slowly to a cupboard in the corner of the hot room and removed a jug from its dark interior. 'Gin?'

Martha nodded and was given a full measure before Jane poured some for Nona and James, handing it to them. They took the cups eagerly as they were thirsty, but moments later were choking. 'What's wrong wiv 'em?' The large women indicated towards the children with a nod of her head.

'They've never had gin.'

'What? Never?' Jane looked amazed. 'Drink up, it'll put 'airs on yer chest.' And she indicated with her cup for them to drink, which they did. The children found the liquid sour but afterwards, although flushed, they looked more relaxed.

'Now tell me whatcha doing back 'ere, Martha.'

Martha took a deep breath and sighed. 'Dear William died and we had to leave the village.'

Jane frowned, knowing Martha to be of stronger character than that.

'I'm sorry to hear that, Martha, yer were so looking forward to a better life.'

Martha smiled ruefully at Jane and then indicated her children. 'This is Nona and this is James.'

'My, my, aren't yer just like yer father?' James looked at his mother, who nodded agreement and smiled. Jane continued, in what she thought a posh voice. 'Pleased to meet yer both.' She nodded to them. Then, understanding that Martha wasn't going to reveal more in front of the children, she refilled their cups.

'Is the house full, Jane? We're in need of a roof.' Martha asked hopefully.

'Well, I'm sorry to say that it is. I've two families sharing the large room at the top.' Her eyes rose to the ceiling, 'The O'Neils and the O'Sullivans. There were over twenty of 'em at the last count.'

Martha looked at her children. Their eyes were drooping with the heat and the gin. 'Can they lie down, Jane?' She stood and lifted James up from his chair before he fell from it.

'Put 'em over 'ere in the corner, Martha.' Jane unrolled a straw mattress that lay along a wall. Nona and James lay down without a murmur and the two women returned to their conversation.

'We have nothing, Jane,' Martha whispered. 'I have managed to find work for Emma and Robert.' With pain striking her heart she spoke the next words for the first time. 'My baby died.'

Jane nodded; she had lost several herself, as had most women, but it didn't ease the pain. 'I'm sorry, really sorry, Martha.' She allowed a little silence before carrying on. 'Have another gin while I get us some cheese and bread.'

'How many are you now, Jane?' Martha asked for polite conversation.

Jane had to stop and think. 'I'm not good at counting, as yer well know, so l thanks Gawd for small mercies,' and, putting her hands together, she looked again at the ceiling. Then, counting on her fingers, said, 'There's our eldest, Charlie, then Edith –

she's in service – William, known as Bill, Buller, Pit, who was Paul, Sid, Joe – his twin sister, Joy, died. Then Ruth and Ethel, they went to the mill.'

Martha tried to keep count on her own fingers. 'I think there's about eight of you living at home.'

'Really, is that all?' Jane screwed up her face. 'Maybe I missed one.' As the food was laid upon the table, a connecting door opened next to the range, revealing the interior of the shop. A young man with long brown hair pushed his head around the door. 'How much meat do y'want, ma?' he asked.

Jane thought a moment, then turned to Martha sitting on the other side of the table. 'Will you stay for food, Martha?' Martha nodded, grateful that they would at least be fed today. Jane made a clicking sound at the side of her mouth, raising her cheek and screwing up her eyes as she calculated an amount. 'Better give me five chickens and some pork.' He was about to bob back into the shop when she called. 'And tell Mister Gimbell we 'ave a visitor from the past.' When the door was shut she looked straight at Martha. 'Now tell me all about it.'

Martha told her of the way William had settled into the work at the big house, working for the Laddisbrocks. How they had managed to rent a terraced cottage, where James and Charity were born. They'd had plans for their children. They would go to school. The boys would follow William as carpenters, perhaps forming a business. But everything changed with William's unexpected death. She'd got behind with the rent. She told of Barney Beemer, and as she spoke she was trying to decide whether to mention what he'd done to Nona. But as that was the real reason she had left the village she would have to tell Jane. Making Jane promise not to speak of it to anyone, she continued with the story. Jane was angry as she heard about the rape and cheered when she heard what Martha had done to Beemer.

She smiled at the look on Martha's face as she recounted their life on the farm with Andrew Tate. But became worried when she realised that the man Beemer might take his revenge, and might even be looking for Martha right now. But then, she thought, she should be safe in London, where it would be like looking for a needle in a haystack.

The day wore on unnoticed by the two women, who were reminiscing about the past, and soon the candles had to be lit. The children awoke and sat by their mother, as a tall, thin boy with long brown hair slapped five chickens and a large piece of pork on the table.

'Nona, James, this is Charlie,' Jane said. He grunted and barely glanced at them before returning back through the door.

The women sat at the table with the children and plucked the chickens. Nona pulled at the feathers half-heartedly, making a face and blowing away the feathers that floated to her nose but was afraid to moan in front of the strange woman. James attacked them with vigour and tried to gather more feathers than his sister. When five naked birds lay before them, Jane gathered the feathers into a sack. The meat was put to cook on the jack and the children shared the turning. The long table was set with dishes and bread. One by one Jane's family arrived for their supper and were introduced to Martha and the children.

Nona and James gasped loudly as the first two boys walked in through the back door, their clothes and skin covered in blood.

'Get back out and wash yourselves, we 'ave visitors,' Jane bellowed, and the boys quickly obeyed. 'The small one with brown hair is Sid and the taller one with the fair hair is his younger brother Joe,' Jane informed them.

'Have they had an accident?' James asked from behind his mother's skirt, making Jane laugh.

'Good Lawd, no. They work at the abattoir in the next lane.' James's face had a blank expression; he had never heard the word before. 'The slaughterhouse,' she tried again without success. 'The place where they kill the animals what come to the butchers for sale.'

Now he understood.

Nona screwed up her face and was about to say something when a noise outside in the street distracted her and she and James ran to a chair and helping each other up looked through the small window into the street.

They were just in time to see bones flying through the air from the shop doorway, landing in the dirt outside. Along with snarling dogs, women and children in rags fell upon the scattered bones, squabbling and screaming while trying to fill pockets and sacks before hurrying away.

Two women with large sacks clipped the ears of the children and tried to take the bones from their hands. The children held on kicking and squealing. The women also tried to take the bones from the dogs and were bitten for their trouble, after which they walked away complaining.

'Who are those women?' Nona asked no one in particular as she and James jumped down from the chair. It had become quiet in the street again and there was no longer anything to see of any interest.

'The women are bone collectors. They sell 'em to the bone man,' Joe said winking at Sid and pulled a frightening face at the children, saying in a strange voice, 'Don't leave yer dead outside in the street or they'll pinch 'em and sell 'em to the glue factory.'

The children's eyes widened in astonishment, even though they didn't know what a glue factory was.

At that moment the door between the house and the shop opened suddenly and a small man with muscular arms entered, commanding instant respect from his family, Martha noted. His tired face did not smile in greeting.

'Oh, there you are, Mister Gimbell.' Jane, who had been calm, became flustered, wiping her hands down her apron several times as though trying to smooth it.

The man ignored her and looking straight at Martha nodded. 'You're back then?'

'Yes, it seems so,' Martha replied cautiously. Nona and James stood unmoving, affected by the atmosphere in the room, which had changed by the entrance of this small man.

'These yours?' he indicated Nona and James.

Yes, these are my children, Nona and James.' Both came to her side and James hid behind her skirt.

'I remember Nona,' he said, 'scrawny little thing.' Martha smiled a thin smile, but didn't answer as she stroked the heads of her children to reassure them.

'Everyone up to the table,' Jane called as Charlie and Bill also entered from the shop.

The meal was full of banter and good humour. Half-way through Buller arrived and took his place at the table. 'Who's this then?' he indicated James and Nona as Jane handed him a full plate of meat and bread.

'They're two of Martha's,' Jane told him.

He nodded at them before attacking his meal. Then looked at James and said, 'How would yer like a day out tomorra? You could come with me and 'elp with the shoes. The toffs'd like yer.' He looked at Martha. 'I could take 'im to Newgate later in the week; there's going to be a fair.'

James's face lit up, suddenly liking Buller. 'I like fairs! Can I go, Mother, can I?'

Martha shook her head and was sorry to have to disappoint her son the moment he felt comfortable in this new place. 'No, James, I'm sorry, it's not the sort of fair that you'd like.'

Martha saw his little face crumple and knew that he wanted to go. He had nothing to do in the house with the women talking and ignoring him all day.

'What sort of fair is it then?' he demanded.

'It's the sort of fair where people dance a jig,' Buller butted in and smiled as he filled his mouth with more meat. And around the table the boys all laughed.

Mr Gimbell's fist hit the table. 'That's enough.' The voice was loud and sharp. Nona and James froze and Buller jumped. Mister Gimbell stared hard at Buller. 'We'll have no more talk of Tyburn or Newgate at this table.'

The rest of the meal was eaten in a strained silence, after which Mister Gimbell and the boys left the table to sit by the fire and smoke their pipes, while Martha and Jane cleared away the plates and bowls. 'Bit silly of me really,' Jane whispered, 'sending all my girls away to work. I could have kept one as 'elp in the 'ouse.'

'It must be hard tending so many grown men, Jane. Why not employ one of the lodgers from upstairs?'

Looking shocked, Jane stopped rubbing at the plate in her hand. 'Do yer know what they'd do to each other if I employed one without another? They'd murder each other. They're like wasps. If yer disturb them they gather in a crowd and scream and shout and come to blows with each other and anyone else around them. They're on the top floor so we can't hear 'em in the daytime. Mister Gimbell put wooden stairs up the back of the house so they can come and go without our seeing 'em. It's more peaceful that way.'

Jane piled the dishes into a large wooden barrel bath on the floor and threw a bucket of water over them. 'Sometimes they even pay their rent, if one of my boys gets 'em before they spend it on gin.' She pulled a plate out of the bath and wiped it on her apron before handing it to Martha, who placed it on a shelf. 'When they first arrived, their men was wiv 'em. The men 'ad some sort of work, but it wasn't long before we realised we 'adn't seen the men and they were getting behind with the rent. There was always some excuse and gradually they became more abusive. The families continued to grow even though there were no men around.'

'Can't you get them out, Jane?'

Jane expelled a long breath in exasperation. 'The boys 'ave a plan,' she raised her eyebrows and held up her hands as Martha's face showed that she was curious. 'I don't know, and I don't want to know what they're 'atching. It won't work and will bring us all trouble and then life won't be worth living.' Jane answered Martha's unspoken question.

It was getting late. Martha changed the subject. Her children were looking tired and she still had nowhere to go.

'Jane, could we stay here tonight? It's too late to drag the children around the streets looking for a bed.'

The answer came back without hesitation. 'Of course yer can. You can sleep down 'ere in the corner on the pallet. Take the sack of chicken feathers for your 'eds. If yer need anything else, yer know where we are upstairs.'

In the dead of night Martha lay on the uncomfortable straw mattress and remembered when she and William used to live in this house. They'd had a corner of the room on the top floor where the Irish families now were. She and William had shared the floor space with a family called Edgeson. Mister Edgeson was a wood turner by trade and it was he who had got William an apprenticeship. William had been a natural with the wood and was quick to learn. She remembered him being so proud of the wren that he had carved for his examination piece. They'd been happy here and had planned their lives in that room at the top of the house. William felt close to her tonight and in the warmth of the kitchen with its unfamiliar smells she fell asleep wondering what life had in store for them.

Next morning the children and Martha were covered in bites and she realised that the chicken fleas were still in the feathers. Getting up she put a log on the fire, then hung the bag of feathers well above the heat so as not to catch fire, and hopefully the smoke would kill the fleas.

With the leftover meat from the night before, Martha made some of her small pies, stuffing them with herbs and putting them in the oven beside the fire. Then she thought that she would go into the garden and welcome the day. Many years ago, she had planted herbs in this garden and hoped that they were still there.

When she opened the door to the garden she found it full of children. Some were barefoot and two boys were urinating on the plants while half a dozen girls fought, screaming and pulling at each other's dark hair. She sighed; these must be some of the children who lived on the top floor. Going back inside, she shut the door firmly.

Jane was first down and Martha and Nona helped her set the table while James concentrated on scratching the bites on his arms and neck. Breakfast was eaten as people arrived. Sid and Joe were first and gratefully took a pie each and sat to eat them. 'These are good,' Sid told her, while Joe just nodded in agreement, his mouth stuffed. He was still eating as they hurriedly left the house.

Pit shuffled heavily into the kitchen pulling on his jacket and just wanted ale. Martha poured it for him and offered a pie for his pouch; he took it, nodding sleepily, and went off to his work.

As Martha sat the children at the table, the rest of the family arrived. 'Umm, smells good, what is it?' Charlie wanted to know as he poured some ale into a pot and took a seat.

'Meat pie.' Martha put one before him as he cut some bread. He breathed in the smell with his eyes shut tight and smiled.

When he arrived, Mister Gimbell sat in his usual seat and waited for his ale, then ate a pie in silence. After breakfast, as he walked through the door into the shop, he looked back at Martha and nodded. 'Those pies are very good.' Then, seeming not to be able to cope with giving a compliment, he turned angrily on his boys. 'Come on, Charlie, Bill, get to work,' and the door was closed.

'Praise indeed,' Jane muttered. 'Thanks for yer 'elp today, Martha, they take a lot of feeding and it is good to 'ave something different to give them.'

'I hope you don't mind me asking, Jane, but why does a woman in your position not have a maid servant to help in the house?' Jane looked uncomfortable and screwed up her face.

'I've tried, Martha, but they don't stay. It's not that they're not paid well enough; there just isn't the room.'

'But you've put us up.'

'Yes, but I can't expect someone to work and sleep on the floor for very long.'

Martha understood, but was sure that there were plenty of starving people who would be glad to work for Jane and sleep out in the lane if they had to, but she could see that Jane had standards.

Buller arrived last, throwing his leather jacket on the empty seat next to him. He wasn't in any hurry because he worked for himself. As he took a pie from the dish he asked, 'Could I take James with me today, Martha? It would get 'im out from under yer feet? I think the toffs'd like 'im; 'e could be good for business.'

'Can I go, Mother, can I?' James whined, his face alight with expectation. Martha wasn't sure. Her children were used to being able to wander in lanes and fields in safety. To wander here would have a different outcome altogether and she was afraid for her small son, who wasn't used to crowds or villains. Her children were gullible and would be easy pickings for the quick-witted rogues of London. 'I don't know.' She shook her head.

'I'll look after 'im and teach 'im the trade.' Buller was quick to step in. 'The little fella will be fine with me. Really, Martha, he will.'

'All right, Buller, but you must keep an eye on him. James, you mustn't wander off it's not like Haddenford, where you knew everyone and they knew you.'

But James wasn't listening as he whooped and danced about the room. And Buller laughed with him. When they had gone, leaving the three women alone, Martha helped Jane with the tidying and noted how her friend stopped often for a swig of gin. 'How can you drink that stuff?' Martha asked. 'It'll rot your insides, Jane.'

'It 'elps me through the day.' She placed the jug back on the shelf and sat down heavily at the table. 'Whatcha going to do now, Martha?'

Martha could see how tired Jane was. Life had taken its toll, but like all Londoners she had a strong backbone. Giving in even to tiredness was not an option.

'I have to find work, Jane, or it's the workhouse for us. I can't look after my children otherwise.' She was beginning to face the fear that had been steadily rising in her heart since arriving in London. The fear in realisation that the responsibility of their lives was hers and hers alone. That word, 'alone' had never before held such meaning. She was, on her own and it was her own fault that they were in this position. It weighed heavily on her, and she felt old; she was old, at nearly thirty, and today she felt it keenly.

Jane broke into the hopelessness that was starting to flood her mind.

'What sort of work can yer do?'

Martha could see that Jane wanted to help, but also knew that the children would be a problem.

'Like most women I cook, clean and mind babies.' Martha would like to have said that she had a skill, but she hadn't. Marrying young, she had no skill other than running a home.

Jane frowned. 'Those that can afford 'elp around 'ere only take cheap child labour. They're not going to take a woman with children. You wouldn't be able to live in, and living out you wouldn't have money for rent. You couldn't leave them alone, they're too trusting. They ain't in any way streetwise, Martha.'

'What should I do, Jane?' Her position seemed impossible and she found it difficult to hold back the tears. Swallowing hard, she lifted her head bravely, looking to Jane as though she would have all the answers.

'You gave me an idea this morning, Martha. Why not cook small affordable pies and ask Mister Gimbell for a little space in his window to sell 'em?'

Martha considered the proposition. 'That would be wonderful, Jane, but it would be your meat and your heat and ingredients that I'd be using.'

Jane was enthused now, possibly with the effects of the gin, but also because she'd had an idea, and Martha was actually thinking seriously about it. She felt proud of herself as the blood rushed through her veins in a way that had not happened in a long time. Her face was flushed as she said, 'Work out a price with a profit. Offer Mister Gimbell 'alf the profit and that could also cover yer rent.' She got up and went to the jug for more gin.

'But I don't know where I am to live or how much the rent may be.'

It had been a good idea but Martha could see that, even if Mister Gimbell agreed, they still had nowhere to live.

'You can stay 'ere with me. I enjoy 'aving yer company.' It was said quickly and was probably fuelled by the drink. But Jane didn't care, she loved having Martha here. It had brightened up her whole hard life and she had to admit that she didn't want Martha to leave. But Mister Gimbell would be no pushover and Jane had to think carefully how to approach him with her idea.

Martha threw her arms around the large woman. 'You're a good friend and one day, Jane, I'll repay you.'

'No need,' Jane laughed hugging her back. 'First we have to convince my husband.'

~

Buller set out his stool on Fleet Street and was soon busy. It had been a long walk for James. The first gent took his place on the stool and Buller passed the time of day with him in a friendly manner. He took his time in cleaning the shoes so that it made

219

him look busy for longer. The gentleman was very pleased with the result and after paying gave James a farthing.

'Thank you, sir.' James stared at the coin in his hand. 'Look, Buller, money.'

'I'm going to set yer to work, young James, now yer earning.' Buller smiled. 'I want yer to put the polish on the brushes for me and keep the cloths in the right order like this. Now can yer do that?'

'Oh yes; it's easy and will I get paid, Buller?' He looked excited, his eyes expectant.

'Well, I can tell that yer 'ave an 'ed for business, little 'un. We'll see how it goes. Yer can keep yer tips.' Buller was pleased. The boy was a quick learner and well spoken: the toffs'd like that.

James took to the work and liked speaking to the posh gentlemen, who tipped him well. When they returned home, James ran to Martha and showed her his money. 'Look, Mother, I've earned money.' He placed it in her hand.

'Oh, James, I'm very proud of you,' and she cuddled him up into her arms. Smothering his small face with kisses. 'I'm very, very proud of you and pleased that you did as you were told.'

'You have it, Mother, for my keep, just like Buller.' And he wriggled from her arms. Martha found it hard to keep her emotion under control as she spoke to her small son as though he were a man. 'Thank you, James, this will be a great help.' And she smiled gently as he pulled himself up taller.

~

That evening, when they were alone in their room, Jane watched her husband go through his bedtime routine and awaited her moment. It was no good trying to talk to him when he got into bed, for the man worked so hard he was almost asleep before his head hit the pillow. Just as he approached the bed she said, 'Mister Gimbell, I had a thought today that might bring some profit to us and at the same time help Martha.'

He stopped beside the bed and looked at his wife. 'You had a thought?' Jane ignored the surprise and derision in his voice. Too much depended on her plan. 'I thought that as Martha cooked such wonderful pies that she could have a small space in the window to sell them at a reasonable price to the poor.'

'To the poor? How do you think that they will be able to afford pies? You've seen how they try to kill each other over the bones I throw into the street.'

Jane was not going to give in so easily. 'But, sir,' she continued as though he'd not spoken, not all the poor are that poor, as you well know. It's them she will be aiming at.'

'You mean those that buy my cheapest scrag end and bones with a bit of meat on?' He pulled the cover back with more vigour than was needed. 'Don't you understand that that's my profit? Managing to sell what could be thrown away is money in our pocket.' He sat heavily on the bed, swung his legs in and pulled the cover up. She had to be quick.

'Please let us try, Mister Gimbell, it might bring more business to us, what with competition from the other butchers. We'd 'ave something they didn't 'ave and couldn't copy. You've tasted how good 'er pies are.'

He teetered, his back and head lowering towards the head rest. 'She 'as three days, woman,' he said. As his head hit the pillow, his body relaxed and he was instantly asleep.

She'd done it! Jane smiled to herself. My, my, how things were changing. She almost wanted to go downstairs and tell Martha the good news but good sense prevailed and for the first time in many years Jane fell asleep with a smile on her face.

Martha could hardly believe it next morning when Jane told her that Mister Gimbell had agreed to let her have a little space in his window and she heeded his warning about what would happen if it affected his trade. She was not by any means on a solid footing, but it was a chance that Martha prayed would work.

Next morning Jane left the door to the shop open, just a little, so that the smell of pies cooking would drift innocently into the shop. Customers began enquiring about the smell and when told that there would be small affordable pies on sale soon, they formed a crowd.

Martha's first batch of pies sold before getting into the window and she and Jane turned around and started the pastry all over again. Four batches of pies were sold during the day and Martha was pleased and Mister Gimbell was politely surprised. The following day there was a crowd outside Gimbell's shop waiting for him to open. But only a few came in.

'They're waiting for pies,' Charlie told his father when he asked.

The butcher frowned. 'Make two queues, one for meat and one for pies, before they start pushing and shoving. I don't want a riot in my shop.'

The new arrangement worked and the queues grew daily as the news of affordable pies and how good they were spread. While people came for the pies they also stopped to buy the meat. Mister Gimbell was happy when he realised that his profits were rising.

On the third evening, as the meal was about to be served, Sid and Joe staggered in through the back door looking ill and weak-legged. Clinging to each other, they looked as though they were about to die. 'My Gawd, what's wrong with yer?' Jane cried out in shock. 'Mister Gimbell, they've caught something. What shall we do?'

Their father stared at his white-faced sons and squeezed his eyes up for a better look at what was oozing from the lumps on their faces. When he shouted, Jane flinched. 'Is this a joke, for if so it's not funny, with so many dying of the typhoid.'

The boys laughed. 'It's all right, Father, don't fluster, it's only flour and fat.' They wiped their faces, laughing harder at the expressions around the table.

'Whatcha playing at, scaring yer mother like that?' Their father's face flushed angrily.

'We did it for a good reason, sir,' Joe said trying to stop laughing. 'We 'ave a surprise for Mother and for Martha. The lodgers are gone. Now yer can let out the upstairs room again, sir.'

For a moment everyone stared at the boys open-mouthed, trying to take in the enormity of what they had just heard.

'So, this is what yer've been planning, the pair of yer.' Jane laughed. 'Break out the rum, Mister Gimbell, this is a celebration.'

Rum was taken all round and raised to the ceiling for it was the best news they'd had in a long while. Now they could let the upstairs and get some rent, without all the hassle from those women, who, in truth, although Mister Gimbell would not admit it to anyone else, had scared the living daylights out of him. He couldn't understand a word that they said when they were angry and they seemed angry for one reason or another all the time.

Later that night before bed Jane asked, 'Mister Gimbell, would you mind if Martha was offered the room upstairs? She can afford the rent and she'd be no bother, I'm sure.'

'Ummm,' was the muffled reply from the nightcapped figure beside her. Not a complete yes, she smiled, but at least they would be sure of the rent and that was all that her husband would care about.

Martha and the children settled in upstairs and life once again began to look good. Fresh herbs were planted in the garden, the others having died away through neglect and abuse. Chickens, newly purchased for their eggs, were kept in a long pen to keep them off the vegetables and herbs. Martha worked hard with the help of James, who ran errands, and Nona, who had learnt how to make pastry. Martha gave thanks privately to the Goddess.

25.

Claydon House

The squire, a well-dressed, thickset man in his sixties, arrived around noon on a spirited black horse. He was accompanied by two of his gamekeepers, Knowles and a young man called Lett. They had been sworn in as his deputies and witnesses. They arrived at almost the same time as Horace Whitaker, the local doctor, in his smart carriage. Dr Whitaker, a rotund man, constantly dabbed at his perspiring, purple-veined face with a lace-edged handkerchief, although the day was not hot. As the small party crossed the field, he, having difficulty in walking on the uneven ground in his soft shoes, dragged behind in his tight breeches that strangled his portly belly.

Alf led the silent group through the forest to the shallow grave. The body, after being released from the ground, was identified as Polly by Alf and by Lett, who had hoped that one day he and Polly would walk out. Visibly shaken after seeing the body, Jimmy Lett sat pale-faced beneath a tree, his hands covering his eyes to shut out the horror. Alf sat with him until he recovered enough to do his duty. Then Lett and Knowles carried the body, wrapped in a shroud and placed on a stretcher, out of the forest and across the field to Alf's cart. It was then taken by cart to the doctor's home, where he examined her more carefully.

Having settled the squire in his spacious drawing room with a brandy, the doctor got on with the gruesome work. An hour later, having washed and replaced his jacket, he also poured himself a brandy as he sat in the drawing room facing the squire.

'Well?' the squire asked sharply, his face lacking its usual intensity of ruddy colour.

'There was no foul play exactly, sir.' The doctor downed the brandy in one gulp and poured another. 'She died in childbirth, not an unusual occurrence.'

'How can you know that?' The squire frowned across the top of his glass. Always amazed by men of science, he needed to know how.

'The placenta was still in place, indicating a birth. It's a very good thing that we have no hogs in the forest or there would have been nothing left to identify.' He sat down heavily in his leather chair and drank the brandy a little more slowly.

'But the question remains' – the squire frowned as he poured another drink for himself – 'who buried her in the forest and why, if there was no foul play?'

'That's not the only question, sir,' the doctor said, studying the squire over his glass of brandy.

The squire raised his eyebrows and waited for the doctor to explain.

'What has happened to the baby? Where is it?'

The squire shook his head. Of course. Where was the baby? There were too many unanswered questions here and he didn't like it. There were a lot of things that he didn't like about Claydon House, and at the top of the list was the mistress and the gossip, although there was always an element of truth in gossip, he had found. Weighing up everything they knew, which wasn't much, he said, almost to himself, 'I shall have to speak to the staff at Claydon and Miss Brack; someone must know something.'

~

A day later the squire's presence filled the library, where he questioned Nell, Emma and Alf for more than an hour. But there was nothing they could tell him about Polly's death, only how she came to be found. Alf had thought it prudent not to mention the master and warned Emma and Nell to say nothing about him. After all, he thought, no one but Emma had seen him, and, knowing the master as he did, Alf knew that he would not have been hanging about in the forest. It just didn't make any sense. They didn't know what to say about the baby that Emma had seen and decided to say nothing about that either. That was up to the mistress. After all, they had been told nothing officially about a baby.

When the Squire had left, the three sat alone in the kitchen wondering what would happen next. 'What are we going to do?' Nell was agitated. 'The squire will tell the mistress and she'll find out you're still here, Emma. We're all in trouble now.'

'Never mind that,' Alf spoke quietly. 'What has the master got to do with Polly being buried in the forest? He knew where she was. Why hasn't he come forward?'

'Maybe he killed her, that's why he's run off.'

'But he hasn't run off, has he, Nell, not if Emma saw him in the clearing?'

Nell covered her eyes with the heel of her hands and sighed deeply. 'I just can't understand any of this. A missing master who's still here. A dead maid, a baby that none of us but Emma saw is dead, then buried alive in the earth, but wasn't there at all. It's all too much. I don't know how we will explain all this to the mistress when she returns.'

The happiness of the past few days had sunk into a gloom that sat once more over the house, spreading its tentacles into every corner of every room, filling the occupants with uncertainty.

The coach, pulled by two sweating horses, arrived at the front of the house two days later. Matt helped Amelia down from the coach. She was still dressed in deepest mourning, her face covered by a thick veil that concealed her face.

Nell stood alone on the step awaiting her, but she swept passed without a glance, going straight to her room. Nell was worried. It was unlike the mistress not to give instructions on her return and a feeling of imminent disaster settled on Nell's shoulders as she bustled back to the kitchen.

Matt was about to drive the coach to the stables when Alf caught the reins. 'Get back as soon as you can, Matt, there's trouble afoot,' he warned.

In the kitchen, Emma didn't know where to hide and Nell was in a fluster; only Alf made any sense when he came in saying, 'We don't know how much she knows, so let's act normally until we do, Nell.'

'What's normal?' The colour had drained from Nell's face. 'She usually gives me instruction about tea or lunch or sends for me to unpack her things, but she hasn't said a word. I don't think I should knock on her door, do you?'

'No. Perhaps not,' Alf agreed. 'We'll wait for her instructions. Get the ale, Nell; Matt will be here as soon as he has the horses settled.'

Emma was afraid of the mistress's reaction to her still being in the house and wished with all her heart that she were somewhere else. The squire would have mentioned that it was she who had found the body and, yet, another emotion was filling her with warmth. Matt had been away for so long that she could hardly hide her newly discovered feelings of love, and joy that he was back.

As he entered the kitchen her heart jumped and her face flushed. But she kept her head down and continued to slice the hock for their meal.

'Long journey, Matt?' Nell went to her son and put a hand on his arm.

'Yes, Mother, a long journey; she didn't stop for refreshment.' His boot fell to the floor, almost in slow motion.

'Did you hear that Polly had been found dead, buried in the forest?' Nell blurted it out and started to cry, dabbing at her tears with her apron. 'It's a terrible business. That poor little girl must have suffered.'

'No!' Matt exclaimed, looking at each face, trying to make sense of what he was hearing. 'Polly is dead?'

Nell pointed at Alf, who stood with his back to the fire, looking chilled. 'Alf was with the men who dug her up, Matt.'

'But who would have killed her and buried her in the forest?' His voice sounded sceptical before he added quietly, 'How did she die?' Each face he stared at looked back blankly, unable to answer his question. 'All the time that she's been missing and she was buried in the forest?' He shook his head, unable to believe it as Nell started to weep again. 'What happened to her? Who did it?' He put his arm around his mother, whose face was wet with tears.

'We don't know what happened,' Nell spoke between the sobs.

'Dr Whitaker took the body to examine it and we haven't been told how she died.'

Alf, who had been quiet, cut in. 'But it had to be someone local who buried her in the forest. Someone who knew it.'

'Could it have been Jake Poleshore that night he went mad?' Matt asked.

'He don't act like a man who done it, more like a man who saw it done, I'd say, or maybe he saw Polly's body.' Alf shrugged. 'Guess we'll never know, as he's never uttered a word since that night. His head seems completely empty; there's been no change in him since I found him.'

They all shook their heads and stared at each other in silence. Nell could no longer stand the tension in the kitchen and changed the subject. 'How are your burns, Matt?'

'They're fine, Mother; they were dressed each day at the house by one of the servants.' A gentle look came over Matt's face that did not go unnoticed by Emma, who frowned and cut at the meat with more vigour.

'The mistress doesn't seem herself; does she know what's happened here?' Nell ventured as Matt dropped his second boot on the floor by the door.

'I think so, Mother. We all thought it strange that the squire from here should visit the Shillabeers'. He spoke to the mistress for some time, after which I was instructed to get the coach ready for home the next day. And the strange thing is that Mrs Shillabeer's baby, who Emma thought died in the fire, is alive and at the house with its family. It was never here, Emma.'

'So, didn't we have a baby in the house then?' Nell asked, putting a mug of ale before her son. 'Emma thought she saw the evidence.'

'I picked the baby up when it was crying,' Emma tried to justify herself. 'There really was a baby, there really was.' She looked from one to the other, hoping to see their belief in her.

Matt shrugged, 'Dillys, one of the Shillabeers' upstairs maids, said that their baby had stayed with Mrs Jolly, Mrs Shillabeer's sister, the whole time she was with us. It's now back with the family.'

'My, my, this is getting stranger and stranger.' Nell shook her head in confusion and sighed. 'So, whose baby died in the fire, if indeed there was a baby?'

'If there was one, it wasn't Mrs Shillabeer's,' Matt said with conviction. 'And what would a lady of her standing be doing with a baby if it wasn't hers? And even stranger,' he continued, 'is that she was looking after it herself. Where was her nursemaid?' Nell frowned and was going to speak but changed her mind. 'I'll tell you where the nursemaid was,' Matt continued, 'she was looking after the Shillabeer baby, who was fit and well, at the house of the Jollys.'

Nell was shaking her head and thinking there couldn't have been a baby upstairs, that Emma must have been mistaken.

Alf placed his arms on the table and asked, 'Has anyone thought how strange it is that Mister Oliver is hanging around in the forest? Why didn't he come back while the mistress was away? It's his house.'

Nell sighed and seemed to shrink. 'It's all too much for me and right now I'm more afraid of what the mistress is going to do to us. I didn't say anything before you left, Matt, but she was threatening to let you go.'

'What, is she mad?' Matt was wide-eyed now.

'I'm beginning to think she is.' Nell sounded worried. If Matt went, who would look after the horses, and would she, still be kept on?

It was around six o'clock that the mistress rang from the drawing room and three minutes later that Nell knocked timidly on the door and awaited her fate. But the mistress seemed preoccupied with her own thoughts. 'Mrs Ames, I should like something light to eat before I retire.'

'Yes, ma'am.'

'And would you send Ames to me immediately?' Nell's sense of doom increased, washing over her in a tidal wave, rendering her muscles to jelly.

'Yes, ma'am.' She backed slowly out of the door, saying no more. It was with tears in her eyes that she told Matt that the mistress wanted to see him straight away.

Moments later Matt stood before his mistress awaiting his fate.

Amelia spoke quickly. 'I want you to travel to London and fetch Mister Redfern; it is a matter of great urgency. I have a letter here that you must put into his hand. Not that of his clerk, but *his* hand. Do you understand?'

'Yes, ma'am. Should I go now or in the morning when it's light?'

'You will leave now. I wish you to be at his office when he arrives tomorrow morning.'

'I'll leave right away, ma'am,' he answered, even though he felt too exhausted to ride to London.

In the kitchen, Nell and Alf waited, hardly able to look at each other. If Matt went, it was the end for them all. The door opened and he strode quickly across the floor to his boots. 'I have to get a horse ready. The mistress wants me to ride to London to fetch her solicitor.'

'Tonight, Matt?' Nell was ruffled. 'But you've only just got back.'

'I know. Don't worry about me, Mother.' He reached for his greatcoat, hanging on the door. 'Just get me some food together, she hasn't offered any money for somewhere to sleep or food. I shall have to find some shelter where I can.'

'I'll get you some food, Matt.' Emma ran to the larder and with shaking hands wrapped ham, bread, cheese and an apple in a cloth. As she returned to the kitchen he was fastening his coat.

'Thank you, Emma. I'm sorry that we haven't had time to talk; things are more than a little strange.'

Minutes later the door closed and he was gone.

'No mention of you, Emma, or getting rid of Matt,' Nell said grimly, knowing that this situation was not yet finished. 'We will have to wait and hope.' She poked at the fire vigorously with the poker and sighed again.

Alf settled himself into a chair next to the heat, unable at the moment to think about his work in the garden. 'There's nothing for it but to wait,' he said, closing his eyes, while Nell filled a kettle and Emma prepared supper for the mistress.

~

Matt didn't hurry, saving his horse that had already travelled a great distance that day. It was some hours later that he reached the outskirts of a farm. In the distance he could see a barn and, beyond that, a stark house surrounded by a collection of drab buildings. He sat quietly, letting his horse rest, and wondered if he should creep into the barn and sleep in the straw, or ask permission of the farmer. When he eventually rode into the farmyard and approached the house it was dark. He knocked nervously on the door, hoping that the farmer wouldn't see him off with a gun.

It was some time before a candle moved behind the window in answer to his intrusive knocks. A sleepy-eyed boy opened the door slowly, his face grey in the candlelight.

'I'm sorry to disturb you but I'm travelling to London and find myself with some distance still to journey. I wondered if your father would let me use the barn for the night to stable my horse.'

'I don't have a father and the farmer's asleep.' The boy started to close the door, withdrawing the candle.

Matt halted the movement by saying quickly, 'Could you ask him if I could sleep in the barn? I've travelled a long way today.' The candle came back to the opening and the boy stared at him with a serious face. The candle left dark shadows around the boy's face and it was hard to see how old he was. But when the boy spoke again he was polite.

'I can't ask him, sir, he's asleep.' Then looked over his shoulder at the sound of a door opening upstairs.

'Who is it, Robert?' A man with unkempt, greasy hair and beard, his features lit eerily by his own candle, stood on the stairs behind the boy.

'It's a traveller, Mister Tate, sir, he wants to stay in the barn with his horse overnight.'

Andrew Tate walked to the door and pulled it open, thrusting his candle at Matt's face. 'Well, let's get a better look at you. What brought you to my farm?'

'I was passing, sir; my horse is tired. I have to be in London early in the morning and it's getting too dark to travel. I'm not asking for food; I have food for my journey, just rest and water for my horse.'

Andrew put his head out of the door and saw the horse standing in the yard, its head drooping.

'You can put it in the barn yonder and water it, then get yourself in here where I can see you.' Andrew's voice was gruff, suspicious.

'Yes, sir, and thank you for your hospitality.' Matt was grateful. He didn't think that he or his horse could go much further. As he hurried to get the horse settled, he wondered why the farmer sounded so aggressive.

On returning to the kitchen he could see by the light of the candle offered to him that unwashed pans were piled on top of a low cupboard. Plates and mugs were scattered about the table. Clothes hung on the backs of chairs in the shadows of the room and boots were scattered on the floor.

The farmer spoke wearily. 'I'll show you where to sleep.'

Matt was taken to a room upstairs in which two small beds stood, both neatly made. 'I won't see you in the morning unless you start early.' And with that the farmer left, closing the door, which didn't shut properly. Matt heard the man's footsteps moving along the landing and watched through the half-open door as the darkness gave way temporarily to the farmer's candle before closing in behind him.

Matt only half undressed and lay on top of one of the beds. He slept until the morning, when light gleamed through the window. As he opened his eyes, he wondered for a moment where he was, then remembered the young boy with the candle and the aggressive farmer. But he'd had a good sleep and hopefully so had his horse.

Standing in the cold morning air Matt drew water from the well in the yard and splashed his face. Finding the water was sweet, he drank deeply. In the barn his horse was standing and ready, having eaten from a rack near the door. After watering the animal, Matt saddled up. Just as he was leading the horse out of the barn the boy appeared, driving a cow out of the milking shed.

'Good morning,' Matt called to him. The boy nodded. 'Would you thank the farmer for his kindness?'

The boy nodded again and slapped the cow's rump with his hand to move her on.

Looking about him in the light of a new day, Matt could see that the place was run down. In the distance he could see that there had been a fire and that half their open barn had been lost. He wondered if they might need another worker. It might be somewhere for him and his mother to settle.

The farmer suddenly appeared from the other side of the yard, pushing a cart of pig muck to the heap that stood steaming in the cool morning air.

'Good morning, Mister Tate,' Matt called, walking his horse in the direction of the farmer. 'I wonder, sir, if you need any more workers. I may be looking for work myself soon.'

Andrew didn't look up as he shovelled the muck from the cart onto the heap. The smell made Matt's eyes water. Horse muck was so much sweeter, he thought.

'I'm not looking for a worker,' Andrew replied irritably.

Even though the man sounded uninterested and his tone seemed final, Matt continued, 'I'm a good worker, sir. I can mend fences and muck out any animal. I'm good with horses. That's my job.' He stared at the farmer's back as he continued the muck shovelling.

'I don't have room for another worker.' Andrew's voice accompanied a grunt as he hefted a full shovel of wet shit to the heap.

'Not even if I work for nothing but my board until you can afford to pay me, sir?'

'*Not even then*.' The farmer threw the spade forcibly into the empty barrow and walked away, not even looking in Matt's direction. The man's actions, Matt felt, said it all. He'd been dismissed.

As he mounted his horse Matt called, 'Thank you for your hospitality, sir. On my way back from London might I call again?'

In response, Andrew shrugged. Matt took that as a yes and rode on happily, waving to Robert as he left the farm.

~

As Matt rode across the Thames, with its dark water littered with rubbish, he wondered how deep it was and noted a narrow shingle beach. There were an assortment of ships in full sail, and he watched mesmerised as men worked furiously to get the masts lowered before they reached the bridge. Then felt dizzy as they sailed smoothly below him, the ship appearing bit by bit, until it was clear of the bridge and the men were again raising the masts. He was, though, more impressed by a shallop, painted red and gold with a single mast being rowed at speed up river. There were many boats, and oars spewed the water, as strong men rowed goods and businessmen to their destinations along the river. Perhaps he could do something like that, he thought. Larger barges packed with goods pulled smaller barges behind them in which horses were housed, ready to be disembarked and harnessed up to pull the boat through shallow tides or along a towpath. His knowledge of horses might stand in his favour here, if he could get a job. He nodded his head thoughtfully, storing what he was seeing for the future.

London would have enjoyed the late autumnal sunshine had the rays been able to penetrate between the tightly packed houses and narrow streets. He had never seen so many horses and carriages. How, he wondered, did they not crash into each other? The noise was deafening: with horses neighing, horseshoes clattering, wheels rumbling and rattling and street vendors clamouring for the attention of passers-by, shouting against each other, selling their wares.

A man in a long red coat was selling oysters to a queue of people from a barrow at the side of the road. And an elderly woman in a blue shawl sat on the steps of a church selling

235

flowers from a basket as the church bells rang out over the street noise. Stopping the horse, he watched as two blackened men delivered coal to a house from the back of a flat cart, and a man in a tattered hat adorned with feathers walked the edge of the street, selling ink. Poor men in clogs were out on foot and rich men were travelling in their carriages. All before him was constant sound and movement. He wasn't sure if he was excited to be in London or frightened.

As he travelled further into the town, he passed through tight darker back streets where the roads were of hard-packed earth and the buildings leant against each other for support. Dirty children with large eyes and sharp cheek bones that played and argued in these back streets looked nothing like the children he saw in the countryside. Coming upon an open square that divided four narrow streets, he stopped the horse. He was trying to make up his mind which street to take when his horse suddenly shied away from three growling dogs. Muzzles drawn back, sharp teeth exposed, they made the horse nervous and it almost trampled the people around it as it backed away. Matt tried to gain control, ignoring the shouts of anger aimed at him. The flea-bitten and hungry dogs fought ferociously over a bone in the gutter, dispersing a cloud of flies. Covering his mouth and nose against the awful stink of this place, Matt rode his nervous horse onwards, not knowing where he was. Around him, adults, men and women, hung about on street corners smoking their pipes and yelling to each other in voices that were harsh to Matt's ears.

After asking directions twice, he found his way to Bloomsbury, where magnificent houses surrounded pristine squares, edged with newly planted trees, so different from what he had earlier passed through. Here, the sun caressed the windows set in the white painted facades of three-storey houses. Recently washed steps were as clean as bedsheets, while highly polished doorknobs and nameplates glinted in the morning sunlight.

He knew that Mister Redfern's office was secreted in a building on the edge of Bloomsbury Park. And on finding the address Matt rang the bell. A young maid opened the door but at seeing him she looked annoyed.

'Get yourself to the tradesmen's entrance at the back' she shouted and began to close the door, muttering, 'Some people just don't know their place.'

Matt put his foot in the doorway and pushed against the wood with his hand. 'I have a message for Mister Redfern from Mistress Brack of the Claydon Estate.' He raised expectant eyebrows.

Her face became flushed with anger, her jaw tightened as she almost spat the words. 'Then take it to the back of the house and give it to his clerk.'

Matt stood his ground. 'I'm sorry, but I have strict instructions to give the message direct into Mister Redfern's hand.'

The girl sighed. 'Have you made an appointment?' Her eyebrows were now raised as she glared at him.

'No, there was no time to make an appointment.' He was already feeling out of place in London and this haughty maid was making him feel like a naughty child. She thrust her face forward, eyes bulging like a toad, and spoke slowly, emphasising each word as though he were stupid.

'Then go to the back of the house... and see... his clerk.' She closed the door loudly, and with a finality that dared Matt to knock on it again.

Walking back down the steps he found a passage that ran at the side of the building leading into a yard surrounded by a high wall. The back of the property wasn't nearly as prosperous-looking as the front. The yard had been filled with rubbish, including broken furniture where rats had made nests. There was only one door and Matt noted that the paint on it was poorly applied. He pulled the black bell handle fixed on the wall beside the door and stepped back. Somewhere in the distant dark passages beneath the house, a bell resounded. Matt waited patiently. It was some minutes before the door was opened by a small man with a large pox-pitted nose and tired red eyes.

Matt looked down upon the man's thin hair and noted his scuffed shoes and ink-stained hands. 'I'm looking for Mister Redfern's clerk,' he said hopefully.

'You found him. I'm Lack, Mister Redfern's clerk. How can I help you?' The voice was stiff, his pale face unwelcoming.

'I have a message from my mistress, Miss Brack of Claydon House.'

'What form does the message take?' The little man sounded impatient and for a moment Matt stared at him, not knowing his meaning. 'Letter or word?' the man spoke sharply.

'A letter, sir, it's in the form of a letter.'

Lack held out his hand. 'I will see that Mister Redfern receives it.'

Matt stood his ground. 'I'm sorry, but my mistress, Miss Brack, insists that I deliver it into Mister Redfern's hands myself.'

Lack sighed and turned stiffly, saying, 'Follow me.'

Stepping into the narrow passage, Matt closed the door and followed Lack into a room where a tall desk and stool were surrounded by heaps of papers and books. The room smelt musty and even at this early hour candle smoke from a large candle on the desk crept across the blackened ceiling. Piles of books with well-worn covers formed uncertain columns against the walls; some leant perilously.

'Wait here.' Lack indicated his office and carried on up the passage.

Matt stood as indicated, beside the man's desk, as Lack shuffled away to speak to his master. He heard muffled voices as he noted that the writing on a piece of vellum on Lack's desk was written beautifully, artistically, with many of the letters exaggerated with embellished swirls. How Matt wished that he had gone to school and learnt to write. Where would he be now if he could write like that?

A cough made Matt look up. His face automatically flushed with guilt. He knew what it must look like. He defended himself quickly. 'I wasn't reading it, sir. I can't read. But it is the most beautiful script I have ever seen.'

'Thank you, sir.' Lack's tiny eyes stared suspiciously a moment longer than was necessary before he spoke again. 'Mister Redfern will see you now.'

The room on the other side of the partition wall enjoyed the only narrow window through which light might once have penetrated. Matt was sure it had never been opened, as the only piece of its glass showing above the books and papers piled against it, was covered in a curtain of thick, grey cobwebs. Candles permanently lit Mister Redfern's room, as the amount of wax covering what must once have been candlesticks, and now appeared as bizarre wax sculptures, showed. His large desk was also surrounded by paper and books, just like his clerk's. Bookshelves lined the walls from floor to ceiling and the leather-bound books upon them gave the room a cosy copper hue in the candlelight, even though it was early morning.

The solicitor, dressed in black, looked up from a large document that almost covered his entire desk and raised an eyebrow expectantly.

'My name is Ames, sir.' Matt bowed in respect. 'I bring a letter from my mistress and employer, Mistress Brack of the Claydon Estate.'

Although the man behind the desk wore a long white wig, his face was not old. Holding out a delicate hand, he took the letter in silence. He read it solemnly while Matt waited. Mister Redfern sighed deeply and, folding the letter, placed it in his desk drawer. Then, folding a large sheet of paper into eight, he proceeded to cut along the folds with a knife as Matt watched with interest. Taking an eighth of the cut paper, he began to write, dipping his pen often in the blue glass ink-pot that sat on his desk. After blotting the letter, he folded and sealed it with wax before handing it to Matt.

'You will carry this letter to your mistress, Ames.'

As Matt bowed, Mister Redfern delved into his jacket pocket. 'And here is a penny to get yourself something to eat, young man.'

Matt, whose stomach had been growling for the past hour, was grateful for the man's kindness. 'Thank you, sir.' He slipped the penny into his own pocket as the man acknowledged Matt's thanks with a nod and went back to studying the document on his desk.

~

On his way back through the winding streets, Matt passed a coffee house filled with well-dressed men partaking of breakfast, drinking and undertaking business transactions, some loudly and others secretly in dark corners. He moved on, thinking that his penny would not be enough for food in that establishment. He was doing well finding his way back until a broken cart blocked his way in one narrow lane and a fallen house in another made him detour until he realised that he was completely lost and became worried for himself and his horse. People jeered and jostled him, calling out, 'Oy, toff, 'ow much d'ya want for the 'orse?' Greedy, sunken eyes, set in dirty, pitted faces, watched his progress and he was glad not to be on foot even though riding was difficult in the tight spaces. After seeing so much poverty in the town he vowed never again to think himself poor.

As he passed down Hare Lane he noticed a butcher's shop with rabbits hanging from a pole above the shop window and chickens in full feather hanging from hooks by their scrawny feet around the doorway, but it was the smell of food cooking that drew him to the window, where cooked pies were on sale for a halfpenny each. Getting down and holding tight to the horse's reins with one hand, he bought two of the small pies from the woman who was placing them in the window. She had the most beautiful black hair and fleetingly reminded him of someone, but he couldn't think who. She called over her shoulder as she picked up paper to wrap his pies. 'Nona, please bring more pies as soon as they're cool.'

'Yes, Mother,' the voice of a young girl answered from somewhere inside. Another woman looked through the opening of the inner door, saying, 'Martha, we will have to send James to order more flour.'

The woman, called Martha, finished wrapping Matt's pies and handed them to him with a kind smile. He took them, but couldn't take his eyes from her face. She stared back as though reading his thoughts. 'Take the next turning right and then walk past the next three turnings on your right. Don't turn left and you'll come to the bridge over the water.'

He thanked her for her advice but it wasn't until he was on his way with one of the pies in his hand and the other safely stored in his pouch that he realised that he hadn't asked her a question.

26.

Haddenford

Andrew had been silent and moody since all the changes and John Brisket could only guess at what was going on in his head. To have lost a wife and child was bad enough but to also lose the farm would be the end for Andrew Tate. John felt unsettled. Would he soon be looking for work elsewhere? He had no family to which he could return and each morning he wondered if the farm and his job would survive.

It was while he and Robert were clearing the charred straw and wood from what was left of the barn that John saw something flapping in the wind on the thorn hedge. Going over to it for a better look, he found that it was a piece of material.

'What you got there, Mister Brisket?'

'Not sure, Robert, but it looks like a piece of someone's coat.'

Robert came nearer and John held it out to him. 'Looks like someone caught their coat on the thorns, Mister Brisket, but who would be walking in this field?'

'There're some heavy footprints too,' John said, as he scratched his chin.

'I've seen material like that before, Mister Brisket, but I can't remember whose coat it was.'

'I think we should take it and show Mister Tate, Robert, see what he thinks.'

They found Andrew in a far field with a horse and a flat cart. Standing on the cart, he had his back to them, throwing manure from a pitchfork onto the ground.

'Mister Tate, sir,' John called. 'I think we've found something.'

Andrew slapped the horse's rump so that he moved on a way and carried on forking the muck.

'Sir.' John came abreast of the cart. 'I found this piece of material caught in the hedge near the barn while we were clearing.' He handed it up and Andrew bent down and took the material, staring at it before shrugging his shoulders and handing it back.

John pulled his hands away, refusing to take it. 'There were also footprints leading from the hedge to the barn,' he said pointedly.

'So, it was deliberate then. Someone means to ruin me.' Andrew frowned, trying to understand why anyone would want to ruin a farmer already struggling to survive. Unless of course they wanted to make an offer for the land at next to nothing on the pretence of easing the poor farmer's burden from debt.

'It seems so.' John's voice broke in over Andrew's thoughts. 'What shall we do about it, sir?'

'Let's find him first and then think about who to tell. We have to prove it. We can't just go accusing people.' He turned to continue spreading the muck when Robert, who until now had stayed silent, suddenly remembered something.

'Mister Beemer has a coat like that.' Robert sounded excited.

'Beemer?' Andrew said looking at Robert. 'Why would it be him? He is a pillar of the church and has no truck with me.'

'He has a coat like this.' Robert pointed at the material. 'I know he has.'

'No, Robert.' Andrew shook his head. 'You must be wrong. But I will go and see the vicar tomorrow. He sees many people on his daily rounds and he might recognise it.'

At eleven o'clock the following day Andrew Tate was standing on the vicar's doorstep, having rung the bell. It was the

Draycotts' housekeeper who answered the door. Her voice gave away her surprise.

'Mister Tate! Please come in.' She held the door wide, smiling.

Andrew hesitated. 'Is Mister Draycott at home?'

'Yes, sir, he's in the garden. Please come in and wait while I fetch him.'

Andrew was shown into a large and comfortable, although shabby receiving room and at that very moment Ernest Draycott arrived, wiping his hands on an apron.

'Please excuse how I look, Andrew,' he smiled 'I like to help the gardener. A little physical work gives me a great deal of pleasure.'

Andrew attempted a smile. He knew about physical work and it didn't give him any pleasure.

'As you may know, sir,' Andrew addressed the man, 'we had a fire and I lost a lot of valuable winter feed kept for my stock.'

'Yes, yes indeed, Andrew, a terrible business,' and then continued quickly. 'If I can help in any way please let me know.'

Andrew coughed and continued. 'While clearing the ground after the fire my foreman found this piece of material impaled on a hedge in our field leading from the lane to my barn.' He handed the material to the vicar, who stared at it and wondered why it was being shown to him. 'As no one but myself and John should have been in that field, this had no reason to be there in the hedge.' He took a breath before saying, 'I believe that my barn may have been set alight on purpose sir.'

Ernest look shocked and then worried. 'You realise the implications of what you are saying, Andrew?'

'Yes, Vicar. Someone may have started it deliberately and I want to find that person.'

Ernest ignored him, and his face was grave as he continued. 'The implication of pointing the finger at an innocent man, Andrew, is grave indeed. The law says that setting fire to a building, or even just a sheaf of straw, is now a hanging offence.

And, if proved, the likely consequence will be that someone hangs.'

Andrew considered what he had just heard. 'I didn't know that, sir. But it makes no difference. If someone is out to destroy me and my livelihood, then he must face the law.'

Ernest opened his mouth to speak but at that same moment his wife entered and seeing her husband busy she smiled at them both. 'Oh, I am sorry, I didn't know that you had a visitor, Ernest. Good morning, Mister Tate,' she acknowledged.

Emily's eyes fell on the material held in her husband's hand and her face became wreathed in an excited smile and she clapped her hands in joy. 'How wonderful,' she exclaimed. 'Where did you get that? It's just what I need.' Both men stared at her, bewildered. 'Oh, please forgive me.' She looked uncomfortable. 'I didn't mean to interrupt. It's just that Mister Beemer had torn his coat and left it for the charity. Mrs Pendell was going to mend it with some wool, but we hadn't managed to find the right colour and here is the very piece.'

Alarmed by their change of expression, Emily stopped and looked at one man and then the other. 'Have I spoken out of turn, sirs?'

'No, no, not at all,' Ernest assured her kindly. 'Would you ask Mrs Pendell to bring the coat here so that we may examine it, my dear?'

'Yes, of course, Ernest.' She sounded puzzled and Ernest could see that his wife could not understand how a piece of material could bring about such seriousness in both men.

When Mrs Pendell bustled in carrying the coat, she was also very pleased to see the piece of material held in Ernest's hand.

'This coat will make such a difference to someone this winter, Mister Draycott, sir. I understand that you have the material that is missing.' And she held the coat up by the shoulders so that the men could see the gap that matched the material in Ernest's hand.

The men looked at the coat and then at each other with faces that did not hold the glee that she felt. 'I'm afraid, Mrs Pendell,' Ernest said, 'that we have to keep the coat for a while.'

Her smile fell away and she sounded almost petulant as she exclaimed, 'But sir!' Her eyes didn't leave the material in the vicar's hand until she said, 'Why?'

Ernest did not feel like giving her any more explanation. He didn't want gossip spreading around the church or the village; after all, Beemer might be innocent. He might have an explanation. So he said, 'You may have it back when we are finished with it. Thank you, Mrs Pendell.'

The little woman turned abruptly, her skirts rustling her dissatisfaction as she left the room. She did not like being dismissed in such a manner without explanation. It wasn't like the vicar to be so sharp, and he a man of God. It must, she decided, be the influence of that disagreeable man from Tate Farm, and she banged the kitchen door hard behind her to show her displeasure.

'Where is Beemer to be found?' Andrew asked angrily.

I'm sorry, Andrew, but he has left the area. I understand from the widow Fearling that he may be on his way to London.'

'London? Why?' Andrew was puzzled.

I really don't know. After he lost his job he lost his home. We gave him a room here; we felt it was the duty of the church to support him. I gave him a little work keeping the parish records and such, but perhaps it wasn't enough for him.'

'When did he leave?'

'Only yesterday,' Ernest said quickly, as Andrew turned away sharply and was already making for the door. 'Remember what I said, Andrew,' Ernest called after him. 'You have to be certain.'

On leaving the vicarage Andrew didn't know what to do next. But, by the time he arrived home, he had decided to talk it over with John before he made any decisions.

John was in a field harnessing the horse to the plough, calling to it to steady as it kicked against the chains. 'Robert was right, John,' Andrew said coming alongside him and stroking the horse to calm him. 'It was Beemer's coat.'

'But why?' John was amazed. 'What reason would Beemer have had to set fire to our barn?'

Andrew shrugged, also bewildered. 'We only see the man in church. He has nothing to do with us at all. I don't think that I have ever spoken more than two words to him in passing.' John looked as puzzled as Andrew. 'I don't know why' – Andrew's voice was sad – 'but he's gone, moved away or run away, what difference does it make?'

'Where has he gone?' John asked.

'To London!'

'Mother's gone to London.' Andrew hadn't seen Robert approaching and ignored the boy.

'Should we pursue him or tell the constable?' John asked, standing up straight and stretching his back. At last the horse was attached to the plough.

'I don't see the use of telling anyone now that Beemer is out of the area, John.' Andrew chewed the side of his face, feeling helpless. 'And we can't leave the farm, there's too much to do.'

'I could look after the animals,' Robert said, trying to be helpful.

Andrew's smile was thin as he looked at Martha's son. 'No, not on your own you couldn't, Robert, there's far too much work here for one person, even if it is only looking after the animals until I get back.'

'I think, sir,' John said, 'that we should tell the constable and show him the evidence, just in case Beemer comes back here and tries something else. At least we have proof he was in our field.'

Andrew pushed a hand through his hair and looked desperate. The word screaming in his head over and over was *why?* 'My head's buzzing, John. Let's leave the decision for a while. I have to think it through.' Andrew hadn't felt this low in spirit since the day that he had considered taking his own life. And at this very moment he knew that he didn't have a fit mind to work out the best solution to this problem on his own, any more than he had the last time, when Martha rescued him from his intended fate. However, something had changed in him, a determination to keep his farm, and his inheritance.

27.

London

Beemer stood uncomfortably on the bridge overlooking the Thames and felt out of place in his Sunday best. On both sides of the river there were buildings as far as the eye could see. A muddle of houses, a jumble of roofs and church spires, the like of which he could not have imagined, spread before him. He had never seen so many houses or people in one place. How would he find the Tilby woman amongst this mass of people, and they walked so fast; where were they all going? Even the Thames was a width of which he could never have dreamt and it was also full of people in boats. Walking to the end of the bridge, he approached a man and asked if he knew Martha Tilby.

'Sorry guv, never 'eard of 'er,' and the man walked on without stopping. Barney walked around all day trying to catch sight of Martha and as the day came to its close he realised he would have to sleep somewhere and eat; he was hungry.

Entering one of the many taverns, he bought a dish of broth, some bread and some ale. It was more expensive than he had imagined and he soon realised that unless he could make a friend he would have to return home sooner than he'd hoped. The tavern was noisy, full of traders and sailors and the gin and ale flowed like the river outside. He ordered a small beer as women moved around the tables in low-cut gowns, their faces heavily flushed with rouge. He smiled to himself as he wondered what Mrs Fearling would say at the sight of them.

'Allo, darlin, just come up from the country 'ave we?' He felt her arm slide across his shoulder and looked up into what might once have been a pretty face but was now heavily painted with rouge and paint to cover the sign of the pox.

'You're very perceptive, madam; indeed, I have just arrived from the country and am looking for a cheap place to stay for the night.'

'Ooh big words, and polite. I like you, darlin', do you 'ave any money?'

'Yes, a little,' he said, touching his pocket. 'I have enough for a room.'

'Well, you just come along with me, I 'ave a room where we can be cosy 'til morning.' Winking at him, she nodded towards the door.

Finishing his beer in one swig he followed her into the street, feeling pleased with his good luck. She took his arm, smiling up at him with yellow teeth. Her breath almost made him reel. Staring down at her heaving breasts as they walked, he felt a thrill of movement starting in his breeches and was already planning what he would do to her.

'Up 'ere,' she said, turning him into a dark alley, 'I live up 'ere.' He'd only taken three steps into the dimness when two men hidden in the shadows slammed him against the wall. Taken by surprise Beemer didn't have time to lash out before a blow to his head sent him reeling. When he came to his senses he was lying in the filth of the alley floor with rats running over him as though he were part of the slimy ground. He jumped, as whiskers touched his face. Standing up quickly out of fear, he held his pounding head, feeling dizzy, then sick. It was as he leant on the wall for support that he noticed that his clothes were in disarray and that he'd been robbed. He cursed himself for going off with the first person that offered him help and felt stupid and angry.

He stood at the corner of the alley looking out at the street. If he saw her again he'd give her what for. He'd teach her very quickly what he was made of. From the shadows he watched a drunk weaving along the street, singing softly to himself. Then two men stepped from a doorway and grabbed the hapless man, dragging him off towards the river. Barney sank back into the darkness; he hadn't realised that London was such a dangerous place.

A voice behind him said, 'That's 'im done for, off to sea to fight the Frenchies, never to be 'eard of again, I s'pect.'

'What?' Barney turned quickly and could just make out the face of a man sitting under a cloth in the dark shadows.

'Them sailors wait for the drunks and then drag 'em off to work on their ships, never to be seen again by kif nor kin,' he said through broken teeth.

Barney indicated uselessly at the state of his clothes. 'I was attacked, my money's been taken,' he grizzled.

'Yeah, I saw 'em do it.'

'You saw them and you didn't help me?' Barney was incredulous.

''Elp yer? Huh, not me, matey, I don't want to die. Yer was lucky they didn't cut yer up wiv a knife. Only yesterday I saw 'em cut up a...'

But Barney wasn't listening 'I don't have anywhere to sleep tonight,' he whined to the man in the shadows. He had never felt so lost, or alone.

The man under the cloth laughed, a harsh sound that forced its way through his hollow body, escaping through his broken teeth into the night air. 'That's both of us then, matey, and many more,' and pulling the cloth over his head he disappeared into the pile of waste in which he lay.

~

Barney awoke around midday with a start. He thought he'd been awake all night, watching the street, unnoticed, but somehow,

251

he had almost lost a day. He felt disorientated as he sat amidst the rubbish, feeling exposed to all who passed by, waiting for someone with a knife to come and cut his throat. The man under the cloth made him nervous with his loud and constant snoring.

Barney was hungry and his back was stiff as he walked from the alley. His clothes were now crumpled and stained but when he realised that he was beginning to look like everyone else he felt better about it. His Sunday best had been a mistake.

He walked aimlessly towards the river, not knowing what to do or where to go. A hungry stranger in his own land. Squinting against the sun's glare on the sparkling surface of the filthy water, he had to remind himself of his goal. She's here somewhere and I will find her. But first he needed to search for food and he would, get some; whatever it took, he would get some.

Some hours later and still hungry, Barney sat on the edge of a horse trough watching the people and waiting for an opportunity to steal something. But he had competition. There were many street urchins working the crowds.

He took a long drink from the water trough. It helped to fill his stomach. As he came up for air, his face dripping with water, he saw her, a woman in a tatty red dress stalking a man. The gentleman, who was fashionably dressed, had just alighted from a coach and was standing with his bag at his feet. Barney watched as she circled her unsuspecting prey like a cat waiting for the mouse to move.

The man looked up at the buildings before bending to pick up his bag, and as he did so, she was there and gone in a trice with his wallet. Full of admiration, Barney followed her along the street and saw her turn into a passageway between an alehouse and a shop. Although he had hurried after her, by the time he arrived the high-walled passage was empty.

He walked its length, finding that it ended abruptly, cut across by the wall of a house. Looking about he saw that there were only two doors at ground level and one above reached by wooden stairs. Hiding beneath the stairs, he settled down to wait.

His stomach was groaning mercilessly by the time the door above opened, revealing a woman in a red dress, who flounced down the stairs that creaked beneath her shoes. At the bottom she gave a little swish of her skirt, revealing a dirty lace petticoat beneath, and walked lightly towards the street. But she didn't reach it. Barney launched his body out of the shadows beneath the stairs, knocking her against the wall. His thick arm pressed across her neck with ease, choking her. He smiled knowingly into her face and was surprised that she was younger than he'd thought.

'I saw you today stealing from a gentleman.' She made no move. 'I know where he is.' Barney's face was so close to hers that his saliva fell on her mouth. 'Now I know where you live. I could get a constable. Tell him what you did. Unless, that is, you let me in on it.' He released the pressure slightly on her neck so that she could speak, but she didn't answer him, only stared defiantly into his face.

'Well?' He could feel anger sweeping over him. How dare she look at him with such derision?

'Go then, get the constable,' she spat back, eyes glaring, chin pushed forward. 'I'd like to see yer try it.'

Barney was unsure what to do next; he had never come up against such a woman. To show her who was in charge he started to lift her skirt with his spare hand. His breath came hot and fast on her face as he spoke. 'Perhaps,' he smirked, 'this will teach you to be more civil to your betters.'

The girl smiled into his tiny eyes and watched in fascination the confusion that crossed his sweaty brow. 'Goodbye,' she said coolly.

Before the surprise he felt had even reached his face, he was felled by the iron hand of Scarlet Bateman, the girl's mother, chopping into the side of his neck with a hand that could belong to no delicate lady.

Much later he awoke, lying on a floor, his feet tied together and with his hands tied to the legs of a bed. He groaned at the pain in his neck and ear.

'So yer awake. I should cut out your tongue for attacking my daughter.'

A voluptuous woman in a red dress stood over him. But what he noticed first was the knife held in her hand that was pointed towards his throat.

'I'm hungry woman. I will do anything to get food.' Anger rose in his chest; no woman would have him at a disadvantage. He nodded towards Moll Bateman. 'I saw her steal from the gentleman and thought I could have some of it.' The younger woman stood behind her mother, watching Barney with interest.

The older woman looked at him with distaste. 'Did yer?' She raised an eyebrow in mock surprise. 'Well, yer ain't going to get your own way 'ere and threats will only find yer floating face down in the river.' She placed a dainty boot on his thigh and pressed down. 'Understand?' He squirmed, but said nothing. Moving the heel of her boot into his groin she twisted it, pressing down. 'Do yer understand, or ain't yer listening?' Her voice was low, her eyes cold.

'Yes,' he groaned reluctantly. 'But for pity's sake, give me some food.'

She turned to her daughter and nodded towards their captive. 'Get 'im some broth, Moll, but don't untie 'im.'

The girl moved to a pot hanging over the fire and poured brown liquid into a bowl. Taking some bread from the table, she knelt on the floor beside him, putting the bowl to his lips. It was warm and he drank it fast. In all his life he had never been so hungry. The bread pushed bit by bit into his mouth had never tasted so good and he wondered as he ate, how he was going to get the better of these two women. But Scarlet was talking to him again.

'Now, what are we going to do with you? We can't let a dangerous man who knows where we live go free, now, can we?'

'I won't say anything.' Barney mumbled through the bread. 'I just needed some food.' He struggled against his bonds, but they were tight, and he cursed.

'What's your name?' Scarlet asked. But Barney tightened his lips. 'Don't want to say, eh? Well, it doesn't matter for now. We've to go out; when we come back we'll decide what we'll do with you.'

Barney watched in fascination as the two women dressed themselves in gowns, hats and stoles, clothes that they took from a trunk. When they'd left, he struggled against his bonds, but lack of food had left him weak and the small amount of food he'd consumed had made him sleepy.

Waking some hours later he watched the two women, who were now sitting at the table with their backs to him, giggling as they tipped out a purse and investigated the contents. Moll held up a gold watch and chain. Something was obviously funny as they laughed a great deal, but Barney couldn't work it out.

'You'll take these things to the Jews in Duke's Place tomorrow, Moll. A good haul with the thirty guineas from the purses.'

'He's awake, Scarlet.' Moll had noticed the movement on the floor as Barney tried to get a better look at what was on the table.

'So 'e is. Well, Mister Nobody, we have decided that yer can work with us. We need a man to accompany us around town.'

'Doing what?' He wasn't sure that he wanted their company; after all, they had threatened to kill him. He didn't want to spend the rest of his life looking over his shoulder. He just wanted to find the Tilby woman.

'It's nothing too much for such a frail creature as yourself, Mister Nobody. All we want you to do is walk with us in the park.' And they laughed like it was a joke.

'Untie me, woman.' He was angry now: no woman was going to treat him like this. 'I'm getting cramp in my legs,' he whined.

'Sorry. Yer ain't to be trusted. Scarlet smiled with a raised eyebrow. 'Yer might take it into your 'ead to murder us frail women in our bed.'

'I won't. I promise.' He tried to smile, but his small eyes and slack mouth told a different story to the women, who were well aware of the treachery of men.

Scarlet looked at him, Barney thought, for an uncomfortably long moment before saying, 'Moll, tie 'im by 'is neck to the hearth in the other room. He can lie there fer tonight.'

With hands and legs still tied, Barney was dragged unceremoniously by the women into a small room and made to lie face down on the floorboards beside the hearth. A piece of cord was put around his neck and he was tied by many knots to a black metal ring in the wall of the hearth.

The night passed uncomfortably for Barney, who ached in every muscle and feared choking himself on the rope. The women arose late next morning. It had been light a long time before he heard them moving about in the next room. He listened to the fire being raked and pots dragged across the iron bars. He flinched as the front door banged shut, and heard footsteps on the wooden stairs. It was some hours before the footsteps returned and Scarlet opened the door to his room.

'Well, Mister Nobody, I hope yer had a comfortable night?'

Barney ignored her; what he wanted was to know his fate and get his hands around her neck. 'What are you going to do with me?' he growled.

'Well, ain't you the chirpy bird?' She untied the knots at his neck. 'Come and eat, I 'ave something to discuss with yer.' She helped him to his feet and he followed her, shuffling with difficulty into the main room where he was surprised to see the table was now full of food. Meat, bread, oysters and ale were offered to him as he sat down.

One hand was released and they watched with disgust and amusement as he attacked the food, pushing it into his slack mouth by the handful until he was full. Feeling better, he turned to Scarlet. 'What do you want me to do?'

Scarlet tutted loudly. 'Yer've already guessed what we do.' Her index finger stroked the front of her neck as though she was still debating. 'We need a man to accompany us so we're not recognised. Do yer want to play?'

'What's in it for me?' He was still angry, but interested, aware that he needed somewhere to stay and that he would not last long without friends.

She nodded. 'I will give you a place to stay and food.' She watched his face closely.

'What do I have to do?' he repeated. He wasn't going to make any quick decisions; he could go along with them, lie to them, steal their loot and live a better life; they were only women.

'Just walk with me in St James's Park, that's all.' Scarlet smiled sweetly and moved to the trunk pulling out some gentleman's clothes. 'I'll untie yer if yer agree. But any funny business and you'll feel me knife in yer innards.' Her face had become a serious mask as she spoke. Her eyes were cold and he believed everything that she said. He could see that she really believed that she could get the better of him. He nodded agreement; he'd agree to anything to be free of the bindings that were cutting off his circulation.

When Moll had removed his bonds, Scarlet threw the clothes at him. 'Put 'em on, let's see 'ow yer look.'

The clothes he noted were expensive, there was even an ivory-topped cane. And when he was dressed, washed and clean-shaven the women liked what they saw. Moll dressed up as a servant, while Scarlet pushed a bundle under her petticoats and, pulling on a smart coat and hat, was transformed into a pregnant woman.

As Barney walked with Scarlet and Moll in the park he felt good, although apprehensive. There were crowds of people walking between Spring Gardens and St James's Park. Happy people taking the air. Scarlet had chosen the place well.

Suddenly, and with great dignity, Scarlet folded and fell to the ground wailing. Barney didn't know what to do while Moll in her role as servant bent over her mistress and called for help. A crowd surrounded them and, while they all gave advice, Moll cut purses from cords and lifted gold watches. Scarlet recovered, thanking everyone for their kindness, and was helped away by Moll as Barney called a hansom cab. Inside the cab Scarlet got rid of the bundle beneath her petticoats, throwing it out of the window to the poor.

Back home they spread the haul on the table. Barney was shaking with a feeling that he had never experienced before; it had been frightening and exhilarating; he wanted more. The women worked through the proceeds. Four gold watches, five purses, two wallets and a gold buckle inlaid with diamonds. The purses and wallets netted them one hundred and twenty guineas. Barney stared at the rich pile on the table and his eyes grew greedy. The money was put to one side and Moll was instructed to take the buckle to Duke's Place and get a good price. Gathering it up, she left the room.

'What do I get?' Barney asked sullenly.

'You know whatcha get.' Scarlet's voice was soft as she gathered the money to count it again.

'Yeah, well, it's not enough if I'm risking my neck.'

'Yer as guilty as us now, Mister Nobody; food and roof, that was the agreement and I'm going to call yer Nobby, as yer won't tell yer name.'

Moll came back with money from the haul and then she and Scarlet went off together to buy more food and clothes, taking the money and leaving Barney to think.

The following day, Scarlet, dressed as a lady, Moll as her servant and Barney dressed as a footman approached a genteel home in the East End of town. The two women had been watching a narrow townhouse for some weeks. It was a small house, occupied by a woman and two servants. The woman's husband, they had found out, worked away on the ships.

From the park opposite the house they watched as the cook and the maid set out for their usual afternoon stroll.

Scarlet and Moll approached the house and Scarlet feigned a faint on the bottom step of the property. Moll knocked heavily on the door in a panic. The mistress of the house, a gentle soul, opened the door herself and looked alarmed. 'Please could you help us? My mistress has fainted,' Moll sobbed.

'Oh dear.' The woman looked up the road for her servants but they were not in sight.'

Moll could see that the woman was flustered, being alone, and not knowing what she should do. Scarlet moaned loudly and as they had hoped the woman asked them in. 'Come in and sit awhile until you feel better.' Her hands fluttered, she looked pale and at a loss.

Scarlet was taken to a front parlour and, while the gentle woman looked in a room upstairs for smelling salts and remedies, Scarlet was searching through the drawers of the furniture downstairs. Moll, who had made her way to the kitchen, removed a pepperbox and silver-topped salt cellar along with six silver spoons, placing them in her bag.

Barney arrived with a hired landau as arranged and waited at the door. Scarlet then revived very quickly and thanked the woman, saying, 'You have been so kind; you must dine with me next Thursday. I can think of no better way to show my gratitude.' Moll helped Scarlet into the landau and they laughed all the way home with their hoard, it had been so easy.

As Barney drove them through the streets, neatly avoiding oncoming carriages, he watched for Martha. One day he would see her and he was ready; not only that, but he had a plan, a plan that made him smile and would probably bring Martha to her knees, and he would enjoy that.

'What do you think,' Barney asked Scarlet, on their return, 'about the help of a child?'

'What do yer mean, a child?' she frowned.

'We could change our image again, look like a family with a child.'

'I like that,' Scarlet nodded. 'Yer earning yer keep, Nobby, it won't be too difficult to get a child. There's plenty of hungry urchins out there and parents what would sell 'um.'

'Good,' Barney smirked. 'I will get the child.' It was left to him.

Several days later, the trio were out working the streets when they came upon a crowd in Covent Garden Market watching a street entertainer. Moll couldn't pass up an opportunity and as she lifted a gentleman's coat tail an off-duty Bow Street Runner saw her in the act. At his warning shout she ran off through the crowd. A woman turned and looked at Scarlet. 'Ain't she with you?' she shouted accusingly, getting the attention of those nearby.

'No.' Scarlet shook her head. 'Yer mistaken, madam.'

'I'm sure I seen you two together t'other day.'

'You are wrong, madam, I ain't never been 'ere before.'

The woman ignored Scarlet's denial and turned to her husband. ''Ere, Reg.' She tugged at her husband's sleeve. 'Ain't this the woman yer saw 'anging around with the young un who just ran off t'other day?'

Others in the crowd were turning to look and Scarlet started to leave.

'She looks guilty as 'ell,' the woman shouted. 'Let's see what's in 'er purse.' The woman's hands, covered in sores, moved to pull Scarlet's purse from her, as Barney faded away into a back street.

'Yer touch my purse and I'll call a Runner and 'ave yer for theft,' Scarlet spat at the woman and stood her ground, eyes flashing and defiant. She saw the woman hesitate and realised that she wasn't sure, perhaps Scarlet was innocent and taking her purse would, look like stealing.

'Leave 'er, Gladys; if she's a wrong un, the kid'll squawk when they put a noose round 'er neck.'

Her husband dismissed the incident with a look of disgust and he and Gladys turned back to the entertainment.

Barney and Scarlet met back at the room. It felt hollow and silent without Moll and Scarlet paced the floor at speed.

'Perhaps we should get out,' Barney said nervously. 'It seems daft staying here waiting for the Runners to come and find us.'

'No.' Scarlet's voice was low. 'I ain't going without knowing what's 'appened to Moll.'

The tension rose as the hours went by. Afraid to light a candle, they sat in the darkness. Scarlet silently made plans and worried about Moll. In the unnerving darkness Barney thought only of himself. He wanted to make a plan but his brain had frozen with fear. Nothing came to him. He should run while he could, but somehow, like a moth attracted to a flame, he waited.

It was in the grey early hours that a sound froze the blood in their veins. A movement outside the door, a shuffling and then silence.

'What do you think it is?' Barney had paled; he knew he should have run hours ago and now wished that he had.

''Ow the 'ell do I know what it is?' Scarlet hissed. 'I can't see through wood.'

At the faint sound of scratching along the bottom of the door, Barney caught his breath. Fear filled his throat and prickles of sweat ran uncomfortably across his head. 'It's a dog, or cat,' he whispered, trying to convince himself.

'I'm going to open the door.' Scarlet stepped towards it.

'Are you mad?' He hissed and grabbed her arm; his sweat streaked his face. She shook him off roughly, pushing him away.

'If it was the law they'd be in 'ere by now,' she said, opening the door a crack, then with a gasp she flung it wide.

Moll lay covered in blood on the wooden landing, her face as white as chalk. There was no one in the passage, all was quiet as they pulled her inside and lay her on the bed. Scarlet grabbed a jug of gin and some cloths, washing Moll's bloody face, arms and legs she exposed deep wounds.

'Here's the cause of the blood; she's been bitten.'

Barney looked at Moll's arms and hands, pieces of flesh were torn away or hanging loose and blue tooth marks were raised on her legs.

'Lay the skin back and tie it down tight with this material,' Scarlet instructed Barney, while tearing up a white shirt. 'We can only hope for her.'

Moll groaned as the gin stung through the darkness of her unconscious mind and the material was pulled tight over the wounds. 'At least my daughter is alive. There's nothing else we can do but wait.'

Not convinced that she wasn't followed, Barney kept watch at the window for the next hour, while Scarlet didn't leave Moll's side. Next day Moll was hot with fever and they could do nothing but put gin-soaked cloths on the bites and give her plenty of gin to drink. By the second day her fever had gone and she slept peacefully. 'I think she's through it,' Scarlet voiced her thoughts as an hour later Moll opened her eyes for the first time. 'I'm sorry, Scarlet, I wasn't careful enough,' she spoke through swollen lips.

'Hush now, no matter, yer home safe.' Scarlet stroked her daughter's brow and smiled into the pale face that lay on the pillow.

'I got away;' Moll said weakly. 'They couldn't run as fast as me but the Runner had a dog. It didn't give up and trapped me in a dead end.' She winced as she moved her arm to look at her wounds.

'They're clean, don't move you'll open 'em up,' Scarlet instructed with a gentle force. 'Nobby, get in the passage and see if there's a dog hanging around.'

Barney looked shocked but went and looked, going slowly down the stairs. He didn't feel safe; he didn't like dogs. There wasn't a dog hanging around and he returned quickly to the room.

On his return Scarlet looked at him as though making up her mind about something. 'You got something to say to me, Nobby?'

Barney looked her square in the face and wondered if he should say what he was thinking or just disappear into the crowd, which might be safer.

It was Scarlet who spoke first. 'We're leaving for Liverpool, me and Moll. Taking a boat, probably hide out in Ireland for a bit. We'll come back when everything calms down. You can come with us if yer want.'

'No, sorry,' he said without even having to think. 'I have plans.'

28.

Haddenford

It was early afternoon. Matt, seated astride his horse, looked around the deserted Tate farmyard. The muck in the yard was thick and dry, reaching everywhere, and he could see that this was a farm that was struggling. The boy Robert suddenly appeared and nodded at him. Matt was happy to see the boy and called to him. 'Good day, Robert, may I water my horse?'

'Yes, sir.' The sky was bright and the boy squinted up at him as he approached.

There was no sign of the farmer today so Matt asked, 'Is Mister Tate about?'

'No, sir, he's mucking the fields with John. Won't be back till late.'

'Would you mind, Robert, if I ate my pie here?'

'No, sir,' Robert replied as Matt got down from his horse and led it to the trough where it drank gratefully. Opening his pouch, Matt removed the second of his pies. The geese approached him in a tight gaggle, holding out their short wings and hissing. They watched him menacingly with small, eager eyes. 'You'd better eat it inside,' Robert said, opening the door, and Matt once again stepped into the untidy kitchen.

Trying not to sound too obvious as he looked around at the mess, Matt asked, 'Where is your mother, Robert?'

'Gone to London, sir.'

Matt nodded and smiled before Robert could read his mind about the dirt. 'London?' he questioned. 'To visit relatives?'

'No, sir. She's just gone to London.' He eyed Matt's pie. 'My mother used to make pies that size for us.'

Matt nodded, his mouth full of meat. 'This is the most delicious pie I have ever eaten.' He looked at the contents and commented, 'It's full of greenery!'

Robert had a look. 'They're herbs. My mother used to put herbs in her pies. It looks just like one of hers.'

Matt noticed that Robert's face had become sad. But it wasn't unusual for a child of his age to be living away in a trade. 'Do you miss your mother, Robert?' Matt wanted to make conversation with the boy. He didn't know how old Robert was but had sympathy for him, having himself been working from a very young age. But he'd been lucky to have his mother with him.

'Sometimes I miss her, sir,' Robert said softly, 'but I couldn't go; I have to stay here and learn how to be a farmer.'

Matt understood. It was important for Robert to have a trade if he was going to survive in this world. It was something his own father had impressed on him and he felt a sudden sadness both for himself and for the boy. 'You've done the right thing in staying,' he assured him. Robert nodded, but didn't seem convinced. Matt brushed himself down and, smiling at the boy, said, 'Well, Robert, thank you once again for your hospitality. I must be off now to Claydon House.'

Robert became suddenly alert. 'Claydon House? That's where my sister works. Do you know Emma?'

'Emma is your sister? Yes, I know Emma; she works for my mother and works very hard,' he added.

The boy's face lit up. 'Please tell her where I am and that Mother, Nona and James have gone to London; they didn't have time to get a message to her.'

'I will be pleased to give her your message, Robert; now I must take my leave.'

'Will you come again?' Robert's small face was hopeful as he followed Matt into the yard.

'If I'm passing this way again, Robert, I promise to come in and bring a message from Emma.'

As Matt made his way home, his heart felt light; Emma had been rather cool with him before he left for London and she would be happy to receive Robert's message.

29.

The room felt cold as Matt stood before his mistress and handed her Mister Redfern's letter. Her voice was terse as she took the parchment from him. 'You may go, Ames.' Grateful that she had nothing else to say to him, he left and headed for the kitchen, looking for Emma. He found her in a cool room beating cream into a junket. 'Emma,' he spoke joyfully, 'you'll never imagine who I met this afternoon.'

'No, Matt, I could not imagine who you met this afternoon, as I know so few people.' She did not look up from her task.

He smiled wickedly, enjoying having the upper hand. 'I met your brother Robert.'

Her eyes widened and the hand that held the whisk stopped its beating.

'How did you meet my brother?'

'I happened upon Tate Farm when I needed to rest my horse.'

'Tate Farm! Is Robert well?' She was eager for news of her family.

'It seems so.' He nodded, deciding not to tell her about the dirt of the yard and the filth of the kitchen. For all he knew, that was normal.

'And my mother?' Her face was excited, her eyes shining.

'Robert said that she'd gone to London.'

Emma's face was no longer smiling and Matt felt confused; what had he said to make her frown? So, he added quickly, 'Robert said that Nona and James had gone with her.'

'Did he not mention Charity?' She put the bowl down heavily on the table, a look of fear in her eyes that Matt could not understand.

'No, only the names I mentioned.' He couldn't understand why it mattered that her brother might have forgotten to mention one of her siblings.

A spear of fear tore through Emma's heart and she bit at her lip as though she were about to cry.

'Perhaps he just forgot to mention your sister?' Matt tried to reassure her.

'Yes, perhaps he did, please excuse me.'

Wiping her hands on her apron, she ran to her room, holding her skirt up and taking the stairs two at a time. Closing the door, she locked it. Kneeling before her altar, she lit a candle to the Goddess and placed a bowl of water to the side of her special stone and lit a candle.

'I ask the Goddess for her help in reaching my ancestors, whom I honour.' She spoke in a small soft voice, concentrating on the candle flame. Her eyes began to water as the aura of the candles light increased, deepening in colour. As she felt a comforting presence enter the room tears dampened her cheeks. 'May I ask if Charity is on the other side, and, if so, is she with you?'

A whisper caressed her ears, filtering into her mind. 'Yes, child, she is here. She is not alone. Do not mourn for she is happy and safe.'

Emma felt her ancestor depart, leaving the room empty as though a cloud had passed over the sun removing the warmth. Continuing to concentrate on the candle, she said. 'I honour the Goddess,' she spoke quietly, placing her hands on the stone. 'Please bring me your wisdom. Help me to find my locket. Let me know when it is safe to look for it and lead me to where it is hidden. I ask this in your name of love and peace.'

Placing her hands in the bowl of water, she wiped her face with the liquid before drizzling it over her hair and sprinkling it over her altar.

'In the name of the Goddess, so mote it be.'

A feeling of quietness filled her heart and sitting back, she remembered her sister, picturing her curly blonde hair, her little arms and her sweet face. Then she thought of her mother's loss and cried for them both.

~

Two days later, Nell opened the door to Mister Redfern, who had arrived in answer to Miss Brack's letter. She showed him into the morning room, where her mistress received him gushingly, offering tea, which he refused, and wine, which he accepted, having had a long and hard journey from London.

'Have you heard from my brother, Mister Redfern?' Her voice held a level of concern that she felt proud of.

He shook his head. 'I have not, and his creditors are becoming restless.'

'Do we let them have the farm and the land that they have clearly won in these wagers?' she asked.

'It would be better if your brother were here to sign the parcels over to them.' He looked troubled.

'But my brother is not here and I wish to get rid of this debt as I would like to leave the house and go abroad to France, where I once lived. I have friends with whom I shall be staying; the climate of France suits me better than the dreary cold of England.

'For how long will you be away, madam?' He looked concerned.

'Indefinitely, sir.' She walked to the window and looked out at the forest. 'I will leave a retainer here to look after the property. I would like you to make sure that he receives a small wage from the estate.'

'Miss Brack.' Redfern's voice was solemn. 'I must inform you that, as your brother has not drawn on his allowance, or been seen at his club or by any of his friends, I am concerned that something may have befallen him.'

Her heart felt a stab of fear for the first time but she held her nerve. 'I'm afraid that I don't understand, sir.' She stared at him with eyes as innocent as a childs.

'Your brother was known as a character who loved life, Miss Brack. He was a man with many friends and, perhaps, some enemies. It seems that he has... disappeared.'

Her hand fluttered up to her throat. 'What can we do about this, sir? I don't understand how Oliver could disappear. Surely there is someone who knows where he is?'

'I came today to inform you that I feel we should put his continuing absence into the hands of the authorities.'

Her throat constricted. 'Well, of course you must do as you see fit, Mister Redfern.' She was aware of a change in her voice, and hoped that he would put it down to fear, it was fear, but not for the reasons that he would believe. Her heart was racing. How far would the authorities go in searching for her brother?

Redfern felt sorry for the woman before him. Her plight was dreadful. How could Oliver have left his sister in such a position, without funds in a large property and having to carry his debts? He kept emotion out of his voice as he replied, 'This is a matter of normal procedure, madam, in cases of this type. Please do not worry yourself. I will do all that I can to find him.'

'I'm sure that you will, sir. But if my brother cannot be found, what will happen to the estate?' This was something she needed to know, as one day she might need to sell it. France would not be without its expenses.

He nodded sagely, grimacing at having to speak of the possibility that he felt may well have to be faced by this lady. 'If a body is found, the estate will go to the next of kin. If there are no other male relatives, then it will revert to yourself.'

'And if a body is never found?' she raised an eyebrow and kept her innocent gaze level.

'Then that will take a lot longer and will have to be brought before the courts, where his disappearance will have to be proved.'

'Proved?'

'Yes, madam. Proved.'

'How can one prove someone no longer exists, if there is no body?'

'You must understand that we have to be very sure that Oliver will not be returning before signing the property over to yourself if no male relative can be found.'

'Yes, I can see that, Mister Redfern, but Claydon House is not in good repair, as you can see. Surely it will only become worse and decay. What will there be for Oliver to come back to or for me to inherit?'

'I do understand the difficulties that you face, madam. I will release some of the estate money for the upkeep of the property in the absence of Mister Brack and yourself, if you are living abroad, until this is settled properly.'

'Thank you, sir. After all, there must be something for Oliver to come back to.' She tried to smile.

'Yes indeed. With your permission, madam, I will arrange for a surveyor to look at the property and see what repairs are essential and he will inform me of the cost, whereupon I will release the money and find the tradesmen to do the work.'

'You are very kind, sir. Thank you.' Amelia was feeling a little relieved. She would just have to wait. The sister in mourning would go abroad. She never wanted this house anyway and to be truthful didn't care if it rotted; she had never been happy here. But she did know that she would need money to support her in France, and that she couldn't sell the Claydon Estate until Oliver was found, which irked her because if that day came there would be a huge inquiry.

~

Nell bustled into the kitchen, where Emma had started scrubbing the floor. 'That Mister Redfern is a real gentleman,' she spoke to no one in particular.

'Is he here now?' Emma asked, brushing her hair away from her hot face.

'Yes, they're in the morning room; I'll get some lunch organised in case he stays that long. I am sure that he will need to eat before he takes the road back to London.'

Emma stood up and wiped her hands on her apron. Now was her chance to search for her locket. It might be many months before anyone else came to call and took up the mistress's time. 'I'll be back soon,' she informed Nell.

'Where are you going, Emma?'

'To look for my locket, Mrs Ames, while I have the opportunity.'

'Oh my life. Oh dear no. Oh dear.' Nell's fingers drummed on her chin and she suddenly looked very old. Emma had not before noticed the wrinkles on Nell's face or the bags under her eyes and she was sorry for all that this dear woman was going through.

'Please don't get caught, Emma. I don't know what she'll do to you.'

'I won't get caught,' Emma called over her shoulder as the door closed behind her. Having left the safety of the kitchen, she lifted her skirt and walked with determination towards the servants' stairs.

The mistress's bedroom was musty and dark and in need of tidying. This would, she thought, give her a reason for being in the bedroom if caught. She stood for a moment, not knowing where to look first. Scanning the dressing table, she could see that her locket was not sitting on the surface. She lifted the lids of the many little pots that held pins and hairnets, but found nothing. Opening drawers, she searched through the clothes, but again found nothing. Emma looked under the pillows, in the bed and under the bed. But didn't find it. It had to be somewhere here. Although afraid of being discovered, she took a moment to stop and calm herself. I asked for help, now is the time that I need that help, she thought. As she concentrated on the face of her grandmother, the door to the dressing room swung open. Emma caught her breath, expecting the figure of Miss Brack to appear. When no one walked through the door, she made her way cautiously in that direction, peering slowly around the doorframe. The room was empty. Relieved, she realised this must be a sign from her grandmother. If I were going to hide something, where would I put it? she thought, looking around the small room. There were the wardrobes. But a servant would be expected to hang clothes in there. There was the top of the wardrobe, but a servant would be expected to clean up there. The door to the wardrobe opened easily to her touch but creaked and Emma again caught her breath. The bottom of the wardrobe was full of shoes and beautifully embroidered purses, some decorated with pearls and shiny beads. Emma fell upon the pile of purses, opening them all in turn. One, a purse so beautiful it was fit for a ball, attracted her more than the others. Inside was a smaller silk purse and inside that she found her grandmother's locket. Emma kissed it with joy, holding it in the palm of her hand, where it threw out sheens of colour in acceptance of the wearer. A voice like a gentle breath caressed her ear. *'Emma, make haste to leave this place.'* Quickly pushing all the purses back into the wardrobe, she obeyed the voice immediately. The servants' door closed silently behind her just as her mistress stepped foot on the landing.

In the kitchen she found Nell cutting some cold meat and hurried to her. 'Nell, I have it. I have my locket.'

Nell's hands started to shake and she put the knife down as she was in danger of cutting herself.

'Oh, my Lord.' Nell's voice held a tone of fear and she swallowed hard.

'Please don't worry; it is mine, Mrs Ames.'

'Yes, I know. But you took it without permission, Emma.'

Emma was dumfounded at her reaction. 'No, the mistress took it without my permission. Why should I get permission to take back what is mine? And who should I get permission of, Mrs Ames?'

'In a court of law, Emma, your word will mean nothing beside hers.' Nell felt sorry for the girl, who was such an innocent soul.

'I have to leave, Mrs Ames, and I must go right now.' She clutched the hand of the woman who had replaced her mother and made her so welcome. 'I will miss you.' She tearfully hugged and kissed Nell. 'Thank you for taking care of me.'

Emma had taken one step towards the door when it opened and their mistress stood menacingly in the doorway.

Emma and Nell stared with mouths gaping, unable to move, their feet locked as in a nightmare. The tall, elegant woman stepped slowly into the kitchen and seemed to fill it with the width of her brown satin dress. Amelia's stare was hostile as she looked from Emma to Nell. 'So, you blatantly disobeyed me, Mrs Ames.' Her eyes glared at Nell. 'I cannot employ a servant that I cannot trust. I am afraid that I have to let you go. You will of course not expect a reference. I am sure that you understand why. But you can of course say that you worked here if you wish.' Her voice rose sharply as she turned her attention on Emma. 'Mistress Tilby. Against my orders you are still here.' She took a step forward. Her voice rose. Emma couldn't move. 'Show me what you have in your hand.'

For a moment Emma's limbs were immobilised with fear, but then lifting her chin in defiance she held out her clenched fist. She would run out of the door before this woman could touch the locket again. 'Turn it over and open your fingers.' The voice demanded and Emma obeyed, unable not to.

Looking down at her open hand, Emma gasped. The locket had gone. Her eyes widened; she must have dropped it but resisted looking at the floor in case it was there beneath her skirt. 'You will leave this house immediately,' Amelia shouted, her face now flushed with anger.

It was then that Emma found her voice, although with the fear that was jumping around in her chest it didn't sound like hers at all. 'May I get my things, ma'am, before I leave?'

'No, you may not. You will leave now.' Emma looked at Nell, who stood pale-faced and round-eyed, staring in disbelief at the sight of their mistress in her kitchen.

Emma opened the door and walked out into the yard. Her heart was pounding in her chest and her legs felt weak with fear as she hurried away with no idea where she was going. But she wasn't going far, and for a moment hid in the laundry room wondering what was happening to Nell left alone in the kitchen with that monster? There were tears in her eyes as she decided to find Matt.

Hurrying to the stable block, she found him forking clean straw into an empty stable. 'She's dismissed me, Matt, and your mother,' she cried in her shock.

'What? Is she mad? What could have happened?'

'She blames Nell for keeping me on.' Emma felt sorry for all the trouble that she realised that she had caused. Poor Nell, what would happen to her? Matt looked shocked and then defiant.

'Well, I'm not staying, not without my mother. So I don't know how she'll run this place.'

'*Mister Ames!*' The loud voice turned them both around. 'Miss Brack would like to see you in her drawing room.' Mister Redfern looked out of place in the stable yard in his white wig, black coat and shiny buckled shoes. He indicated the house with a sweep of his hand. 'If you would be so kind.'

Matt threw down the fork that clattered on the cobbles and walked ahead of the solicitor with long, determined steps in the direction of the house.

Amelia was seated silently beside the fireplace when Matt and her solicitor entered the drawing room. Alf was already there. Standing like a statue before Amelia, turning his battered hat round and round in his hands. She didn't acknowledge Matt's attendance. And it was the solicitor who addressed them looking first at Matt.

'Your employer, Miss Brack, in the absence of your master, is closing the house and will no longer need your services.'

'And what will happen to the horses, sir?' Matt spoke quietly.

'They are to be sold. They will stay in the field until that time.'

'But there's no water in the field, sir; someone needs to see to them, they can't just be left.'

'That will be taken care of, Ames. You will be paid until the end of the week, when you will leave with your mother.' He turned towards Alf. 'Mister Freeman, Miss Brack would like you to stay on as caretaker; you will receive a small retainer from me each month. You will keep the gardens dug and planted with whatever you see fit. You will sleep in the house, looking after the fabric of the building.'

Alf looked confused. 'You want me to look after the curtains and furniture, sir?'

'No.' Mister Redfern's faced twitched. 'I'm sorry,' he spoke kindly. 'I didn't make myself clear. You will look after the building by seeing if any repairs need doing. You will tell me by messenger and I will get a tradesman to do the work.' Alf nodded that he understood.

'That will be all.' They were dismissed as though it was an ordinary day and they had been given their daily tasks.

Matt and Alf returned stunned to the kitchen, where they found Nell in a dither. 'What will become of us?' she asked Matt.

'Don't worry, Mother. I will find employment.' He didn't feel confident on that matter but for her sake he pretended that all would be well.

'But they may not take me. I'm not getting a reference.'

'You are my mother and we travel together. I'm being paid to the end of the week, so we'll have a bit to live on with what I have managed to save.'

'What will happen to Emma?' Nell asked shakily

At that moment the back door opened and Emma entered. 'Oh, my Lord, Emma,' Nell cried out. 'Don't come in, don't come in.'

Emma shut the door behind her. 'I'm not going without my things and my locket, Mrs Ames.'

'But, Emma,' Nell pointed, 'the locket is hanging round your neck.'

Putting her hand to her chest, Emma could hardly believe that the locket was hanging there. She genuinely didn't know where it was after it left her hand. 'You're scaring me now, Emma; how did you do that?'

'I… I don't know,' she stammered. But in her heart she knew she'd had the help of those watching over her. No longer caring what the mistress thought, as she had already been dismissed, Emma left the kitchen, running unseen along the passage and up the back stairs to her room. She collected her few possessions, but most importantly her father's bag. Everything was pushed into it including her special stone. Back in the kitchen she gave Nell a hug and wished everyone good luck. Walking as quickly as possible down the lane behind the house to the road, she stood, not knowing what to do next.

The road was quiet, apart from the birds twittering loudly in the hedgerow. She stood thinking. Should she go to London and find her mother? Surely, she would be able to get a position there. On the way she could take a small detour and call at Tate Farm and visit her brother. Stepping out at a good pace, she walked strongly, a person with a destination, a goal. She almost skipped as she swung her bag, feeling happy and released from the tight fist of Claydon House.

The day, although autumnal, was warm as she started the long walk towards Haddenford. With a little money in her pocket, her father's bag and her locket tucked into her bodice, she had all that she owned with her and her spirit was light.

As night fell, Emma was deep in the countryside with no food and nowhere to stay. Hungry and exhausted, she curled up in a field, using her bag as a pillow and her jacket as a blanket. It was just getting light when she awoke to the sound of creaking cartwheels on the road. She stood, shakily smoothing down her clothes and picking up her bag she made her way to the grass verge and waited.

It was Lady and Mim Buckle that came around the bend under the shadow of overhanging trees. Emma was so glad to see someone that she knew that she ran towards them waving. Lady was pulled up as Mim stared into the weak sunlight that was just fudging up over the treetops and tried to see who it was running towards him.

'Are you going anywhere near Tate Farm today, Mister Buckle?' she called out as she ran. 'If you are, could you take me, please?'

Mim looked shocked. 'What're you doing out here in the middle of nowhere at this time of the morning?' He pulled Lady to a halt, looking down on Emma.

'I was walking to visit my brother at Tate Farm, but it was further than I remembered.'

Mim's pipe moved from one side of his mouth and back again as he stared at her. 'Come on up then.' He held out his hand. Gratefully she climbed up, sitting upon the front seat, where she silently thanked her ancestors for Mim Buckle and his old horse.

Later that day Emma stood in the dirty yard of Tate Farm. Apart from the chickens and geese the place was silent and still. She peered into the barns; all were empty. She could hear cows somewhere in the fields and the smell of pigs led her to their pen, where she stood and watched them nuzzling in the muck.

30.

The voice that accosted her was loud and demanding. 'What are you doing near my pigs?' Emma jumped and turned to look down the long barrel of a gun, behind which stood an unkempt, bearded man, his eyes glistening with suspicion.

Emma's knees almost buckled as she tried to ignore the gun and answer the question. 'I was looking for my brother, sir.' She didn't take her eyes from the barrel pointed at her face.

'And you thought you'd find him in my pig pen, did you?'

'I was just looking at your pigs, Mister Tate.'

'You know who I am?' He was taken aback. He didn't know this young woman; why should she know him.

'Yes, I know you, sir. My mother worked for you.'

His voice was gruff, cheerless. 'Many mothers have worked for me.' He did not lower the gun and continued to stare angrily.

'Martha Tilby is my mother, sir,' she said quickly. 'I'm Emma and I am looking for my brother Robert.'

The gun was lowered slowly, fully revealing the eyes and tanned skin of the bearded Andrew Tate. The eyes that watched her were red-rimmed and tired. His hair hung in greasy lengths from under a wide-brimmed leather hat. But he spoke more civilly to her. 'Robert is off with the cows. He'll be back later. Your mother has left for London. I'm sorry.' He turned to walk away.

'Oh, but excuse me, sir,' she called after him. 'Can I wait in your house for my brother's return?'

He didn't exactly answer, but nodded and walked away as though he had all the troubles of the world on his shoulders.

Emma opened the door and stepped into the dirtiest kitchen she'd ever seen. For a moment she stood, unable to believe that her mother could have lived in this place. Sitting down carefully in the chair by the hearth, she looked around the room. It was worse than the pigsty, with dirty dishes and food piled up on every work surface. Flies buzzed at the windows, trying to get out. Maggots crawled on surfaces where uncooked meat had been left.

Unable to continue to sit in the mess, she threw open the windows, letting the flies out, and filled a bucket with water from the well. Rescuing the fire from its small glow she put a kettle over the fire to heat the water. How, she wondered, was her brother not ill, or dead, living in a place like this?

Gathering the dishes, she scraped the contents into a bucket, then washed everything in the room. Finding some flour in a tin and some fat that smelt fresh, she made some scones, putting them to cook on the flat iron that hung over the fire.

Later in the day the door opened and Robert stood mesmerised in the opening.

Looking up, Emma smiled at the look on Robert's face. 'Come in and shut the door, Robert,' she called from where she bent over the fire.

'Emma!' He ran to her, throwing his arms around her waist. 'I didn't think I would ever see you again.'

Emma was taken aback; he had never thrown his arms around her before and in that moment her heart went out to him; he seemed so small and alone as she stroked his head.

'I brought this rabbit home for cooking tonight, Emma.' He laid the carcass on the table with a thump.

'Give it to me; we'll skin it and put it on the jack. You can watch it carefully while we have something to drink and eat. Do you want to turn the spit or shall I?'

When they were seated she said, 'Now tell me, Robert, what has happened since I went away.'

Sadness showed in his eyes as he replied, 'We had to leave the cottage. I don't know why because Mother and I were working, and we had the money for the rent. We came to live here and Mother looked after the farmer's children as their mother had died. It was all right while Jack, George and Sarah were here but after Sarah and Charity died everyone had to leave.'

'Everyone?' she looked expectantly at him for more information.

'Yes, first Jack and George, Mr Tate's children, and then Mother, Nona and James. I think Mister Tate was too sad to have them stay.'

'But he kept you.'

'Yes, I work for my board. He told Mother that he couldn't really afford John Brisket, the overseer, but he can't do all the work himself.'

'Would you like a scone Robert? They are cool enough to eat.' Getting up, she fetched a couple of golden rounds to the clean table and placed them before her hungry brother.

'Mister Tate doesn't know how to cook, and he doesn't have time, there's too much to do.' Robert said as he took a scone from the dish.

Or keep a clean house, Emma thought, but said nothing.

Andrew arrived home later in the evening. He entered the kitchen and, without removing his muck-laden boots, crossed the floor and slumped into the chair by the fire, and without removing his hat shut his eyes. Moments later he opened them to find Emma standing before him with a mug of ale.

'Your food is on the table, sir; please come and help yourself.' She spoke quietly, slightly fearful of the man behind the beard.

'You're still here!' His voice was tired as he stood slowly moving towards the table.

They sat in silence, and after he had eaten Emma asked hopefully. 'I wonder if I can call upon your generosity, sir, to allow me to stay until tomorrow.'

Andrew looked at Robert, whose face was hopeful. He thought of his own children and felt sorry for the boy.

'You can stay.' He stood slowly, nodding at Emma with what she imagined to be thanks as he left the room.

While she had been cooking Emma had been planning and now put it to her brother. 'Robert, I'm going to London to find Mother. Will you come with me?' She thought to rescue him from this place and his company would be appreciated on the long journey.

His immediate reaction wasn't what she expected and he looked very serious, like an old man, as he replied, 'I don't know, Emma. I have to learn a trade and Mister Tate needs me.'

'Yes, I understand, of course you're right.' She was sad. 'Think about it until tomorrow, Robert. And at least I know where you are and can come back and get you, if our fortunes change.'

Next day, taking a scone and some cheese, she set out for London on foot and alone. An hour later she was sitting cheerfully on the back of a very full flat cart swinging her legs and looking up into the trees. 'Are y'all right back there?' the soft Irish voice called back to her.

'Thank you, sir, yes, I couldn't be better,' she called over her shoulder.

The tinker laughed; 'Sir, is it? Well, haven't I suddenly gone up in the world?' He smiled, thinking how good it was to have helped a fellow traveller and to have some company, as footpads could appear at any time and they might think twice with two people on the cart instead of one.

It was late afternoon by the time they reached the bridge over the Thames and Emma was speechless at the sight of its many arches and stone pillars and the number of people crossing it.

She was also not ready for the noise and the smell, which was so different to the countryside.

'I'm sorry mistress, I have to drop you here, so I do. I'm not crossing the water today, y'see.'

'Where do I go for London, sir?' She looked round in confusion as the cart pulled up in front of some large black-and-white buildings.

'Cross the bridge, mistress' – he nodded towards the bridge – 'and you'll be in London town herself.'

Getting down into the road, she looked up and thanked him. As he pulled away waving his hand above his head, she watched him go, feeling the loss of his company.

Walking slowly across the bridge, she felt afraid. The water was so wide. How did the bridge not fall into it? Stunned by the sight of the interwoven mangle of houses, and so many streets on the other side of the water, she wondered how she would find her mother. But, first, she knew that she must see to herself. Where would she stay? She could hardly walk the streets at night and she felt like crying. London was so much larger than the village. There were hundreds of people here and she knew no one. She really wished that Robert had come with her.

When she reached the other side of the river, she approached a man in a red coat who was selling oysters. His voice was loud, rising above the surrounding noise. 'Oyst–ers,' he shouted. 'Oyst–ers caught fresh to–daaay,' he called. 'Last few left. Come on, mistress, don't make me throw 'em back in the Thames.'

'Excuse me sir,' Emma asked politely, 'Could you direct me to a place where I might take a room for the night?'

Looking down, the red-coated tradesman saw a pretty girl in an ugly brown dress that must have been passed down to her. The girl was holding on tightly to an old canvas bag in which he guessed was all that she owned.

'Well now' – he paused – 'it's not good for a young person such as yerself to be alone in London and wanting a room. Safe rooms are expensive; you could try an inn.'

'Sir.' She made herself stand taller. 'I'm thirteen and I'm looking for my mother, who is in London somewhere, and I just need a safe place to sleep until tomorrow.'

He stared at this young girl who had no idea how much danger she was in and sighed. 'Oh, come with me, my Ethel will put you up; she'd kill me if I left you on the street. There ain't nowhere 'ere that's safe for a girl on 'er own.' The last remaining oysters were tipped into a bag. 'With an extra mouth to feed we'll eat these ourselves. I'm Bert.' He smiled down at her. 'Known as Oyster Bert or Red Bert 'cos of the coat.' He held out a filthy hand that smelt of fish. Emma looked at the proffered hand and hesitatingly shook it. There was something in his eyes that she trusted, and she smiled back.

'Thank you, Bert, thank you very much.'

~

Bert's home was off a narrow passage that smelt of urine. Emma held her hand over her mouth, following carefully in Bert's footsteps as he picked his way through the muck. Opening a weathered brown door, he called. 'It's me, Effie. I brought a visitor.'

The room that Emma entered was small, warmed by a fire on one wall and furnished with a meagre amount of furniture. A table with four chairs that didn't match, a faded armchair beside the fire, and a box of logs. In the corner of the room a cupboard hung on one wall and on another a picture of the king. Emma, who was expecting to be met by Bert's wife, was surprised to come face to face with a pale child no older than Robert, who stared shyly at her.

'Emma, this is me daughter, the apple of me eye. Effie, this is Emma; she's going to stay with us for the night.'

Emma smiled at Effie, who she'd noted was very thin. The girl was about to speak when suddenly taken with a fit of coughing that racked her small frame. Reaching for a chair, she lowered herself slowly onto it. 'Is she ill?' Emma asked Bert, alarmed at the deathly colour that had come upon Effie.

'No more'n anyone else around 'ere; now sit yerself down at the table while I cook these wonderful oysters fer our tea. Effie, you fetch the bread.'

The oysters were an unusual taste; she'd not had them before and wasn't sure if she liked the feel of them in her mouth. But the bread was good. Not as good as her mother's, but she was grateful to Bert and Effie for sharing the little that they had with her.

'This bread is very good, Effie. Did you cook it?' Emma looked about the room and wondered how it was cooked for there was no brick oven next to the fire.

The girl smiled. 'I makes the dough and takes it up the alley to be cooked in the oven at the forge. We all do along 'ere.' She stood slowly to clear the table and another fit of coughing gripped her. As she collapsed back onto her chair, Emma noticed the dark circles around Effie's eyes and that her skin was damp.

Bert took a small jug from a corner cupboard hanging on the wall and poured liquid into a cup. ''Ere, 'ave a swig of this, it'll make it better.' Effie took the cup from her father and sipped at the drink visibly relaxing.

'What is it?' Emma asked, indicating the cup.

'Gin,' he replied.

'Gin!' Emma was interested; she hadn't heard of it before. But this was London and more went on here than in the countryside. 'Is it made from herbs?' she asked.

'Do yer know, I think it is.' He nodded. ''Ave a drop yerself.'

Taking the cup offered, Emma experienced her first taste of the drink that was the ruin of many Londoners. 'It's very strong, Bert,' she spluttered, screwing up her face as the sour liquid caused her mouth to become dry.

He laughed. 'You'll do. Take a cup when yer thirsty; the jug's there.'

'Thank you, Bert.' She tried to be polite and noticed that the gin had stopped Effie coughing.

'You're very pretty,' Effie said, staring at Emma directly. 'Why are yer out on the street on your own. Where's yer family?'

Emma blushed, ignoring the compliment. 'It's a long story, Effie. I'm looking for my mother. All I know is that she came to London with my brother and sister. I didn't know that London was so big, or that there would be so many people and houses.'

Effie continued to stare at her; the serious expression on her face reminded Emma of an elderly lady. 'Where're yer going to look?' the girl asked.

Emma shrugged. 'I don't know; I've only just arrived in London.'

'It's going to take a long time. Maybe for ever,' the girl embellished.'

'If yer tell me about 'er, I can look out for 'er when I'm selling the oysters.' Bert joined in.

Effie's face was suddenly covered in excitement. 'Maybe I can 'elp yer look. I knows me way around some of London, the theatres, Covent Garden and such.'

'Thank you, that would be a great help.' Although Emma was doubtful that the girl had the strength to help her look, she was grateful for the offer and her company would be a comfort.

The evening was spent with Emma telling them about life at Claydon House. She enthralled them with stories about the food they ate and of Nell, Alf and Matt. She also told them of the frightening Miss Brack, but not about the body in the forest, because she didn't want to relive it.

'I think you've fallen in love with Matt.' Effie had a gleam in her eye.

'No, I don't think so. I'm a bit too young for love or to marry, Effie.' Although she was trying to convince herself that she was too young for love, her heart was sad at the loss of Matt's company and she wondered what he was doing now, and if they would ever meet again. But it was her secret, something to keep close, a feeling that was hers alone, something to give her comfort when she felt lonely.

'Well, yer nearly old enough to marry.' Effie's voice broke through her thoughts. 'Tilly Bennet got married last year; she said she was nearly fifteen, but Dad wasn't sure that she was that old.' Her mother couldn't remember what year she'd had her and there weren't no father to ask.'

Emma nodded; she was getting an idea of what it was like living in London. Looking around the sparsely furnished room with its damp patches on the walls and the ever-constant smell of mould, she thought, poor Tilly. That won't happen to me. I want more than that and hopefully more than this, she thought guiltily and, looking around the room, she wondered what conditions her mother was living in?

Bert held out a rug to her. 'Yer can sleep 'ere by the fire grate, Emma, and if yer get a bit cold put a small log on the fire. Better to keep it alight; it's a faggot to get going again if it goes out.' He snuffed out the candle, leaving the room lit cosily by the firelight's glow, and moved to the other side of the room, where he unrolled a bed on which he and Effie would sleep.

As they all settled down for the night, Emma held her locket and fell asleep, thanking the Goddess for this shelter.

Next day, Emma and Effie searched the streets and sometimes sat watching the passers-by. They followed the same routine for days, but saw nothing of Martha, Nona or James.

Emma felt guilty for eating the little food that Effie and Bert shared with her. It was, she thought, time to do something for them for they hadn't asked her to move out. When they were all together that evening, she said, 'I can't stay here any longer eating your food and contributing nothing. What can I do to help?'

Bert scratched his head. 'I've been thinking of taking another pitch and getting more oysters. Could the pair of yer work it together?'

'We could, couldn't we, Emma?' Effie's face lit up. 'We'd also 'ave a different place to look for yer mother.' Emma agreed, although she had to be shown again how to open the oysters with the sharp knife.

Bert chose a site half a mile away where no one else was selling shellfish. On their first day the stall sold out before noon, leaving the girls to spend the afternoon looking for Martha. The streets were narrow and the air thick in places with wood smoke from chimneys and fires built on street corners by the homeless. One afternoon they'd just reached Hare Lane when Effie started to cough and couldn't go on. 'I'm sorry, Emma, I 'ave to go 'ome; it's me chest.'

'It's all right, Effie, we've done a lot today.' Emma put her arm around the girl, feeling the thinness of her shoulders through her clothes. The frailness of this new friend whom she was becoming very fond of worried her.

They had walked back slowly and were pleased with the amount of money that they had to show Bert that evening when he got home. Gradually, Emma and Effie started to get regular customers. Housekeepers sent maids with usual orders, along with one or two innkeepers who bought them and sold them again, cooked, at a good profit.

'Our fortune changed when yer came along, Emma,' Bert said one night as they counted the day's takings. 'Here's yer money, yer earned it.'

'Thank you Bert but isn't this too much?'

'Yer earned it, take it, and 'ere's yours, Effie.'

Effie looked at the money spread out on the table and then stared into her father's eyes. 'I don't need money like Emma,' and she pushed it back into the centre of the table into the pile that was left to pay the bills.

'You're a real trooper, my girl. I didn't want yer to feel left out,' and he leaned over and kissed her head.

Emma looked at what he had given to her; it was more than she had ever seen, although she knew another person might think it not very much. What did she need money for? 'I can't take this money, Bert,' she said slowly. 'Keep it for my roof and board, for which I am very grateful,' and she also pushed the coins back across the table.

'Yer a good girl, Emma, and I thanks yer for that. It was a blessing the day yer crossed that bridge. This,' he said, looking at the money, 'will buy a blanket for Effie to keep her warm come winter and help with the rent.'

31.

A mile away, Buller and James were getting ready for another day of shoe cleaning. Arriving at his usual spot, Buller set out his pitch and the tall chair that he carried on his back, ready for his clients. James set out the brushes, cloths and the polish in a neat row. The brushes were standing to attention and the cloths neatly folded when the first customer arrived. He was a chatty gent and Buller kept him in conversation, it being better to have a client than an empty chair.

Across the street in the shadow of an alley, a man was stirring from the place where he'd slept with the rats that no longer worried him. He stretched and looked around, thinner now and no longer as hungry as he used to be. As Barney left the alley, he barely noticed the shoe boy, until a voice called, 'The black polish, James, if yer please.'

Barney squinted across the thoroughfare at the two young boys cleaning shoes and recognised James straight away. Ducking back into the alley he gave thanks for this lucky day and tried to come up with a plan. He sat hidden in the alley opposite them all morning, watching. While the populace of London rushed passed relentlessly, he waited for his chance to move.

At noon there was a sudden increase in the number of people passing by, they seemed excited, laughing and joking but none stopped to have shoes cleaned. 'Where are all these people going, Buller?' James asked.

'From the direction they're going there must be a hanging at Newgate,' he replied in a matter-of-fact tone.

'Shall we go, Buller, and have a look?'

'Well,' Buller said watching the masses pass by, 'I might get more custom if we follow the crowd. Pick everything up, James; we'll follow them.'

The throng outside the large black doors of Newgate Prison was swelling by the minute. James and Buller set out their pitch behind the crowd that faced the Debtors' Door, where the scaffold with its skirt of black fabric had recently been erected. Other tradesmen mingled with the throng, pushing their wares with loud shouts. The streets were crowded and above them men and women hung out of windows looking down on the gallows and calling out to those below, laughing. To James it was jolly, like a fair. But no one was interested in having their shoes cleaned. Many in the crowd didn't have money for luxuries, but Buller hoped that a gentleman might have come for the fun and would stop to have his shoes polished.

The mournful sound of the prison bell rang on and on, calling people from all over London. The gallows, set on a platform high above the crowd, was ready to receive two people, as the empty coffins on the edge of the platform suggested. Eventually two men were pushed up the wooden steps at the back and stood looking down at the crowd. They seemed to Buller momentarily taken aback by the noise, which rose as they were pushed roughly forward by the hangman towards the centre of the stage to stand beneath a thick beam. 'Who's for the drop?' Buller asked a woman.

'Martin Clench and James Mackley for murder,' she replied, her eyes sparkling with an anticipation that reflected the mood of the crowd.

Being small, James couldn't see anything as a wall of human bodies blocked his view. The crowd heckled and cheered as the two men, their arms secured behind their backs, waited on the platform. A heavy noose already hung around their necks as the priest administered the last rites to the men. After pulling a cotton bag over the head of each prisoner, the hangman climbed a ladder propped against the centre of the main beam holding each rope in his left hand. Each rope had an eye hole at its end and these were forced over the points of two butcher's hooks screwed tightly into the heavy beam above the heads of those about to die.

The crowd was cheering when suddenly, and without warning, the platform collapsed, sending the priest, hangman and officials tumbling below the scaffold, landing them in a confusion of arms and legs below the jerking feet of the murderers. A mass gasp emitted from the crowd a second before they screamed with excitement. The roar was tremendous as the crowed jumped up and down, pushing and shoving for a better view. In the melee Barney struck. Sweeping James up and placing him under one arm, he made off unnoticed by Buller or the animated mob.

By the time that Buller thought about James it was too late. He asked everyone near him if they had seen the boy. But none had. He searched for hours and as time passed dread and panic seized him. James wouldn't be the first child to have been lost in the crowd, swept away up a side street or – he didn't want to think the worst, but someone could have made off with him. Small children were easy prey for villains, who used them in crimes or sold them for profit. As it got dark he gave up the search. There was nothing to do but make his way home, and he was afraid. There was, he thought hopefully, the chance that James would already be there, having remembered the way back.

Unseen by Buller, a shadow dogged his footsteps. It darted from cover to cover in the darkening evening light and as Buller reached home the shadow moved speedily away.

The Gimbells' kitchen was busy, as it always was at this time of evening, when the shop was shut.

'Where 'ave yer been, Buller, and where's James?' Jane's voice was sharp.

'I lost 'im.' The boy was near to tears.

A stunned silence fell upon the kitchen and then the sound of complete horror exploded from the women.

''Ow did yer lose 'im, yer wretch?' Jane clubbed his ear.

Buller held his reddening ear. 'Martha I'm sorry, 'e was there and then 'e wasn't.' Buller was distraught, his eyes pleading for an understanding which he knew he didn't deserve.

Sid stood up. 'Where were yer? We'll all go and look.'

'It's no use, I already looked, 'e's nowhere to be found,' he sobbed as his tears flowed.

Martha howled. '*Oh no. Please* no. Anything could be happening to him.' All feeling had left her as the enormity of the situation sunk in and her body shook uncontrollably with fear. Her baby, her baby was lost and alone. She sat down suddenly on a chair, almost unable to breathe.

'Where were yer, Buller?' Jane also asked.

'Newgate,' he admitted sheepishly.

Mister Gimbell shouted above the noise. 'Newgate! That isn't yer area, boy. And didn't I tell yer not to take the boy to any hanging?' His face, red with rage, was now transformed into an inhuman mask.

Buller shrank before the fury of his father. 'We didn't 'ave much work 'cos of the hanging, so we followed the crowd.' Buller wiped a tear from his face with a polish-stained hand. 'We stayed at the back hoping for some business, but there were so many people.'

Martha had her head in her hands and Nona, who was frightened, hung onto her mother's arm and cried.

'We'll find him.' Jane tried to comfort Nona and rubbed her back roughly with her large hand, while Martha enclosed Nona in her arms and sobbed into her daughter's hair.

The tap on the door was barely heard above the din. It was Pit who opened it, to a small boy who stood barefoot and ragged in the candlelight thrown out into the dark street.

'I 'ave a message for Missus Tilby,' he said nervously.

'Come in.' Pit held the door open.

'No!' The boy shook his head and took a step back away from the opening.

'Come in and 'ave some food.' The quick-thinking Pit opened the door wider and indicated the table. The hungry child, unable to resist, entered, looking at the occupants of the room with suspicion. Sid gave him meat as Martha said, 'I'm Mrs Tilby; you have a message for me?' He nodded, at the same time stuffing his mouth with meat.

'Well, what is it?' she almost screamed.

'Yer're to come to the Embankment tonight at eleven. A man 'as somefin for yer.'

As he spoke food dropped from his full mouth and his eyes bulged with the effort of breathing and talking.

'Do yer know what 'e 'as for 'er?' Charlie asked.

'No.' The boy shook his head and stared at the meat plate.

'Do yer know the man?' Sid asked.

The boy shrugged. 'Well, do yer?' Charlie picked the frail boy up by his torn shirt. The boy's eyes were huge with fear, but he didn't drop his food nor stop eating.

'Where on the Embankment?' Martha asked.

'Walk opposite Parliament, I'll find yer and take yer to 'im.' Wriggling from Charlie's grasp, the boy ran for the open door, grabbing a handful of meat from the plate as he went.

'What'll we do?' Jane looked at Mister Gimbell.

But he was staring at Martha, his brow furrowing. ''Ow does 'e know yer name?'

For the first time Martha felt a deep fear. Perhaps James had given it to him. She looked at Jane, her eyes pleading for support.

'You should tell 'im.' Jane indicated Mister Gimbell with a nod of her head. 'He may 'ave found yer.'

'Who's found 'er?' Mister Gimbell demanded, his face red with anger.

Martha looked at Nona. 'Jane, I wonder if you could take Nona upstairs and get her ready for bed.' Jane nodded.

'I don't want to go, not without James.' Nona began to cry again.

Pit called across the room. 'We'll find 'im, Nona, don't yer worry yer pretty little 'ead.'

As she passed through the doorway with Nona, Jane shot Martha a sympathetic glance. She knew that she would have to tell the family the truth and a woman shouldn't have to speak of such things to men.

Hot tears rolled over Martha's cheeks as she faced the man and the boys before her in what had seemed a safe place. Her brain was working quickly; what should she say? The butcher watched her expectantly, noticing the struggle that she appeared to be having. Eventually he said, 'Boys, I want yer to go upstairs. I'll call yer when I know what we're dealing with.'

They moaned, but did as he asked. 'Now, I want to know exactly what sort of trouble you've got yerself into and who yer hiding from in my 'ome.'

Martha faced the man who had never been very friendly towards her. She'd never felt him approachable and certainly the last person that she would want to confide in. But fate had played its hand and she had no option.

'Would yer like a drink?' He offered the jug. It was the nearest that he had ever been to caring and Martha was grateful. She took her time and chose her words carefully as he poured the gin.

'It all started when William died. I couldn't face the possibility of being parted from my children. I wanted to keep the family together and tried to live on our little savings and our vegetables. But it wasn't long before I couldn't pay the rent. I got help from the Poor Fund, a charity set up by the church elders in the village. But it wasn't enough for rent and to feed us.' Her fingers twisted her apron as she remembered. 'I got work for

Emma as a maid and a job for myself and Robert in the fields and that helped. The rent collector, a Mister Beemer, was often impolite to me and I feared at times for my honour.' She took a swig of the gin and trembling, continued. 'When he gave me time to pay I thought that he was being generous and I did find the rent money eventually. What I didn't know was that he…' Her voice died away and a sob left her throat as her eyes became moist again. 'He was doing what he shouldn't with Nona.' Martha was shaking, twisting her hands in her lap. Tears ran over her cheeks as she looked at Mister Gimbell for understanding and struggled to carry on. But he didn't speak, only watched her in stony silence. After a moment she said, 'Beemer told Nona that he would let us stay in the cottage if she kept their secret, telling her that it was her way of helping me. One night I found bruises on the top of her legs and at first thought it to be a boy.' She poured another cup of gin and took a long drink before she could continue. 'So, on the day that he was to collect the rent I sent my children away and lay in wait for him. He searched the cottage, looking for her, but found me waiting with a knife.'

Now Mister Gimbell looked disturbed but didn't interrupt.

'I knocked him out with a pan and cut many times into that part of his body which had violated my child and robbed her of her innocence.' She broke down sobbing. The butcher flinched but didn't move; he had no idea how to handle a weeping woman. Eventually Martha managed to continue. 'I rubbed salt into his wounds, then dragged him out into the lane and left him there.' She wiped her tears on her apron. 'I didn't think of the consequences,' she said reflectively. 'I just wanted to hurt him as he had hurt Nona. After that I couldn't stay in the cottage and took refuge at the farm where I worked, looking after the widowed farmer's children. I wasn't paid. He was as poor as us. But we were fed and were safe. After the death of my baby and his daughter, I was asked to leave and, as I had nowhere to live and was afraid for my children, I left the village and came here.'

'I see,' Mister Gimbell said slowly. "'E's a villain and is taking 'is revenge.'

Martha nodded. 'I had hoped to be invisible here in London.'

Mister Gimbell poured himself a large drink. In the silence the liquid poured noisily from the jug as he said, 'You'll 'ave to go and meet 'im, Martha, but we won't be far away; we'll get James back, never fear.'

He'd not used her name before and she felt an overwhelming sense of gratefulness. She said quietly, 'Thank you. But he mustn't see you.' Her face was creased with worry. She had never imagined that she would ever need to be grateful to this man who, in the past, seemed to disapprove of her and had openly and pointedly avoided her.

'He won't see us, Martha.' His face twitched, a quick grimace, a wry smile that came and went suddenly across his face, 'until it's too late,' he qualified. 'We'll be as silent as the grave. Shadows in the moonlight.'

He poured more gin.

~

The Embankment, Martha noted, was less busy this late in the evening. People who had been taking the evening air were returning home. And the homeless were finding a safe spot to sleep, gathering their children under their arms. Martha pulled her shawl around her shoulders against the cold evening air and walked on in the direction of Parliament. The night was cloudy but now and again the clouds parted and the moon showed her face upon the water. Martha leant on the Embankment wall, taking in the sight of the moon that she'd loved for so long. Her shawl slipped, revealing her shoulders, as she let the light of the moon wash over her. With every fibre of her being she sent out an earnest plea; 'Help me.' In answer, the moon disappeared behind a cloud and Martha walked on feeling abandoned.

In the distance, a gentleman leant against the wall, also looking out over the water, and she wondered his reason for being there, before tears of fear for her son crept into her eyes, blocking out the view.

She felt the presence of the boy before he appeared suddenly at her side. He said nothing, but beckoned her to follow and they crossed the road, turning into a wide street. The boy walked quickly uphill and Martha kept hard on his bare heels. He stopped suddenly, pointing into a dark alley. Martha hesitated. 'Is my son in there?' The boy didn't answer, just shrugged his shoulders.

'Go to the end, missus,' he said, and turned away.

Martha stepped into the walled alley that ran between two houses. Finding her way cautiously in the darkness, she strained her eyes for a sight of James. 'James,' she called in a whisper and listened. There was no reply. With no idea of how long the alley was and with her hand following the wall to steady her, Martha moved slowly. In the overwhelming darkness she suddenly felt hot breath on her face before an arm wrapped roughly around her throat and dragged her backwards into an angle of the wall. Her heart thumped in her chest as the arm pulled her head backwards and booted feet were pushed between her own until they were so far apart she couldn't take either of them from the ground to kick her aggressor. Hot lips crept down her neck and hot spittle, falling upon her shoulder, ran down her back. Her attacker's breathing was loud in her ear, panting in short, exaggerated bursts of excitement.

'You don't know how long I've waited for this moment,' the voice hissed. Martha's eyes widened in silent terror as she recognised the voice of Barney Beemer. His free hand ripped at the back of her bodice, yanking at the material, his fingernails gouging into her flesh. She felt the material give and his hand move slowly to the front of her bodice, feeling her breast. She tried to struggle against him but he gripped a nipple so hard between his fingers that she groaned with the pain. 'Like that, do you? Well, you're going to enjoy this even more,' and his free hand moved to the back of her skirt, pulling it upwards, wedging the endless amount of material between his stomach and her back. Martha stiffened as his hand touched the bare flesh behind her knee, moving quickly to her thigh and around her buttocks. The only movement available to her was to push her buttocks hard into him. But this movement only seemed to excite him more. 'So you like it, Martha. I always knew you did and I'm going to give you a taste of what I gave your daughter.'

As she convulsed her body he became angry. 'Don't struggle, you little witch, or you won't see your son again,' and his thick arm tightened around her neck until she could hardly breathe.

~

The gentleman who had been walking along the Embankment had seen a woman in the distance stop and lean upon the wall. He observed her shawl fall from her shoulders and the way that she had almost bathed in the light of the moon and his heart had quickened beneath his fashionable clothes. As he watched, he saw a child appear beside her like a shadow. She turned and followed the boy, crossing the road quickly, not looking left or right but hard on the child's heels. The man was curious and stepped into the road to follow. Stopping for a hansom cab to pass, he noticed a group led by a short man with large arms slinking along the railings opposite. They looked furtively into the street and followed the woman and the boy. He stood frowning; something was happening. He watched the group come abreast of the boy, who seemed to know them. The barefoot child pointed up the street before running away at speed and the men moved on, removing knives from their clothes that flashed in the sudden moonlight. The gentleman turned and hurried back along the Embankment.

Barney was trying to loosen his trousers with his free hand and was having difficulty because Martha was pulled so close to him. His fingers struggled through all the material of her skirt and Martha prayed that her son was not anywhere close to see what was happening. She felt Barney's body stiffen, but her head was at such an angle she could see nothing but the sky between the roofs.

'Go away; this is mine,' she heard him hiss. At that very moment a cloud moved away from the moon, lighting the alley and revealing the sharp butcher's knives held by a group of five men confronting him. Barney realised he was in trouble and turning Martha towards them he used her as a shield. Moving slowly backwards up the alley he pulled Martha with him. But his arm was so tight around her throat that she couldn't breathe and passed into unconsciousness. As her knees buckled, her limp body sank against him, becoming too heavy for him to drag. Dropping her, he turned to run and was stopped in mid-flight by an iron fist that felled him in one sure movement. The gentleman had brought a constable and they had entered from the other end of the alley. Now, seeing the group of men bending over Martha and thinking the worst, he laid into them. The fight was hard but brief. The gentleman, the constable and the short man, were the last men standing and the constable held Mister Gimbell against the wall by his thick neck.

'I'm detaining all of you until I know what's going on; attempted murder, I wouldn't mind thinking,' the constable said loudly, the fight and the outcome having excited him. 'What's your name, sir?' he shouted with authority as Mister Gimbell raised his hands in submission.

'I'm Gimbell, the butcher from Hare Lane, and these are my sons.'

The constable looked closer at the man before him. 'I've heard of you, sir; my mother buys pies at your shop. I thought as how you were a law-abiding gentleman.'

'I am, constable. I can assure yer that I am.' A tinge of worry about his reputation and his business was now being realised and Gimbell didn't like it.

'But it doesn't explain what you're doing attacking this woman.' The constable indicated Martha's lifeless form on the ground, where the gentleman was bending over her.

As her head was lifted, she stirred. 'She's alive,' the gentleman called to the constable. 'We must get her home.'

The constable tightened his grip on Mister Gimbell's neck. 'No one is going anywhere.'

'Sir,' Gimbell said, 'I know yer must do yer duty but we're not the villains. That man' – he pointed to Beemer's inert body – 'as stole 'er son and 'as 'im 'idden somewhere. She was lured 'ere by that foul wretch. We came to protect 'er. We arrived too late.'

The constable stared into Gimbell's face, his eyes searching for evidence of the truth. 'She lives with us. She's Mrs Tilby, the lady who bakes the pies in my shop.' Gimbell's tone was getting desperate.

The boys were now recovering, beginning to stand. Realising that he was outnumbered, the constable became nervous.

'I think that we can believe them,' the gentleman said, looking up. 'Let them take her home and we'll find out where this man has hidden her son.'

The constable nodded. There were too many for him to handle anyway, and he knew where to find the Gimbell family.

It was only a short time later that Barney stood before the Justice of the Peace. The man was unhappy, having been called from his mistress's warm bed. When Barney refused to speak the constable was ordered to incarcerate him in the nearest prison until he could be put on trial.

It was well after midnight when the Gimbells returned home, carrying Martha through the front door. When Jane saw that Martha was unconscious and her clothes ripped, she cried out in dismay. 'Oh, Gawd 'elp us, what's happened and where's

James?' She stared horrified at the state of her family covered in blood, with swollen faces and black eyes forming.

Martha's inert body was placed on the table a cushion under her head. Having done that the men seemed at a loss as to what to do next.

Pit looked down at the floor and mumbled. 'We didn't get 'im.'

'Yer came back without the boy?' Jane was worried.

'He wasn't there. We searched the area after they took Beemer away.'

'After who took 'im away?' Jane was confused as everyone spoke at the same time and the kitchen was filled with a blur of noise.

'A constable and a gentleman who came to 'elp,' her husband said, touching the bruise on his face tenderly. Jane sat down heavily, then, seeing Martha's pale face, poured some gin onto a cloth and wiped her mouth with it.

Her eyes fluttered and when she saw where she was. Martha looked about her with wild eyes, hoping to see her son, and when she didn't see him she cried out in agony, '*No! James!*'

Jane put her arms around her only friend, stroking her head as though she were a child. 'Don't yer worry, m'dear, we'll get 'im back.' But in her heart Jane knew that it was rare for an abducted child to be found alive in London.

32.

In the early hours of the morning a brazier of hot coals burnt brightly in a small room at the front of the prison. Beemer screamed as his manacles were welded in place. The heated metal burnt into his wrists and ankles blistering his flesh. The sound of his screams echoed through the passages to the cells below, sweeping over the ears of the prisoners, who had heard it all before.

Beemer shuffled with difficulty, as he followed the jailer, down the windowless passages, where a terrible stench invaded his nostrils. The man, holding a large bunch of keys, eventually opened a small door and pushed Beemer roughly through the opening and into darkness. His manacles were secured to a chain and the cell door was slammed shut. The hollowness of that sound danced upon every nerve in Beemer's body, turning the contents of his stomach to acid. He couldn't see the size of the room, as the darkness was complete. But the heat and stench, along with his fear, made him retch. As the fluid fell from his mouth, a man's voice, very close, moaned and cursed. Barney took a step forward and kicked something and was cursed again. Taking a step to the side, his foot came across someone else and he was punched in the leg with the demand to stand still or die. He stood still for the rest of the night in fear of who was in the darkness.

Morning's light fell upon the cell floor from a narrow, barred window high up on the opposite wall. The horror of his position was well founded. A jumble of human limbs was spread across the floor and he discovered that he was not the only one standing. Men and boys slept leaning against the wooden walls. Some had their hands or legs shackled to long chains that hung from rings in the ceiling or floor. Slowly the human mass began to move as the incarcerated awoke; some staggered to their feet, their heavy chains hampering movement. A man suddenly grabbed at a boy, putting him upon his shoulders, and leant against the wall. The boy then held his arms through the barred window, begging passers-by for food. Other men did the same and soon the wall was covered in men and boys. Barney was interested to see a boy brought down from a ragged man's shoulders, and the food taken from him, before he was pushed back again to ask for more. When a skirmish broke out in a corner of the cell, Barney feared for his life. Three men rolled on the floor punching and pulling at each other; tangled up in their chains, they screeched and growled like animals. He watched, unable to see the reason, until an arm rose up out of the melee, a squirming rat clutched tightly in a bloody hand. As the man extricated himself from the others, he crouched with his back to them, biting the head off the creature, and proceeded to pull off its fur and eat the bleeding meat while its legs still moved. Barney knew he was going to be sick.

A man was discovered dead. He was chained to the floor, his ankles a bloody mash of flesh into which his leg irons had rubbed. Barney turned his head away as several men descended on the corpse, pulling at the clothes, over which they then fought. The victor shuffled to the door, calling the jailer, hoping to exchange the clothes for food. Two jailers opened the iron-grated door to remove the body, leaving a dirty bucket of ale well away from the opening. As the inmates squabbled over the drinking rights, the body was removed. The door banged shut. Barney was hungry and asked a frail man with a ragged flesh wound that ran from his eye to his mouth when they would be fed. A mirthless laugh left the torn mouth. 'You want food, yer has to pay for it, or get it somehow.'

304

'I don't have any money.' Barney was near to tears. The man shrugged, uninterested, and turned away to watch the man with the rat.

Several women, young and old, pushed food through a hole in the inner wall for their imprisoned relatives during the morning. But, apart from bringing the bucket of ale and removing the body, the jailers hadn't been seen.

'I need food.' Barney addressed the half-hidden face of the jailer through the bars on the door.

'What yer got?' the jailer in the candlelit passage asked.

'What have I got?' Barney didn't understand.

'Yer 'ave to buy food in 'ere, me Lord.' He laughed, exposing uneven yellow and black teeth.

'But I don't have any money.'

'Then you'll probably be one of the lucky ones who don't make the gallows,' and he laughed again as though he had said something funny.

'Tell me what I must do to earn food,' Barney shouted as the face disappeared from the grill. The man had returned to his chair and was leaning on the table, his face now yellow in the selected light from the candle.

The jailer's sweating expression moved into a sneer, his eyes calculating. The door was opened and Barney's shackle was unhooked from the ring in the wall and he stepped through the door into the passage. The nightmare lasted for half an hour. In that time he was raped and flogged alternately until he couldn't stand. At the end, the laughing jailer threw him some bread and a piece of stinking fish, which Barney stuffed into his bleeding mouth and swallowed without chewing. Back in the cell, he lay prostrate upon the floor where he'd been thrown, ignored by the inmates, who'd seen it all before.

The blood trickling into his mouth tasted good until he began to reflect on how low he had fallen from the church, how his life had changed, and it was all the fault of that Tilby woman.

The rest of his day was spent reviewing his hate for Martha, and what he had done with the boy. He knew that she would never find her son's body, and tried to imagined the pain that she must be feeling. Her possible anguish lifted his spirits.

During the afternoon he was taken to a small room in which stood an inspector and a gentleman in a fashionable blue coat. The inspector stood beside a table, but the gentleman, who had his back to Beemer, continued to stare at the writing gouged into the thick wooden wall. The jailer pushed Barney into a seat at the table.

'Thank you,' the inspector said as the jailer retreated, closing the iron door with a clang that made Beemer blink. 'Mister Beemer,' the inspector continued. Beemer looked surprised. 'Oh yes, we know who you are, sir, and what you have done. What we don't know is what you have done with the boy.' He raised an eyebrow and waited for Beemer to speak but Beemer stared sullenly into the face of the inspector and said nothing.

'You do know, don't you, that what you've done is a hanging offence?'

'I didn't do anything.' Beemer's voice was barely audible.

'Tell us where the boy is,' the policeman said in an agreeable tone of voice.

'What boy?'

'James Tilby.'

'I never heard of a boy by that name.' Beemer stared straight into the man's eyes, just for a moment, before looking down at the table.

'I think you have, and you abducted him.'

There was a slight twitch at the side of the inspector's mouth but not enough to be thought of as a smile.

'You can't prove anything,' Beemer spoke quietly with his head bent.

The inspector changed the subject. 'Do you know a woman by the name of Martha Tilby?'

'No!' Beemer looked up, anger showing in his battered face. His cheeks were flushed with a sudden heat and his eyes became slits. He sat very still like a trapped animal, watching and waiting.

The inspector turned to the gentleman who had stood all this time with his back to them. 'Sir, would you like to speak to the prisoner?'

The man in the blue coat turned slowly to face Beemer, whose eyes, now set in deep black sockets, widened in disbelief.

'Would you like to tell me, Mister Beemer, that you have never heard of James or Martha Tilby?' he said through tightly drawn lips.

'Andrew Tate!' Beemer's mouth was dry.

'Yes, Beemer, and I know just who you are and what you are capable of. Now tell us what you have done with James Tilby.'

'I don't know anything about James Tilby.'

A weak smile crossed the inspector's face. 'We are holding a child who says that you do.'

'What child? I don't know any children.' Beemer looked unsure.

'The one sent to Gimbell's shop with a message for Martha Tilby from you.' The inspector leaned forward over the table. 'The child you sent to lure her to the Embankment.'

'If he says he knows me he's a liar.' Beemer seemed to regain his strength. 'You can't believe a gutter rat before me.'

'We didn't say it was a boy.' The inspector raised an eyebrow. 'Did we?'

Beemer was agitated, his eyes darted here and there around the room as he looked for a way out. There was none. 'Don't try to trick me,' he shouted.

'We are trying to find James Tilby before you add murder to your list of felonies,' the inspector shouted back.

The blood drained from Beemer's face. 'What felonies?' This was a word of which he knew the consequences.

'Shall we try stealing a boar and arson?' Andrew stared into the bruised, ugly face of the man he had seen for so many years in church.

'You can't prove anything. It wasn't me. It's your word against mine, Andrew Tate.'

'But we have proof, as you will see at the trial.' Andrew was calm.

'Trial? What trial?' Beemer couldn't believe they were using words like trial.

'Your trial, Beemer, for stealing my boar and burning down my barn.'

Andrew felt no satisfaction as he faced the man he had been looking for ever since he had arrived in London some weeks ago.

The awful predicament in which Beemer found himself showed on his face as it began to sink in. 'Where's your proof?' he snorted into Andrew's face.

'You'll see soon enough.' Andrew kept his voice level.

Beemer shrugged. His mind was working overtime. What proof could they have? He'd been careful. 'I think you're setting me up for your own purposes, Tate, and I demand to know about the proof.'

Andrew looked at the inspector for guidance. He nodded and Andrew continued. 'We have a section of your coat found near my burnt barn and your footprints are in my field.'

'Where is this piece of material?' The bruised face twisted crudely.

'In the hands of Ernest Draycott, along with your coat. I feel that the judge will believe a man of the cloth, don't you?'

Beemer knew that he was finished but he wouldn't answer their questions.

'Now, where is James Tilby?' the inspector shouted, suddenly banging on the table and making Beemer flinch.

'What's in it for me?' Beemer whined as saliva dripped from his mouth.

'What do you need?' the inspector asked, sitting back in his chair.

'I need food. I need money for food and board. If I can't pay my board I'll be flogged as a debtor.' His face was morose. 'I have no relatives to bring me food, like some.'

Andrew thought about it. 'Tell me where the boy is and I will give you money each day for food until your trial.'

'You didn't listen.' Beemer spat out the words. 'You always were unapproachable, Tate. I need money for my board or I'll be flogged and worse.'

'You're not getting any help until you tell me where the boy is.'

'I don't know where the boy is and you can't prove that I do,' Beemer sneered.

'Then so be it, sir. I leave you to the jailers.' Andrew was disappointed; he'd thought that Beemer would tell in the end and hoped for the sake of the boy that hunger would soon drive Beemer to confess.

The following day Beemer didn't get the chance to earn his food. Three jailers arrived with a priest and called the names of three men and two boys, who shuffled obediently towards the door. 'Where are they going?' Beemer asked no one in particular, but, secretly thinking they were going to get food, he wanted some of it.

'They're for the drop; they're being taken to the chapel to ask God's forgiveness,' a foreigner called Jeykle informed him. 'The sexton reads them the burial service while they sit in the Black Pew looking at their coffins and tonight they stays in a separate cell. *The cell to Hell*,' he said, and he spat on the floor.

The blood in Beemer's veins ran cold and he felt numb. Is that all it took, your name called out and you go obediently to your death? For want of conversation, he asked what they'd done.

'The little 'un stole a loaf of bread. He was hungry. The tall man stole a pig.' He shrugged and stared back at the wall.

Beemer thought about Andrew Tate's boar, but no one could prove anything. No, he would get out of this hole, he was sure of that. He just had to be clever. Hunger raged in his stomach and he called the jailer, but the straw-strewn corner of the passageway where the jailer's table stood with its little candle was empty.

The next day a single bell tolled sorrowfully. The monotonous sound slid through the deep darkness of the prison passages, and voices were quieted in the cells. A hush fell over the prison, causing a heaviness of heart and fear. At eleven o'clock a multitude of excited voices was heard. Slightly muffled by the thickness of the walls, a great roar of excitement reached the inmates' ears. The crowd roared and twenty minutes later the roar and the toll of the bell continued. 'What's happening?' Beemer asked.

'Expect someone's taking a long time to stop jigging,' a naked man chained by his feet to a large ring in the floor answered. 'They take bets on it.'

'Who does?'

'The crowd, they bet on who'll croak first or last the longest. They bet on all sorts of things.'

Beemer was sober now. The seriousness of his position had become very clear and his heart thumped in his chest. Although, he thought to himself, they can't prove anything without a body. They can't prove I know where James Tilby is. Even then, how would they prove it? Then he remembered the urchin and swore under his breath. But then, who would believe a street urchin over him, an educated man who'd been trusted with large sums of money and never found stealing? Also, he smiled, wasn't he known to be a pillar of the church? No, he assured himself, he would be free soon. But then he remembered the Reverend Ernest Draycott, who had his torn coat, and he wasn't so sure.

33.

It was early morning and Martha hadn't slept. Pain and turmoil ran like demons in her head and in her heart. She'd cried in anger, then fear, and back again to anger until she was weak, wrung out and more exhausted than she had ever been. Her only visualisation was the face of her son, his fear and his imagined loneliness. Martha tried to reach him telepathically in the hope that she would feel what he felt. Perhaps know where he was, that in some way he might feel her presence, her love. She felt only emptiness.

In her distress she cried out to the Goddess, but her anguish overrode any guidance that might have been forthcoming. A hollow blackness was eating into her soul and she could no longer feel anything but her own suffering. For the first time in her life she felt detached from everything and everyone, not eating, not sleeping and unable to think.

The day after James disappeared, the Gimbell family had taken it in turns to search the busy streets. Martha also walked the streets, at first with determination, staring at people and buildings, crying out his name and crying in fear for his life as the hours passed. But it was a hopeless task. There were so many houses, so many streets and alleys, as well as the length of the river.

On the fourth day, Jane kept Nona busy making pies, while Martha, hollow-eyed and desperate, continued to search for her son. She hardly felt the coldness of the wind that blew from the north with a bitter bite that cut through her clothes.

She thought that she saw him many times that day. At windows, walking, sitting on the back of a cart, but each time it wasn't James. By the afternoon she was so distraught that she felt she was going mad. She wanted to scream, tear at her clothes and fall on her knees in desperation, begging everyone to help her. Weak and unable to go on, she sank down beside a stack of barrels. With her head in her hands she sat on the ground and sobbed uncontrollably. The inhabitants of London passed by without giving her a second glance. There was nothing odd about some poor wretch sitting on the ground howling: today it was this woman; tomorrow it would be someone else.

~

On the fifth day Andrew Tate visited Beemer in prison, as he had each day. As Beemer walked slowly towards him, pulling the heavy chains to the cell gate, Andrew shook his head at the man's dogged stubbornness. Beemer had lost weight. His once-full belly hung in a flattened ruche of empty skin between his hips. Sores and welts covered his now bony shoulders. His chin lay upon his chest, where his loose mouth seemed even flabbier as it hung at the corners. Andrew knew, if he didn't get the answer today, by tomorrow Beemer wouldn't care if he lived or died and perhaps it was already too late.

'Beemer,' he spoke quietly with sadness in his voice, 'you can get some ease by paying for food. Just tell me where the boy is.'

Beemer stood unsteadily. When he lifted his head his small eyes were dead and showed no recognition of the face before him on the other side of the bars.

'Did you hear me? I can get you food and money to ease your suffering. Just tell me where James Tilby is.'

Andrew quickly covered his nose with his arm as the unimaginable, gut-wrenching stench from the mortuary below the cells pervaded the corridors on a sudden draft of air mixed with that of the unwashed prisoners' bodies. 'Do you hear me?' he said again, trying not to retch.

Barney moved his cracked lips but no sound emanated from his mouth.

'Jailer,' Andrew demanded of the man who sat watching from a table with a bunch of keys hanging from his belt, 'give this man a drink.'

The man shrugged. 'It'll cost yer, sir.' His face held no expression as he awaited a reply.

Andrew held out a coin and a metal cup holding thin ale was pushed through the hole in the wall. Barney grabbed at it like a mad man, tipping it up so shakily that the liquid spilt over his face and ran down his bare chest. He drank in great gulps.

'Now,' Andrew said when the cup was empty, 'what was it you were trying to say, Beemer?'

'I want the ordinary.' The voice was gruff, almost unheard.

'You can see the chaplain, if you tell me where James is,' Andrew persisted.

'I want the ordinary,' Beemer repeated, as though Andrew hadn't spoken.

'Jailer, send for the ordinary,' Andrew demanded.

'Yes, sir.' The man scurried away, pocketing another coin, to carry out Andrew's demand.

Half an hour later the chaplain bustled along the passage, his black robes flowing around his short fat body. Swinging a small orb on a short chain from which fragrant smoke escaped, he looked frightened.

Andrew walked towards him to be out of Beemer's hearing. They nodded a greeting to each other.

The chaplain noticed Andrew's glance at the smoking orb. 'Protection,' he said, 'against lice and jail fever, sir. Now, who is it that wants to speak with me?'

'His name is Beemer, but I must come with you, sir; I have to find out where he has a child hidden.'

'I cannot allow that, sir'. The man looked askance. 'I am on God's business and a man's confession is between himself and his Maker.' He'd taken a step back away from Andrew and his voice was pious.

Andrew felt his anger rising but for the sake of James spoke softly. 'A young boy's life depends on my knowing where he is, sir. Surely, God, and the church would care about the life of a missing child.'

The chaplain waved the orb, emitting more fragrant smoke and covered his mouth with a cloth as a wave of putrid stench passed up the corridor on another blast of air. Looking terrified he nodded his agreement. 'Stand near the hole in the wall out of his sight. I will repeat what he says loud enough for you to hear. But I cannot tell you directly, sir.' He held out his hand with a meaningful look. Andrew angrily, placed a coin into the fat hand, which was studied before being dropped into a pocket hidden in the man's robe. With a nod to the jailer the cell door was opened and the chaplain entered and spoke with Barney, while Andrew put his cheek to the damp wall and listened at the hole.

34.

Emma awoke with a feeling of fear running through her body. Something was wrong, she could feel it. Was something going to happen today, or had it already happened? She lay very still, listening. She could hear Bert's heavy breathing, but she couldn't hear Effie. Getting up from her mattress, she moved to the other side of the room and looked down on the frail girl. She was very still. Emma reached out a hand and touched her. The skin was cold. Suddenly the eyes popped open and the girl screamed out. Emma jumped, and Bert snorted awake. 'What's going on?'

'Oh, Emma, you gave me a start.' Effie's eyes were wide with shock.

'I'm sorry, Effie, I thought you were…'

'I was what?' Her face flushed and her eyes held suspicion.

Emma didn't know how to say it. 'You were very still; I couldn't hear you breathing.'

'Yer thought I'd kicked the bucket, didn't yer?'

'No!' Emma lied in vain.

'Yes, yer did. I can see it in yer face.'

Emma was embarrassed. 'I'm sorry. I can't explain it, but I feel that something is wrong.'

'Where?' Effie asked, concerned.

'I don't know.' Emma wanted to change the subject now that it was obvious that all was well here. 'Let me prepare some food for you both.'

She turned back into the room to prepare food for the start of the day but the feeling of dread continued and she wished she hadn't woken Effie, for now she had no privacy to consult with her ancestors.

The morning selling oysters dragged on. Customers came in dribs and drabs to the stall. Emma unconsciously scanned the buildings that stood around them, looking hard at passers-by for clues to her fear. She found none and was almost in tears by mid-morning and Effie could feel it too.

'Emma. Do yer think it could be yer mother?' Emma's tears rolled like a dam overflowing.

'I think it could be. I have to find her.' She sniffed and dabbed away a tear, relieved that at last she had been able to speak of her fear.

'We're very slow 'ere today; why don't yer go and look?'

'No, I can't leave you here on your own. I don't know how long I'll be.'

'Let's give it 'alf an hour, then we'll pack up early. We're not doing much today.'

'Effie, you are my dearest friend, thank you.' She hugged the girl tightly and felt her bones through the thin clothes.

Before setting out, they sold the remaining oysters to the innkeeper at the Cat and Tinker for a good price. Not feeling so bad about the morning's work, they set off.

'Do you know which way to go, Emma?'

I don't. I just feel it could be this way; it seems as good as any other.'

They walked the streets for an hour, glancing down alleyways, looking up at windows, watching people passing, until Emma noticed that Effie was limping as they stepped into yet another road. 'What's wrong?' she asked, aware of the girl's frailty.

'A small pain. Can we stop?'

Stepping back from the road, they stood a while on the corner. Emma felt anxious that the search would be finished before it had begun. An urgency had risen within her that she couldn't explain. She needed space to think, to link in, but there was no space, no silence and no privacy on London's streets. Somehow she had to shut everything out and feel the energy, but how? The noise was extraordinary, with people calling out, horses snorting and whinnying and carriage wheels rumbling. Just then Effie let out a gasp, crying, 'No! No!'

Startled, Emma grabbed the girl 'What is it! What's wrong?'.

But when she looked in the same direction as Effie's fearful eyes, she also held her breath in fear. A small puppy was running around in the road as the horses and carriages thundered past in a melee of wheels, hooves and dust.

'Oh! It's going to be killed.' Effie gripped Emma's arm, her nails leaving marks on the skin.

They both wanted to shut their eyes and not see what was inevitably going to happen. Yet somehow they couldn't look away. It was only seconds before a hoof caught the pup, sending it tumbling into the air, where it was hit by the chest of another horse before falling limply to the ground. As horses and carriages raced past, Emma picked her way precariously across the road. Stepping neatly between the fast-moving carriages, she bent quickly, gathering the pup from the dirt, where it was howling in great distress. No one stopped. Emma took the pup back to Effie. They sat at the side of the road, with it lying in Effie's lap. Emma ran her fingers lightly over the small creature, examining it. It shivered and whimpered as she ran her hands over its body. 'I don't think anything is broken, but it must be bruised.' The pup looked pathetically up at Effie and laid a soft paw on her arm.

'Oh, dear little thing; Don't worry, we'll look after yer.' The pup, seeming to know it was safe, licked her arm. For a moment Emma thought that this was the end of her being able to look for her mother, but then the seed of an idea formed in her mind. She hoped that she wasn't deceiving Effie when she suggested the idea.

'I think it would be best if you took the pup home, Effie, and looked after it. We can't leave it here on its own.'

'But what about searching for yer mother? I feel bad leaving yer, Emma.'

'I'll carry on. You take it home and care for it,' and she patted the pup's head as it wagged its tail in response. Emma smiled and kissed its nose. 'Thank you,' she whispered in its ear. It responded by licking her face.

When Effie and the pup had disappeared into the crowd, Emma stood very still. What to do now? She stepped into the road, but then stepped back frowning. Turning to her left, she followed an instinct and started to walk.

She passed establishments that she would dearly have loved to be able to enter. The apothecary, with all its coloured jars in the window and seats at the long counter. The draper's shop on a corner of two streets, with its window decorated with bundles of coloured cloth and delicate lace. A shoemaker's window displayed ladies' shoes in coloured leathers and exquisitely embellished leather bags. Also displayed were fine leather boots for the gratification of those who could afford them. In-between the shops that she passed were busy yards where horses were stabled and carriages housed, some with wheels being mended, and all the time she looked beyond what she saw, looking for her mother. There were taverns with music and riotous laughter emanating from windows and doors, and barefoot, dirty-faced children hanging around the entrances. She passed coffee houses, where more educated gentlemen were talking and smoking. But it was the constant noise that made Emma feel alien to this environment and wondered if her mother could survive in a place like this.

Passing an alleyway beside a tavern, her breath was suddenly taken away by a physical blow to her back and she grasped a wall for support. 'Allo, darling, 'ave yer 'ad too much?' A man, unsteady on his feet and reeking of alcohol laughed as he wrapped one arm around her waist and tried to kiss her. Feeling the danger that she was in, she placed her hand beneath his arm and pushed as hard as she could. He tumbled to the ground, a look of surprise on his face. Once down he seemed unable to get up and started to sing. 'She was me lov–aly, that lady in *re-d*, and I was *sooo 'appy*, when she came *tooo* me *be-d.*'

Two more men staggered from the tavern, blocking her way. To escape them she ran into a narrow passage. It wasn't until she reached some wooden steps looking for a way out that she realised that she had run into a dead end. There was nowhere to go. The three men were making their way unsteadily towards her, grinning and leering at her as she started up the wooden staircase that rose from the passage to a landing and a door. By the time she had reached the top she had talked herself into enquiring of the occupants about her mother, as an excuse as to why she was on their step. Taking a deep breath she knocked somewhat timidly on the door, and waited. There was no answer. One of the men was now at the bottom of the stairs, looking up at her, grinning stupidly. Knocking twice more she tried the door; it opened to her touch. Without another thought she stepped inside and shut the door. The silence inside the property was unnerving. What would she say if the owner came back? Trying to contain her fear, she looked about her. Most of the room was taken up by a large bed, with drapes half pulled. Worryingly, the bedding was gathered up in the middle, as though someone had just got out of it. There was a small table beneath a window, accompanied by two chairs, and a slight smell of perfume on the air. There were cooking pots on the cold grate and a dish of half-eaten food on the table. But, apart from the insects that scurried across the floor, the place was deserted.

Taking a deep breath to settle her nerves, she wondered again what would happen if the owner came back, and how she would explain her presence in their property.

'Why am I here?' she asked herself uneasily.

'*Wait*,' a whisper formed in her head. But the cold silence of the unfamiliar room and the fear of being caught here crept like a snake up her spine, chilling the back of her neck. In this state of fear she ignored the whisper and turned to leave. But it was already too late. The sound of heavy boots on the stairs outside drummed like a heartbeat in her ears. She froze, staring at the door, waiting, horror reflected in her eyes. There was nowhere to hide. She'd stopped breathing by the time the latch lifted and the door creaked slowly open. A tall figure entered stealthily, a pistol in his hand. Letting out a low moan, Emma fainted.

~

The body of a girl on the floor wasn't what Andrew Tate had expected to find. He approached her carefully. Bending, he felt for a pulse in her neck and was relieved to find her alive. Lifting her from the floor, he laid her on the bed. There was something about the face that was familiar, but he couldn't know her: he knew no one in London and young women rarely came into his life. But what was she doing here? Beemer hadn't mentioned a young girl and where was the boy? He searched the room and the small room that led off it. The place was silent and empty and had been for some time. He returned to the main room just as the girl was stirring. He stood back, not wanting to frighten her, and watched as her memory returned. Her body convulsed and her head turned towards the door. From the fear that showed on the young face, he could tell that she knew he was in the room. She moved slowly, pulling herself to the top of the bed between the heavy drapes. Large, fearful eyes stared at him, but not a word was spoken.

'I'm sorry to have frightened you, mistress; I understood that this property was empty.'

Emma stared, her mouth open, her brain moving fast. So this wasn't the house owner, she thought quickly. He must be a robber; that's why he had a pistol. Believing herself to be in danger, Emma rolled from the bed and made for the door, but Andrew was quicker, getting to it first.

'You know where the boy is, don't you?' he shouted.

His voice was accusing; his words made no sense to Emma, who stood before him trying to think of a way to escape.

'Where is he?' Andrew shouted. 'Tell me and I will try to make your crime easier for you.'

Now Emma came to life. Words exploded in her head. *What crime? What boy?* 'What boy? What crime?' she managed to speak at last. 'I have just arrived here myself, sir, and there was no boy.'

Andrew's temper flared to the surface and, pointing his pistol at her, he demanded harshly, 'Tell me what you have done with the boy.'

Emma was afraid as she stared into the barrel of the pistol, but stood before him solidly, her chin raised. 'You may shoot me, sir, for I cannot tell you. I know of no boy. I am looking for my mother.'

Suddenly Andrew knew who stood before him. Martha's daughter. He lowered the pistol. 'I'm sorry, Mistress Tilby. I realise now who you are.'

Emma was taken aback so much that she had to clutch at the bed drapes.

'You know me, sir?'

'Yes, you're looking for your mother, Martha Tilby.'

Emma swallowed hard. 'Do you know where my mother is? For I must find her and see that she is well.'

'She is not well,' he sighed, 'and will be very pleased to see you. She is looking for your brother, James, as am I. Your brother was abducted by Mister Beemer, who appears to have followed your mother to London.'

'For what reason would he follow my mother to London, sir?'

'I do not know, unless it is revenge, she being a target in my stead.'

Emma was mystified; her mother was a calm, wonderful woman who always saw the other person's reasoning and made allowances. How could she have made an enemy? 'Revenge for what, sir?' Her voice was slightly raised, bewildered.

'That, mistress, you will have to ask your mother.'

Emma's heart was racing with fear. 'If you know where my mother is, please take me to her as fast as is possible, sir.'

Andrew opened the door and as they left she asked, 'Do I know you, sir?'

'No!' he shook his head sadly. 'No, you don't know me. No one knows me.'

~

Trade at the butchers was as busy as usual and no one would have realised the drama that was playing out behind the dividing door. Jane and Nona had been keeping their spirits up, furiously making pies that had become so popular they were finding it difficult to keep up with the demand. Buller was still walking the streets looking for James, only stopping to return home for food and sleep. Pit was keeping watch for James as he worked his way around the city delivering coal. Charlie and Bill took it in turns to leave their father in the shop, while they searched the bank of the Thames and the narrow alleyways leading from it. They asked questions at the warehouses that edged both the south and the north bank of the river. Everyone's thoughts, day and night, were for the boy and his mother. Martha was dying before their eyes. Her face had become sunken, her eyes circled with a blue shadow, her beautiful hair now hung dull and uncombed. Out all day, only returning to see if he'd been found, she refused food and hardly slept.

Jane was worried as she watched Martha's mental state change and for the first time in her life she was feeling completely inadequate.

A thick fog descended on London, trapping the smoke of a million fires and the gas from rotting sewage and detritus beneath it, a miasma that attacked the lungs and eyes of all who ventured out into the unsafe streets.

It was early evening when Nona answered a knock at the door. Her scream filled Jane with dread and she ran to the door, pulling it from the girl's grasp. Before her stood a man in a blue coat and a young girl in a brown dress. He politely lifted his hat and nodded a greeting.

'Whatcha want?' But Jane's sharp enquiry was ignored as Nona flew into the young girl's arms.

'Emma,' she sobbed. 'Emma, we've lost James.'

'I know, Nona.' Emma enclosed her sister in her arms, saying, 'We've come to help find him.' Turning around to include the gentleman, she found him gone, disappeared into the fog that hid the rest of the street.

'Where is he?' she asked, unable to believe he had delivered her and walked away without speaking.

'Come in.' Jane held the door wider. 'Don't let the foul air in or we'll all be ill.' And she shut the door behind Emma with purpose, locking it as though the fetid stink could still enter the premises and choke them.

Nona's face was bright with excitement as she held Emma's hand tightly. 'This is my sister, Emma, Mrs Gimbell.'

'I thought as much.' Jane smiled, raising her eyes to the ceiling and thanking the Lord for small mercies. 'Now sit yerself down and tell me 'ow yer got 'ere.' But Emma ignored her words, needing to know of her mother.

'How is my mother, Mrs Gimbell? I'm very worried about her and about James.'

'We're all very worried about them both, but how did you get to know something was wrong?' Jane was puzzled. 'And who's the gentleman and how did he know where we live?'

'I don't know who he is, but he knew where my mother was

living and brought me here. I'm so grateful; without him I would not have found you.'

Jane was thoughtful. 'I wonder if 'e's the same man who called the constable.'

'The constable?' Emma looked puzzled.

'Gawd. It now seems such a long story and I don't 'ave all the pieces of it. But I will tell yer some of what I know.' She winked.

Emma wasn't sure if this strange woman was communicating something silently or whether she had an affliction. So she nodded and smiled.

'Nona' – Jane bent down to the girl holding tightly to her sister's hand – 'get the jug and some pies; we must offer Emma some refreshment. She must be very 'ungry.'

When Nona was out of hearing, Jane leant forward and whispered. 'There's something I can't tell yer. It will be up to yer mother.' Emma didn't understand, but nodded in accord and worried all the more. 'The something I can't tell yer,' she whispered, "appened while yer mother was out of the 'ouse working in the fields with Robert. I understand that yer mother then took 'er revenge on a man called Beemer.'

Emma was amazed and shook her head. What she was hearing was so unlike her mother. But she let Jane continue.

'Your mother later realised that she'd made an enemy and for the safety of 'em all 'ad to find somewhere else to live. She found refuge on the Tate farm after the farmer's wife died suddenly. At first, all was well until a spate of bad luck 'it the farm. Mister Tate, who 'ad been struggling to save 'is farm, was not a rich man. In fact, 'e only 'ad the farm because it 'ad been passed down through 'is family.'

Jane took a swig from the jug and wiped her mouth on the sleeve of her dress before continuing. 'When 'is daughter and yer sister Charity died, 'e could take no more, and sent 'is children away to live with 'is sister and asked yer mother to leave. She made 'er way 'ere, 'aving nowhere else to go and believing that she was safe from Beemer in London. But the evil must 'ave burnt deep in the 'art of the man, 'cos 'e followed 'er 'ere and some'ow 'e's found 'er. It was 'im oo took yer brother and, although 'e's in prison, he won't say where 'e's got the boy 'idden. It was six days ago that 'e was taken.' Her face had a meaningful look.

'Six days!' Emma was concerned. 'I must go and look for Mother and James.'

'What can yer do that the rest of us 'aven't done?' Jane shook her head, and sitting back in her chair pushed the jug and a pie towards Emma. 'First eat. This is going to take the luck of one of us being in the right place at the right time. The more of us who are out there looking the better for young James, the poor little mite.'

35.

When Andrew left the Gimbells' home, he moved cautiously through the fog and into the main street. His heart was pounding, his whole being stimulated at being so close to Martha. He wanted to run and shout with the amazing feeling in his body that even the fog could not suppress. He mumbled under his breath, chastising himself to keep control of his wits. He believed that he had never before been in love and this feeling that he was experiencing was both beautiful and painful.

His wife, Margaret, had lived in the village and she'd seemed like good stock for a farmer's wife. After they'd married there had been nothing else but the daily running of the farm. It was all that he thought about and it had worked. It was a good partnership. He didn't know then that there could be anything else. A working partnership is what he had witnessed with his parents and his grandparents. What he felt for Martha was disturbing, debilitating and at the same time stimulating beyond his imagination. She was different, not just because she didn't attend church, to the annoyance of others, but because whatever she believed in she would not be bullied into something that she did not. He admired the way she dealt with life and realised he'd never heard her complain. From the fields he'd observed her walking on the edge of the forest. He had seen her standing in the moonlight, her hair loose to her waist, doing nothing, just looking at the moon. He had seen her when she'd thought she was unobserved, holding a flower up to the sun before placing it into a pot or into the ground. He had imagined that this must be for her husband and he had respected that perhaps her heart was elsewhere. A flush came to his face as he smiled at the vision of her naked in the candlelight of his kitchen, and he thanked her for the painful joy that was now in his heart. If only he could hold her, bury his face in her hair, lie with her, he would be a happy and fulfilled man. It was unbearable for him knowing that Martha was suffering for the loss of her child. Her sadness lay upon his shoulders like a yoke, driving him to find the boy.

As he entered his lodging, his landlady, the imperial Mrs Moody, moved her frilly plumpness into the hallway and twittered like a bird.

'Oh, Mister Tate!' She leant against the doorframe of her own private rooms and smiled seductively at him in her low-cut dress and lace-edged bonnet. A heavy rope of amber beads lay like miniature golden eggs on her heaving bosom, drawing the eye, whether it wanted to look or not. Her fat fingers, adorned with many rings, touched her face, a sign of her affluence, which she flaunted. The scent she wore permeated the hallway, competing with the smell of fish that had been cooked for her earlier by her maid, Eliza.

'Mrs Moody.' He tipped his hat as he'd seen others do in London. She sighed; her heart fluttered: such a handsome gentleman, so well built.

He made for the stairs, his room being on the third floor. But, changing his mind, turned suddenly towards the woman. An expectation of what might be to come took her breath away and the desire showed on her face.

'Mrs Moody.' He smiled. 'My friend, new to London, has lost...' he chose his words carefully... '*his*... child. I wonder if you might know where he might look, having looked everywhere he could think of,' he added quickly.

'Oh, my dear sir,' she breathed heavily. 'Has he tried the graveyard?' She walked towards Andrew, holding out her chubby arms in sympathy.

Andrew took a step backwards, shaking his head. 'Perhaps not, madam.' He had definitely not thought of the graveyard. That would have given into defeat and was certainly not the message he wanted to take to Martha.

The woman's heavily made-up eyes suddenly opened with an idea. 'What about the church, sir? They seem to know everything.'

'A very good idea, thank you, Mrs Moody.' He turned again for the stairs.

'What is the poor child's name?' she simpered. 'It is my pleasure in this line of business to know many people, sir, who would be very glad indeed to help us in this search.'

'His name is James Tilby, madam. He's about eight years of age, fair-haired and small for his age.'

The emotionally fluttering hand that touched his in sympathy was warm and wet, the upturned face framed in its little bonnet adoring. Andrew felt suddenly hot and uncomfortable with this show of adoration, something that he had never experienced before.

'If you'll excuse me, madam.' He bowed, and turning again for the stairs took them two at a time as though the Devil were on his heels.

As he reached the landing she called after him. 'You could always try the workhouse, sir.'

Early next morning Andrew awoke to the sound of furious knocking on his door. 'Mister Tate! *Mister Tate!*' Mrs Moody's voice was muffled behind the door. 'Mister Tate, please stir yourself. I have news of the boy and you must hurry.' The knocking became more demanding. '*Mister Tate!*'

Andrew answered the door to a lady who was genuinely agitated. 'You must hurry, sir, if you are to save him. My acquaintance who works at the docks has found the boy, but he has been taken onto a ship bound for the Indies. It sails on the tide.'

Andrew was suddenly wide awake, grabbing at his outer clothes. 'Has the boy been conscripted, madam?'

'No, sir, I understand it to be a merchant ship called *The Eagle.*'

'Where do I go, madam, and how long do I have?'

'You have less than an hour sir before it sails.'

Borrowing a horse from Mrs Moody's yard behind the house, Andrew rode the truculent mare, which hadn't had its breakfast, through the quiet streets to the docks, which were crowded with packets, their masts standing erect in a maze of rigging. The halyards and shrouds cracked and smacked a discordant tune with the movement of the water. The quayside was busy with ships some being unloaded and others loaded. The passage of men between gangplank, dockside and warehouses was endless and noisy.

Andrew sat astride the horse, watching the scene before him. There were more than ten ships, some still out in the river with small boats ferrying cargo and men to the shore. He called to a man in a thick woven tunic. 'Can you tell me, sir, where *The Eagle* is berthed?'

'I'm sorry, sir, I can't.' The man hurried on.

Andrew rode the horse amongst the baskets of potatoes, barrels of salted fish, caskets of tea and porcelain. He moved the horse carefully between the articles stacked upon the dock, piles of wood, coal, marble and slate, while all the time surrounded by working men who frustrated his need to find the ship quickly. Stepping his horse neatly over ropes and swerving around men who cursed him and his horse, he came across a man sitting on a pile of canvas smoking a pipe outside the sailmaker's workshop.

'Could you tell me sir, where *The Eagle* is berthed?' he called down to the man.

'Aye, that I can,' the man nodded. Removing the pipe from his mouth, he pointed with it towards a ship that, having raised its signal, was pulling out into the river.

'She just set sail.'

Andrew's hopes and expectations dropped like a stone to his boots. Fear for the boy and Martha drained every cell in his body. He watched helplessly from the side of the dock as the ship, with sails raised, glided slowly out to the middle of the wide river, its eventual goal the sea and the other side of the world. As men on board *The Eagle* rushed about the decks pulling at ropes and climbing the rigging, Andrew hoped to get a sight of James, but the sides of the ship were too high for a small boy to be seen. As he watched the ship go he made a decision. He would follow the ship along the river in the hope that he could get close enough to shout to the crew.

Without food or thought, he rode the horse for hours, sometimes along the towpath, which became narrow in places and was often overgrown. He would have called out to the boat but the river was wide and many ships sailed between them. Sometimes he rode through dark, overgrown woods, having left the town's housing behind, and felt more at home passing small fields. Often he had to ride inland away from the wide river to avoid marshy ground, where his horse whinnied and staggered and refused to go on. Sometimes Andrew rode the horse at a gallop around small hamlets, where frustration and fear of losing sight of the ship raged within his being and always, somehow, he found his way back to the water. By midday, with the clouds scudding at speed overhead and the light turning a muddy yellow, he realised that the ship was slowing, lowering her sails.

A strong blast of cold wind, with the smell of rain and seaweed upon it, tugged at Andrew's coat. As he looked towards the distant sea it became clear why the ship had lowered her sails. The sky ahead was black and threatening as it caressed the horizon. Within its dark depths the warning rumble of a storm already playing out at sea could be heard. The sound rolled menacingly across the flats and marshes, sweeping up the channel as though an army on horseback approached. The strong wind whipped up the waves, giving each a frothy white head that ran swiftly before the storm and crashed against the land.

Andrew put his hands to his mouth and called, 'Hello, *The Eagle*. Can I come aboard?' No sound came back from the ship, where men were busy on the deck, and then Andrew saw that the anchor was being dropped. 'Hello, *The Eagle*, can I come aboard?' he tried again. In the gathering darkness the movement of a lamp showed Andrew that someone was still moving about the ship. He called again. 'I have business with the captain of *The Eagle*. Can I come aboard?'

'Hello, the shore, what is your business?' The voice carried well between the squalls of grasping wind.

'I must speak with your captain, urgently. It… is… in… his… interest.'

The light moved slowly to the back of the ship and disappeared from view. Andrew waited patiently while his horse munched on the grass at the base of a tree.

A small boat was lowered over the side of the ship and two men rowed with difficulty through the rough water towards the shore. Tying the horse to the tree and stepping into the boat, Andrew sat nervously, looking at the angry water and hoping that he would again feel the land beneath his feet as the small craft rose and fell pounded by the waves in the now-turbulent estuary.

As Andrew stepped upon the ship's deck, men the like of which he had not encountered before surrounded him. They fitted his idea of a band of cutthroats very well and for a moment he wondered if he had done the right thing; after all, he didn't even know if James was aboard.

'I should like to speak to your captain.' He addressed the nearest man, as the wind took his voice away over the side of the ship. They stared at him as though deaf to his words and he stood awhile longer surrounded by the silent crew.

The crack of a whip made Andrew flinch, and the group of men parted to reveal the captain in all his splendour. He wore a wide-brimmed hat, decorated with plumes of exotic feathers and worn at a jaunty angle. A strand of red leather held his long black hair behind his head, where it curled at length down the centre of his back. He was unshaven and the most handsome, flamboyant man that Andrew had ever seen. The captain stood with his feet apart, his blue eyes appraising Andrew; one eyebrow was raised, awaiting an explanation.

Andrew took in the long wine-red coat of good quality and brown breeches, his expensive leather boots and the whip that lay stretched out between the man's hands. 'May I speak in private with you, sir?' Andrew shouted over the wind.

The captain turned away and Andrew took it that he should follow. Below deck the captain's cabin was well-furnished, with an oak table that had strange animals carved on the legs. Two chairs and a carved bunk were against one wall. Deep blue drapes woven with patterns in gold thread hung at the bunk and window. A walnut tallboy with six deep drawers and three small ones in a row at the top had been built against a wall, and the deep polished surface was rich in colour. Seemingly out of place in these surroundings was a tall highly polished red cabinet on which, painted in black, were scenes of mountains, rivers and fantastic creatures. A table with an overlarge top sat under the window on which lay a chart. An ornate lamp swung from a chain in the centre of the cabin, housing three candles. Other lamps holding candles around the cabin walls had been lit giving the room a cosy feeling. Andrew felt anything but cosy.

Lightning crackled through the rigging, followed instantly by thunder that crashed above the ship. The rain, which had been tapping upon the window, now hammered so hard that the captain drew the drapes across it. Andrew flinched at another crack of thunder and the captain mumbled, 'Right overhead.' Raising both his eyebrows he stared at Andrew, awaiting his explanation.

'I am Andrew Tate, sir, at your service,' he said, composing himself quickly and bowing, unsure how to speak to the captain of a ship.

'Captain Taymar.' The flamboyant captain nodded towards the table for Andrew to sit. 'Would you take some wine with me, sir?'

Andrew was relieved at the captain's apparent friendliness. 'Thank you, sir,' he said. 'It has been a long day in the saddle.'

The captain took a flagon from the red cabinet, along with two goblets and half-filled both with a deep red wine, the best wine Andrew had ever tasted.

The captain's amused eyes assessed Andrew across the table. He could see that, although well dressed, Andrew was not a gentleman by birth. Looking at the rugged hand that held the goblet, he was even more intrigued.

'There was something that you wanted me to hear urgently, sir?' Captain Taymar said, lowering his goblet and placing it on the table.

'Indeed, please forgive me. I have never before tasted such wine.'

The captain smiled. 'I travel to many countries and buy for myself that which I like.' He held his goblet betwixt finger and thumb, twisting it.

Having had a life of constant struggle and pain, Andrew found it hard to envisage that anyone but a nobleman or rich landowner could just buy anything that he liked. But he had to get down to the business of finding out if James was on the ship.

'Sir, I believe that you have a boy working on this ship who should be with his mother.'

The captain inclined his head and looked thoughtful. Andrew continued. 'He was abducted at a hanging by a man who at this moment is in prison awaiting the gallows for that and other offences. The boy's mother is distraught and the constables are trying to find the boy.'

'The boy's name?' Captain Taymar gave nothing away.

'James Tilby.'

The captain stood and walked to the door. 'Jonah,' he called. A man was at the door instantly. 'Do we have a boy on board by the name of James Tilby?'

'Yes, sir. The one we've named Jolly.' Jonah looked into the room and frowned at Andrew.

'Bring him here.' The order was obeyed quickly and Jonah's feet could be heard on the stairs. 'It appears that you are right, sir, we do have a boy by that name aboard.' Andrew looked relieved. 'But I can't let you have him, if that is your intention. I need every hand that I have hired for this voyage.'

'I am willing to pay for his release.' Andrew had known he might have a battle, and had thought it out on the long ride and how much he could afford.

'As I said, I need every hand that I have hired.' The captain held the flagon up, offering more wine.

Andrew declined, asking, 'How much are you paying the boy?'

The man looked amused and avoided the question as they continued to weigh each other up across the table. 'What is the boy to you, sir?' the captain said thoughtfully.

'In the absence of the boy's mother through illness because of his loss, I have become his guardian.' Andrew felt himself becoming hot beneath his coat at the lie that had come so readily to his lips but stared steadily at the captain. He had never in his life had to tell an untruth and could never have imagined that he would be in such a position as to have to do so. He was, however, determined to get James back to his mother even if he himself had to stay aboard until they reached the Indies.

The cabin door swung open and a small boy was pushed into the room. Ragged and barefoot, his face, showing the anxiety of his position, eyed the whip that now hung on the wall beside the door.

'James Tilby?' the captain asked in a quiet voice.

James looked from the whip to the captain. 'I didn't do anything, sir.' He looked and sounded distressed.

'I know. I want to ask you if you know this gentleman.'

James had been so engrossed in the whip that he hadn't noticed the other man in the room.

Andrew stood up. 'Hello, James, I've come to take you back to your mother.' For one awful moment Andrew thought that James didn't recognise him. And why should he, dressed as he was now?

'Mister Tate? Mister Tate!' The boy started to shake and tears rose into his eyes. 'I want my mother. It was Barney Beemer, Mister Tate, I didn't know the way home.' he sobbed, and would have run to Andrew if Jonah had not been holding him by the shoulder.

'It's all right, James. It's going to be all right.' Andrew stepped forward to comfort the boy but was stopped by the captain.

'Jonah, take the boy on deck,' the captain ordered with a nod at the seaman. Jonah immediately obeyed, pulling James out into the passage.

When they had gone, Captain Taymar sat back at the table. 'So it seems I have your boy.'

'With your leave, sir. I would like to return him to his mother.'

'That would be at a great loss to me. I am sure that you understand.' Taymar's smile did not reach his eyes.

Andrew knew what he could afford and hoped that it would be enough and, if not, he had another idea up his sleeve that might get him killed or abducted. 'I will pay three guineas for his release; after all, you are barely started on your voyage.'

The captain's eyes twinkled as he considered. 'It will leave me having to find another boy. Perhaps fifty guineas would see me right.'

'Sir.' Andrew's voice held no threat, yet it was strong and not intimidated. 'As I told you, this boy has been abducted by a man who at this very moment is awaiting the gallows for that crime. I feel sure that, if you make away with him after I have informed you of his ill fortune, you may also be seen by the magistrate as an abductor.'

Captain Taymar could see the logic in this and nodded his head slowly. He held out his hand towards Andrew. 'Three guineas it is, sir.'

Andrew was elated as he sat in the small rowboat with James sitting between his knees. As the small boat left the shelter of the large ship, man and boy shivered against the salt-laden wind and spray as the craft rose and fell with the waves. The strong wind blowing up the channel made rowing difficult for the two crewmen and the boat rolled at an alarming angle. Large waves washed over the boat and Andrew held onto James, who flinched at each flash of lightening and cried out at each crash of thunder. He tried to comfort the child, exactly as he would have with any of his distressed farm animals, holding him close and shushing him. It seemed to Andrew that they were making no headway in the swell until as lightning cut a jagged line of fire through the dark sky he was relieved to see that the land was near. A land that disappeared from view just as quickly as the waves broke over their heads and filled the boat with water. At a loud rolling boom right overhead James let out a cry and Andrew prayed in earnest. He was a man of the land, not the sea. 'Dear God, please save me and the boy this night,' he mumbled as the boat rolled alarmingly.

36.

That evening, when Martha returned home exhausted and cold, she could hardly believe her eyes as she saw her eldest daughter standing in the centre of the room while Nona prepared the supper.

'Emma! Am I dreaming? How did you come here?'

'It's a long story, Mother. But come sit by the fire; you are cold.' Emma was horrified at the sight of Martha's frail body, as she obeyed and moved towards the fire, looking glad of its heat.

'You look well, Emma.' The girl smiled in response, but noticed that there was no real interest in her mother's voice. It was only what a person said when being polite.

'Come eat with us, Mother, and we will tell our stories.' Emma took her mother's cold hands in hers and rubbed them, feeling the bones protruding at Martha's wrists.

'I cannot eat; I'm tired, that is all. I will go to my bed.' And she pulled her hands away, turning for the door.

'Mother, you must eat. I insist that you eat. Without strength, how will you be able to keep looking for James?'

Martha hung her head and wept. 'I am so tired, Emma. I can't think of anything but James and his suffering.'

With an arm around her mother, Emma led Martha to the table and was dismayed to feel her mother's frailness through her clothes. The warmth and the little food that she managed to eat did much to revive Martha and she now looked at Emma with a tired smile upon her lips.

'I am pleased to see you, Emma.' This time she meant it as she took her daughter's hand, holding it to her face.

'Tomorrow, Mother,' Emma said, searching Martha's face for the woman she once was, 'I will be with you to help in the search for James.'

Martha smiled, glad to have her daughter by her side and then wondered why her daughter was in London. 'Tell me, what you are doing in London, Emma?'

'I have been searching for you, Mother, after I left the service of Miss Brack.'

'Why did you leave her service?' Martha frowned. 'And how did you find me?' She had suddenly realised how incredible it was that Emma was here.

'It seems now to be a long story, Mother, and I hardly know where to begin,' she said quietly. As her mind flitted over the past it seemed like looking down a long road into the distance as she tried to find the beginning. Her mother looked so tired; how much should she tell her about the unhappiness of the Brack family? She decided to start with how she came to be here.

'I was here in London just walking the streets looking for you. I entered a building to escape some drunkards. No one was in there and I became frightened in case I was discovered by the owner. I was about to leave when a man entered with a pistol drawn.'

Martha put her hand to her mouth in horror at the danger her daughter had been in. Emma continued, 'But he meant me no harm, and was surprised to see me there, as he thought that this was where James was hidden.' She saw now that she had Martha's complete attention.

At the name of her son, Martha flinched. 'James? Why is this man looking for James? Who is he?'

'I don't know, but he informed me that in prison Mister Beemer told the ordinary where he had hidden James, and that he had made an arrangement with the ordinary and had overheard what was said.'

'Who is this gentleman who knows where I am living and is looking for my son?' Martha, who had hoped to be invisible and well hidden in the back streets of the East End, now realised that this was not the case.

'I don't know, Mother, but he knew me.'

'He knew you?' It made no sense. Resting her hand on her forehead, she tried to understand why a man on overhearing the ordinary would want to look for her son. Unless he was with the police, yes, that must be it; the constables are helping to find James. She felt some relief and changed the subject. 'Tell me why you left the employ of Miss Brack.'

'Oh, Mother, it was the strangest place, surrounded by a forest without birds.'

Martha's face changed. Emma could tell that she knew something.

'What is it, Mother?' Martha shook her head and frowned but bid Emma to continue with her story.

'On the first day I couldn't get to the house because spider webs seemed to entangle me and I was frightened. As you know, Mother, I am afraid of spiders. I thought that to avoid them I would walk through the forest instead of on the path, but got lost and spent the night under the trees having nightmares. I was really frightened, Mother.'

'My poor child.' Martha reached out a hand to her daughter and felt her shaking as she relived the fear of being alone in the darkness.

'I met a man in the forest the next morning who said he would lead me to the house if I did something for him, and he gave me a piece of silver to put in my pocket, saying that he couldn't go to the house. That Miss Brack had hidden something that was his and he wanted it back. He said that when the silver got warm I would be in the right room and was to hang a ribbon on the outside of the window. I thought it very strange and didn't want to do it, but I was beholden to him for showing me the way out of the forest.'

'Did this happen, Emma? Did you find the room and hang the ribbon?'

'Yes.' Emma felt ashamed and saw that her mother heard it in the tone of her voice. How could she tell her what happened next?

Martha was concentrating on every word Emma spoke and chewed at her bottom lip, worried that her daughter had been in danger and she hadn't known. A mother should feel something when her child is in trouble. 'Who was this man?' She kept her tone gentle, enquiring.

'I saw a picture of him in the house, Mother. It was Oliver Brack, Miss Brack's brother. The house was in great need of repair, and after the fire and death of Mrs Shillabeer and her baby things became worse.'

'A fire and the death of a woman and her baby?' Martha was horrified.

'Yes, Mother, after I put a ribbon on the window of the nursery where Mrs Shillabeer had the baby hidden, the room caught fire and Mrs Shillabeer and the baby died. Matt, the stable boy, and I, were burnt trying to save them. And, while we were being nursed, Mrs Ames, the housekeeper, found Salanda's locket hidden on a shelf in my room.'

'What did she do with it?' Martha tried to keep her breathing centred as the knowledge of a greater horror filled her.

'She took it to Miss Brack, thinking that I had stolen it.' Emma could see Martha's dismay and hurried on with the account. 'I told Mrs Ames it belonged to my grandmother, but she didn't believe me.'

'Is that why you left, Emma?'

'Yes, and no, Mother. I went and asked Miss Brack for it back. But she said that it belonged to her, and that no one would believe a servant would have such a thing. She told Mrs Ames to throw me out. But Mrs Ames couldn't because I was not yet recovered from my burns. So, she made me a bedroom in a room near the kitchen and nursed Matt, her son, and me.'

Martha raised her hand. 'I feel quite exhausted, Emma.'

'I'm sorry, Mother. It's the first time I have spoken of Claydon House.'

'It's all right, dear, just speak a little slower.'

'Miss Brack went to the Shillabeer funeral and Matt was made to drive the coach, even though he was in pain. I searched the house for my locket, but couldn't find it. While they were away I went for a walk in the forest and met Mister Brack again and he indicated that I follow him. When I got to a clearing he stood holding the dead baby.' Nona, who had been listening in wonderment, took a short intake of breath. Emma put her hand on Nona's and continued, 'But it was still alive in his arms; it wasn't dead at all.'

'It couldn't have been the same baby,' Nona interrupted.

'Yes, it was the same baby, a little boy, Nona. He laid it on the ground at his feet and it sank beneath the earth.'

Nona cried out horrified. 'Oh, Emma, no! What did you do?'

'I ran to the spot and started to dig with my hands and...' she stopped, unable to go on. Her eyes glistened as the awful vision once more flooded her mind. She was once again lost in the trauma, looking at the disturbed leaf mould and staring at the ghastly decomposing hand. She could hear screaming and could feel the scream forming again in her throat.

Martha looked at the faces of her two daughters, the younger with a look of fear crossing her face and the other, living somewhere in her mind, a horror that she could not fully impart. Martha's brain suddenly cleared and she took charge of the situation.

'Nona, I want you to go to bed now; we will talk more in the morning.'

'Oh, Mother, do I have to? What about the baby?'

'It wasn't there, Nona. When I dug, it wasn't there.' Emma spoke lightly to cheer her sister before bed. 'When I see you in the morning I will tell you all about life at Claydon House and about Matt and Alf, who also lived there.'

When Nona had gone the two women continued to sit before the fire.

'Can you tell me what happened?' Martha asked quietly.

It was with difficulty that Emma took a deep breath and continued, glad that her sister was no longer listening. What good would it do to frighten her? 'I... I uncovered a body, Mother. It was the maid Polly, who went missing before I arrived. No one knew why she'd disappeared without a goodbye.'

After a silence Martha asked. 'Did Oliver Brack ever come to the house?'

'No, I'm sure he didn't. In fact, the gardener couldn't understand why he didn't, as the house is his, and even if he was afraid of his sister, why did he not return when she was at the Shillabeer funeral?'

'Did you see Mister Brack in the same area each time, Emma?'

'Yes, Mother, each time he was near the river.'

'It is my belief, Emma, that Oliver is not of this world.' Martha leant forward and placed her hand over that of her daughter.

The girl was shaken. 'I don't understand,' she whispered.

'I believe Oliver to be dead, probably in the river or near it.'

Emma stared at her mother, trying to take in what she was saying, but there was no sense in it.

'I saw him, Mother, as plain as I see you now. He was as solid as us, really he was.'

Martha sighed, her voice held the tone of a woman exhausted but trying to do the best for her child. 'Emma, you have a gift, the gift of sight; Salanda had it also.'

'Do you mean that I see spirits, Mother?'

'Yes, Emma, I think that you do. If that dead person wants to be seen.'

Emma frowned and shook her head. 'What about the baby?'

'I think Oliver knew where the baby's mother was buried and wanted to bring mother and baby together again.'

Emma sat quietly in the cosy glow of the fire as it crackled peacefully in their upstairs room, trying to make the pieces fit. 'When Matt came back from the Shillabeers', he said that her baby was at the house with a nursemaid and that it was well. I couldn't understand how that could be.'

'I think, Emma, that the baby that died in the fire belonged to Oliver and Polly. Somehow Oliver and Polly died and were buried by someone in the forest. Oliver wanted the baby to join them.'

A sudden realisation swept across Emma's face and she looked pleadingly at her mother. 'I led that baby to its death. Oh, Mother, It's all my fault that it's dead.' Tears rolled in her eyes.

'You weren't to know what was in his mind, Emma. He would have found a way to get what he wanted even without you. Perhaps now they can all sleep in peace.'

'But, Mother, someone killed Oliver and Polly. What should we do about it?'

'We can do nothing, Emma. How could you explain it? As with the locket, you wouldn't be believed.'

Emma suddenly remembered something else. 'Mother, it was very strange but there was a picture of a man in a dark part of the house. A man with a very kind face, painted sitting in Salanda's garden. I'm sure it was her garden because of the position of the church, although the trees were smaller.'

Martha nodded slowly. 'Was his name on the picture?'

'Yes. It was...'

'Hanwell Brack?' Martha finished for her.

Emma stared in amazement at her mother. 'How did you know?'

'Because we are related to the Brack family and he was the nicest and kindest of them all.'

'We are related? How can that be, Mother?' Emma could hardly believe what she was hearing. 'I am related to that awful woman? You are related to her? How?'

'We are related distantly.' Martha nodded, her eyes not focusing on the room as Emma stared at her and waited for more information. 'It's complicated,' Martha sighed. 'Amelia and I share the same grandmother, Liannda. Salanda was Amelia's aunt. Your great-grandfather, a wonderful, gentle man, whose mind was open to experiences and adventure, took a trip to Ireland. While he was there he fell in love with a beautiful woman, Liannda, who had the gift of sight and wisdom. He married her there before he brought her home to his family. It was soon discovered that she was different, not only because she was below their class. They were afraid of her. In the eyes of the Bracks he had made a fatal mistake in marrying and they made him pay dearly for his love. They turned him away. Cut him off without a penny. All that he had was the cottage that he had bought as an investment. The Brack family turned their backs on Liannda. No pictures of her were allowed in the house. She had three children before her husband died: Oliver Senior; Amelia's father, Hanwell; and my mother, Salanda. Oliver Senior inherited Claydon House on the death of his father, but could not go against his father's wishes from the grave that Liannda and her daughter be dead to the Bracks.'

'Grandmother was sister to Amelia's father and Hanwell Brack?' Emma still could not picture her beautiful, gifted grandmother having anything to do with the Brack family.

'Yes, Emma. Hanwell was a lovely man, just like his father. I could not have had a better uncle. When he was killed in the war, Salanda knew her brother was dead long before any news came back to this country. The Brack family didn't help Liannda and her daughter; they were left to fend for themselves.'

A thought entered Emma's head. 'Did Amelia know who I was, Mother?'

'No, I don't think so.'

'She asked me who my parents were and I did tell her my grandmother was Salanda.'

'She may not have heard of Salanda, for that name was not spoken in family circles when it was found that Salanda had the gift like her mother.'

Mother! Why did the birds not come to the forest? Was Amelia in league with the Devil?'

Martha was shocked. 'Where did you hear a word like that, Emma?'

'In the church, Mother; they say evil people are in league with the Devil.'

'Let me try to explain something to you, Emma. There is no such thing as the Devil. There is energy. People call the energy many things – God, Goddess, Devil – because they want to identify with a face. So they give it human form. It helps to concentrate the mind.'

'But you said there is no Devil.'

'Yes, that's right. It is what I believe, Emma.'

'Then there is no God or Goddess.'

'That is right also, not in human form.'

'I don't understand,' Emma said quietly, a frown appearing on her forehead; it was as though everything that she had believed in was being taken away.

'I will try to explain, Emma. There is an energy. It's neither good nor bad, male or female. It is as gentle and as strong as the person who links into it. It is identified as God or Goddess by different religions. This energy is in every living thing, Emma. For those who can see it, the energy is a light that shines through all things. Animals, humans, rocks and rivers, mountains, beaches and sky. It is neither good nor bad. But can be used by a dark mind or soul for evil purposes, or a clear soul for good. When you look at a forest you see many trees, but it is made up of individuals. When you look at people you see them as individual. But that is not exactly so; we are all linked by the energy that runs through us. We are one with the animals and the plants, rocks and stones. So it was Amelia who, through the blackness of her mind, used the energy to frighten others who didn't understand. She wanted to keep the people from the forest. It's clear that she also has a gift, feels the energy, but uses it in a different way. To have her own way.'

Somewhere, deep down, Emma understood what her mother was saying. She remembered her beautiful grandmother feeding the birds, saw her mother kneeling before the moon in prayer and saw Amelia standing in her room, her eyes filled with hate when people didn't do her bidding. 'Is our being related why Amelia wanted the locket?'

'I don't think so. But even if she knew it was her aunt's, she couldn't wear it. She wasn't the one who was ordained to inherit it.'

'It should be yours, Mother. I want to give it back to you.' Emma slipped it from inside her bodice and gave it to her mother.

Martha held the locket gently in her hand. 'Thank you, Emma. I am relieved to have you both back safely.' Martha stood wearily, feeling that in these last few days her body had aged beyond her imagination. 'It's getting late; we must go to bed and tomorrow we will search together for your brother.'

Sliding her arms around her daughter, she kissed her head, but nothing, not even the closeness of her daughter, could take away the pain that sat like a lump of lead beneath her heart.

~

A horse, head drooping, followed the course of the river, carrying a man and a boy they travelled slowly on waterlogged roads and muddy footpaths towards London. The storm in Kent had left much damage. Uprooted trees were making the journey more difficult and frustrating Andrew, who wanted to get James back to his mother and relieve her suffering,

His heart fluttered as he thought of her. He had not had a moment of peace since seeing her naked body and he wanted to be near her as quickly as was possible, and yet he was afraid. On the long ride back he'd had time for reflection. What if she didn't feel the same for him? What if she was indeed still very much in love with her husband, who was not long dead? These thoughts raged in his head, leaving him silent and isolated from the boy who sat in front of him in the saddle. The unwanted thought came swiftly: *if she could not feel the same, then he had nothing left to live for.* Shaking his head vigorously to remove the thought, he startled the horse but pulled it back to a slow walk. Guiding the animal around yet another obstacle, he knew that he must fight the blackness that sometimes came over him.

~

At the end of a fruitless day looking for James, Martha, Emma and Nona returned to their room and sat wearily and distraught in front of the fire. Jane brought food to them and a jug of weak ale and left the three women to their thoughts and despair. She also had a heavy heart, for she had come to love them all and felt their pain deeply. She was not much of a praying woman, but she had prayed every night, with tears running down her face, for the return of the boy.

Walking slowly and with leaden feet she answered a knock at the door. Tired, Jane opened it slowly, then gaped at what was on her step. The gentleman was back and he held in his arms the limp body of a boy. Her eyes increased in size as she looked upon the white face of James Tilby.

'May we come in?' Andrew sounded weary.

'Oh, Gawd bless us on a Sunday, 'e's not dead, is 'e, sir?' she asked, as Andrew bent to enter the room.

'No, Mrs Gimbell, he's not dead, just asleep with exhaustion and cold.'

'She pulled the door wider. Come in, come in, get by the fire, I'll fetch Martha.' And she hurried away up the stairs.

When Jane had gone, Andrew knew he couldn't stay. He couldn't face Martha's thanks surrounded by other people, being unable to touch her, to hold her. No one must see how much he ached for her and he knew that if he saw her his face might tell it all. No, he was sure she still grieved for her husband. He would rather spend the rest of his life aching for her than to receive her rejection.

Laying the boy in front of the fire, he stroked James's hair. 'You'll be fine now, boy, and one day we will meet again.'

When the door burst open and Martha, Emma and Nona rushed into the kitchen, there was no one in it but James, lying silently on the floor in front of the fire. They rushed to him, kneeling by his side. Lifting him onto her lap, Martha cradled him in her arms, as she had when he was young. She rocked back and forth, holding his light body, the tears rolling over her cheeks unchecked. She kissed his face and kissed his head as Emma stroked his arm. Nona looked on anxiously. 'Is he going to die, Mother?'

Martha smiled and replied huskily. 'No, dear, he's just asleep.'

At that same moment the door opened and Buller came in from his searching. Buller, who had carried a haunted look for days, saw the body of James in Martha's arms and thinking the worst fell to his knees, weeping.

Jane ran to her son and threw her arms around him. 'It's all right, Buller, 'e's not dead. 'E's not dead.'

''E's not?' he sobbed, looking up at his mother.

'No, just exhausted, Buller. Come by the fire and see.'

''Ow did 'e get 'ere, Mother?' he asked, as he looked down on the pale boy, feeling just as responsible as he did on the day James vanished.

'A gentleman brought 'im. I opened the door and there he was holding the boy laid out. I thought he was a goner. It's a miracle, Buller.'

'My gentleman?' Emma looked up.

'Yes, Emma, it's the same gentleman.'

'But where's he gone? Why does he keep going?'

'I don't know, dear, but we 'ave a lot to thank 'im for.' Jane smiled.

'I'm taking James up to my bed, Jane; he will sleep with me tonight,' Martha lifted him easily in her arms. Quietly and smoothly so as not to jar him, she glided across the floor and carried her son from the room.

Jane shook her head; it was unbelievable. Only an hour ago they didn't know where he was, if he was dead or alive. Now here he was home. And who was the mystery gent who kept turning up? She reached for the gin.

~

In her room Martha laid James in the bed and Emma stoked the fire. There was already an improvement in the colour of his face. 'I think he is going to be all right, Mother,' she said gently. 'We will soon feed him up.'

'Yes, indeed we will.' Martha spoke almost to herself.

Emma took her sister's arm. 'Come, Nona, let us sit by the fire downstairs and leave Mother and James to sleep.'

When the door closed, Martha lay upon the bed with James in her arms, unable to take her eyes from his face. He seemed so small. His injured wrists, adorned with yellow and blue bruises, lay limply on the cover. 'Where have you been all this time?' she whispered. But he didn't wake. She stared at him for a long time, a gentle smile on her face, hardly able to believe the miracle. Eventually, her own eyelids, heavy with exhaustion, lowered and she fell asleep with her son still held gently in her arms.

The following morning, the birds had barely risen when Martha knelt in the garden amongst the herbs and flowers, in a space she had made for herself away from the Gimbells' eyes. She placed her offering of three dry leaves upon her slate alter. Raising her hands to the low autumnal sun that was barely peeking over the staggered rooftops, she breathed in the energy of the land, the trees, the grass, the plants, acknowledging every living creature. Then, lighting a candle, she linked into the energy, saying quietly: 'Accept this offering from your daughter, who comes with humble heart to give thanks for the return of her son. I have been in a dark well of despair and have struggled with the emotions of hate, loss and fear. Emotion that was not resolved in my heart before my son was returned. I take these three leaves as a symbol of those feelings.' And picking up the first leaf she held it to the candle flame, where it caught fire briefly. 'I release the hate in my heart,' she intoned. Taking the second leaf, she held it to the flame, where it caught fire, falling as ash to the slate. 'I release the fear in my heart.' Taking up the third leaf, she kissed it and held it to the sun, before holding it also over the flame, saying, 'I release the loss from my heart.' The flame flared, curling the leaf that shrivelled in the heat. She watched it burn until it was no more than dust upon her altar; blowing the blackened powder she said, 'I release you. It is done. So shall it be.'

Then, sitting quietly, she listened to the joy of the dawn chorus and felt the first rays of the early sun upon her closed eyelids, where tears of joy escaped and ran peacefully over her cheeks.

When Martha returned to the room, James was sitting up in bed with Emma and Nona on each side. 'Mother!' He jumped from the bed and ran to her, crying, 'I couldn't find my way home.'

'Shhh now.' She stroked his hair. 'We will sit by the fire and you can tell us what happened while Emma gets us all some food.'

'I was at the hanging with Buller. We stayed on the edge. We hoped for some work. I couldn't see anything, there were so many people. There was a great shout, but I couldn't see why.

And suddenly I was lifted off my feet and carried away. I called to Buller but he couldn't hear me because of the noise. I was carried a long way under the arm of a man, who when we reached the top of some steps put me down and told me to go inside. I could see then that it was Mister Beemer. He pushed me inside and dragged me to the bed, where he tied me tightly. I asked him why he had brought me here and he said to see my mother. Then when it was dark he went out.' James's lip trembled. 'He didn't come back, Mother. I slept, tied to the bed, and the next day I was hungry and thirsty, but he didn't come back. And he didn't bring you, Mother.'

'No, he didn't bring me.' Martha wished in some ways that he had, for they might have defeated Beemer together.

'Go on, James,' Nona said, perhaps too quickly, receiving a frown from Emma.

'I struggled with the twine but it was too tight. I called for Mother, but no one heard. One night it was very cold and in the morning my hands slipped from the twine with only a little struggle.'

'What happened then, James?' Nona's face was bright, enjoying the story without understanding the horror of it.

'I crept down the steps and ran in case Mister Beemer caught me. I ran through the streets. I thought he would find me. I came to the river and watched the men loading the boats. There was such a lot to see. I was very hungry and was going to take a fish from a cask when a man said, "If you take that you will hang on the gallows." So I didn't take it. I was very hungry. I wanted to cry. That night I slept on a pile of sail cloth and next day the same man said, "You still here?" I said I was lost and couldn't find my way home. He asked if I wanted to see inside a ship. I went up the gangplank and it was busy and jolly on board. They gave me a little food and said that they were going to see the world. I helped the men carry baskets on board and they gave me some more food. It was fun. I stayed on board that night, sleeping on the deck. The captain said I would be safer there. Next morning, Jonah said, as I didn't know where I lived, I could go with them to India and work for my keep and a little money at the end of it. I didn't want to go, but they were the only people I knew, and they were kind, so I said yes.' James began to sniff and wiped a tear from his cheek. 'I'm sorry, Mother, I didn't want to go, but I couldn't find you.'

'It's all right, James, go on with the story.' Martha held his hand gently.

'I was working below the deck when the storm started and I was frightened. The ship rolled and things fell off the shelves and rolled around on the floor. I couldn't walk without holding onto something. I thought the ship was going to sink. Then Jonah came and told me the captain wanted to see me. The captain had a whip.' He sniffed.

'Were you whipped?' Shocked, Martha grasped his hand harder.

'No, I was taken to his cabin and Mister Tate said he had come to take me to my mother.'

'Mister Tate?' Martha sat up straight, surprised and shocked all at the same time. *Mister Tate!*

'Yes, Mother.'

'How did Mister Tate, who is on the farm, come to be on the ship?'

'He said he'd been looking for me.'

Martha now had many questions that needed answering as James continued, 'Jonah took me up on the deck while Mister Tate stayed talking to the captain and then we were rowed ashore in a small boat and I was frightened because the big waves nearly toppled us into the water. But Mister Tate held me tight and said we were safe. When we reached the land I slept under a tree in Mister Tate's coat.'

Listening to this, Martha's heart was full of an emotion that she thought never to have again for a man. How could she not love a man who put himself in danger to save her son?

'You've had such an adventure, James.' Nona sounded overwhelmed. 'What did Mister Tate do next?'

'We rode all the next day in the cold wind trying to get back to London. Lots of trees had fallen down and footpaths were washed away, but Mister Tate kept riding. I fell asleep and woke up here this morning. It seemed like a dream.'

Emma put her arms around her brother and hugged him. 'We've all been so fortunate to know Mister Tate. I hope we see him again to thank him.'

Martha smiled; yes indeed, she thought, they had been very fortunate in knowing Mister Tate, who had saved them twice. She wanted to thank him for looking for James and for saving him from a journey to the other side of the world, where he would have been lost to them all forever. Her heart fluttered at the thought of the rugged farmer trying to find her son. How did he know James was missing? And then she remembered her conversation with Jane, and how they had wondered who the gentleman was who'd brought the constable. But that couldn't have been Andrew Tate. Why would he be in London? It was just too much to work out.

37.

A week later Pit rushed into the house just as Martha was removing some pies from the oven. Nona was sprinkling flour on the table and Jane was skinning a rabbit.

'Mother, Martha, I've seen a notice pinned on the wall outside the magistrates' court.' They all stared at him, wondering what was coming next. 'Beemer is on the list: 'e's going on trial tomorrow afternoon.'

For a moment they all stared at him; they'd forgotten about Beemer.

'Right, that's it then.' Jane stood up wiping her hands on her apron. 'We're going to the trial. We'll see that the man gets 'is justice.'

Martha stared at her. 'Jane, the man has his justice just being in prison.'

Janes face flushed, unimpressed with Martha's forgiving nature. 'Don't you go defending 'im, Martha Tilby, 'e's a villain. You know what 'e 'ad in 'is mind.'

'What did he have in mind?' Nona asked placing some dough on the floured boards of the table.

'Never yer mind, young lady,' Jane said a little too sharply. 'Now get those pies over there into the shop. I'm taking yer mother shopping for some decent clothes.' Martha raised her eyebrows, causing Jane to fluster. 'You've earned the money, Martha. You're a businesswoman now and should dress like it. It's time yer spent some of that money on yerself. We're going to the dressmaker and there's no argument.'

Elizabeth Lettuce was a professional young woman trying to make her way in the world with the help of her father. They had started her little business after she proved to be excellent with the needle. Elizabeth sat in her front room surrounded by material, cottons and half-finished dresses as the two women entered. Her tiny frame was clothed in a deep pink dress. Her pale hair, piled upon her head, was set around with matching pink ribbons.

Elizabeth had been sitting quietly sewing, while contemplating whether Bert Cole would ever get around to asking her father if he could marry her, when the door in her limewashed cottage opened. A very large, well-known lady with the frame and face of a man stepped into her small room, almost filling it.

'Mrs Gimbell, how nice it is to see you, and you've brought Mrs Tilby. Welcome to my couture house, Mrs Tilby.'

Jane almost choked with mirth but the young woman was too busy clearing material from a chair so that Martha could sit to notice Jane's merriment.

'Now, how can I help you, Mrs Tilby?'

Martha, who had always made her own clothes, didn't know what to say and looked at Jane, who immediately took charge.

'Mrs Tilby would like a dress and jacket for…' She hesitated, not wanting to give the young woman any information she might share with her other clients. Martha interrupted Jane's pondering. 'Mrs Gimbell has kindly said that she would take me to see a trial and I would like something for that occasion.'

'A trial! How exciting. I went once with my father and it was so entertaining. You cannot believe what we heard. Do you know who is being tried? Is it someone well known?'

'No,' Jane interrupted, perhaps a bit too suddenly, and then continued kindly. 'We're just going for an outing, as Mrs Tilby 'as never been to the courts before.'

'You will enjoy the thrill of it, Mrs Tilby, but I hope that you don't hear anything that will upset you for the rest of your day.'

'I'm sure all will be well, mistress.' Martha smiled uncertainly.

'Then let me show you some designs.' She hurried to a shelf and, pulling a very large book from a cupboard, laid it on the table for Jane and Martha to look through. Getting out her appointment book, she asked, 'Now, when would you like the clothes finished?'

'Tomorrow,' Jane said lightly.

'Tomorrow?' Elizabeth seemed to shrink. Eyes wide with horror, she saw her sale disappearing. 'I don't think that I could make a dress and a jacket in a day, Mrs Tilby.'

Jane looked around at the half-finished dresses hanging from hooks around the room.

'So, these are for your clients are they?'

'Yes. Well, not all. This one is a piece I am working on to see if the style would work.'

'It's lovely.' Jane looked from the dress to Martha.

'It's grey!' Martha looked at Jane. 'Would grey be the colour for a trial?'

'Perhaps we could edge it with this green and add a green jacket,' the young woman suggested. 'I have several jackets already made in various sizes. Let me measure you, Mrs Tilby.'

Martha stood to be measured and Elizabeth was beginning to get excited. One of her own creations was to be worn at a trial and seen in public. 'I have a young girl that I am training and she is very good with the needle. I will bring her in to help me. As so much of it is already done we may be able to get it to you on time. What time is the trial?' she enquired.

'I believe,' said Jane, 'that we will be going in the afternoon as we would need to attend to our own business in the morning.'

'Of course! I understand from my clients that your business is doing very well, Mrs Tilby.'

Martha smiled and nodded agreement but didn't enter into any conversation about her business.

'I wonder if you would allow us to take a little of this green material with us?' Jane asked.

Later they took their time walking along Cheapside looking in the shops and it was Jane who found the perfect hat, matching it to the green material.

The next day at noon the dress and jacket arrived without further fitting. Nona unpacked it with shaking hands. 'Oh, Mother, it's so beautiful.'

Later, as Martha stood in her upstairs room, clad in her new outfit, she looked at the corner where she and William had slept and fashioned their dreams so very long ago. She missed him with every ounce of her being and sighed sadly.

'Don't sigh, Mother. You look so beautiful.' Nona's eyes sparkled with joy. 'You look so different, like a lady, and you are very pretty.'

'I don't think I can wear it, Nona. I'm not used to looking so grand. I don't feel comfortable.' She was about to unbutton the jacket when Jane walked in and stood in the doorway, mouth open at the picture before her.

'My Gawd, Martha, yer look beautiful. Just right for the trial.'

'I can't go, Jane,' Martha removed the hat, revealing the soft black curls piled high upon her head. 'I feel much more at home in my old dress.'

'Martha!' Jane sounded determined. 'You're a businesswoman now and yer 'ave the money to dress the part. Do you want to stay poor all yer life? You were the wife of a carpenter. You would one day 'ave been able to afford a good dress if William was still with us. Why should yer worry about wearing it now that you are the one in business?'

'This isn't me, Jane. It just isn't me. I want to be free. I can't breathe in these clothes.'

'Yes, yer can, just for the trial. Otherwise we'll be in the cage with the penny smellies.'

'Perhaps I would be more at home there.'

'No, yer wouldn't,' Jane laughed, 'until you've been there and seen 'um; yer will 'ave to believe me. Now come on. It's a bit of a walk and we must start out right away.'

And she bustled out of the room, leaving Martha no time to argue and expecting her to follow.

38.

The courtroom was crowded. The windows had been opened to let the fresh air in and the smell of the entertainment-hungry Londoners out. Gentlemen and ladies held pomanders and posies in front of their faces as the poor of London streamed into a wooden caged area, where they stood in disarray, laughing and chattering, waiting for the afternoons diversion to begin.

Two constables brought Beemer up from the crowded holding cell below the courtroom. With eyes squeezed up against the unaccustomed light, he stood, a dirty, bent shadow of his former self. A constable stood stiffly at Beemer's side in the dock.

Judge Mallgride, in wig and robes, grandly took his place in a leather-bound seat boasting the king's coat of arms. The noise in the courtroom did not subside even when an usher banged his staff on the floor and yelled, 'Silence in the court.' When he rattled the staff across the wooden bars of the cage to let the crowd know he meant business, accompanied by a ferocious stare and a shout of '*Quiet... in... this... Court!*' an expectant hush fell upon the room and many eager and dirty faces waited for the deeds of Barney Beemer to unfold.

The court clerk handed Beemer a Bible, and in a passionless voice asked, 'Do you swear on that Bible to tell the truth?' Beemer put a shaky hand on the book, staring at it as though it was going to burn him.

'I do.' His voice held a shadow of the sound it used to carry.

In her new clothes Martha stood with Jane on the edge of the area put aside for the upper class. They both felt nervous about what was going to unfold before these strangers. Unaccustomed to being in such a crowd, Martha felt that the air was too hot and she became uncomfortable. She would like to have left but knew that Jane who stood between her and the door would not let her.

The judge cleared his throat. 'Mister Levett' – he addressed the aged lawyer before him loudly so as to be heard above the noise from the cage – 'we will proceed, when you are ready.'

Martha waited, hardly breathing, for her name to be made public as Levett, the lawyer, stood and faced the judge bowing deeply, his wig almost touching the bench. 'We bring before you the case of Tate versus Beemer, my Lord.'

Not understanding the legal system, Martha was confused: he had it wrong. It should be Tilby versus Beemer, surely. Jane gripped her arm, also wondering what was happening. Neither knew that, if Martha was to have been called, someone would have spoken to her before now.

'The prisoner is charged with the theft of a boar owned by the farmer known as Andrew Tate and of setting fire to a winter feed store on the property known as Tate Farm at Haddenford, diminishing the complainant's livelihood. With your permission, my Lord, I call Mister Andrew Tate.'

A buzz went around the courtroom and the gentlemen of London parted to allow Andrew to get to the front of the court.

Martha gasped, and was hardly able to breathe as her heart thumped in her chest, and she had to hold Jane's arm for support. *Andrew's boar and the fire was to do with Beemer?* She hadn't known, and now felt guilty that she hadn't told Andrew what Beemer had done to Nona. But, even as she thought it, she knew that as a mother she could not have told Andrew, then a stranger to her, that she had taken a mother's revenge for her child.

A hum of excited voices rose from those in the cage, pushing for a better view of Andrew as he walked to the front. The courtroom was also crowded with well-dressed men holding papers awaiting their own cases to be heard. They stood patiently with their solicitors to one side, occasionally flapping their legal papers against the heat.

There were many 'ooos!' and appreciative looks from the women in the cage as Andrew stood before the bench. His hair had been shaped and he was clean-shaven, revealing a tanned, rugged jaw line and the high cheekbones of a handsome man.

'Are you Mister Andrew Tate, farmer, of Tate Farm, Haddenford?' the black-clad Mister Levett, lawyer for the Crown, asked, his bulbous nose, heavy eyelids and low-slung jowl, giving him a sleepy hangdog expression. But his grey eyes were gleaming with intelligence and looking eagerly for the truth.

'I am, sir.' Andrew nodded.

'Do you know this man?' Levett indicated the hardly recognisable Beemer standing shakily in the dock.

'Yes, sir, he is Mister Barnard Beemer.'

'How do you know this man?' Levett nodded in Beemer's direction.

'He used to live in my village, sir, a member of my church.' Andrew's voice was strong. There was a stirring amongst the onlookers at that revelation and Mister Levett struggled to be heard above the mumbling.

'Tell us why you have a grievance with Mister Beemer, sir.' He raised his voice.

'My pigs were released from their sty, which was always locked, and, although all the sows were retrieved, the boar was never found.'

'Was this a valuable animal?' Levett looked pointedly at the crowd. They stood still, waiting in anticipation of hearing the price of a boar.

'Yes sir, it was valuable to me. A good part of my livelihood depended upon its reproduction.'

The rabble in the cage howled with laughter, snorted like pigs and made lewd gestures. A constable stepped forward and rattled the cage with a wooden truncheon and the usher called loudly for '*order*'.

'How do you know that this man was the perpetrator?' Levett asked with raised eyebrows and a serious face for the benefit of the crowd.

'He later confessed it to a constable, sir, while in the jail.'

'I see. You also accuse this man of arson, sir?'

'Yes, sir. I have proof that this man set fire to my winter grain store. After the fire, my foreman, John Brisket, found a piece of material hanging on the hedge near the burnt barn. Footprints led from the barn to a hedge bordering the lane where an entrance hole had been cut, allowing access onto my land unseen.'

The judge looked up and asked, 'Where is the proof?' At this point the Reverend Draycott pushed through the crowd carrying Beemer's coat and the piece of material that had been ripped from it. Both were shown to the judge, who nodded his head. He addressed the prisoner. 'Is this your coat, sir?'

Barney did not answer but stared straight ahead.

'I am informed, Mister Beemer,' the judge continued, 'that you were a rent collector and that you wore this coat daily in your work and that this can be established as yours by your employer of that time.' The judge spoke with passion, staring pointedly at Barney, who appeared to shrink before his gaze.

After a long pause, which had the rabble and Barney holding their breath, the judge addressed him again. 'You have admitted to these crimes and there has been proof of your crime to which you have agreed.' He turned the corner of his papers and looked up slowly. 'There was another lesser case pending against you, sir, of the abduction of a child, to which you have also confessed; this will be noted in the records. In the light of the confession and the judgment I am about to make, I will save the court time and money by not hearing the second case, which is already proved

362

and agreed by you.' The judge held up a piece of parchment. 'I have your admittance to the crime written here' – he shook the parchment vigorously towards Barney – 'signed by you. Is this your signature, sir?'

Mister Levett took it from the judge and showed it to Barney, who nodded agreement that it was his signature on the record.

The crowd became restless in the cage, booing and stamping their feet, disappointed at missing out on the details of the other case. Some of the women, who were drinking, became abusive. The usher rattled the cage with his staff and the judge continued in a louder voice. 'I want it put on record that you did admit to the abduction of James Tilby, who due to your confession was found and returned to his mother.'

Jane threw her arms around Martha. The rabble in the cage continued their discontent loudly, shouting that they wanted to hear the other case.

Several constables approached the cage with raised truncheons and the crowd became quieter, although a mumbling of unrest continued. While the constables were engaged with the rabble, the judge bent beneath his high bench and out of sight took a swig from a flask. Feeling the heat of the rum move to his innards and soothe the pain that had been plaguing him since his large lunch of fatty pork and porter, he felt relief.

The judge, coming upright again, surveyed the crowded room. 'I will now pass sentence,' he said without feeling.

Silence fell upon the court and an excited energy of expectation pounded in many hearts. The judge nodded to the clerk. A little powder from his wig puffed into a stream of late autumn sunlight that streaked through the leaded window above his chair. The usher handed the judge a black cap, which he placed on top of his tightly curled wig.

The crowd cheered. The sudden noise was deafening and Barney shrank before it. Two constables held him up as his legs gave way and his body shook violently.

'Barnard Horace Beemer,' the judge shouted over the din, trying to uphold the dignity of the court, 'I sentence you to be hanged by the neck until you are dead. Your body will then be dismembered and anatomised. Until that time you will languish in Newgate Prison, where you will reflect upon the crimes that you have committed.'

The crowd roared with delight, hissing, booing and snorting like pigs as Barney was led away back to the safety of the cold, wet cells below.

As Jane and Martha stepped outside the courthouse and into the busy street, Martha noticed Andrew Tate and Ernest Draycott waiting for a cab. It was Ernest who saw Martha and made his way towards her. 'Mrs Tilby, how very nice to see you again.' He bowed.

'And also yourself, Reverend Draycott.' Martha greeted him with a nod. 'May I introduce my friend, Mrs Gimbell?' Jane bobbed and Ernest Draycott bowed again.

'My honour, madam.'

A spark of amusement played in Martha's eyes: how grand they all were today, she thought. How London had impressed good manners upon them all. She looked towards the road, where a tall, handsome gentleman in a blue coat stared back at her, unmoving. She nodded to him, her heart missing a beat, her legs becoming weak.

Ernest noticed her acknowledgement of Andrew and called him over.

'Andrew, here is Mrs Tilby, looking very well.'

Andrew could not hide his feelings as he stared at the woman who had his heart. He bowed stiffly, knowing he should speak but not knowing what to say. His heart was beating so hard that it almost took away his breath.

'You are indeed looking very well, Mrs Tilby,' he said at last as she raised her eyes to his.

Martha's heart beat uncontrollably. This was not the rugged farmer that she knew, the silent, worried man in whose home she had lived. It seemed that London and circumstance had changed them both.

'I have to thank you for returning my son to me, Mister Tate. I haven't before had an opportunity and shall forever be in your debt.'

'It would give me great distress to think that you felt yourself in my debt, Mrs Tilby.' His troubled eyes searched hers and he desperately wanted to call her Martha.

'But you rescued my son when none of us could find him, sir.' Her voice wavered. 'Without you he would have been lost to us forever.' Tears flooded her eyes as she was still not over the drama through which they had all lived.

Andrew wasn't coping with the emotion that he was feeling. To be standing so close to her, and she with tears in her eyes, was more than he could bear. His voice, when he eventually was able to speak, had a break in it as he said, 'It was my pleasure to bring James home to his family.' His eyes looked deep into her soul and Martha found it hard to find words to reply.

'How can I ever thank you, sir?' An embarrassing flush had appeared on her cheek. Jane and Ernest Draycott were forgotten.

'There really is no need. Is James well?' He changed the subject, feeling uncomfortable. Surely, they would see that he was driven to rescue James because of his love for Martha. A love he dared not express or admit even to himself.

Martha smiled. 'He is very well, sir.'

Looking at Andrew with new eyes, she began to wonder how someone so poor could afford such good clothes.

'You are wondering about all this,' and he opened his arms, indicating his attire.

It was Martha who now looked uncomfortable as she knew that she would have to reply. Looking straight into his face she said quietly. 'Yes, although it isn't my place to know.'

'As you will remember, my farm joined that of the Laddisbrocks.' Martha nodded, and Andrew continued. 'He had been trying to buy my land for some years. I'd always refused his offer, believing that I could make the farm work. Although it was a struggle, I wanted to hold onto the family name. After the damage caused by Beemer, I couldn't go on.'

'I'm sorry.' Martha felt an overwhelming feeling of guilt and responsibility. A flush of heat rose again into her cheeks and she hoped he wouldn't notice.

'No!' he exclaimed. 'None of this was your fault and if in any way it was, then you would have done me a great service. Major Laddisbrock offered me three times what he offered two years ago and I have been able to keep the farmhouse, five large fields and the orchard.'

Martha was relieved he had not lost everything and said, 'May I ask, sir, about my son Robert?'

'Robert has been with the Reverend Draycott and his wife while I have been in London. But I believe he is very well.'

Martha looked at Ernest, who assured her with a smile that Robert had been well looked after. 'My wife and I have enjoyed Robert's company immensely. We have continued with the education that you started, Mrs Tilby, and found him to be a very bright boy. It has made such a difference to an old and dark house to have such a nice young gentleman staying with us. He has, I am afraid, been a little spoilt.'

Martha's heart was glad.

At that moment a carriage pulled up outside the courthouse. Ernest went to speak to the driver then turned to the little group.

'Here is our carriage; may we accompany you to your home?' he asked, looking at Martha and holding the door open.

Martha was about to refuse when Jane stepped in.

'That would be most kind of you, sir,' And she gave Martha a look that forbade her to refuse.

Unable to get under the arch, the cab was pulled up at the bottom of Hare Lane. Andrew and Ernest helped the ladies alight onto the cobbles and Andrew held Martha's hand a little longer than needed. Looking into her deep brown eyes, he feasted on the beautiful face that had haunted his dreams for so long.

'I should like to bring Robert to see you soon, if that would be acceptable, Mrs Tilby.'

'Thank you, sir,' Martha replied softly. 'Yes, I would dearly like to see my son.'

Her heart was eager to see Robert again and to hold him close. Since the return of James and Emma to her, she had missed Robert. It was hard for a mother to release her children while they were so young. To ask them to make their way in the world alone was even more heart-wrenching.

Andrew still held her hand as he looked into the face that he loved, noting every contour, every eyelash and the fullness of her mouth. Martha gazed upon the face of a man who had changed beyond all measure. The gruffness of a man who had struggled for survival had been replaced by a man so handsome and self-assured that her heart swelled in her chest. It was Jane who broke the moment and Andrew reluctantly let her hand go.

'Mister Tate, Reverend Draycott, may I offer my abode for tea on Friday, when yer could bring Robert to see 'is mother? And please, sir, bring Mrs Draycott.'

Ernest inclined his head politely and smiled. 'We will be most pleased to take tea on Friday, thank you, Mrs Gimbell.'

When the carriage departed and they entered the house, Jane was smiling as she let her shawl fall from her shoulders and hung it on a peg behind the door.

'Is something amusing you, Jane?' Martha noticed the secret smile.

'Not my place to say.' She continued to smile as she poured gin from the brown jug that sat on the dresser in the corner.

Martha removed her hat, glad to have her head free, saying, 'You are a strange woman, Jane Gimbell, to be smiling for no good reason.'

'I think yer know the reason very well, my girl, and don't pretend that yer don't.' Jane placed the jug on the table next to two cups and looked with a raised eyebrow at Martha.

Martha flushed slightly, but the moment was broken as Nona came in from the shop and opened the oven door to remove more pies.

'Mother, I'm very busy, even with the help of James.' Can you help now that you are home?'

'I shall go and get myself changed, Nona. Where's Emma?'

'She's visiting Bert and Effie. She's taken them some pies. She says that my pies are as good as yours, Mother. Are you pleased?'

'You've learnt very well, Nona, and I agree that your pies might even be better than mine. You have the lightness of touch that is needed for the making of pastry.'

The smile of joy that suffused Nona's face brought a lump to Martha's throat. Her daughter had been through so much: the loss of her father, the rape, the loss of home, the smell of the butcher's meat, and then the disappearance of her brother. Through it all she had quietly worked in the background, never moaning. She'd grown up while Martha wasn't looking. Kissing Nona's forehead, Martha went to change her clothes.

~

When she was alone in her room, Martha looked at herself in the brown speckled mirror and hardly recognised the woman who stared back at her. This smartly dressed woman with her hair piled upon her head was far more elegant than Martha Tilby. This woman glowed and her eyes sparkled. Martha chewed her bottom lip as her heart pounded uncontrollably. Who was this person who wanted to laugh out loud? What is wrong with me? she thought. But as the vision of Andrew Tate flooded her mind she knew exactly what was wrong with her. I am attracted to him, nothing more than that. But, as she pulled off the jacket and dress and pulled on her old clothes, she felt the need to dance around the room, singing with a heart as light as when she first met William. When she stopped and looked again in the mirror, she saw the Martha that she recognised, but she was different; she was happy.

'I think I am in love with Andrew Tate,' she voiced to her reflection. But she soon became sober, thinking, my life has been full enough of pain. I am sure he helped us find James only because of his connection with Mister Beemer. I am being silly, she chastised herself: why would a man like that be interested in a woman like me? She moved away from the mirror, feeling sad, and sighed. It was nice, but would come to nothing. And, going downstairs, she took over from Nona, rolling out the pastry.

~

Back in Newgate Prison Barney heard the door of the condemned cell close loudly behind him. In the half-light, he sat on the bed, looking down at the Bible that he'd been given to reflect upon. He felt nothing. All his years of going to church and now, being sentenced to hang, he felt nothing. Surely, he should feel something?

~

Andrew sat opposite Ernest in the highway coach that would take them back to Haddenford. As it rattled across the bridge going south, leaving London behind, Andrew experienced an overwhelming feeling of loneliness and loss.

Ernest Draycott, misunderstanding the strained expression on Andrew's face, assured him that he would soon be back at the farm, where he was sure that John would have everything in order.

Andrew nodded, barely hearing the vicar as he chattered on about London and the trial. Andrew's mind was filled with the vision of a beautiful woman with black hair and soft brown eyes, whose eyelashes lay like small fans upon her delicate cheeks, whose mouth he wanted to lay his own lips upon, swooning into a place where nothing existed but the love of a man for his woman.

As the journey progressed, he realised soberly that he had to think about what he was going to do with the rest of his life.

Ernest's voice broke through his gloomy musing. 'You seem as though you have great troubles sitting upon your shoulders, Andrew. Are you not pleased with the outcome of the trial?'

Brought out of his thoughts, Andrew noticed the concern on the face of the good man. 'Yes, indeed I am,' he sighed. 'Although I feel that death in such a way is wrong.'

'Would you have him starve to death for having no money or be tortured as a debtor?' Ernest held his hands up, looking mystified.

'No, I suppose not.' Andrew spoke almost into the collar of his coat as he slumped opposite Ernest. All the life and energy had left him. He was tired.

'Many more, children included,' Ernest said thoughtfully, 'go to the gallows for far less, Andrew. We must pray for their souls on Sunday.'

'Yes, indeed we should, sir,' Andrew responded vaguely and sighed.

'This news will be badly received by our congregation,' Ernest continued, ignoring the lack of response from Andrew as he looked out of the window. 'Mister Beemer, being well known in the church; it will have an effect on them.'

'Yes.' Andrew nodded agreement, but he felt nothing for Beemer.

Ernest's face was serious as he looked across the carriage at Andrew. 'Something is wrong, Andrew. Would you like to tell me what it is?'

'I seem to have lost my way, sir,' Andrew sighed. 'I don't know if I want to farm any more. I don't know what to do with the land. John Brisket has been a faithful employee and I cannot see him suffer. I may leave the village as it holds nothing but sad memories for me now.'

Ernest looked hard at Andrew and could see now that he was indeed suffering. 'I know that life for a farmer is very hard, Andrew, unless you are born rich. But I feel that something else bothers you. What is it?'

'I can't speak of it, sir. It is too painful.'

Ernest nodded sagely. 'Forgive me if I speak out of turn, but I believe that you have deep feelings for Mrs Tilby.'

His words hit Andrew like a physical blow to his body. He looked shocked and his face became pale.

'I'm sorry, Andrew, if I add to your distress, but it was written on your face when you spoke to her at the courthouse and when she alighted from the carriage. I have conducted many weddings, Andrew, and have seen love on many faces.'

'I don't know what to do.' Andrew's body seemed to shrink with the acceptance of Ernest's words. 'I am sure she still loves her husband.'

Ernest's voice was kind as he quietly said, 'Love isn't turned on and off, Andrew. Why should she not still love her husband and be ready to love another? We don't stop loving someone because they die.'

'Do you think, then, that I should speak to her about my feelings?'

'If you do not, how can she know how you feel?'

Andrew was silent; the thought of her rejection of him was unbearable. He knew that he wasn't a brave man when it came to women. He had only known the one, his wife, Margaret, and he had not experienced pain like this before they decided to wed.

'May I suggest, Andrew, that you decide what you are going to do with your life before you speak to her.'

'Yes! Thank you, sir, for your advice. That is what I shall do.'

As he stepped from the coach into the familiar village surroundings, Andrew recognised that his life had changed forever. There was no going back. Now he had to work out what had to be done.

~

John had kept the farm going and even cleaned up the yard. Andrew said little to him apart from letting him know that Beemer had confessed and was to be hanged. For two days Andrew shut himself away in the house, thinking. At night, when he couldn't think sensibly, he walked the fields in the light of the moon and felt peace. John watched Andrew's struggle and said nothing but feared the outcome on his own life. After those two terrible days of torment, Andrew had made his decision and called John to the house.

John stood in the kitchen holding his cap and looking at the floor, waiting for the words he knew would inevitably be spoken. *I have to let you go.* But those were not the first words that he heard.

'How old are you, John?' Andrew asked, sitting stiffly at the table.

'Nineteen, sir,' he replied, frowning, and wondering if perhaps he had it all wrong.

'Nineteen?' Andrew's manner gave nothing away.

'Yes, sir.' John twisted his cap nervously.

'Do you intend to marry, John?'

The words were unexpected and John answered bravely, still wondering what this was about, why Andrew had not said quickly that he could no longer afford to keep the farm. And so there was surprise in his voice when he answered, 'Yes, sir, one day.' It felt strange to be asked, and he was embarrassed not having been asked about his life before, why now, when his life was about to change forever?

'What stops you, John?' Andrew enquired softly.

'I don't have anything to offer a wife, sir.'

'There is always the tied cottage in which you sleep, John. You could bring a wife to the cottage.'

'Yes, sir, but my girl is only just old enough to wed.'

'Who is your girl, John?' Andrew was surprised, not knowing John had been walking out.

'Alice Mott, sir.'

Andrew looked thoughtful. 'The Motts are a good, hard-working family, John.'

'Yes, sir.' John's smile was thin. He realised that when he lost this job he would have to move on to find work and Alice, whom he adored, would never be his.

'I have a proposal for you, John.' Andrew looked intently into John's eyes, studying him. 'I am going to leave the farm and I would like you to stay and run it for me.'

'Me, sir? Alone?' He looked shocked and stared at Andrew, wondering if he had really heard correctly and then, as the words sank in, he wondered how he was going to run the farm on his own when he and Andrew couldn't run it together.

Andrew smiled for the first time, he had a little hope in his heart now. 'I am hoping that you will ask Mister Mott if you can marry his daughter, John.'

For a moment John was speechless, unable to take it in. Confused, he eventually asked, 'How will that help, sir?'

'It might seem agreeable if you were to ask the Motts to move into the cottage. You will move into this house and marry Alice when she is ready and work together on what is left of my farm. You will have to find your own markets for the produce. I will keep the deeds to the farm and it will still be known as Tate Farm. Although it will still be my farm in name, it will be like your own. But I will leave the arrangements to you, John. Not everyone wants to live under the eye of his in-laws.'

The boy grinned. 'May I go and see the Motts right away, sir?'

'No, John! If I have learnt anything in my life it is to take some time to think about it before you make your decision. This is a big step for you. You will be my tenant farmer. You will pay me a quarter of the profit annually and you will employ labour from the poorest in the village when you need help. If you take the farm on for me, I will expect you to agree to these terms and to turn a profit.'

'Yes, sir.' John nodded.

'Now go away and think carefully about this. It's a big undertaking. If the Motts agree, then I will get the legal papers drawn up.' Andrew was in no doubt that John would accept. The boy had character and would have a good, hard-working family to back him up, and on Friday, when they went to London, he would speak to Martha and would then know his own fate.

39.

Martha, Nona, Emma and Jane spent the next few days getting ready for the tea on Friday. Martha was dizzy with fear about seeing Andrew again and looked at herself hard in the mirror every night. There was no doubt that every time she thought of him her face glowed.

'How awful,' she whispered to her image. 'Everyone will know how I feel if I can't control my face better than this.'

Downstairs, Jane's large kitchen had been transformed with soft candles. Newly covered cushions adorned the easy chairs and the large oak-panelled dresser that held all of Jane's beautiful porcelain had been polished until the wood shone. A fire crackled cosily in the inglenook and at four o'clock the guests arrived. At the knock on the door Martha's heart beat so rapidly that she thought that she would faint. James and Nona rushed to the door to greet Robert. 'We have so much to tell you, Robert.' They chattered excitedly as they pulled him into the room.

'Robert.' Martha held her arms out to her son, but he didn't rush forward as he would once have done but held his mother's hands for a moment before saying, 'You look well, Mother.'

Martha looked hard at her son and felt sad, although she didn't show it. He seemed to have grown into a young man while she'd been away. 'You are also looking very well, Robert,' she smiled gently, hiding her pain of loss. 'I can see that you have been well cared for by both Mister Tate and the Draycotts.' At this, Robert nodded and seemed to soften a little.

Taking Robert by the arm, Nona pulled him away, saying excitedly, 'Come, Robert, we have to show you our room.' He went easily, smiling, and Martha was sad that he was not as at ease with her as he was with his siblings.

As the Draycotts entered the room, Martha introduced Emily. 'Jane, this is Emily Draycott,' she spoke with a smile on her face. Emily, a picture in white and cornflower blue, bobbed and took Jane's hand warmly.

'I am very pleased to meet you, Mrs Gimbell,' and Emily's face shone with true warmth.

Relieved that Emily was not the typical wife of a vicar, Jane smiled. 'I'm very pleased to meet yer too, Mrs Draycott, but please call me Jane.'

'Thank you, I would like that; please also call me Emily. Tell me about London, Jane. I have never been here before and it is so large.'

Martha left them talking and turned to help Emma with the tea, but Andrew stood in her way.

'Mrs Tilby!' His face was serious, his eyes searching her features as he nodded his head slightly.

Martha was taken aback by both the suddenness of him being so close and the look on his face.

'May I talk with you? Perhaps later we could take a walk.'

'Yes, I would like that very much.' Her heart rose with hope and dropped with fear. What was it that he wanted to speak about? As the afternoon wore on she found it difficult not to think of Andrew's words.

The tea was jolly and the Draycotts made everyone laugh with stories of the different vicarages in which they had stayed. For Martha, the afternoon was endless. Robert approached her as Jane cleared the plates away.

'Mother, I have something important to tell you.' He looked uncomfortable, and bit the side of his mouth while he awaited permission to speak. While trying to find the words, he stood tall, emphasising the growth that had taken place since he had last seen his mother.

'Yes, Robert?' She waited, marvelling at how grown up he'd become.

'I no longer wish to become a farmer, Mother,' he blurted out with a blush on his cheeks.

Martha nodded and waited, digesting this piece of information and thinking that he could do something here in London. But his next words left her wide-eyed and speechless.

'I want to enter the church, Mother.'

Emily and Ernest, standing nearby, looked uncomfortable. Ernest said rather quickly, 'I really have not influenced Robert in any way, Mrs Tilby. He only told me of his decision yesterday. I… we…' – he looked nervously at his wife – 'will of course help and guide him.'

'I'm sorry.' Martha smiled at the Draycotts. 'I was taken by surprise. Of course, if this is what Robert wants, then I am very happy for him. Will he not need monitory support, sir?'

'He will indeed, and unfortunately…' He looked at his wife with a grimace on his face, his eyes clouded with regret.

Martha spoke gently. 'Mister Draycott, my business has done well and I will be able to support my son.'

Robert seemed to relax and Martha realised then what had been weighing so heavily upon him.

'Thank you, Mother.' His manner changed and he slipped his arm around her shoulders as she patted his hand. This was her son and he was following his path, as were they all, and she felt proud of him for knowing his own mind at such a young age.

'May we take the air now, Mrs Tilby?' Andrew stood at her side.

Shaking with anticipation, Martha rose from the chair, seeing Jane look pleased. Passing Martha a shawl, Jane looked at Andrew with a frown that was obviously fake.

'Now don't let 'er get too cold, Mister Tate, there's a chill on the air.'

'I will look after her, Mrs Gimbell.' There was a softness in his voice that brought a tear to Jane's eyes. Mister Gimbell had never spoken of her that way.

When they were outside in the lane, Martha spoke first. 'Mister Tate, sir, you saved my son's life; I give you permission to... I mean, I would like you to use my given name if you would wish not to be so formal.'

'Thank you, Martha; please also call me Andrew, for I want to speak to you about a very important matter and it would be strange for you not to use my name.'

'Oh!' Her heart quickened.

'In the last few days I have made a decision. I am no longer going to farm my land.'

'Oh, Andrew, you are giving up the farm?' She couldn't imagine it.

A tight smile crossed his face. 'I'm keeping the farm, but letting John Brisket run it for me as my tenant. I'm going away.'

Martha's heart almost stopped beating with the shock. Looking on his handsome face, she felt such deep regret, almost panic, that she would never know it better. He didn't love her. Tears flooded her eyes before she could stop them or look away.

'I am truly sorry that you are going away, Andrew.' She turned her head from him so that he would not see her tears of disappointment. Now she knew without a doubt that she loved him. How could she live the rest of her life without him?

'Martha,' he said softly, 'would you look at me, please, for I have more to say.' His rough hand touched her face, turning it gently to his.

'Please don't cry. I can't bear to see you cry after all that you have been through these last few months. I have something very serious to say and after that I may never see you again. I don't want my last memory of you to be one of sadness.'

'Oh, Andrew, I cannot bear this.' She couldn't hold back the tears.

There was a catch in his voice as he kept his eyes steadily on her face. 'I am taking a passage to the New World. There's plenty of rich farming land there and hardly any restrictions like here. I want a new start. I have the money for a new life.'

Her tears flowed uncontrollably and he smoothed them across her cheek with his thumb, lifting her face to his.

'I'm sorry, Andrew.' She apologised for the tears. 'You have become very dear to me. But too late, it seems.'

'Oh, Martha, I hoped so much that you would feel something for me.'

'You did?' She was more than a little surprised, as he had never shown it.

'Yes, every day, Martha, I see your beautiful face in my mind and I cannot work or think I am so distracted.'

She felt confused. 'Then why are you going away?'

Unable to bear her sadness any longer, he pulled her into his arms, burying his face in her hair as he'd so longed to do. 'Martha, I love you,' he whispered. 'I have never known love before. I cannot bear to live another day without you by my side. Marry me, Martha; come with me to the New World.'

'Leave England?' She pulled back from him; she'd never thought about leaving England. How could she leave all that she knew? What would the New World be like? And, worse, wasn't it full of criminals?

'We would start a new life together.' His eyes now betrayed his fear at the decision she might make.

'But what about my children?' She knew that she could never leave her children. That pain would be greater than losing his love.

'They will come with us, if they want to.'

Martha stepped away from him so that she could better see his face and so that she could breathe. His eyes looked anxiously into hers with such love that she knew wherever she went in the world with Andrew she would be safe. She knew that she had to decide quickly; she didn't want to lose him.

'I would like to marry you, Andrew, for I couldn't live a happy life if you were not a part of it. But I can only do so if my children consent to come with us. They are too young and too precious to me to leave behind.'

'Martha!' He picked her up and swung her around, kissing her face, until their lips met and a feeling of oneness flowed through them, and they were frozen in time. When at last he released her she looked seriously into his face.

'There is something that you must know about me, Andrew, before I accept. You may change your mind afterwards and I would hold no blame over you.' She didn't want to speak of something so precious, but took a deep breath: he had to know. It was better he knew now than his discovering it later.

'There is a reason that I do not attend church.' She stopped a moment to think. 'I believe in God, Andrew, but I don't see God as a man, as you do. I cannot bring myself to pray to a man, holy or not.'

'What are you saying?' He stepped back, frowning. 'Surely God is important in all our lives.' He was taken aback and yet hadn't he suspected something all along?

'Andrew, I am not saying that I do not believe in God; I just believe in a different way.'

He stared at her, holding her at arm's length, the frown deepening on his face. 'Please explain how you see God, Martha.' His tone was serious. He hadn't seen this coming, hadn't thought about their differences.

'I feel God, Andrew. I feel God in every breath of wind, in every drop of rain. I see God in the river, in every tree and every animal. I feel God in every kindness one person shows to another and in the birth of every baby. To me, the world is the church and every living thing in it is the congregation: tree,

380

rock, animal or man. We are all joined together by an energy that runs through us all; the energy that links us is what I call Goddess.' She looked at his serious face. 'I'm sorry, Andrew, but I cannot marry a man who will expect me to find my God in a building.'

There was an awful silence between them and he looked at her as though seeing her for the first time. He turned his head away, frowning. When he turned back to her he spoke softly.

'Martha, I am a farmer. I live with nature and have done so all my life. I understand something of what you are saying. I know that you have been discreet about the way you commune with God and that it must be something special to you. There are many religions in this world, Martha, and who is to know which are right and which are wrong? I love you and believe you to be a good person and I hope that you see the same in me. It will not be my intention to change you in any way and I believe that you would not want to change me.' He looked at her critically, one eyebrow raised.

'My understanding, Andrew, is that each person should be responsible for his or her own life and not influence another. For on the day of judgement we cannot blame another for the life we have led. We have free will. I have to ask you this, Andrew. In the light of what you now know, do you still want to marry me?'

She stared, heart pounding, at his handsome face, now crossed with worry lines. When he eventually spoke, she realised that she'd been holding her breath.

'Martha, apart from the love I have of my God, there is no one in the world that I have ever loved in the way that I love you. I ask you again, Martha' – he held her face between his hands and looked with love into the depths of her eyes – 'will you marry me, Martha Tilby, for better or for worse?'

As she put her arms around his neck and kissed him, wetting his face with her tears, she knew that they would never be parted. 'I will marry you, Andrew,' she whispered, and her heart gave thanks to the Goddess, who she knew would be looking upon them.

When they returned to the house, Jane was waiting with a full jug of gin and a flagon of wine. She smiled expectantly.

'Do we have cause for celebration?' she asked the grinning pair.

Andrew put his arm proudly and protectively around Martha and said, 'Martha has agreed to become my wife.'

'Oh, Mother, I am so pleased for you.' Emma rushed to hug her. James and Nona were shocked. They looked at each other, unable to understand how this had happened, while Robert beamed his acceptance.

'We have more news,' Martha said. 'We are emigrating to the New World, which has much to offer. Cheap land, a new life and any of you are welcome to come with us.'

Jane hurried to Martha. 'Oh, Martha, I am going to miss yer.'

Martha hugged her and realised that there was so much she was also going to miss. 'Oh, Jane, I have so much to thank you for.'

'Look, we're friends, Martha; you'd 'ave seen me all right if life 'ad been t'other way around. Buller, Pit, pour that wine, we are going to have a party. Will yer take wine, vicar?'

'Indeed I will, Mrs Gimbell, but only on one condition: that I am allowed to conduct the marriage of the happy couple.'

40.

Inside Newgate Prison a line of four men, a thin boy and a small woman moved slowly upward along a tiled passage towards the gallows. Each had the noose already hanging around their neck, and their hands tied at the wrists in front of their body. Each also had their elbows pulled back tight behind their back by a leather strap.

They had already been prepared for their fate. Last night, after a service in the prison chapel where their coffins had resided on the floor in front of the alter, each had spent the night alone in a cell with a Bible and a candle. This morning the fetter irons had already been removed from their ankles by the blacksmith in the Press Yard. Those who had nothing to dress in for the occasion had been given a clean white smock that hung below the knee, leaving bare calves and feet exposed. Chained together, the silent group shuffled upwards through the passages towards their fate.

Barney could hear the noise of the crowd gathered outside for the spectacle as a muffled cacophony, slightly muted, as it filtered down through the passages. As Barney shuffled forward, his bravado left him. He had said that he didn't care, that he was ready to die, but now fear clutched at his heart. He thought of his mother, who, right to her end, had withheld her love from him. All he had ever wanted was her love, her approval. Suddenly, he had a vision of her face, her hard eyes. He knew if she was alive what she would be saying: '*I knew you'd never come to no good, you worthless empty pot. Just like your father: useless.*' His heart thudded in his chest and he hoped that if there was a hereafter she wasn't waiting for him. It felt hot in the tunnel, sweat dripped from his nose and his breathing became laboured; his legs felt weak. Behind him the boy was crying. The warden shouted for them to stop and moved ahead of them. In his mind's eye Barney saw Martha Tilby standing in her doorway, like a mother hen, protecting her brood. There'd never been anyone to protect him. No one had cared enough about him.

Ahead of them, a door in the side of the passage opened and the priest and three other men, the observers, stepped out into the tight space. The priest nodded to the warden, who pushed the first prisoner forward, and they again moved in procession behind the chanting priest. They moved slowly into the daylight and across a courtyard towards the huge prison doors and the outside world.

Barney could hear the mournful tolling of the death bell. Tears came to his bloodshot eyes as the words played in his head: *it tolls for me. It tolls for me.*

The roar of the crowd grew louder, nearer, as the prisoners hobbled across the yard. As the gate was opened and the priest and the observers stepped through and climbed the gallows steps, the roar of the crowd reached a crescendo of excited expectation.

Barney had not appreciated the full volume of the crowd noise when he had been a spectator. It was a sound that now ripped his soul open and dangled it before the entrance to Hell. He had to struggle to stop his bowels opening. The pain in his stomach almost overwhelmed him and he wanted to shriek like a woman, but instead it was a deep moan that escaped his lips. Slowly and unsteadily, he watched the first man climb the steps onto the gallows' platform. Following him, Barney told himself that he would go without regret; he had made his peace with God.

As the group stood on the platform above the crowd, the bells of London rang above the rooftops and vibrated through the streets with a mixture of deep clanging and fast, rippling peals, almost drowning out the mournful tone of the prison bell. As the priest carried on his chanting, Barney looked down at the crowd, who jeered and shouted vulgar remarks as they enjoyed the entertainment.

Laughing and shouting, the crowd surged forward, trampling some and pushing against the guardrail that surrounded the platform. It quivered, but held them at bay. Weapons raised, the marshal's men stood steadfastly behind the rail guarding the platform and its occupants.

As the priest continued, nervously intoning his prayers for the souls of the soon to be departed, Barney felt a tug on the noose around his neck, and looking up saw that the hangman had climbed a small ladder and was placing the eyehole, situated at the end of the rope, over a butcher's hook set in the main gallows beam.

The crowd jeered and whistled. '*Hats off*,' came the familiar roar from those at the back of the crowd to those in front blocking their view. Barney heard a noise beneath the platform and for a second he felt hope: was someone going to rescue him?

'It's the hangman's assistant,' whispered the man standing next to him. 'He's easing the bolt that'll release the trap door. It will be quick for me. My father's paid the hangman's assistant to pull on my legs so I die quicker. Maybe your family did the same.'

'I ain't got no family,' Barney whispered out of the side of his mouth.'

The priest was still praying for their souls and the crowd was getting restless as the scene around Barney started to swim; his knees buckled but he didn't fall as the noose held him up by his neck. Suddenly, from behind him, a cotton bag was pulled roughly over his head, shutting out the scene before him. He panicked; he couldn't see, couldn't breathe; he heard crying; he wished that the person would stop. It took him a moment to realise that the voice was his own. His mouth was dry and his legs were unexpectedly hot with liquid. The crowd laughed with approval. Then he was falling. The roar of the crowd smothered him. The noose tightened sharply around his neck. Instinctively he tried to move his arms to hold the rope, but they were still tied behind him at the elbow. He jerked and gasped, felt his neck swelling, his tongue and eyes protruding. He continued the jerky dance of death in the gloom beneath the platform boards until he felt the arms of the hangman's assistant around his legs. The man hung onto them with all his weight, pulling Barney down. 'Courtesy of Mister Tate,' the man grunted as Barney sank, desperate to live, into the permanent darkness of death.

41.

As those same bells rang out over London, Martha stood next to Andrew in a church near the docks. Behind them stood Emma and Nona, dressed for travelling, and behind them James, George and Jack. In the pews, the whole Gimbell family watched the proceedings, having closed the shop for half a day. Jane was crying with happiness. Everyone was smiling except Mr Gimbell, who from time to time looked sternly at his wife.

'It is with the greatest pleasure,' intoned the Reverend Draycott, 'that I pronounce Martha and Andrew man and wife and wish them much happiness in their life in a new land.'

Emma and Nona hugged each other and the Gimbell boys cheered. Jane blew her nose loudly and dabbed furiously at her eyes with her handkerchief.

The wedding party retired to a tavern near the dockside for the wedding breakfast and last meal that the Tates and Gimbells would ever eat together.

Later that afternoon the Gimbells stood on the quayside, waving and calling goodbye as the passengers boarded a ship. The Tate family looking down responded by waving from the deck. 'Goodbye, Jane; I will write to you.' Martha called.

'Yer better 'ad, my girl; I'll be waiting for it.' Jane dabbed at her eyes as the children hung over the side, waving. 'Goodbye, Nona, James, yer be good for yer parents,' Jane shouted as she waved her handkerchief furiously.

Andrew and Martha went below deck and stowed their bags in their two cabins as the ship prepared to leave England.

The children stayed on deck and continued to wave to the crowd standing below on the dockside as the sound of the bells continued to peal across London.

In their cabin, Martha was keenly aware of Andrew's nearness, as she busied herself sorting out the bedding. She saw the desire on his face and knew that he wanted her. Her own heart was beating faster in her chest as she also became aware of her own erratic breathing and need for him. Surely it would be impractical in the confines of the space that they would share with their children on the long journey.

Andrew's arm slid around her waist and as she turned to him he buried his face in her neck 'We're on the threshold of a new life, Mrs Tate, are you ready to find land and perhaps start a new dynasty?' he whispered.

Looking into the rugged face of her husband, Martha's desire was written on her own flushed face as she answered him. 'Yes, Andrew.' Her voice came as a sigh and the strength of her kiss told him all that he needed to know. She wanted him.

'At last you are mine, Martha,' he whispered. 'I have loved you for so long.' He pulled her body tight against his and felt his muscles harden as his kisses fell hungrily upon her lips, her face and her ear. Beneath his fingers, her neck and shoulders were like silk to his touch and it was all that he could do to stop himself tearing off her clothes and taking her. He knew by the way that her body responded to his touch that she felt it too. They were almost lost in their need for each other when they heard the voices of the children and feet on the stairs outside.

'This is not the time, Andrew, but we will find time and space to be together on this journey.'

They smiled at each other as they pulled apart. They had the rest of their lives and for now it was enough to be together, to be man and wife.

Bibliography

The Book of London	St Michael. AA
Everyday Life Through the Ages	Readers Digest
The History of Tea in Britain	Tea Council
Pagan Feasts	Anna Franklin & Sue Phillips
Old Cooking Utensils	David J. Eveleigh
Police Uniform and Equipment	A.A. Clarke.
Hangmen of England	Brian Bailey
The Chronicles of Newgate 1883	Arthur Griffiths
Assistant Surveyors 1689–1823	British History Online
Miller's Antiques	1989/1999/2000
Early eighteenth-century newspaper reports	
Newgate Prison	Rictor Norton
Ever Wondered Food.	Open University 1780.
The Chronicles of Crime, London 1887.	Camden Pelham. &T Miles & Co.
Herbal Healers.	Glennie Kindred
Sacred Celebrations.	Glennie Kindred
The Housekeeping Book of.	*Susanna Whatman*
A History of English Criminal Law and Its Administration 1750 VOL.3.	L Radcinowicz. Stevens & Sons.
Transportation & London Barges.	Georgianindex.net/Londonbarges

Read on for an extract from the sequel, 'Between Classes.' The Tate family have been in Australia for twelve years and Emma dreams of returning to England's green shores and cool air, but when, through a terrible circumstance, she returns to England, she finds that she no longer fits in. Living with a husband who doesn't love her, in-laws who don't accept her and her only confidant, her sister Nona, is acting strangely.

Between Classes
The New World 1802

Emma urged her horse on, yelling crazily as Black's hooves thudded into the dirt track that had been shaped over the last twelve years. The drumming of his hooves vibrated through her tense body, blotting out all feeling and thought. Earth spewed out behind them as she rode Black hard. Her tanned legs hung free and bare below her skirt that lay in folds around her thighs. Her body stretched forward. Her face, almost touching the animal's neck, was lost in the mane that flew wildly about her head mixing with her own loose sun-bleached hair. Reaching a group of eucalyptus trees, baked dry by sun and fire, she encouraged the horse through them. Crisp leaves, crushed beneath his hooves, released a strong smell that she did not like. This was never a place she wanted to linger. The trees, unlike those at home in England, had thick roots that lay humped and dipped like huge snakes on the surface of the land. The blue-grey bark was cracked and dry like an old man's skin, peeling off in strips, revealing patches of yellow beneath.

Leaving the graveyard of trees, they zig zagged through the brush until they reached the top of a rise and here, she pulled the animal up. Black's body steamed as he pranced in the sparse vegetation, eyes bulging, muscles twitching. Exhilarated, Emma bathed in the smell of her horse and patted his neck to calm him. He whinnied in reply and dipped his head sharply, nearly unseating her.

She wanted to scream, as the psychic stress that had built-up within her body during the day was released, but she dared not spook her horse. There seemed no reason for her feelings, yet she knew herself too well not to believe that what she felt would come to pass. If only she could know in advance what it was, she would be better able to prepare for it.

Below her, the territory that she viewed stretched for miles in all directions over the never-ending flatness towards the west and the distant hills in the east. Within it she saw nothing to account for the feeling of unease which had grown slowly within her over the past two days until she could stand the feeling no longer. In desperation she had taken Black from his paddock, racing him out across the land. The wildness of their flight had, for the moment, overridden the feeling of approaching doom that had gripped her all morning. Filled only with the exhilaration of the ride, she now observed the distant Tate homestead. The cabins, the surrounding barns and water towers, appeared in miniature from this distance. Nothing moved in the heat haze that blanketed the land and choked the day.

Her brother, James, and stepbrothers Jack and George Tate, now all in their teens, had been away for several days on their horses somewhere off towards the hills looking for stray bullocks. Her mother, Martha, and Emma's stepfather Andrew, had also been away for two days checking the health of their bullocks and goats.

Her sister Nona, had left hours ago with their flat-back cart. She was heading for the small township that had started to take shape some seven miles up-river. The township consisted of a dozen houses, a tavern and a general store from which she would collect their supplies, accompanied as always by her dog Bart. Spread out along that stretch of the river settlers had built makeshift homes on poor soil and these inhabitants were barely surviving as the growing number of mounds in the area set aside for burials was testament.

It had taken the Tate's two years to understand the weather patterns in this new land and they were thankful to John Brisket, their tenant farmer on Andrew's farm back in England, for sending the rent regularly at the end of each year. Without it they would not have managed.

Unlike England, this New World was hot and sometimes arid and when it rained, it rained so hard that the land was unable to absorb the water quickly enough. Deep gullies opened filling with water. Rivers appeared where no rivers existed before, death traps for animals and humans who could be swept away on a frothing red surge. The steamy silence after a torrential downpour always excited Emma. Cleansed, the land seemed to vibrate with expectation, waiting, hormonal, pregnant with hidden promise. In the following days after the infrequent rain, the land was awash with colour. A sea of red, yellow and white flowers spread like a carpet across the earth and both Martha and Emma gave thanks to the Goddess for this occasional beauty.

Emma searched the sky for an indication of a change in the weather but could see nothing to cause worry. Her brow furrowed, as she looked east towards the hills and then west, her eyes following the direction that Nona had taken earlier. There was no movement in the landscape.

It was getting hot. She'd taken off without her bonnet; a stupid thing to have done she now realised as the sun bit into her neck and arms. Seeing nothing in the landscape to alarm her she eased her horse back down the slope guiding his feet away from the holes in the dry ground. This far out from the homestead her life depended on his fitness. At the bottom he pranced ready to be off again running wild and she gave him his head.

On reaching home she returned Black to his paddock. The ride had given her some relief, even though it had been a fruitless journey.

As she entered her cabin, the coolness of the dark interior washed over her, sucking the heat from her body. She was grateful that just before her marriage two years ago, Andrew and the boys had built her a home with thick walls to keep the heat of the day at bay.

Now standing in its stillness her thoughts turned to her husband Richard. He was younger than she by five years and at first Martha and Andrew had been happy with their match. The stranger calling himself Richard Ladd had arrived one day when they needed extra help with branding and harvesting. They knew nothing of him but he had convinced them that he was a good worker and that he was not a deportee from Britain. That he was certainly not a criminal and came from a good family, although he never said who that family was until the day of the marriage. Emma knew that Martha and Andrew had agreed to the union having long since realised how few neighbours they had and there being little possibility of their girls finding a decent law-abiding husband.

She pondered sadly how, at first, Richard had worked hard alongside Andrew, and how after the marriage, the call of the township with its bar and gambling room had become a bigger object of desire. Emma believed that she loved Richard, but was becoming tired of placating the family when he wasn't pulling his weight.

She sighed as she washed her hands in a small bowl of cold water. She was twenty-five and had still not settled in this hot country. She longed for the greenery of England. The cool dark lanes, their banks filled with flowers and herbs, the forests of recognisable Oak and Chestnut, Beech and Willow. The snaking silver rivers that ran gurgling gently between fields and under trees. She wanted to see again the gold and bronze of autumn, see the beautiful whiteness of a hoarfrost and feel the coldness of a snow filled day.

It was during the afternoon that she felt the pang of impending doom again. The worry of the unknown about to be visited upon her was as real to Emma as the table at which she sat sewing.

Going to the door she looked towards the horizon and waited. It was coming, approaching fast and yet she could see nothing. Every muscle in her body was taut, her stomach cramped with anxiety. For an hour she stood watching, and then, through the heat haze she saw a shadow, a distorted blue grey movement that disappeared as quickly as she had seen it. She waited, her mouth dry. It appeared again a little closer, the outline of men on horses. Dust rising from the ground told her they came at speed.

Opening the drawer in the dresser that stood by the door, she snatched the pistol that lay covered by a cloth. She had no means of firing it as ammunition was on Nona's list of things to buy, but the feel of it in her hand gave her courage. This was a lawless land and she was alone.

Running outside she hoped that they were sufficiently far away not to see her. Taking Black from his paddock she led him into the barn tying him loosely to a post in case she needed to escape quickly.

Standing in the shadow of its large warm interior Emma observed the fast-moving group. As they came closer she saw another horse bringing up the rear, moving slower, throwing up more dust than the first group and knew it was pulling a cart.

The horses thundered into the yard stopping in front of her cabin. As the dust settled she recognised them and her heart thumped in her chest. The Logan brothers; what could they want out here on Tate land?